J.R. VAINEO

Kings of Muraine

The Journals of Ravier, Volume I

Second edition

ISBN: 978-1-7340315-1-5

Editing by M. Gray
Cover art by Dissect Designs

This book was professionally typeset on Reedsy.
Find out more at reedsy.com

Luke Leland Bridge:
"Never again! Until the next time."
October 1992 - December 2014

The greatest gift, the best tribute, I could ever give to you and your wonderful family is a whole story bled out into words made into sentences, sentences rearranged on the page, pages ordered to a disorderly sort of perfection. Altogether? A book. Perhaps not started for you. But, instead, completed in your honor. See you on the other side! –J.R. Vaineo

Contents

III   The Victor

Acknowledgement

J.R. Vaineo—of JRV Books, LLC—would like to give special thanks to a few people who made this book possible.

J. VaineoHurst, for always being a listening ear; encouraging the continuation of the story, even when it was hard; and being an all-round good guy.

M. Gray, for being an amazing editor. Ever so patient with all questions and concerns. She's a super editor. Up there, with the greats!

T. Barber, of Dissect Designs, for crafting an absolutely stunning bespoke book cover. J.R. Vaineo couldn't have found a better cover and digital designer. His work is that finishing, breathtaking detail that brings the story to life before the first page is even read.

So many other people, in more minor ways, have contributed to this journey of a finished product: J.R. Vaineo's debut novel. Nevertheless, J.R. Vaineo still gives you her thanks.

I

Lies & Truth

It only takes one night.
One visit, from two strangers,
And everything changes forever . . .

1

A Year to the Day

"I know you, but I have never spoken to you. Familiar as my own face staring back at me. How can that be?"

With a notebook resting in my lap, the fountain pen's nib scratches on the lined page. It pauses in my hand, waiting for more words to come. Deeper. It digs into the paper, and blue-ink bleeds away like frost icing over a window. The pen quivers in my hand, begging for continuation. But I lift it away. Letting it balance in my palm, my thumb runs over the gold engraving.

To my son, Tyler M. Ravier. May you write of many adventures, with and apart from me, as you discover your own story. Your loving father, Lance O. Ravier.

Like winding a watch, I turn the pen over and over. Struggling to win this battle against tears, my chest aches. Then words come, and forceful blue strokes prick the page.

"Happiness is vanquished and love is lost. Sadness arises, before hatred turns to anguish. Fear is near, when reflection confirms it. But resolve can mend?" I shake my head. "Total nonsense!"

Ripping the page out, I crumple it. Out, it is thrown into the murky lake. Fury turns to the pen. In my crushing grasp, it almost snaps in half. My hand lifts. I'm about to throw the pen. But my breath catches, and pain surges down my throat.

Something stops me. Fear? Guilt? Anguish? I do not know.

My hold loosens. When I flop into the long, flattened grass near shore, and watch the paper sink into the lake's darkness, my chest is freed of tension. My eyes close. A smile tugs at the corners of my mouth.

I whisper to the forest, "Tyler Malik Ravier. Fourteen and fatherless."

Blue-ink traces into my palm lines. The pen tip doesn't lift, until I'm finished. Now etched in blue, the 'M' on my right palm tells the story of what my name should have been. Malik. It's the name Mother wanted for me. In the end, Dad's choice won out.

"Not a family name," I state. "Not an Iraqi name. Not a catchy name. Just. Plain. Tyler."

Crawling to the edge of the lake, I thrust my hands below the cold water's surface to grate my nails over the pen marks. Then beckoning is the mocking reflection, asking me. Again. To search for any trace of him. No pale skin, or copper-brown eyes. No platinum-blond waves. No evidence that I am my father's son. Only proof that Amira is my mother. Same black waves. Emerald eyes. And dark olive skin.

I smack the water, and the reflection distorts.

"Gone a year. Dead a year," I seethe. "Why does it still hurt like it happened today?"

Sunrays of noon, on the calm lake waters, often bring me comfort. But this day is shaded by despondency. By a deep yearning to join the discarded poem on the bottom of Mirror Lake.

Time still goes on.

Never-ending, like the rhythm of a breath and the heartbeat.

The only constants—the companions—unable to leave.

Even in death, they may follow.

Still too much of a coward to test the lake's current, I ease up from the damp knoll.

Birds sing the chorus.

Squirrels chatter the song.

Adding to the companions.

For now.

Each step. Each turn. Every slope takes me closer to home. But farther from where I want to go. Eyes shut tight, my mind strains to remember his sharp features. One in particular: his contagious smile. Now a feeble reflection of what it was.

If only he were here.

We would still fish at Mirror Lake, after he got home from a trip.

We would still escape life's monotony, with fantastical stories imagined together.

And he would still sneak me out to the movies, with friends, on a school night.

Lance Ravier was one of those dads my friends laughed with and teased like he was one of them. All who met him, couldn't help but love his kind yet teasing nature.

"I would give anything," I whisper, "to see his face. Hear his laugh. Feel his embrace. Just one last time."

Save for the forest creatures, no one replies.

Hot tears trickle down, again, making me feel the sting of sorrow. At that moment, my foot catches on something. I'm sent sprawling to the ground. Glancing back, I see my offender. A broken tree now lying across the beaten path I take every day. Sweeping my fingers over deep claw marks in the bark of this tree, then its pliable leaves and branches, my gaze travels down its twelve-foot length.

How'd this get here? I wonder. *Could be some Galloway stable hands playing a prank. Trying to distract me this day. Of all days.*

"Or," I whisper, "is it something else?"

Chills bite at the back of my neck, propelling me into fleeting glances of the area.

No footprints.

No paw-prints.

Or drag marks.

The broken tree seems to have been dropped on the path, by an invisible hand.

"They swept away their tracks." I shrug. "That must be it."

From behind, a branch snaps. My breaths quicken. Then the forest plunges into silence.

I call out, "Who's there?"

When the forest song restarts, my shoulders relax. Continuing my steps, I rant on, "Mom's worried about me. Still thinks I need a shrink. But why? I'm not depressed. Just angry. My clothes? All black. Sometimes a white shirt to change it up. It is a new me. Devoid of color."

A kamikaze sparrow almost smacks my head, right then, attempting to get its fill of the gnat swarm ahead.

Swatting at the little pests, I pass their valley and begin again, "I don't need the shrinks. I need him. Did he have to go the Middle East that day? It was supposed to be a business trip. Instead, it was a bombing. It could have been anything, but telling people my dad died in a terrorist attack is different. It's foreign and unreal, until it happens to you."

Breaching my agony is the jabbering of a woodpecker on a tree. Through the thickness of the trees, his red speckling peers out. Grinning at his jackhammer head, onward I go. Drifting farther from my destination, I move closer to where he would want me to be.

Home? The barn? With people? Anywhere but alone.

* * *

With chores done, I wipe sweat off my face and grip the warm barn latch. That's when one of the horses protests my escape, with pawing at the gate. Down the cobblestone walkway is my dad's red Shire, hanging his head over his stall gate.

I amble back to stroke him, and hair flies off in clouds. "Need a good brush down, don't you?"

Ginger Snap's nose pushes me away, just enough to nibble on my pockets.

Grinning, I pat his neck. "No treats today, Snap."

After gathering brushes, currycomb, and a step stool from a nearby cabinet, I toss them into his stall. In I go, closing the gate behind, and up perk his ears. With currycomb in hand, the grooming commences.

Scratching his cheeks first, my fingers run up behind Ginger Snap's ears, as my dad's used to do. Then each stroke of the stiff-bristled brush sends plumes of Snap's reddish-brown coat behind us in streams.

"Be glad I convinced Mother to keep you. While you're not worth much to anyone, you're everything to me. First Dad's. Now mine. I'm not too bad, am I?"

A deep groan escapes him, and I laugh. "I'll take that as, 'you're not the same.' What about your conversations with her? The sobbing on your shoulder. Confessions of loneliness to you. The pain she sees in my eyes every day. How scared she is that we'll never find the same happiness again."

Done with the brush, I fling it away. It smacks the half-wall separating the stalls and scares the neighboring horse. But I just shrug. "What do you think, Snap? Will it ever stop hurting?" I glance into his content brown eyes, before ruffling his mane and continuing the grooming in silence.

Latching the barn for the day, I cross the expanse of twenty-two steps from barn door to back door. When I reach for the kitchen knob, I spot it: the coarse coat of Ginger Snap all over me. Brushing off what will release its hold, I crack the door open.

With no sight of Mother, I stroll into the newly beach-themed kitchen. Its soft whites, beiges, teals, and blues pop in contrast to the dark walnut floor. The best part of it all? The painting of a windmill on a coastline, now hanging on the wall by the dining table.

She finally hung it up.

It was a birthday gift for her. That, and money to renovate the kitchen. They had planned the kitchen revamp, for the end of last summer. Two months after he died. Took her almost a year to go through with the renovation. She couldn't bear to do the work without him, so she saved more and paid someone else to do it.

Through the archway, but before the hallway and living room, I stand at the bottom of the steps. Thirteen steps. Every other one's a member of the silent seven. The rest? The squeaking six. Up the worn metal rail, my hand travels. The coolness of it soothes my callused, clammy palms. But on goes the count of steps.

The number fascination started a year ago. This day. The very day he died. Within months, it twisted to an obsession. A distraction from the thoughts. From the truth. I will never see him again. Only frozen images and archaic videos will keep him in focus.

Still, I count the steps to the first door on the right, even though I know there are seven strides to the bathroom beside my bedroom. Greeting me are its stark-white walls. Bleached of emotion. Who needs color for their dwellings? Mine are now as they should be. White bathroom. Black bedroom. A calm blankness. Void of happiness.

Shedding the filthy clothes. Climbing into the stall shower. I set the stream to lukewarm. Water splashes on my face, as I hold my breath, depriving my lungs of air until they ache. A long, controlled breath severs their cries for relief, though it does nothing for the pain in my heart.

Images of aftermath. Footage of bombings. They torment the canvas of my mind. Toppled buildings. Disfigured cars. Dust refusing to settle. Fire with endless fuel.

There were bodies, too, but the news never showed them. Never showed him.

Teeth clenched and anger rising up, I'm powerless to stop myself. The handle twists to steaming hot. My head ducks out of the way. Scorching water hits my back like angry hornets. Still, the spray's sting is a fraction of the stabbing pain in my heart. Too stubborn to free my back of the Hot hornets of water, I press my hands to a cool shower wall and then ball them into fists.

When tears flow down my cheeks, I know the ritual isn't enough.

One-two. Three-four. The handle turns all the way, until only the exterior sting paints across my thoughts. The tears stop. Replacing the shaking breath is a half-smile. In that moment, I have my victory. The battle won, the handle jerks to icy cold. Shivering and frozen inside, I scrub down.

Five-six. Towel round waist, I open the squealing door to the favored vision of my bedroom. On the matte-black walls are pieces of his collection:

the blueprints of ships, fighter jets, and submarines.

Seven-eight. The door closes silently. My focus goes to what the rising sun touches every morning: his hand-drawn blueprints of gardens, homes, and skyscrapers watching over my desk.

Nine-ten. My hands search two black dresser-drawers for the usual choice: white tank, up top, paired with black, down below. The boxer-briefs and cargo pants. They're about all I wear, these days. Same everything. Contrasting, yet colorless.

Eleven-twelve. The drawers glide shut. The clothes slide on.

Tapping on the scuffed dresser top, I speak two words: "Thirteen. Done."

Darting to the mirror, my gaze lingers on the three-inch black hair atop my head. Another cause for dissatisfaction. Iraqi surfer-waves staring back at me. Every day, I hate them a little more. Every day, their owner bores me to an endless pit I cannot escape.

"Will it ever end?" My voice cracks. "Will you fade away? Will you die a second death? The death of my memories?"

A pocketknife, resting among the clutter on my dresser, begs to lop the hair off. To free me of it. But then … my stomach grumbles, and I flick the knife away. Again, a distraction saves the broken boy for another day.

Two-one. The bottom step squeaks.

The same time each day, like clockwork, Mother's knife hacks into a cutting board. Then that knife scrapes food into an oiled pan and it sizzles. Sometimes, though, it spits and provokes a frustrated growl from Mother. Today is one of those times.

Smiling, I put off the inevitable and turn the corner to take eight steps to my dad's study. Gracing its tall ceiling are wooden beams. Wrapping its walls are walnut panels blending down with the floor planks. For most, the deep colors might be too dark. Yet, for me, they briefly bind the bleeding heart.

Three steps, to cross over the big, scrolled rug he brought home from India. Then seven, to the blue-and-green curtains half-shielding the bay window behind his desk. Into his large chair, I sink down and grip the armrests. By the door is a grandfather clock, on one side. Then a built-in desk, on the other. Covering the walls are paintings of exotic birds. But what study would be complete without bookcases suffocating two walls? Shelves filled to the edges, they tell of his obsession: knowledge.

Grasping the picture from his desk, the copper gaze of a smiling woman mocks me. On her lap is a grinning boy with hair matching her sandy-blonde locks. "Aunt Miriam and Cousin Alec," I proclaim. "Never met them. Probably never will."

The photo shows them celebrating my cousin's fifth birthday. They're in costumes for some Renaissance faire in England. Or so my dad told me.

"Even missed the funeral, Aunt Miriam." I scoff. "Although, you made every excuse imaginable for not being there. Guess you two were never close?"

Just then, the study door creeps open, and Mother pokes her head in. Forcing a smile, she announces, "Dinner's ready."

* * *

Tonight's a table full of his favorites: Teriyaki noodle stir-fry. Spring rolls. Crab Rangoon. Finished by candied ginger.

As I scoop food onto my plate, Mother avoids looking at me. After stacking several letters next to my water glass, she takes her seat and fills her plate, saying, "Presumably, birthday cards."

One is from my only living grandparent. The mother of my mother. Haven't met her, either. Then some are from distant friends. But no birthday would be complete, without Aunt Miriam's pathetic excuse of a card.

At last, I get to the one from the twins: Jed and Jaxson Craven. Thicker than most, their card sets off the suspicion radar. I pull it out to reveal one of Jaxson's graffiti-type drawings with the words, *What you want most for your birthday ...* on the front.

When I peel it open, Jed's boisterous voice begins the twin-rant.

"To hear our voices, while we're on vacation!"

"And forty dollars!" yells Jaxson, from the card.

"About that," protests Jed—every 'about that' is followed by Jed's finger lifting to make a point—"I tried convincing Jaxson that we should give you twenty and pocket the other half. See if you notice it's different from other years."

"I told him you're too smart for that," states Jaxson.

Jed continues, "Why our parents insist we give twenty a piece to our friends for their birthdays is beyond me. When Jaxson and I want a new video game for *our* birthday, they give us twenty, *one* twenty. That's not enough for a new game. Obviously, our parents favor our friends more than they do us."

"Not true," corrects Jaxson.

"We'll debate that later. Happy birthday, Ty-Ty! Hope it's a good one."

"Jed, stop calling him that. You know how he hates it. Anyway! Love ya, bro."

"Dude, that's gay!"

"Whatever!"

Although I can't see Jaxson's face, I know he's rolling his eyes at Jed.

Cringing, I slam the card closed, musing, *Should've opened that in my room.*

"Those boys are crazy," states Mother.

"They can be."

For several minutes, we eat our dinner in silence. Then Mother fiddles with her napkin, seeming unconcerned with eating.

Twirling more noodles on my fork, I ask, "Something bothering you?"

She smooths her napkin out. "Are you sure you don't want anything for your birthday? I remember what you said last year, about not wanting to celebrate it anymore, but there's something I've been aching to give you."

Telling me more than her words are her green eyes. Hopeful, anxious, and excited wrapped into one.

Reluctantly, I nod. "I'd be all right with that."

"Wonderful! Be right back." Before I can change my mind, she races out of the kitchen.

While I wait, I search for Aunt Miriam's card. But not for long, as hers is the smallest yet again. I tear the envelope open, to a black note card with green scrollwork. Edged in silver are white stickers spelling out *Happy Birthday.*

I startle at the hundred-dollar bill tucked inside and … words. More words than the usual, impersonal '*Happy Birthday. Love, Aunt Miriam.*' My gaze skims over the pen strokes.

Happy birthday, Tyler. I am sorry we have never met, these past fourteen years. One of these days, I will find my way to London, Kentucky, to visit you and your beautiful mother. Until we meet. May it be sooner, rather than later.

Love, Aunt Miriam

Something unknown tugs at me. Is it excitement? Or longing? Frustration? Who can know? Sliding the card back into the mangled envelope, a persistent thought refuses to be quiet. *I know you, but I have never spoken to you. Familiar as my own face staring back at me. How can that be?*

I whisper, "What does my poem have to do with anything?"

* * *

Anticipating my reaction, Mother's expressionless and folding her hands to stillness on the table. I call this action her Chess-Bluff.

Resting on the card pile is a petite silver-wrapped box with a black bow on top. The wrapping tears. The black box's lid lifts. Then the room spins a moment. Nestled inside, it ticks the rhythm of time: his black-and-gold divers' watch.

"I thought he was wearing it when he …" Trailing off, I lift it out and run my fingers over the watch-face crystal.

"It was being repaired," replies Mother. "He wanted it like new, before giving it to you."

On my right wrist, it clinches just as Mother's Chess-Bluff breaks into bliss.

"Thank you." I grin.

She eases her chair out, saying, "I wish it could be more."

Agony to my soul, her broken smile makes mine fade, as I reassure, "It's more than enough."

I didn't believe him, when Dad said seeing loved ones in pain is sometimes worse than your own pain. No effort to defy or crush her could be made. Not by me. I often wanted to scream at her to leave me alone, but thoughts never became actions. All I did was hide myself away or fight the urge to hold her and share her pain. Some days, though, I couldn't share the pain. It was too much to bear.

I know she needs one, but I resent them—hugs.

"Still a bit big." I shrug.

She tightens a hand on my arm, saying, "You'll grow into it."

Standing almost eye-to-eye with her, I wrap my arms around her waist and pull her close. Resting my chin on her shoulder, I whisper, "Couldn't have had a better gift."

She pulls away, letting that Chess-Bluff spark return. "I'll have a better one, next year."

I tap the watch-face. "What could top this?"

"Wait and see."

"Or snoop and find?" I tease.

"You do and I'll hire someone to take a belt to your backside."

"She makes threats again? I've missed that all year."

"Tyler Malik Ravier! Go to your room."

I grin. "What? No help with dishes?"

"And get more of your teenage sass? I'll do it myself. Be gone with you." She waves me away. "Do something fun. Mother's orders."

Five steps to the kitchen archway, then ten to the front door, and many more to where my heart longs to go. Mirror Lake. To swim there again? To almost drown? To test the divers' watch? So many options.

Like a mind reader, Mother points the accusing finger. "By fun, I don't mean sleeping out at Mirror Lake again."

I sigh out, "Yes, ma'am."

"One more thing, Tyler?"

I turn around to her mutter of, "Put a shirt on."

Tugging at the tank top hem, I defend, "This is a shirt."

"If you're a gangster."

"I'm not going anywhere."

"Doesn't matter."

Groaning, I charge up the thirteen and into my room.

Again. The defiance evades me, as I yank a button-down on and flop to my bed in disgust with myself. I inspect the divers' watch. As soon as it's set to the current time, my eyes fight to stay open. Like a drug, sleep calls to me. Calls for me to think of him. So much for fun.

***

A tortured screech in my head jolts me awake. Except for moonlight casting a faint glow through the blind slats, the room's blanketed in blackness. Pressing the watch's light button, I see the time. 11:33 PM.

Faint in the distance is a distressed horse's screech, as I peer through the slats and strain to spot anything amiss. Nothing seems out of place, though my breaths are ragged. Then—beyond the barn—a white creature flashes by the forest edge. At the sight of it, my chest stings. Three breaths and five heartbeats later, a green glow floats in pursuit of the large creature. Waiting for the light to fade into the forest, I open my blinds to unlatch the window. A cool breeze caresses my face, as I listen.

It shrieks once more, from deeper within the forest, and I sigh. "Again. I must disobey, because this is too interesting to pass up."

Snatching my flashlight off the nightstand, I slip it into my pocket and then fight with the tangled laces of my military boots. When they refuse cooperation, I commit blasphemy in Mother's eyes by tying them in knots and tucking their ends away. The screen of defiance pops out, and thought becomes action as I pass over the windowsill.

"Deep breath," I whisper. "You do this all the time. It's no different tonight."

In response, the sudden crackling in the forest tells me otherwise.

Slinking to the roof's edge, I grip it and ease down with shaky arms. When I let go, something crunches. Now mangled beneath my boots, Mother's freshly planted flowers condemn me. "No way to hide that and my disobedience." I wince. "But I'll promise an appeasing Shrink-Visit."

From the house, lights stretch to the barn. But no farther. During my weave between the night-cloaked trees, I click on the flashlight. After minutes of running, I stop and realize that I know this forest. Out goes the light, before I slip it away to listen and let blackness replace sight.

Save for my unsteady breath, all is ordinary.

Rustling leaves.

Creaking branches.

Hums of crickets.

Swarms of gnats.

Shattering the ordinary, an eerie light shines from Mirror Lake's direction. Creeping toward it, until about fifteen-feet away, I peek from behind an old oak tree. The bright light reflects off the tranquil moonlit water, to illuminate a cloaked figure standing at the shore. One palm glowing, the figure touches something hidden from view, and sparks fly like welding-spatter.

A horse cries out in pain.

That's when fury burns, calling me act. Yet thoughts mock me: *What are you going to do, Tyler? No weapon. No training. Dad never taught you. Never got the chance.*

I'm defeated, crouching down, while the horse's screams torment me. Desperate to do something, I face the light again. But a twig snaps beneath my hand. Holding my breath, I grimace. The welding stops.

The figure's attention jerks to look in my direction. As the light dims to glimmering, the figure looks back to the horse. Whipping a long cloak off his shoulders, he lets it fall over the horse like a feather drifting on the breeze. Moonlight touches his face as he whirls around, and his glowing, citrine-yellow eyes look into me.

I swear that's when my heart, literally, stops.

Even hidden by nightfall, he knows I'm here.

Afraid they are my last, thoughts race. *Will I see him, when I die? Will Mom's heart break to disrepair? If I'm going to die, I want it to be on my terms. Not some stranger's. Certainly not by some welding beast with citrine eyes.*

Confidence ruling his every move, the man saunters toward me with a sadistic smile on his face. Seeming to relish my fear, he jeers out one word: "Afraid?"

Panic pushes me up into a sprint. I dare not glance back. Mid-run, my wrist is caught in an icy grasp. My legs buckle, unable to find a foothold. I'm left at his mercy, when his long and slender fingers catch my other wrist.

Braving a look up at him, moonlight paints across his straight nose and high cheekbones. His almond-shaped eyes of blue are intent on me. Instead of menacing, however, they're eyes of a victim petrified of a captor. Yet I'm the one held captive.

Blue eyes? Not yellow. Two men. One's sadistic. The other one's terrified. When his grasp tightens on my wrists, I muse, *Maybe not so terrified, after all.* As I struggle to break free, the youthful one creases his forehead. In concern? Or confusion? What would he have to be confused about?

"Please," he begs. "I don't wish to hurt you."

I shout, "Then let go!"

He releases me. "Apologies for scaring you, Tyler Ravier, but we couldn't let you get away. You see—"

"How do you know my name, and what are you?" My heart pounds faster. I take a step back.

Swallowing hard, he replies, "You were described by your father, Lan-Soren—"

"My dad? Lance. You know him? You spoke to him. When?"

"The day he died …" The youth trails off.

Nausea consuming me, I ask, "Then he *is* dead?"

The youth slides his white hood off, revealing his sandy-blond hair of medium-length. It falls across his face, when he bows his head in sorrow. "I'm afraid so. We tried healing him, on Muraine. But whatever wounded him here wasn't human. Meaning, someone from Muraine was after him."

Thoroughly confused, I manage to say only one word: "Muraine?"

"It's the planet your father and I are from," he clarifies, while straightening his long, tailored coat. "The land of Paragon. Paragonians. Listen, Tyler.

We can't stay much longer. Thought to bring you the young horse LanSoren raised. Unfortunately, she ran away from us and got tangled in a … fence? I think that's what you call it."

The youth traces a forefinger from behind one of his ears. Then along his sharp jaw line, as my dad had always done when trying to remember something. "We caught up with her here. She's mostly healed now."

I glance to the white horse behind.

The sadistic eyes of citrine-yellow stare back.

"Who's he?" I ask.

"Ryco." The youth beams. "Second of The King's Guard. My Guard, actually. Still getting used to—"

"You're a king?" I ask.

Grinning like a serial killer, Ryco states, "King Talok of Paragon."

In reaction to either the title or grin, Talok just grinds his teeth and fiddles with four black-and-white buttons of one coat sleeve.

I ask the sadist, "You were healing her?"

Ryco, his brown hair cut in military style, nods his head once. Then he splays out all five nimble fingers, to reposition one of his three-fingered white gloves.

What's he going to do, I wonder, *wring my neck with his magical healing-hands, then bring me back to life? That's what a sadist would do.*

A gnat swarm picks that moment to engulf Ryco, as I brave the question, "What's with the archer's gloves?"

Swatting at the swarm, Ryco narrows his eyes at me. "The Son of LanSoren knows archery?"

"A little."

He shakes his head. "A little is not enough."

"Enough to what?"

"Come to Muraine." He smirks.

"Did I say I want to go?"

"Your face did."

Definition of Ryco: arrogance made into flesh and bone.

Shrugging, I ask, "What does the Second of the Guard do, exactly? Wield a bow and arrow. Heal random creatures. Make assumptions. Did I miss anything?"

In response, the citrine glow ends. Dressed in a black version of Talok's coat, Ryco grips his opposite wrist. Aside from the somewhat exposed skin of his face and hands, he now almost fades into the night.

Talok pulls at his coat's high collar. "The Second of the Guard leads the offense. While the First of the Guard holds defense."

Right then, the resting horse softly glows to illuminate the thin cloak covering her body and wings.

Catching Talok's anticipating look, I ask, "You're not giving me a winged-horse, are you?"

"Told you he wouldn't be interested," states Ryco.

"Is that what I said?" I hiss.

"I admit," interrupts Talok, "I was hoping you would take care of her for a while." Pausing to unbutton his coat's center front, he continues, "Right now, she's not safe from Zymarc, King of Vitiosyns."

"We're working on a cloaking spell—"

"With Jasper of the Greyvons," Talok interrupts, finishing for Ryco.

I look away, as questions fill my mind.

Talok sighs. "I wish we could stay longer and answer your questions, but we must be going soon."

How can he read me like an open book? There's something strange about him. The more he talks, the more I begin to trust him. But I never do that. With anyone.

Squirming in the awkward silence, Talok exclaims, "Almost forgot! You'll be needing this."

Out of his inside coat pocket, Talok grabs and relinquishes to me an eight-point star. Like glitter in glass, the dark-iridescent metal glimmers. Over the center-symbol on the circular part, I run my thumb. That's when pain surges into the fingers of my right hand. I toss the star away. Its points are now curved like claws.

Rubbing my five little injuries, I ask, "What is that?" To myself, I think, *It's a possessed ninja-star. Yes, absolutely. That is what it is.*

Coughing once, Talok replies, "Your father said you'd need it, to find one of his journals and other belongings scattered around the area."

"Some of the items are in your house and barn," states Ryco.

Talok continues, "He tried saying where the others are, but—"

"He was unable to finish," Ryco cuts in to say. "In the end, confusion consumed him."

"How did he die?"

"We don't know." Talok's eyes dull, the way hers do whenever she's reminded of him.

In this moment, mine only burn with the battle. *If he didn't die in an attack, how did he die? I must know. If only to distract myself.*

Talok sucks in a breath. "Let me show you how the possessed ninja-star works."

I flinch. "Can you...?"

"What?" Talok glances from me to Ryco.

"Nothing." I clamp my mouth shut. *Read minds? What if he can? Freaky! Could Dad read my mind? Can Mother? That would explain SO much! Maybe this isn't real. How to be certain?*

Talok swallows hard. "You all right, Tyler?"

Nerves calming, I state, "You were going to ... show me something?"

"Right!" Talok beams. "But first, give me a moment."

He holds out his hand. Swirling between his palm and the star is a whitish-blue mist. Up, the star rotates to meet his right palm. Grasping it, Talok presses the center-symbol. The curved points straighten to their original form. When he turns the center-circle clockwise, the eight star points clink away. Staying suspended in the air, all points have different shapes on their opposite ends.

Talok states, "Between the journals and other belongings, LanSoren said there are thirteen items." Focusing on the star pieces, Talok raises his left hand up to it and spreads his fingers wide. Closing his fingertips together, he forms a fist.

Still suspended, the star pieces revolve then snap together with a loud, *Pop!*

Hesitating, I ask, "How am I supposed to do that? Or find the locations? You're sure he didn't have instructions?"

Stepping toward me, Talok offers the star. "He said they're related to favorite places of yours or his."

"You're forgetting, King Talok, about that last poem of his. If you can call it a poem."

"Right!" Talok nods. "It was something like, 'When one mills in the woods of despairion and dusk, one never acknowledges the ever-present fading light of the sun-eclipse, as it dances and races across the still mirror lake.' Does that mean anything to you?"

"Only the Mirror Lake reference. He and I spent a lot of time here. Called it Mirror Lake because of how its surface is perfectly still, when reflecting the rising and setting sun's light. But I don't understand the rest of it. You're sure he said despairion? It wasn't despairing or despair?"

"It was despairion." Ryco smirks.

Talok adds, "It was the only word he was adamant we understand and convey."

Ryco, ignoring the swarm of gnats and somehow managing not to swallow a mouthful, states, "As I said before, confusion consumed him."

Not noticing the cloud of gnats migrating his way, Talok starts to say, "I'm sorry we cannot—" Stopping short, he spews out a mouthful of the little pests.

Composed, perhaps even bored, Ryco flicks his right fingers like a guitarist plucking strings, and the swarm's engulfed in the flames flooding from his fingertips. Dissipating from Ryco's casting glove is smoke, as he rubs his palms together.

Staring at Ryco, Talok starts forming words. Instead of addressing Ryco, however, he shifts to me. "Will you be all right?"

Peeling my eyes away from the sadistic pyromaniac, I think a moment. *Do I want to accomplish something on my own? For me? For Dad? Or do I just want to prove myself to this sadist? But why would I? He is nothing to me.*

"I'll be fine," I reply. "Anything else, besides taking care of this horse-thing?"

"Just that." Ryco cracks his knuckles. "Think you can handle her?"

"She's only one horse."

"A dragon-horse, who can use magic," corrects Ryco.

"She can't be that bad."

"That's what they all say."

Talok fiddles more with his coat buttons, saying, "If you want, I can send someone to check on you and Awngeleik."

"That's her name?" I ask. "Awngeleik. Did my dad name her?"

Talok peeks back at the sadist. In the middle of a yawn, Ryco shakes his head. After Talok mutters something under his breath, Ryco's citrine eyes shift to neon and alert. Then Talok replies, "I'm not sure, actually. It's always been her name."

I ask, "He couldn't go with something simple like Angelic or Angel?"

"He hated the word Angelic." Talok rubs his neck. "Always said it was too cheerful."

"He would say something like that."

"What do you say?" Talok looks down to the top of his black high-boots. "Will you take care of Awngeleik?"

Feigning confidence, I reply, "Sure."

"Wonderful!" Talok exclaims. "I'll send someone to help you—"

I cut him off with, "I'll be fine. My dad died. Remember? I don't think it can get much worse than that."

"Don't be too sure," states Ryco.

Holding my head high like the sadist, I clasp my hands behind my back. When my grip tightens over the watchband, it pinches in. *The pain is real. Is this too? If so, he lied to me my whole life. Would he do that?*

Talok smiles a tense grin, but my breath stops at the sight of his perfect teeth and slight vampire fangs.

"Something wrong?" Talok's face turns grim.

"Your teeth …" I hesitate. "Are you some sort of vampire-magician?"

Ryco's citrine orbs dance with mockery. "The little boy is afraid of your pointy teeth, Talok."

"Oh, that!" Talok perks up. "I inherited the trait from my White Sorsryn ancestors. It's useless for us, now. Sorsryns don't prefer to fight with their fangs anymore."

Ryco adds, "I suppose it can still intimidate one's enemies, though."

Seeming lost in thought, Talok just chews on his lower lip.

Ryco continues, "You should see the Death Sorsryns. All their teeth are jagged as spikes. One prick from those teeth, or their poisonous nails. Dead within minutes. Sometimes seconds."

"Ryco, enough," whispers Talok.

"I'm only telling him of the world LanSoren never bothered to share with him. Honestly! Shouldn't he know more about it, before he decides he's going to look after the beautiful menace all on his own?"

"Ryco, you are out of line!" Talok's gaze strikes into Ryco's. "You will never imply LanSoren acted selfishly toward his son again! Do you understand?"

With each spoken word from Talok, Ryco winces and sinks farther to the ground. "Forgiveness, my king. I meant no insult to LanSoren. Only that Tyler, his son, is not prepared for this task as he should be. If it pleases you and Tyler, send someone in two weeks' time to check on him and Awngeleik. We would *hate* for anything to go wrong."

Talok circles to me, his gaze softening. "How does that sound, Tyler?"

Afraid of upsetting them more, I comply with, "That's fine."

Standing to glare at me is Ryco, stating, "We should get Awngeleik to safety."

After replying, "The barn next to my house will be fine," I hold Ryco's gaze, and muse, *Interesting, how your king so easily prefers me to you. I can't imagine why. With your charm and winning personality.*

Talok glances to me, then Ryco. "Yes, Ryco, interesting. Is it not?"

Terrified that I spoke aloud, I ask, "What's interesting?"

Talok shakes his head. "Nothing."

"One more question. Any chance you can fix my mom's flowers I crushed while sneaking out here?"

Talok simpers. "That should be easy for you, Ryco. Seeing as how you have no difficulties practicing magic here on Earth."

Talok flashes a patronizing grin.

Ryco's face merely sinks to boredom.

"My Second of the Guard. Take us to the barn, please."

"Of course, my king," replies Ryco, with a wry smile.

He snaps the fingers of his left hand. Surrounding objects blur beyond recognition, akin to suddenly spiraling in the air. Nausea eats at me. My body shakes, then begins to burn. All subsequent sensations overload my mind, until …

Lights out, Tyler.

2

The Count of Despairion

From the barn hallway of cold cobblestone, I ease up. Disoriented, as if clubbed by a gang while sleeping, I rub my temples. Head and body throb, in pain. Last night's events rise through the fog. "Crazy dream," I mutter. "Vampire-magicians? Not real. But the name, Awngeleik? Where'd that come from?"

That very second, the rising sun's rays pour through the barn windows and sting my eyes to bleariness. I groan. "Morning. And the never-ending cycle of tending the beasties like temperamental plants."

Despite everything, my autopilot turns on. Without the typical calm, however. I run from stall to stall, thoughts racing, *This day, life may be hanging on by a millimeter. Or an eighth ...*

"Again, with the numbers, Tyler," I scold myself.

During my mad dash, some horses paw at their gates. But most toss their heads—snorting, neighing, or clambering away.

"Thirteen beasties? Done. Fed. And watered." I nod once, then turn to leave, but something nudges my back.

Turning around, I swipe a hand through the air. It catches on something cold. Invisible, a smooth cloth stirs beneath my outspread hand. Gripping its smoothness, I bravely rip it off like a bandage. Now exposed is the winged-horse: Awngeleik. Her surprised blue snake-eyes narrow on me, like a child caught in hide-and-seek.

Suddenly dizzy, my legs buckle. I reach for her head that's dotted with tiny white feathers and patches of fur. But my hand slips right on down the pearlescent scales coating her amused face. I start to lose my balance again. But she stretches her long neck out, just in time to catch me on my back, and lifts till I'm standing upright.

Straightening yesterday's clothes, I'm about to assess what's happening to my life. Something wallops my backside. Whatever it is stings all thought away, except those of agony, during my launch across the walkway. Cracking against a stall gate, my ribcage explodes with pain. Clutching my side, only the sounds of my wheezing fill the barn. Just when the pain subsides, her clacking hooves sound behind me. I hold my breath. Afraid of what this feathered thing will do next, I brave a glance back. Yelping, I'm unable to stop the inevitable: her wet muzzle in my hair.

Knew the surfer-hair should've died yesterday, I muse.

"Seriously!" I whine, while shoving her head away. "You try disfiguring me? Then use my hair as your rag?"

In answer, she nips at my shirt buttons. But I smack her head away.

Either insulted by my swat or simply playful, she rears up to flap her wingspan of nine-feet.

Meanwhile, I cower against the gate. Heart threatening to leap out of place, I hold up hands of surrender. "Mercy!" I call out.

Her flapping wings blast me in the face with wind. Down, she goes clacking on the cobblestone, prancing like a proud Galloway dressage horse. She tucks away her wings, behind the stiff, long feathers guarding her rib cage. From these feathers, it blends into short hair of white-and-gray; but tight, white scales of the underbelly and chest—the shoulders and withers too—protect her vitals. Intermingled with the silky-white coat is a mosaic of tiny feathers embellishing her neck, back, flanks, and legs; together, they glisten like fish scales in sunlight.

"So … you're a dragon, horse-bird-hybrid, thing?" Rubbing at my brow, I continue, "If you're real, the rest was too. Talok. The Sadist. Muraine. My dad's journals. That despairion poem … And magic."

I look at her again. Though her form is majestic, it's her gaze that captivates the most. The snake-eyes of blue, boring into my soul, for a split second swirl with aqua.

Unsure of whether that's a good or bad sign, I sigh. "Just don't make me regret my acceptance of *King Talok's* request to look after you."

* * *

In a vacant stall, still holding *evidence* of a visiting horse's stay, the cloaked dragon-horse is sealed away with the sliding shut of the barn door. Knocking twice above the handle, I speak two words: "Thirteen. Done."

Revolving around, I face the chasm of twenty-two steps. And, whether I want it to or not, the counting starts.

One-two. I begin the sneak toward the house.

Three-four. Marking the halfway point, at eleven, is Mother's workshop.

Five-six. Striking out from her workshop, I hear a hammer smashing metal.

Seven-eight. *Problematic! Can't escape the view of her 'watchtower.' Intentionally had Dad build it that way. Sneaking in or out of the house? Impossible.*

Nine-ten. When metal strikes begin again, I go for it. Past the door. Almost to safety.

But eleven is cut short, by Mother's strained voice exclaiming, "Tyler! Where have you been? I was starting to worry."

Caught again, the count stops. Cringing, I pivot a full one-eighty and let her scowl at me from the doorway. Though the emerald gaze blazes, her face is plastered with blankness. The Chess-Bluff in full force, she waves me in and then withdraws.

Guilt collapses in on my chest, tightening it to discomfort, even though I was not to blame this time. When I amble toward the shop doorway and peer inside, the ritualistic scolding-routine commences.

At her bench, she tinkers with a half-finished English saddle. Her once grungy workshop boasts of its Immaculate-Articulation: bridles, saddles, and horse tack polished to gloss; woodworking and leather tools aligned to perfection; shelves and pegs cleared of dust. Even the raw cedar planks, stacked in the loft, have been sanded.

The Immaculate-Articulation can only mean ... First was worry. Then was outrage, by way of absence. My *absence.*

Though she's armed with the Chess-Bluff, I have Recoiled-Remorse: eyes down and brimming with unshed tears, quiet voice, hands in pockets. She's fooled every time. I mutter, "Fell asleep at Mirror Lake again."

The Chess-Bluff fades to pity. Whether for me or at the remembrance of when everything changed forever, who can know for sure?

"Regardless," she says, "you get to groom the Galloways' horses today, instead of me."

Relief starts sweeping through. Until I remember. *She* will be there. Gemma Galloway. The spoiled Rich Witch.

Arguments are futile. Yet. Why not, for old time's sake? "But Gemma will be hounding me every painful second I'm there. You know how I hate her bragging about being rich and how she's the best at everything. Get enough of her pompous attitude at school. I want to enjoy the rest of my summer free of her."

"Should've thought that through, then, before sleeping out again, when I *specifically* asked you not to. Told Mr. Galloway you'd be happy to muck out the stalls too." Mother grins her sweet-devil smile, before turning on her heel to finish etching the Galloways' initials onto the saddle.

Another customized saddle for the Galloways? How many do they need? Thirty, in two years?

"If you finish early, be back for dinner."

"Yes, ma'am." I sulk out of the workshop. *Good thing she didn't notice the flowers.*

The kitchen door opens. My steps tread across the floor. Up the thirteen, they stomp and squeak, then end in the calm blankness of matte-black.

But *I* am not calm.

A breath turns to ten. The heartbeat accelerates to ninety. Slamming my bedroom door, I state, "Quick change. Then, off to the Galloways."

Tucked between the folds of clothes stacked on my dresser, I spot a small brown envelope pleading to be slit open. The pocketknife, there on the black surface at all times, waits to lop off the surfer-waves. Today, I will appease it with paper. "Maybe," I state, "this is an explanation from those Paragonians?"

In long calligraphy, that weird despairion poem-rant is written on one side. When the pocketknife slices the seal, a pang pulsates over my head. Like the one in the barn. Only far worse. Eyesight blurring a moment, I unfold the letter of crackling heavy parchment to read its penned words:

Son of LanSoren,

Talok and I waited over an hour for your unconsciousness to break, but it was for nothing. I must say, for being the progeny of one as strong as the Great LanSoren, magic is hard on you. Do us a favor? Don't come to Muraine. You weren't raised here. You don't belong here. Like your father, you will only get yourself killed. In your case, it will be because you are young, weak, and stupid. In his case, he was killed for one of the many secrets he kept. I would bet my life on it. Since you will never see the face of Muraine, I need never make that bet.

Another warning. If you do make it to Muraine, by a stroke of luck, and dare to call me 'the Sadist,' you will join your father in the grave. Take that as an empty or serious threat. The choice is yours.

Before we depart, I will answer your silent question. Yes! We can read minds. Yours is easy. Talok can't read mine, though, because I'm not young ... weak ... and stupid. Like you. Even as he heals your mother's flowers, he has no idea of what I'm writing. No idea that I'm not tucking you into bed as instructed. Unaware that I've transported you back to the cold barn walkway. After practicing a bit of magic on your supercilious, little head, that is. Should have a massive headache for a day. A gift to remember the Sadist by. You're welcome.

Forever NOT at your service,

Ryco of Paragon

P.S. Search for your father's belongings, if it makes you feel better. Doubtful that it will, but you never know.

Crumpling the letter, I throw the parchment wad and watch it hit my closet door with a pleasant *thwack.*

"Wish it was your face, Ryco."

Stuffing the despairion envelope in my pocket, I stare at the crumpled letter in front of my closet and try to think of a good fate for it.

"Later," I mutter, as dread replaces rage. "Have to survive a Gemma encounter first. It's seventy-seven percent more likely to happen. Because of you, Ryco of Paragon."

* * *

Sunday means no Galloway stable hands wandering about. Just me, stomping my way to the whitewashed stables and place of my penance.

"He thinks that letter will stop me from going to Muraine? He's dead wrong. I'll get there, along with everything my dad left behind. If for no other reason than to prove the Sadist wrong."

Determination rising to the forefront, I put aside the seething. As soon as I spot *them* on one bleached wall, I know the fanatical stable master is back to fill in for the rest of the summer, while the usual one is on his yearly vacation. The tools are in perfect alignment to each other. Five shovels, three rakes, four buckets, and two pitchforks. They dare someone to break the master's placement.

While memorizing each piece's position, I muse, *Do I dare?*

Leaving my decision for the end, I begin the penance.

The pitchfork, taken off a gleaming steel-peg and then tossed to the wheelbarrow, clangs against the metal. Over to the nearest stall I steer. With each rattle of the barrow, the diver's watch slides down. Shoving it back up, I can't help but wonder, *Were you ever going to tell the truth? If only your watch could tell more than time.*

Down. The pitchfork plunges into the soiled bedding, commencing my punishment.

Does Mom know you weren't from Earth? If so, how could she keep that from me?

Four times, the pitchfork knocks on the wheelbarrow edge.

What if you never told anyone here? How could you hide that part of yourself for so long?

Three steps, then another drive.

What about Muraine? Why would someone from there want to kill you here?

Two metallic knocks.

Why not wait until you went back to Muraine?

Five steps to the next pitch. But my hands stop, trembling before the thrust.

What was your death really like? By the blade, magic, or something else?

"So many questions." I sigh. "But no answers."

"Answers to what?"

Her voice sends tingles down my spine like cold fingers. Hiding a sneer, I swivel around to face her: Gemma Galloway, twirling a lock of black strands around her thin fingers.

The Strand-Twirl, I muse. *How I want to rip that strand from her head! Just to make it stop. Next will be the endless words.*

"Nothing interesting," I state, shrugging yet readying myself.

Here it comes. The Barrage of Gemma. A hailstorm of words: questions, opinions, and judgments on every single *thing!*

Like a black snake lunging at prey, the strands uncoil from Gemma's olive-toned fingers. "Never thought *Tyler Ravier* and *uninteresting* were correlated," she states.

Correlated? Who uses that word, except science nerds?

"Would you say that," I ask, "if I were White, Black, or Asian, instead of Middle Eastern? An assumed Muslim."

To the gate's side, Gemma stands fidgeting with the hem of her pale, sleeveless shirt. "What does race or religion have to do with anything? Besides, I've never seen your mom wear a Burka."

Up go my defenses. And the Ryco-induced headache soars along with them.

"What if she did?" I ask.

Gemma counters with, "My dad wears Kendo robes, when he tests new weapons."

Not what I was expecting.

Gemma curls her shoulders forward, making her frame even smaller. "So what if she wears a Burka?"

For the first time that I can think of, in our entire time of knowing each other since kindergarten, Gemma's almond-shaped eyes are unwilling to hold my gaze. Is it even possible for the Rich Witch to exude … uncertainty?

Taken aback, I ask, "Then what do you find so interesting that you won't leave me alone?"

Perking up, her chocolate-brown eyes meet mine, and she answers, "You're different."

"Like an exotic animal in a circus? Once I'm no longer interesting, you leave me to starve?"

Gemma briefly purses her geisha-red lips, before saying, "You still haven't gotten over that prank my friends and I pulled last year? I've lost count of the *sorrys* I've given you. We didn't know you got the news about your dad a few days before."

My grip on the pitchfork handle whitens my knuckles, as I spit out, "Do you know how much trouble that *prank* got me in? My mom actually believed I bathed your dad's prized white stallion in florescent-purple dye. As a way of acting out. Like I'd be stupid enough to stick around and do the deed myself, if I was guilty."

Gemma pleads, "Tyler, I didn't know your dad had passed away. Do I have to say it again? I'm sorry." Tears pool, threatening to spill down and leave makeup streaks on her porcelain-smooth face.

Cruelty edging my voice, I reply, "You can say it to me a thousand times, Gemma. It will never be enough. The context—my dad dying—doesn't change the fact that you're a bully. Always will be." I throw another heap of dirty straw into the half-filled barrow.

"I'm trying to change." She sniffles. "Haven't you noticed at all this past year?"

"All I see is the rich brat on her porch, waving a dye bottle at me. Her two devil friends next to her, laughing hysterically. Three days after I became … fatherless." Blood boiling, sweat runs down my back.

"Does it make any difference that I'm not friends with them anymore?"

"No. I will *always* hate you."

Almost inaudible, Gemma mumbles, "At least I don't think you're uninteresting."

I stop a moment to prop my hands atop the pitchfork handle, saying, "I wish you would."

"You know what I do, to people I find uninteresting?"

I laugh. "You ignore them."

Gemma's shoulders slump. "You want me to ignore you?"

"Isn't it obvious?"

"I get it." Gemma manages a speck of a grin. "You hate me. Any chance you'll let me make up for the cruel prank?"

"Why would I do that?"

"You give every school bully a chance at redemption. Always get them to regret their actions." Gemma shakes her head. "I didn't believe the rumor that no bully can ever crush *thee* Tyler Ravier. I was stupid for needing to try."

I think it over. *She's right. Could magic have anything to do with that? A spell cast by Dad to protect me. Broken shortly after he died?*

She continues, "I don't know how you do it. I've ruined many reputations. Made lots of girls cry. But getting you in trouble, after your dad died … it was low, even for me. I *was* an awful person for doing that to you."

Tugging at the edges of my heart, her weepy eyes plead that I let the wound go. *Forgive Gemma Galloway? How can I?* Shaking it off, I ask, "What do you really want, Gemma? To clear your conscience?"

"One chance to show you I've changed. That's all."

"I'll think about it. My dad always believed in second chances. I'd dishonor his memory, if I didn't at least consider it."

"Take all summer if you need to." Gemma grins and turns to leave, as she crinkles a brownish paper in her grasp.

So much to consider, I muse, while feeling for the envelope in my pocket. When I realize it's not there, panic cuts into my pulse like a knife into a fish writhing on shore. My voice steady, I ask, "What's that you've got?"

Gemma stops mid-stride to answer, "This? It's the real reason I came to talk. To poke fun at this weird poem, but that's something the old me would do. I think I'll burn it, instead."

The image of the fish flashes again. *What if she has it? I don't have that stupid poem memorized. No way to contact Talok to get it, either.* Calmly trading out the pitchfork with a rake, I state, "That's a bit dramatic. What'd the poem ever do to you?"

"Reminded me of someone from my childhood."

"Who'd that be?"

She hesitates, trying to form words, but none come.

I shrug. "You don't have to tell me. Mind if I read it, though?"

Gemma grimaces, saying, "It's gibberish."

I hold out my hand. "How would you know? Win any writing contests in school?"

"Photography awards. I thought fiction was your thing. Not poetry."

"They're related, at least. But photography and poetry?" I smirk. "Not *correlated* at all."

"Correlated, sort of … came out." Her shoulders curl again. "You don't have to …" She pauses.

"Make fun of you for it?" I finish.

As if it's her last meal, Gemma offers the envelope. "Do you want to read the poem or not?"

I smile a patronizing grin. "You read it. Give it all you've got."

Signaling my success of aggravating the Rich Witch, her eyes blaze. The moment she looks down to the poem, though, my obsession starts. What else can I call it but, the Count of Despairion. My despair? Numbers popping up like mint and dandelions among delicate flowers. Choking out everything else. All thought. Except, this time, there are phrases too.

One-two-three. The count goes. Goes to where?

She smooths out the crinkled envelope.

Four-five-then six. Why stop there?

She begins. "When one mills in the woods of despairion and dusk—" She pauses to swoon.

Seven-eight-but nine is best? Best of what?

"One never acknowledges the ever-present, fading light of the sun-eclipse—" She clenches a fist to her heart.

Ten-eleven. To confession.

"As it dances and races across the still mirror lake."

Twelve and Thirteen. Beginning, end, and all in between.

"There!" Gemma announces. "Told you it was gibberish."

Pushing the Count of Despairion away, I snicker. "Dra-ma queen! Could you say it with any more pizzazz?"

"You said give it everything, so I did."

"The poem," I state. "It reminded you of someone. How?"

"Despairion," she replies. "I've heard it before, from a friend. Of sorts."

Inside, I seethe, *Dad, please no! Would you share truth with Gemma Galloway, instead of me?* Stifling hostility, I ask, "Really? Who?"

Gemma mumbles something. Even with the protection of makeup, she turns bright red.

Twice, I tap behind my ear. "Didn't catch that."

Like rapid-fire bullets, her words spill out, "My imaginary friend. Look, Tyler. Got to go. Think about what I said. Bye!"

She's gone, in an instant, and I'm left hollering, "Wait, Gemma! Come back." Glancing at the time, I groan. "No time to go after her."

In exactly thirty minutes, the fanatical master will come waltzing through the doors.

3

Bittersweet Memories

On my twin bed, I lie sprawled out. Crawling over my scalp are pangs masking all other woes. Not even the shower gave me solace from the Ryco headache. When a whistle sounds through my open window, another throb zaps my forehead. Jolting to sitting, I smack my mattress and then get up on shaky legs. I jerk the blinds up, wishing I could punch Ryco's smirking face.

Grinning up at me is Mother, dressed in some hiking clothes. In one hand, she holds two fishing poles and a tackle box. In the other, she carries a picnic basket. "How does a picnic and fishing at the lake sound?" she calls up.

She likes fishing?

"What about chores?" I ask.

"Already done. Ginger Snap needs gearing up, though." Mother paces for the barn.

That's when my heart springs me into action. "No! I'll get him. Be right down." Each step lights a fire on my abs like a match to withered grass on a hot summer day. Body thrashing down the thirteen steps, I hiss the whole way. Making it to Mother's side, I stop for a few wheezing breaths.

Sadness creeps into Mother's Chess-Bluff. "Tadashi called to compliment you on your good work today."

Before I can respond, a neck cramp launches more woes up my skull. All is swallowed away, save for one thought: *Ryco of Paragon. Just* you *wait!*

Mother reaches into the basket, asking, "You forgot to eat, again, didn't you?"

She hands me one triangular meat pie. Not even tasting it, I devour it in three bites. The Ryco-induced headache diminishes to a sting.

Mother beams for now, erasing her sadness. "Fatayer and Baklava. Two of your favorites," she announces, while her dark rosewood-colored lips curve from a smile to a scowl. "Better not touch mine. Don't want to be tainted by your American pork." She fakes a gag.

"You can keep your lamb. Maybe share the beef?"

"Share with a defiant teenager?" She holds a finger to her chin. "No. I'll be stingy, instead."

Huffing out a disparaging mock of a sigh, I summon more retaliation from Mother: a swift pinch to my forearm.

"Go get Snap, before I snap." Her gaze flicks up toward the barn. "What's that in the loft?"

Rubbing where she pinched me, I look to the loft. Flashing by its opening is a white object that soon disappears. *Awngeleik!* I cringe inside. *You couldn't wait ten more seconds?*

"I'll see what it is."

Before she can respond, I race to the barn. My heart beats like a hammer striking a bell. I burst through the doors, to the sight of Awngeleik trotting down the cobblestone. She waves her floating head, while the cloak conceals the rest of her.

"Do you want Mother to find you? Seriously, horse." I tug the cloak over her face.

From the doorway, Mother chuckles. "They can't understand you, Tyler."

Seven-eight-but nine is best? Curse you, numbers!

Sweat beading on my forehead, I defend with, "I know, but it fills the silence." While stroking Ginger Snap's outstretched muzzle, I try projecting one thought to Awngeleik. One command of: Don't. Move. A. Muscle.

"You checked the loft?" queries Mother.

"Just birds. Probably flew off."

Satisfied with my answer, she goes to the small room below the loft and hauls out some of Ginger Snap's gear. "Tyler, get the saddle."

Pressing my lips together, to repress a guilty squeak, I glance around for the dragon-horse. *Can't see her. Is that good or bad? What if Mother—*

Mid-thought, Mother's foot catches on the cloaked beastie. Then she stumbles three steps, before scowling back at me.

"I didn't do anything," I defend. *Dad's magical horse did.*

I defensively lift my shoulders, while my hands clench onto the saddle. She narrows her eyes, but then continues toward Ginger Snap.

Good thing my thoughts are safe from her ... or are they?

Without further incident, we gear up Snap.

Seeing that everything's in order, but sensing it's not, I look over my shoulder and muse, *Awngeleik.* Please, *stay out of the way.*

To Snap's saddle, Mother ties the poles, tackle, and basket, then she clicks her tongue. Plodding out of the barn with her is the contented Ginger Snap. But that's where contentment ends. When I try closing the doors, something jams between them. Sniffing the top of my boots is the tip of Awngeleik's nose, now peeking out from under the cloak.

Fingernails digging into the wooden door, I rasp, "You can't come."

In response, she steps on my boot. I stifle a scream and then shove her back in the barn and slam the doors.

Mother pauses from petting Ginger Snap to ask, "Need help?"

Wobbling my head, I just say, "Hit foot with door."

She winks. "That's intelligent. You know an injury wouldn't save you from chores."

"Because you're mean like that."

"Get on, Gimpy," states Mother, patting Snap's shoulder.

I shrug. "Won't argue."

"For once." She shrugs back, then jogs to the forest edge.

With the edge behind us, she breaks into a run. Ginger Snap's ears perk up, and his excitement prods him forward into a slow gallop.

Meanwhile, I wonder, *Does she know the truth?* As her story went, she and her parents came over from Iraq, in the 1980s, to escape the destruction of the Iraq-Iran War. She had seen much. Nearly nothing brought her to tears. The night we got the news, though, I stood shocked to silence; it was she who fell apart. In my nightmares, her wails still ring out.

Paralysis preferable to acceptance, I chose to feel nothing. Filled the void with chores, games, and reading. Then the counting. The never-ending counting. I stopped going in the woods. Too many memories, and too much of the obsession. The number-count was worse there than anywhere else.

Over the claw-marred log still lying across the path, Mother leaps. But Ginger Snap slows to a trot and weaves around it.

"Lazy jumper, Snap." I chuckle. "Always will be."

I fade back to that day Gemma Galloway broke my resolve. The funeral had been three days away. In a forced stupor, numbed from pain, I pretended he never died. That's why I didn't notice the dark sheen the shampoo was giving Tadashi Galloway's white stallion. All I was seeing was the footage. The bombing.

His body was never recovered from the wreckage. Talok implied he was taken to Muraine. But what killed him? Though this King of Paragon doesn't know, maybe Ryco does.

It was that day, as I rinsed off the stallion, I was brought back into reality by the sight of the horse's blinding florescent-purple coat. Before thoughts could formulate, the old stable master was screaming, "Why is the horse purple? What have you done? The competition's tomorrow. We're going to be a laughing stock. Tyler! Go home! I can't even look at you!"

He stormed off, leaving me speechless. Running hose and brush still clutched in my hands, I locked onto Gemma and her two devil friends. On the steps of the large mansion patio, they sat laughing. Holding up the dye was Gemma. In mockery, she tilted the bottle side to side and gave that devious grin many others had come to hate. The Victory-Grin.

Until that day, I had evaded her cruelty. Emotions awakening, I abandoned everything. Sprinted the whole way to Mirror Lake. Lungs burning, I collapsed on the shore. At the water's edge, bursting from me were endless tears. That's when my battle against them started. I pounded on the rocky shore, until my fists were bloodied and numb, as distant screams rang out. Shocked, I suddenly realized that those screams echoing around me—as if belonging to another—were being released from me.

In that moment, masculine hands picked me up from the fetal position I had curled into on the ground. Tightly, he held me and accepted each pummel of my fists on his chest. When my raging-strength wavered, I looked up at the man's face, and fear overcame the tears. The usual man of power and sternness was nowhere to be seen; there was only a sympathetic man standing in as my personal punching bag: Tadashi Galloway. Pained and confused, I pushed away and fled to the safety of my home.

When Ginger Snap slows to a halt, I shiver away the memories and let the lake soothe my soul. With the sun shining over it like a blazing fire, Mirror Lake lives up to the name.

Stretching her legs, Mother catches her breath. "Good run."

"Soon to be good fishing," I add, before untying the tackle and basket.

On the same rock he and I frequented, we sit and empty the plates of Fatayer piece by delicious piece. Soaking in the scent of onions and sumac, I savor my last one, then end the silence by observing, "I didn't know you liked fishing."

"Before you were born," she replies, while preparing the hooks with bait, "your father and I fished together all the time. When you got older, he asked that it be something special he did with you."

"Why?" I ask, while wiping my fingers on a napkin.

Seeming to search across the lake for words, Mother casts her line then reels it in a little. "He never gave reasons for excluding me. Guess he thought the summer camping trips and vacations were enough."

"Did he ever ask or"—I join her at the rocky shore—"do anything else a little strange?"

"Like what?"

"Anything."

"There was *one* thing. When I jokingly confronted him, he denied it up and down."

My grip tightens on the pole, as she continues, "Only did it when he thought he was alone. He counted his shirts from right to left, using his left ring finger the way we use our index."

After making my first cast of the day, I state, "That's not *too* odd."

Mother's smile wavers. "His constant denial of it was. Once, I caught him on video. Then I showed it to him on a night out."

"What'd he do?"

"Rolled his eyes, saying, 'Really, Amira?' He was the one lying, yet I felt guilty. Explain that."

"You still have the video?"

Before answering, Mother does the pinky-swipe across one of her black groomed brows. "He deleted it behind my back, during one of his moods."

"Dad had moods?"

"They were frequent, a couple of years after you were born." Pausing, she continues with, "I wanted another. Mostly to please my parents; somewhat for myself. Anytime the subject came up, though, he got upset. Accused me of not being happy with what we had."

"That's why I'm an only child?" I ask. "Because he didn't want any more?"

She nods. "You never cared, did you?"

"Nah. But if you wanted another *me* so badly, you could've taken matters into …" Hesitating, I squirm.

"My own hands?" she finishes, while pink tinges her cheeks.

Good! She's uncomfortable too.

"I did that," she says. "Before you. After you. Until your father wanted a child, we never had any. I know it was in my head, but it felt like he had control over it, and …"

When she trails off, I state, "It hurt."

"Not as much as last year," she adds. "Three months before we lost him, he asked if I wanted our family to have a fresh start. A new home, new job, new friends. New addition to the family."

"Where'd he want to move?" I ask aloud, all the while my mind is asking, *Muraine?* My head throbs, and the pole quivers in my grasp.

Mother reels her line in, proclaiming, "England, to be closer to his sister and her son."

"Aunt Miriam and Cousin Alec?" I pause to think, *Alec? Talok? Could they be? No! Alec is seven. Maybe eight.*

She sets her pole down. "You're awfully jittery, Tyler. Maybe I shouldn't burden you with this."

"It's fine. You have to talk to someone other than Ginger Snap."

"You little sneak." Mother pinches my side. "Your father did warn me of your spying."

"Guilty. Won't deny it."

"Anything else, Mr. Nosy, before Baklava?"

After squeezing sanitizer on her hands, she peels foil off the last plate. Set in place are three triangular pieces of Baklava in the shape of an equilateral triangle; arranged the way they always were, whenever he got home from a long business trip. On every occasion he missed this year, she put out the same arrangement of Baklava. Like an epitaph, it's our constant reminder that he will never be home.

Sitting with knees in front, she bites into a piece of gooey, yet flaky Baklava. Meanwhile, I'm thinking, *Fishing at the lake. Another occasion he's missing.*

Again, I break the silence to ask, "Can I be done with the shrinks? I'm doing much better."

Setting her piece back on the plate, the Chess-Bluff emerges, and she studies my face. "You are," she agrees. "That's why I had plenty of hot water yesterday, while fixing dinner." Adding to the bluff, she folds her hands on her knees like a Chess-player after their winning move.

Caught!

"Can't I deal with it, in my own way?"

"If it didn't lead down a dangerous path, yes."

I drop the pole, not caring if it breaks. "I'm sick of talking to them. It's not fair to make me do it anymore."

Realizing my foot no longer hurts from Awngeleik stepping on me, but that everything inside of me burns like fire, I stride away from the rocky shore. Then over the grass. In my haste on the path home, my boots scatter up dirt and rocks. But, jolting up, Mother blocks my path, demanding,

"Name someone. An adult you'll talk to."

"The one who always helped me is dead."

Her emerald eyes pool like dew on grass. She pleads, "Let me help you, Tyler."

"I don't want—" Cutting my words short is the whirring of my fishing reel. Scrambling, I seize hold of the pole, before it almost slithers into the water's depths. *So, I don't care if the pole breaks one moment. Then care if the lake swallows it up, the next? Yeah, that makes sense,* I mock myself.

While the fish fights, the pole bends akin to a bow about to release an arrow. Echoing next to me is my dad's energetic laugh, like a spirit refusing silence. I look, but he isn't there.

Focusing on the fighting fish again, I wait for its stamina to wane. Then something gives, the pole snaps back, I hit the ground, and the Count of Despairion echoes out one phrase. *Twelve and Thirteen. Beginning, end, and all in between.*

After taking my pole, Mother reels the catch to our feet. In less than a minute, we see it. A gasp escapes her, and down goes the pole for the second time today. This time from her hands.

"What *is* that?" I ask.

She kneels beside it, saying, "Whatever it is, other fish got to it."

Two tentacle-arms are torn off from what looks like a large, eight-point starfish. Longer than most starfish are the four tentacle-arms and two remaining shorter ones. When the creature thrashes and wriggles, two wide triangular-points of the creature's smooth, seahorse-like head poke out farther from underneath a longer tentacle. Altogether? It appears to be some kind of water-fox with three fins on its neck.

I rest my left hand on its rising and falling chest. Leathery scales of bluish-gray reflect a deep-iridescent turquoise and burgundy. Where the two tentacles were chewed off, even its blood runs an iridescent red.

Mother whispers, "I've never seen anything like it."

I ask, "Think it will live, if we toss it back?"

"It's lost too much blood."

Aligned on opposite sides of its head, at a forty-five-degree angle, are six black slits—three on each side—struggling to open. Under its head, I slide my hand and stroke the longer scales above its eyes with my other. Wider, the black slits open. Each set of three evolves to be two horizontal snake-eyes, with pupils of white staring into my soul. When its chest descends, not lifting again, all air escapes me.

The forest goes silent.

I steal a glance at Mother, afraid she can't breathe too. It's worse than that. Seeming frozen in time, she's not moving at all. My hands shift from the creature to her. At least, they try. In front of me, my fingers appear to glitch and blur in the sudden heaviness in the air; heavier than water. Like a slow drip, air creeps into my lungs. The dizziness subsides.

Starting from the center, its pupils, the creature's eyes swirl to pure white. Its gaze burns into mine, yet I cannot look away.

It's dying. I feel it in my chest. A cold sadness sinking down into the pit of my stomach. *I want to save you, but don't know how.* Why *do I even care?*

"When the time is right," my father's voice rings out, echoing in my head, "tell him everything."

As the creature's eyes fade to gray, its resonating metallic-voice quivers, "You care, Son of LanSoren, because I have the answers to what you seek. Though, I have not breath or magic enough to tell. Forgive that all I have is how much he loved you. Enough to die for you."

Why would he have to die for me?

When it doesn't answer, my mouth goes dry. "Love is not enough. I need more," I cry out. My hands tremble over the creature. "How did he die? Who killed him? Tell me."

"Thirteen. Done," it resonates. Then its eyes go black.

The heavy air shakes, rippling over the lake waters, before it's gone.

Retreating to a paleness are the creature's deep colors. On its face, I lay my left hand. Humming and chattering all around are voices too distorted to understand. Just then, a shock from the creature's face stains my fingertips black, like spilled ink.

As fast as they disappeared, the chorus of forest creatures returns. And Mother shakes her head, saying, "It's lost too much blood."

She already said that, I muse, while feeling my hand now absent of the ink stain. After searching around to see that nothing's changed, my breath settles.

"What's it doing?" Mother leans over the creature.

Its scales harden into stone. And its tentacles writhe to a star position. The two short ones point north and south from its head; at a diagonal from them, are the longer four.

"Dying," I whisper.

Running out like black oil on the rocky shore is the rest of its blood, turning to ash and riding the wind. Yet the creature remains a stone and shrinks to the size of an eight-inch starfish.

Mother cocks her head, saying, "Interesting."

"Which part?"

"Your father used to have a stone like that, except it had all eight points."

"Used to? He lost it?"

"Disappeared about two years ago. Never thought it was once a real creature."

"What happened to it?"

Mother rushes to gather our trash into the basket. "We should head back."

"What about the … star-stone?" I ask.

Her words spray out like water from a leaking pipe. "We're taking it home. Find out what it is. Why it's in our lake. Why your father had one."

This creature has unnerved her, I realize. *Why? Did it speak to her too?*

4

Predator or Prey?

"Tyler, get Snap cleaned up," commands Mother. "I'll be in the study researching this … star." Ending with that, she heads straight for the back door and slams it behind her.

Clicking my tongue, I state, "Done it now, Dad. Made Mom mad too."

To the barn, I lead Ginger Snap. While listening for Awngeleik, no sounds are out of place. Still unsure whether that's good or ominous, I lift each piece of tack off Snap. Calm like falling snow, his breaths echo as the currycomb sweeps over his sweaty back.

I begin my monologue. "Wonder what that creature was. And why he kept one lying around for Mom to see. Could Dad have been the one Gemma was talking about? Some imaginary friend charading around. But why share a piece of Muraine with her, and not me?"

Fuming inside, I stomp out of the stall. Slam the gate. Then throw the currycomb down the walkway. "It's not fair, what you did! You lied, and now you're dead. Can't talk your way out of this one. Because … you're not here."

I press my back against the gate, trying to control the red rage. When Ginger Snap rubs his cheek on my shoulder, the red subsides.

Petting him softly, I continue, "Gemma has that despairion poem. His last words. Her own piece to the puzzle. What else does she know? How can I wrench it from her mouth? How can I focus the witch's words into the ones I need to hear?"

Just then, a sound drifts out from the tack room. It's a sound I know all too well. Horse teeth grinding and munching on something. *Awngeleik.* Whom else could it be, but the dragon-horse desperate for a snack? Pushing off the gate, I tiptoe toward the room. In a heap at the doorway is her cloak and, at her sides, her wings hang like slumping shoulders; all the while, she sniffs her way over everything in the basket.

Beneath one of her hooves is the crumpled foil. But it's the Baklava flakes strewn across the floor that pings me forward to shove her head away. "You ate all of it?" I complain. "Didn't save even one?"

When she nibbles at my pockets, I point a scolding finger at her. "There's no more. You should've savored them."

She sulks out of the tack room with a snort.

I sigh. "Found your weakness. You have good taste."

Hoping there are more pieces of heaven in the kitchen, I check the basket one more time and spot a flaky triangle Awngeleik missed. *No slime,* I muse. *Should be safe.* Dissolving in my mouth, the first bite melts away the strain of today.

That is, until Awngeleik reappears in the doorway. Her squeals clang like cymbals next to my head, as she backs me into a corner. After she blocks my every dodge, her pupils grow to that of a pleading cat's.

"This piece is mine," I holler. "You Baklava Fiend!"

Huffing in the way of a spoiled child, she prances away.

"I suppose, I shouldn't be surprised. You've been cooped up too long. Two more bites. Then I'll find something for you to do."

Intently watching me are those eyes. Then her long neck stretches high, just shy of three-feet from her shoulders. Slowly, her wings lift. Before I register what she's doing, she flaps a hard gust and knocks the unfinished Baklava piece from my grasp.

Like a starved gray-creature fondling a ring, I dive for it. Cupping my hands protectively over it, I hiss, "Mine!"

Lingering over my protecting hands, her nose twitches and scrunches. Then comes the sneeze. The hot, sticky snot plasters itself to my hands.

But it's the smell of rancid fish that overwhelms me. I fight the gags and wipe my hands on the closest thing to me. My *black* shirt.

In victory, Awngeleik swallows the remaining Baklava whole.

I tear my shirt away—buttons popping and everything—before tossing it. "Do you do this to everyone who looks after you?"

Her response is tongue smacking that drowns out all other sounds.

The Ryco headache picks that moment to reemerge, and so does the Despairion Count of, *Seven-eight-but nine is best.*

I groan. "Why won't these numbers go away?"

Awngeleik's gait is heavy. In remorse, she approaches with her head hanging down. She drops something metal, and it clangs onto the cobble floor at my feet.

I pick it up like the possessed object it is. "The ninja-star? Eight points like the creature." Turning the star over in my grasp, her saliva on the metal slimes my hand. But I sigh in relief. "At least your spit doesn't smell like nasty fish."

On a tack room shelf, I place the star and my musings. Wiping the hand *ick* on her shoulder, I glance at the bridles hanging on one of the walls.

"Want to get out for a bit?" I ask her.

She nods.

"You like to run?"

Faster, her head bobs.

Needing to be sure, I ask, "My dad teach you English?"

Her response? Head bobbling like a jackhammer.

"What?" I shout. "He taught you a whole language, but couldn't find the time to tell me one ounce of the truth?" Shaking my head in frustration, I stride for the barn door. "Stay, Awngeleik. I'll be back to take you out. Just need to make sure Mother doesn't come looking for me anytime soon."

With that, I grab my gross shirt, and leave the barn. Quickly, the chasm of twenty-two steps is behind me. Jerking the kitchen door open, I pace on the usual path to my room. But at the foot of the stairs, I collide with Mother.

She stifles a gag. "Tyler, *what* is that awful smell?"

"Dead fish scent Snap got on himself, at the lake. Then me, obviously."

"Go shower, before you spread that rank all over the house."

Clutching my shirt tighter, I ask, "Right now?"

"Yes, right now! Afterwards, please try to be quiet."

"Why?"

Wearily, she sighs. "Because I'm going to bed early. It's been a long day."

I ask, "Did you happen to find that star of Dad's?"

"No. I'm not sure what he did with it. However, I did find some short history articles about similar stones. Let's talk about it, in the morning, when you don't smell so … ripe."

"Sure thing." I nod, with more enthusiasm than I feel. "Night, Mom!"

After a small smile back at me, she ambles up the stairs. Then I hear her head into her bedroom and close the door.

* * *

Now in *my* bedroom, I quickly change into a fresh tank top and shirt. Quietly leaving the place of matte-black, I make my way down the stairs. But I only make it as far as one of the squeaking six, before Mother's voice calls through her closed bedroom door, "Tyler! I didn't hear that shower running!"

I holler, "I was just getting some water."

Her door jerks open. Dressed in her satin-peach bathrobe, she crosses her arms and stares me down from the doorway.

Staring back awkwardly, I finally say, "But I'll take a shower first."

"Good." She smiles tensely. "Before you do, however, I wanted to ask you something."

My mind searches for what she could possibly have to ask, but I draw a blank and just say, "Okay."

"Please stop wandering in the woods, at night."

I feel my eyebrows close together in deep confusion. "But I'm not scared of the dark."

She rubs the side of her face, in thought. "It's not the dark that I'm worried about. It's what I heard the other night."

Oh no! What if she heard the Paragonians or Awngeleik or worse? What if she caught a glimpse of Ryco not *tucking me into bed? Leaving a nasty note for me, instead.* Calmly, I ask, "What did you hear?"

"A large dog sniffing around the house two or three nights ago. When I went outside, to shoo it away, it spooked and ran off. But I caught a glimpse of it, as it disappeared into the tree line."

"A dog?" I ask. "So, I'll take an air horn to scare it away."

"No, Tyler. You don't understand. It had to be huge. Its breathing was much deeper than any dog I've ever heard."

I suggest, "Then maybe it wasn't a dog. Maybe it was a horse."

"It couldn't have been. Its gait sounded nothing like a horse, but no dog is fast enough to run from our house to the tree line in seconds."

"Well, what else could it have been?" I ask. *She had to have heard Awngeleik running away from Talok and Ryco, all while I was sleeping too.*

She bursts out, in frustration, "I don't know, Tyler! We can argue all night long, about what I did or didn't hear, but the fact is I don't want you wandering in the woods at night. I'd rather you not leave the house at all, after dark, but that order isn't likely to be honored by you. So, all I'm asking for now *is* no more woods after dark. Understood?"

Sighing, I reply, "Yes, ma'am. Can I go shower, now?"

"Yes, of course! Goodnight, Tyler."

"Night," I call back.

Tiredly, she retreats into her bedroom and softly closes the door.

As soon as it's shut, I start a routine of deception. I fake getting fresh clothes in my room, by opening and closing my dresser drawers but not taking out anything. Then, off go the boots and socks.

Next, I search for a paper and pen. When finding both, I grab them. After taking the steps to the stark-white bathroom, I close myself in and turn the shower handle to extra hot. As long as she hears that water running for ten minutes, she'll be happy ... hopefully. Meanwhile, as the hot water depletes itself in the empty shower, I write down my short excuse. The plan is to be back before it's dark. But in case I'm not, I have to make her think I got up super early to do chores.

Satisfied with the short note, I lean my head into the hot water jet. Cringing the whole time, I scrub the water over my scalp and then soap on my arms. After quickly rinsing my feet—careful not to get my pant legs wet—the suds are next to be washed off. I cut the singeing stream's supply, then lazily grab a towel to pat my head and arms dry. Leaning my hip against the small vanity, I fold the note and tuck it into my pocket.

Upon exiting the bathroom, I decide to make the ruse even more convincing. I stop in front of Mother's bedroom door to whisper, "You awake?"

"Yes!" she hisses.

Cracking open the door, I peer in at Mother curled up under her dark-blue covers. Illuminated by lamplight, she is most certainly glaring at me.

"All clean," I announce. "Happy now?"

She looks away, replying, "I suppose." Longingly, even brokenly, she focuses on the empty spot where he would sleep next to her every night he had been home.

Ignoring the sudden surge of pain in my chest, I state, "I'm going to turn in early too. I might even get up before you, to do chores in the morning, and then go for a walk in the woods. After it's light, of course." I grin. "Night, Mom."

Her gaze softening, she replies, "If you go for a walk, make sure to leave a note saying what time to expect you back. And don't forget to eat. I don't want a third hospital visit this year. Do you?"

I just shake my head apologetically.

After a weak yet triumphant nod, she says, "Sleep well, Tyler."

With that, I close her door.

* * *

After adding *7:00 AM* to the note, I left it by her teakettle. I also devoured some leftover Fatayer and Baklava in the kitchen, before checking all of the door locks, and making my way back to my bedroom.

Now with my socks and boots back on, I'm standing in front of my open window. The screen's already hidden away in my closet. All I have to do is pass over the windowsill, traverse the roof, and then land in the flowerbed, without crushing any flowers this time. But guilt grips my throat and I think, *Is the large dog story her new way of manipulating me into obedience? I have to admit, it's creative. But what if she wasn't kidding? What if it wasn't Awngeleik she heard? Should I risk staying out all night? What's the worst she could do, to punish me, if I'm caught in a lie?*

Shrugging off uneasiness, I ease through the window and close it as far as it will go.

Before long, I'm back in the barn, ripping a bitless bridle off the peg by the tack room door, and saying to Awngeleik, "You need this on, if I'm going to take you out."

When I approach, she backs away. Side to side. Her head sways to tell me of her uncertainty or, perhaps, to dare me to go ahead and try.

"Promise it won't hurt. See? No bit." I hold it up for her inspection.

She stretches out her neck, keeping her body as far away as possible. When her breath quiets to the calm before a storm, I yank the bridle back a little too late.

Teeth clamping onto it, she tugs it from my grasp. Then begins our chase. Down the barn walkway. Into the empty stalls. Up the loft. Down again. I watch in horror, as she flies over the stall railings. The horses' screeching erupts with banging and kicking; only Ginger Snap stands like a stoic statue.

I sink to the cold walkway in defeat, propping my chin on balled fists. *How to outsmart obstinance in the flesh?*

After the noise stills, my gaze flicks to Ginger Snap standing motionless. At the top of the bridle, he bites down. Next to him, almost half his size, Awngeleik waggles her head into the bridle awkwardly. When her ears catch on a strap, they lay squashed on top of her head. She shrugs my way as if to say, 'Are you going to mope or help me, dumb-head?'

Down, she bends her head to let me release the scaly ears from their captive strap.

"Was that so hard?" I ask. "Now I know why Talok needed someone to babysit you, Walking Terror."

Oblivious to my nickname for her, she uses her lips to fiddle with the reins. If this is a sign for anything, it's the premonition that she will be the ride to insanity.

* * *

During my petulance, the watch twists round my wrist. "An hour, Walking Terror. That's how long it took us to get here. Would've been a thirty-minute jaunt, if you hadn't insisted on sniffing every branch, leaf, and rock."

Too ecstatic to notice my grumbling, Awngeleik splashes in the sparkling waters of Mirror Lake, as ducklings do on their first swim, while the smoky light of dusk resists the call of darkness.

I state, "So long as you don't start quacking like a duck, we'll be okay."

Though the ashes of the star-stone are nowhere to be found, its words replay in my head: *You care, Son of LanSoren, because I have the answers to what you seek. Though I have not breath or magic enough to tell. Forgive that all I have is how much he loved you. Enough to die for you.*

Not enough magic, I muse. *Is there magic in the waters? Why wouldn't it have enough magic?*

My gaze zips over the lake that's the size of two football fields, during Awngeleik's dive underwater.

"Twelve and thirteen," I state. "Seven, eight, and nine. They keep coming. Twelve and thirteen were with Gemma. Then here. Before catching the star. What if it wanted to be caught? So it could speak to me?"

As smooth as glass, the lake glistens. Then Awngeleik disturbs the surface again, and I continue with, "Thirteen numbers. Thirteen hidden items. Could the star count as twelve or thirteen *and* is the other *item* in the water or the trees?"

Pulling my boots off, I jog into the cool lake. But a pang in my heart and a throb across my head stop me from diving in and sinking to the one place

I've wanted to go all year. Shaking away the fear, I state, "No diving gear to go deep. He must've hidden it near shore."

Hours passing, the search goes well past dusk. Like an outstretched hand, the flashlight rays fan out one last time to my favorite fishing spot: the resting place of the star-creature. Giving up the water search, I pull the boots back on. Next are the rocks, trees, and anywhere feasible to hide something.

Several yards from shore, I flop down on the long grass and complain, "Hours of searching, Awngeleik, and nothing to show for it." The sun breaks over the horizon, just then, and my yawn turns to a groan. "Stayed out again. Good thing I planned for it."

As the sun breaks up more shadows of the trees, Awngeleik saunters out of the radiant waters. Her flapping wings scatter droplets of water that miss me by two steps. In the mannerism of a wet dog, she shakes her body. That's when the large side-feathers, and tiny dotting ones all over her, puff out to appear as a balloon being inflated and then popped.

The sight is too much to stop my chuckling, as she comes to join me in the flattened grass. Sprawling out, she proceeds to munch on its long blades.

I spring up, exclaiming, "Don't eat it! This is my favorite napping spot."

Awngeleik side-glances at me, with grass poking out of her mouth like pickup sticks. Out, she spatters the pile of green vomit.

"Gross!" I frown. "You could've finished that."

As she eats her nasty vomit, the watch reads 6:22 AM.

"Think I can ride you back? Or are you going to insist on smelling every flower?"

When Awngeleik stands, her wings droop to the ground. But I hesitate. When I ask, "You going to play the game of Cat and Mouse again?" she remains still.

Taking a deep breath, I test my footing on a scaly part of her wing. When she boosts me up, I grip the reins in relief. "Here we go."

At first, her gait's an unsteady trot of fast to slow to fast again.

"You going to run or what, Awngeleik?" I prod.

At the digging of my heels into her sides, she bolts. Her body zigzagging in between the trees, we blur past everything. My grip tightens on the reins, and I press against her neck as she lengthens her strides. Hitting my nostrils hard is the air likened to winter, and I can't breathe. With no saddle to hold me, I feel the arc of her back. Not like a horse at all, but everything like a sprinting cheetah, she amazes me. Somehow, through it all, I manage to stay on her.

A small creek flows ahead. Spotting it, Awngeleik leaps from the top of a grassy knoll to glide several feet over it. When her hooves pound back on the ground, her strides are no different from the glides in air. Over within minutes is the usual thirty-minute walk, as she slows by the forest edge.

Sitting there on her back, out of breath, I state, "Your antics, Walking Terror, are worth it."

* * *

Searching over every barn stall, I weigh my options. "Whom shall I put you with, so there's no chance of you leaving *evidence* in an empty stall?"

Seeming to want something, Awngeleik drops her cloak at my feet.

"If you didn't have that episode with the bridle, the others might like you."

She tilts her head and blinks her eyes like a ticking clock.

"Ginger Snap's the only one who likes you. Don't know if he's willing to share his stall with the Walking Terror, though. Think you can be nice to him?"

She hangs her head, in shame, like Gemma refusing to look me in the eye.

Interesting, I muse. *She has feelings.* I wave my hand and say, "Go on."

One leg at a time, she steps on the slats of Ginger Snap's gate. On the top board, she manages to balance all four hooves, before jumping down and tumbling to the stall floor. The whole time, Snap stares at her blankly.

"How can you be so majestic?" I roll my eyes. "And this awkward all at once?"

Not a care in the world, Snap goes back to drinking his water. Meanwhile,

I lean my arms over the gate.

On a hunch, I speak, "Awngeleik. Seven-eight-but nine is best."

She scrambles up, screeching, and I open the gate. Heading straight for the tack room, she returns with the ninja-star. Dropping it at my feet, she begins gnawing on Snap's gate. Before I can scold her, she runs to a shadowy stall corner and pops in and out of the darkness.

Thoroughly confused, I continue, "One-two-three. The count goes."

Behind Snap, Awngeleik hides and then bursts her head up like a Jack-in-the-Box.

Now you see me. Now you don't, I muse, before continuing, "Four-five-then six. Why stop there?"

She plants her hooves wide, while moving her head in a full circle and flapping her wings once. She repeats it twice, then stops.

When I fiddle with my watch and say, "Ten-eleven. To confession," her nose smacks the watch.

"The watch?" I ask, and she nods. Though my heart pounds, I continue, "Last one. Twelve and thirteen. Beginning, end, and all in between."

In the trough, she head-bangs the water and soaks Snap's head. Now wearing his trough water, Ginger Snap ambles away and lies down.

"Water?" I ask. "But I already checked the lake." After chewing on the inside of my cheek, I sigh out, "How to get that poem back from Gemma to figure all this out?"

I muse, *Who would've thought that I'd be desperate to see Gemma Galloway?*

Giving up for now, I click the barn lock into place and then pivot around to face the chasm.

My heart jumps with a thrill of dread, at first, and then delight. Standing in the front yard is my former horse, Goliath. At eighteen hands high, the black stallion could never disappoint his rider. No longer mine. He belongs to the Galloways. More importantly, to Gemma.

In victory, my mouth stretches into my wicked grin. *The prey comes to the predator. No need to feign confidence. This time, I'll be asking the questions.*

5

The Bear-Wolf

The back door opens to reveal Gemma and my mother, sitting at the bar-height table. Their backs face me. Propped against the kitchen archway are Gemma's riding boots resting next to her helmet.

Been here a while, Gemma?

"You have a good start, Gemma," states Mother. "Here's everything I found on that star-stone last night. I was going to show all of it to Tyler, this morning, but he went out early."

"Do you know when he'll be in?"

"He said *7:00 AM*. But these days, it could be whenever he feels like it."

From twenty-feet away, I can almost hear her grinding teeth. I slam the door, announcing my presence.

Whirling out of her seat, Mother exclaims, "Tyler! Didn't hear you come in. How are the horses today?"

With one terse word of, "Fine," I stand at the sink and slather soap from fingertips to elbows.

Her unusual reserve gone, Gemma turns in her chair to look right at me. "I was telling your mom about the article you agreed to help me write. You know. For our school newspaper, when school starts again."

I reach for the faucet knob, thinking, *So much for being in control of the conversation. At least the headache's gone. As for her, I'll play along. Only because of ulterior motives.*

The knob twists, and I ask, "Remind me what that was again?" Under the streaming water, I dunk my forearm in. For a moment, the water stings like needles of ice. Then, in a split second, its true nature comes out and scalds my skin to almost blistering.

I yelp once, as Mother clears her throat to say, "It seems we need a new water heater. Can't keep hot water in the house, lately. Had to turn it up all the way. Was going to tell you this morning." Mother's Chess-Bluff shifts to the Assassin-Smile. So innocent is it, so sweet, it could melt an assassin's heart for a second and give her enough time to stab him, then make her escape.

For once, Gemma gives a welcomed interruption with her uneasy continuation, "It's about the mysterious creature sightings. You know. In the Kentucky forests."

My reply of, "How could I forget?" is as icy as the water now rinsing the soap away.

While Gemma's eyes plead with me, Mother's gleam with victory. *In Dad's words: Amira-Tyler. Two to zero.*

"You may," states Mother, "use the study, to do research for Gemma's article."

"Doesn't your culture"—Gemma squirms—"call for a chaperone? Or something?"

Chaperone? You afraid to be alone with me?

"You forget, Gemma, that I came to America when I was eight. I remember how stuffy it is to be supervised every second. Besides, with a father like Tadashi, neither of you will be stupid enough to try anything."

Devoid of a response, Gemma purses her lips.

Mother turns on her heel, announcing, "I need to work with the horses for a while. Tyler, we'll talk later."

Gemma waves. "Have fun, Mrs. Ravier."

"I will enjoy every second, Gemma."

More like, you'll enjoy the picture of me enduring the Barrage of Gemma. News flash! It's wanted, this time. Amira-two. Tyler-one.

In her departure, the front door scrapes shut.

"Your mom told me about the remodel." Gemma glances around the kitchen, before meeting my scowl. "Looks nice. The windmill painting gives it the final touch, though."

Flatly, I state, "Study's this way."

Grabbing a canvas satchel, Gemma hunches her shoulders and then follows me. Through the living room. Then left and four steps past the stairs. At the study's carved oak double-doors, we stop and I open them, stating, "Guests first."

As Gemma enters his spacious study, her shoulders relax. "*This* was his study? It's like something out of a Dickens book."

The doors click, before I ask, "What brings you here this early, Gemma?"

"I was hoping"—she casts her eyes down—"that you'd help with the article."

"But?"

Hands fumbling inside the satchel on her shoulder, she says, "Shot some pictures last night, for photography this fall. Rode Goliath to the hills, overlooking a patch of forest, not far from here. Though it was dark, something was casting a light in the lake. Got a better angle, and voila!"

She tosses several photos on my dad's desk. When it registers that I'm looking down at images of Awngeleik playing in Mirror Lake, the room spins. *This can't be happening!*

"You were riding Goliath at night? In the forest?" I ask, with a surprisingly steady voice.

The irony that I've done the same is not lost to me. And Gemma seems to sense this. Folding her arms, she retorts, "I find it hard to believe you've never done the same thing. Besides, it was almost dawn."

Too tired for any witty response, I just shrug; it's the go-to, when words aren't enough.

"Point is," states Gemma, "I took pictures of a glowing winged-horse. By the time I got there, it was gone. But I followed its tracks, to the edge of the forest by your house."

"And?" I press.

"I was wondering"—she pauses, to do the hem-fiddle—"if you've seen anything strange."

Where was I, while Gemma was being an amateur photographer? I wonder, but shake my head and give her one innocent word of: "Nope."

That's not lying, right? It's not like two space-wizards came to Earth. Told me my dad lied then died. And proceeded to give me his dragon-horse: the Walking Terror who plays Charades.

"That's too bad," Gemma mutters. "I still want your help with the article, though."

"Still?" I straighten, before rubbing my itchy left hand. "I never agreed to it. Wasn't I supposed to be thinking of a way for *you* to make things up to *me*? Why's it the other way around?"

"I know! I'm sorry." Gemma huffs. "Your mom and I started talking about the star-stone. One thing led to another. Next thing I knew, she was volunteering you to help me with the article. I tried talking her out of it, but she insisted. Your mom is *scary* convincing. How could I say, 'no, I don't want Tyler's help.'?" Pausing, she bites her lower lip and then whispers, "When the fact is, I need it."

Although she's at least three steps away, her whisper tickles inside my ear.

Was that Gemma's thought?

"How badly," I ask, "do you *need* my help?"

"I said I *want* your help. Not, that I *need* it."

My pulse races. *It was her thought! There* must *be magic in the lake. How else could I read her mind?*

Gemma rushes for the doors. "I see that you're mad. I'll leave. I don't want to make things worse than they are."

"Wait!"

I take the three steps, to push on the door, as Gemma gawks up at me. Letting my hand slide to rest against my thigh, I state, "I'm not mad. Only confused. I keep waiting for the old Gemma to come back full-force, but she seems to be gone."

Her defense wavering, her grasp leaves the handle.

I shrug. "I'm sure the ruse will end. Once school starts."

Got to get the poem and pictures from her. So far, I'm slaughtering my chances. "Tyler, it's not a ruse."

"Say it's *not* a ruse. That I believe you. What happens then?"

"I'll make it up to you. Anything you want—"

My mouth opens, to cut her off, but she raises a finger, saying, "Within reason."

With my wicked grin tugging at my mouth, I state, "Be happy I'm not Jed. He would've had it out, as soon as you got to 'anything.'"

"Jed Craven?" She lowers her chin to dejection. "Another person I've wronged."

"Don't even think about apologizing to him. Jaxson secretly loves you for what you did. He'll deny it, if you ask. Don't believe him."

Slowly, Gemma nods. "Think of any repayment you want from me?"

Like a midget to my dad's six-four frame, his big chair swallows me when I sit in it. Twisting the watch round my wrist, numbers come again, counting, *Ten-eleven. To confession.*

Ignoring the Count of Despairion, I sweep my gaze over to where he may have hidden a journal.

So. Many. Books.

So. Many. Cases.

Could take hours to search all of them. Unless Gemma helped. Pushing the thought away, I reply, "I have."

Expectantly, her voice rises, "Well?"

"Like a genie and three wishes." I clasp my hands and rest them on the desk. "I want three favors from the witch."

"I think," she mutters, "you mean something rhyming with *witch*."

"I won't say it." I grin. "But you're welcome to."

"No, thank you. I'm trying not to be a *witch,* anymore." Grating nails on one of her forearms, Gemma asks, "What are the three favors?"

"First favor? Recite that poem again. Then tell me about the imaginary friend."

Gemma objects, "That's two favors."

"Then just the imaginary friend story."

As Gemma rocks side to side, weighing her decision, Aunt Miriam and Cousin Alec beg for my attention. More importantly, the older man in robes of blue-and-white, standing behind them in the picture, while holding a silver staff and adjusting his wizard hat. No longer able to look at it, I stuff it in a drawer.

"It's a long story," states Gemma. "Will you be able to handle the rambling?"

I reply with, "It'll be entertaining enough to suffer through, this time." *Don't make me strangle it out of you. That'll go over well with Talok and the Sadist. Banned from Muraine, before I even get there.*

"If you must know," states Gemma, "like a lot of five-year-olds, I had imaginary friends."

Interrupting, I proclaim, "I didn't."

"Do you want to hear it or not?" she snaps.

"There she is. The Drama Witch. Sorry. Go on."

"One of them was different. More real than all the others."

"How many did you have?"

"Irrelevant." She flicks her fingers. "The first time I saw him, he was sort of carving on a tree."

When she hesitates, I scratch my temple, asking, "Sort of?"

She continues, "A floating, glowing object was following the motion of his hand. Doing the actual carving."

"Sure you're remembering it right?"

"I'm not positive." Pink tinges her cheeks. "But I've replayed it hundreds of times. It's the same every time."

"What did this imaginary friend look like?"

"Black hair. Green eyes. Greener than yours. Symbols on his hands. It's the symbols and object I can't remember clearly."

Couldn't be my dad, I muse. *Looks nothing like him. But it could have been his killer.*

Bringing me back is her continuation of, "Thinking it was a magic show, I clapped in delight. But his concentration broke, then the object exploded.

Carving on the tree disappeared too."

"Where's the tree?"

"Not far from the lake," replies Gemma. "After the explosion, I cried. Then he knelt down to my level, and his kind eyes comforted me. I remember them so clearly, swirling right then with fiery colors. His fingertips shimmering with the same shades. When I went to grab his hands, mine passed right through. Like he wasn't there."

"What's his name?"

"Soren," she replies. "The only imaginary friend who bossed me around."

"What sort of things did this … *Soren* ask you to do?" Waiting for her answer, my mind continues trying to make sense of what she's telling me. *Soren? Talok called my dad LanSoren. Are they related?*

Finally, Gemma responds with, "He wanted me to memorize things—words, phrases, locations. I—don't remember most of them, however, despairion came from a story he told me."

Resting my chin on my thumbs, I muse, *Hate to admit it, but Gemma may be useful in all this. Somehow.*

Without prompting, she recites, "There was once a girl from the land of Muraine."

A spasm in my chest makes, "Muraine?" blurt out before I can reel it in.

"Odd name, right?" She smiles. "To and fro, she searched for the piece of darkness till, alas, she found it. It spoke to her—told her to hide herself in the woods, till the dragon is slain. In the woods of Despairing Marion. She waited and waited, then died never knowing the dragon had snuffed out her piece of darkness."

I ask, "That's how the story ended?"

She knows more of the truth than I do. Totally oblivious to it, though. Brutal.

"I don't remember the rest," Gemma admits.

"Where does despairion come in?"

"It was me mispronouncing, 'Despairing Marion.'"

Remaining calm, I ask, "When did you last *see* Soren?"

"Eighth birthday. It was the first time I saw him somewhere other than the woods; had on a modern suit, instead of his usual medieval coat too.

When I blew out my candles, I wished to see him again."

"Why? Was he special?"

"At the time, he was," replies Gemma. "That night, I crept down the stairs to sneak eating leftover cake. Some men were arguing in my dad's office, until I made one of the steps creak. When I got to the kitchen, he was sitting at the island with hands folded on the granite. Beside his hands, a piece of wood rested on a silver platter."

"Wood? Not cake?"

She nods. "He gave me a special fork, claiming it would change the wood into The Cake of a Thousand Mysteries. After that, he wished me a happy eighth birthday, gave me a small children's book, and then left."

"You still have the book?"

"Disappeared last year. I remember the handwritten poem at the end, though. It's nearly identical to my recited one from yesterday."

"How could Soren give you a physical book?"

"Maybe it was a gift from someone else. I don't know."

"He specifically wished you a happy *eighth* birthday? How did he know your age?"

"Imaginary friend, remember? Created by my five-year-old mind. I know my age. Therefore, my imaginary friends know it."

"Seems legit. Figuratively speaking. What was the poem?"

"You will find me," she recites. "The one who mills in the woods of Despairing Marion. At dusk. To reverse the clock, you must acknowledge the ever-present yet fading light of my eyes. Death and time will flee between the sun and solar eclipse. As we dance and race across the still Mirror Lake."

"Despairing Marion." I nod. "Have anything to do with the earlier story?"

"He never said and I never asked. Does that satisfy Favor One?"

"More than," I reply. *Bonus! Got both favors, without her noticing.*

"What about Favor Two?" Gemma presses. "Anything for that?"

An idea formulating, my wicked grin flits across my face. In the mirror, its practice is to perfection. Now number one in my arsenal of instruments against Mother, it's utilized on special occasions. *This, I decide, is a special occasion: to make Gemma Galloway squirm.*

She grimaces, saying, "I'm not sure I like what you're going to ask."

"Favor Two: Next year. Pool party. Your house. My birthday."

"That's it?" She sighs in relief.

All innocence, I state, "Invite my friends, of course." Then I turn devious, saying, "And the nerds. The Goths. The outcasts from school."

"This is a test." She folds her arms. "To see if I've changed?"

"Yep!"

"Don't know if I can do that."

"Why? Are they not cool enough for you?"

"How long, until I have to decide?"

"Christmas break," I blurt, then wonder, *Why do I have to be fair all the time? So infuriating!*

"Fair enough. Can we work on the article now?"

"What've you got?"

"Articles. Testimonies of strange animal sightings. Have several phone interviews lined up, too, with people claiming they saw winged-creatures and bear-wolfs. Mind doing research on your dad's computer?"

"You did all that, in a few hours? Did you sleep at all?"

"Been on it for two weeks. Getting the pictures of the winged-horse, though, was the icing."

"This one time, I'll help you," I state. *Only because of what you may know.*

"I promise to never ask a favor again."

"You may not have to," I complain. "If you chat with my mom whenever you need something."

"Are Amira-Chats off-limits?"

"When I'm not around? Yes."

"Noted," states Gemma. Right then, her hands dig around in her satchel. Held in her grasp, the writing tools and expensive gunmetal Aviridian devices emerge one by one—laptop, tablet, phone, and a myriad of pens; on the secondary desk, by the door, they now rest.

That's how you spell: Spoiled. Rich. Witch.

Gemma starts her interviews, ticking away the questions. Though her voice is steady, her fingers slam on the keyboard like an angry pianist; meanwhile, I wait for my dad's eight-year-old relic to boot up.

At last, the browsing begins.

Mythical creature sightings. I scroll the web page down to nothing, musing, *Garbage articles, photo-shopped images, and bogus videos. Oh my!*

Winged-creature sightings. Worse. Looking at the time, I whine inside, *Only been thirty minutes!*

When Gemma goes quiet, I ask, "Anything good?"

Groaning, she drops her phone to the desk like a dirty piece of laundry and declares, "Total fanatics! They're all on shrooms."

I laugh inside, but say, "Not surprised. It's the nature of your subject. Most witnesses of the *supernatural* want to sound fantastical and important."

"I know. You find anything useful?"

"Nothing legit."

Taking up the phone again, Gemma states, "One more person to call; definitely the most intriguing, but he's an old friend of my dad's. I'd hoped to get enough without him."

"Why? Shouldn't you start with the promising ones?"

Gemma stares up at the ceiling, defending with, "Don't want things getting weird. Almost everyone wants to impress my dad. This guy may not be genuine, not after hearing the name Galloway."

"When's the last time he saw you?"

"Years ago. Wouldn't even know who he is, if my mom wasn't constantly talking about him. She dated him in high school, apparently, before dating your dad in college."

My dad's chair flies back, slamming against the bay window. "Wait! *My dad dated your mom?*" Inside, I seethe, *Another secret! Except Mom must know about this one.*

"Your dad never mentioned it?"

Ignoring the question and trying to ignore her Black-Strand-Twirl, I suggest, "Why not use a different name?"

The twirling stops. She briefly tilts her head. "That might work. Thanks!"

"Don't mention it." I pause to roll the chair back in place and ease down, finishing with, "To anyone."

"Afraid Jed will find out you're helping me?"

"Maybe. Or I just don't want 'Gemma' and 'Tyler' said in the same sentence at school."

"Again, noted." Gemma starts dialing. "Jack Wayeland? This is Gemma … Greyson. Do you have time for an interview about your Bear-Wolf sighting?"

When she side glances at me, my wicked grin reappears, and I whisper, "Gemma Greyson?"

Covering the phone, she hisses, "It's the first that came to mind," then she calmly resumes the interview. "It's for an article in my middle school's newspaper."

Fingers to the keyboard, I summon new browser results with:

Jack Wayeland and the Bear-Wolf.

The results explode with headline after headline.

Jack Wayeland: Face-to-Face with a Bear-Wolf.

Bear-Wolf Strikes Again!

Bear-Wolf: Fact or Fiction?

Gemma reassures, "You're not crazy, Mr. Wayeland. A few Kentucky residents claim sightings of it. There was only one, until two years ago. Since then, five more people have made reports."

Just then, the memory of the marred tree on the path to Mirror Lake makes my hairs stand on end. *The Bear-Wolf? Is that what Mom heard the other night? What if it's from Muraine, but here now? Watching us?*

Gemma continues, "Only one other person had a close encounter. She has a low-quality picture to prove it. Not much else. Were you able to get any shots of it?"

Skimming a blog-article, I glean that this Jack Wayeland was out hunting coyotes, during his week off from work. When I spot the date of his encounter, my heart stops.

June sixth? I muse. *My birthday.*

He came back to camp, for lunch, but something had ransacked it. Not scaring easily, he documented the scene with phone pictures—large claw marks in his gear and a shredded tent like a cat's plaything. But what scared him the most was his truck's tailgate that had been ripped off and was cold to the touch, even though the air was stifling hot that day.

Gemma's shoulders slump. "Your phone, that had all the pictures, disappeared?"

I read on. While he was packing up to leave, and making a voice recording, a low growl sounded from behind. Searching for the source, he raised his gun. Among a patch of trees, the horse-sized wolf watched him. Like a sleek and agile cat, but with the bulk of a bear, it sauntered out. When Jack pulled the trigger, it sprang at him. Reaching him in one lunge, Jack was pinned to the ground. Too terrified to scream, he stared into its black eyes.

"You have something better than pictures?" Gemma's clicking pen stops and she straightens. "A dash-cam video? That was never reported."

I save the article to a document, before shutting everything down. Pulling out the picture of Aunt Miriam, I study Cousin Alec's sandy-blond locks and blue eyes.

"I would love a copy," states Gemma. "Let me give you my—"

Jack interrupts, then she answers, "It's in London, Kentucky. Why do you ask?"

Alec's smile doesn't show his teeth, but Aunt Miriam's are normal.

"You live an hour away?"

My musing continues, *Alec and Talok could be related. An older brother. A cousin of a cousin? Except Dad only has one sibling. Or does he?*

Gemma's voice strains. "You're meeting Tadashi Galloway. In London. Today? You don't say."

Returning picture to drawer, I amble to the tall bookcase close to Gemma.

"I meet up with his daughter there, all the time. Look forward to seeing you." Gemma ends the call.

Leaning against the case, I ask, "Dash-cam. What else?"

"Quality isn't good, but it shows the Bear-Wolf knocking him to the ground."

"Where are we meeting him?"

"Morning Bliss at three." Skepticism contorts Gemma's face. "You want to go with me?"

"How else should I pass the time, before *the talk* with my mom?"

"Again. I tried."

"Then stop trying." I smirk.

With each Aviridian device, Gemma stuffs her satchel to bulging and gripes, "Turns out he's on his way back from somewhere, and meeting my dad there before continuing home to Hazard, Kentucky."

"What a coincidence."

"Not likely." She gives a long sigh. "My dad. Always one step ahead. I told him about the article a week ago."

"If it helps, I found a blog-article on Jack Wayeland."

"Nice!" Gemma scribbles on the desk notepad. "Send it to my email later?"

"Sure."

"Be ready by two thirty." With that, she leaves the study.

Slouching into the chair once occupied by Gemma, I run a finger along the peacock lamp residing on a corner of the desk and cup my face, mumbling, "Maybe she's not so bad."

* * *

"Tyler!" Mother shakes me awake. "You're going to the interview with Gemma, dressed in those dirty clothes?"

"What?" I chase away the mind-fog.

"It's two thirty!" she exclaims.

I bolt up to my room, as if a wasp-swarm hovers overhead, and change into the freshest clothes I can find. Next is the body spray encasing me like repellent.

"Probably overdid it," I hiss. "Too late now."

Tossing the B.O. repellent on the bed, I'm about to leave. But the sound of a crinkling paper stops me. As I reach for it, my left hand aches.

Son of LanSoren.

One day, I will tell you all I know of your father's death. Until then.

—Forever at Your Service

Dropping the paper back on the bed, I moan. "What's happening? No time for that, now!" Racing down to the car, I jump in, musing, *Off to London, Kentucky! The berating of Mother to follow. At least I have ammunition: Ginger Jones dating Dad. My dad!*

Most of the ride is silent.

Her grip of death assaulting the wheel, Mother seethes like a viper; meanwhile, I'm plotting how to confiscate Gemma's pictures of Awngeleik.

Ripping one hand of death from the wheel, Mother cranks up the AC and turns my nose to ice.

"Sorry," I whisper, "about using all the hot water."

She snaps, "That's not why I'm upset. I mean, I'm upset about that too. But you can tell your new therapist what it is you do with all the *scalding* water."

"I have a new therapist?"

"You will."

"When?"

She glances from the road ahead, to glare a warning at me.

"Yes, ma'am," I mumble, folding my hands. "What did you find out about the star yesterday?"

"Enough that I'm going to the library, during your interview."

"How'd you know about the interview?"

"Tadashi and Gemma stopped by. But I told them I was going into town anyway and I'd take you myself."

When we pull up to the Morning Bliss, I ease out.

"Tadashi and Gemma will take you home. Don't wait for me," states Mother, before driving off.

I take a deep breath and open the door of the Morning Bliss. Gemma sits at a window booth, while Tadashi flips through a magazine. Seeing me, she stops her chatter and waves me over. When I approach, her nose wrinkles. Then there's Tadashi smelling his coffee, while looking at me, before taking a long gulp.

I hold up a defensive hand. "Better I smell like this, than fish or the lake."

"At least you care about hygiene," states Tadashi, with a grin.

"Maybe you should sit next to me." Gemma bites back a laugh. "Don't want Mr. Wayeland passing out from the fumes."

While studying Tadashi, I wonder, *What is it about him that's always terrified me? Slight sternness to his voice. But no accent. Oriental eyes full of kindness. But a sharpness to his face that seems to belie the kindness.*

Tadashi slips a fifty over to Gemma. "Be polite, and get something for Tyler. I'll be over there." He points. "Making myself *scarce.* Good to see you, Tyler." He claps a hand on my arm, and then retreats to scarcity with his magazine and coffee.

Gemma slides out, asking, "What do you want?"

"Spiced cider," is my reply, while slithering into the booth.

"Apple turnover too?"

In disdain, I make a face and say, "Mushy, mutilated apple pieces swimming in my mouth? No, thank you."

Gemma's laugh is like music, free of tension and full of bliss.

Trying to ignore the visual allure of her dark, lacy sleeveless shirt, I prop my elbows on the table and reply, "Cinnamon roll with cream-cheese frosting is fine."

"That does sound good." She goes to order at the counter. Tapping the whole way there are her tan flats, on the tile floor, and swaying with those steps are her small hips concealed by white skinny jeans.

In that moment, I scold myself with, *Stop looking, Tyler! Don't be like Jed.* Despite my efforts, I take a second glance. *How is anything even there, when she's so rake-thin?*

Sensing a glance my way, I spot Tadashi's scowl. I gulp, as our eyes lock. Then he looks down, and goes back to flipping through his magazine. Startling me, Gemma sets my cider on the table and proceeds to slide in and barricade any escape of a certain Tyler Ravier.

Now imprisoned. No going back.

Gemma stirs her own cider, commenting, "I'm surprised you came."

"I said I would. Maybe it's to see you crash and burn."

Seeming to bite back a retort, Gemma just smirks. And I sip my tangy cider. That is, until she commits blasphemy with one touch. My left forearm, to be precise. Up, the pain surges to my shoulder. Oblivious of my discomfort, she points to the napkins in the holder. I begrudgingly give her one. The wait for food is short, as two servers bring Gemma's order. Piece by piece, the trays are emptied on the table.

Staring over the vast expanse of food, I *am* speechless. Halfway finding my voice, I squeak at first, then clear my throat. "You're not … throwing me a belated birthday party? Are you?"

"Don't be silly." She gives me the cinnamon roll.

"Then who's going to eat all this?"

"Jack Wayeland, you, and me," she replies, while spearing strawberries and kiwi from a monstrous bowl of yogurt topped with granola.

"Speaking of Jack Wayeland." I point to the tall man being handed a drink at the counter. "Is that him?"

Gemma sucks down the food in her mouth, before coughing.

"Do you need a Heimlich?" I ask.

In one swift motion, Gemma shoves at my shoulder and glides out of the booth, calling, "Mr. Wayeland?"

"Yes?" replies the slender man.

"Gemma Greyson." She holds out her hand.

Jack shakes it and then settles in across from me. He drifts his gaze over the food-mountain, before asking, "Will others be joining us?"

Gemma replies, "Just my neighbor and classmate: Tyler Ravier."

"Ravier?" Jack's brown eyebrows shoot up. "You wouldn't be Lance and Amira's boy, would you?"

When I nod in confirmation, his massive, gripping handshake tightens to crushing. After an eternity, he lets go. I rub the tingles away underneath the table.

"What a small world." Jack grins. "Good college days with Tadashi and Lance. Ginger and Molly. Amira and … little Kathryn. May she rest in—"

Gemma interrupts, "I ordered extra. Help yourself." She pushes the empty bowl away.

"Ate on the way. Now, to business. The still-shot from the video, as promised." Jack gives her a folder, then a micro thumb drive from his pocket. "And the video itself."

After flipping the folder open, Gemma begins with, "Tell us about your experience coming face-to-face with the Bear-Wolf."

I lean closer to Gemma to peer at the picture, which she distractedly relinquishes to me. Dwarfing Jack Wayeland is the massive wolf pinning him down. Although it's reminiscent of a wolf, its long legs bulge like a lion. With its mouth wide open, the longish snout hovers over Jack's head. Disguising what is fur or muscle is its black coat. Altogether? It's a beast of terror.

For twenty minutes, Jack relays his experience. The only differences from the article are the fear in his recount and the terror in his eyes reliving it.

"When it roared in my face," he says, "it was all-surrounding. Eerie. Like five different creatures at once. I thought a pack had surrounded me and were about to tear me apart."

Finished with her ham and Swiss croissant, Gemma probes, "What happened next?"

Jack just shakes his head a moment. "From several yards away, a black bear roared. And the beast lunged off me, cracking a rib or two. That's when I blacked out."

I ask, "Why do you think it let you live?"

"Maybe it likes its prey to fight a bit. The bear would've provided that better than me." Jack pauses to eye the food-mountain—now half-gone—before he continues. "Looking back, what disturbed me more than the encounter was finding the black bear dead on the road home. Fish and Game later told me the bear was killed near my campsite. Then dragged over three miles, to where I found it on the road."

"Why's that more disturbing?" I ask.

"Because," replies Jack, "I think that beast knew the way I had to take to get home. The bear only had wounds: two nasty gouges on its sides, with a deep bite to the back of the neck. Whatever killed it wasn't interested in food. Everything hints at it being intelligent. Intelligent, conniving creatures are far more terrifying than those driven by an instinct to survive."

"Agreed," states Gemma.

"When first seeing that bear on the road," continues Jack, tapping on the table thrice, "I thought it was sleeping. It caught me off guard. Later, it terrified me that something went to the trouble of *posing* the bear. When I went to check my phone signal and make a call, my phone was gone. Never did find it."

I glance out the window, to the street, musing, *An intelligent monster? If people knew, widespread panic would erupt.*

Gemma breezes through the rest of her questions for Jack, while I continue looking out the window.

When I spot Jed and Jaxson Craven walking down the sidewalk, their mouths yapping, my attention snaps back to Gemma and Jack. *Haven't thought of an excuse for hanging out with Gemma yet. Jed's going to kill me.*

Although horrified, I remain motionless. From over the top of the booth, I watch the Morning Bliss door admit Jed and Jaxson. As if searching for something, they glance around. And I duck my head low. *Looking for me, most likely.*

"That's everything I need, Mr. Wayeland." Gemma stands to shake hands.

Naturally, the twins pick that moment to pass our booth.

Jed stops to announce, "Gemma Galloway! Fancy seeing you here. Tyler too?"

If flames could shoot from Jed's eyes, I'd be turned to ash in seconds. Not much better are Jaxson's furrowed blond eyebrows. All I have for them is a pathetic hand-wave. No words. Just the wave, a cringe, and my own thoughts: *They shouldn't be back from vacation yet. What gives?*

"Turned to the dark forces, Tyler?" Jed folds his tanned, freckled arms. "Wondered when Gemma would entice you. Thought you were immune to the popular, pretty girls."

Only too calmly, I reply, "I still am. Weren't you supposed to be on vacation a little longer? Why are you back early?"

Jaxson starts to say something, but Jed cuts him off. "Bro, don't tell him. He's sided with the enemy. Look at him sitting by her."

Jaxson blurts out, "We came home early, because of him."

"Jaxson, you traitor of a brother! Tyler's going to find out what happened now because, whenever Ravier is curious about something, he *always* learns the truth. Thanks, you backstabber."

Knowing it's a feeble statement, I still say it. "You've been gone for over a week, and I got bored."

"That's your excuse for betrayal?" Jed spews. "Me and Jax weren't here to fill every second of your summer? Who was there for you, through the worst of it, last year? It certainly wasn't her."

Gemma scoffs. "Jed, you're such a whiner. Stop taking it out on Tyler. It's not his fault I refused a date with you."

Barely maintaining his cool, Jack Wayeland holds his spontaneous smile at bay. Lacking any words, I just shrug at him; meanwhile, Gemma and the twins argue over her prank on Jed.

Next thing we know, Jed is shouting, "I'm over it, Gemma!"

"You don't sound, *over* it," she proclaims. "It was just a bit of fun."

"A bit of fun?" Jaxson fumes. "You led him on. Got him to think you liked him. Then recorded refusing him and posted it on social media for everyone to laugh at. It was cruel, and you know it."

"Bro"—Jed smacks his brother's arm—"I can defend myself."

Jack Wayeland interrupts with, "I'll let you teenagers hash it out. Let me know how it ends, Gemma. Send the article, when it's done."

Absently, Gemma responds, "No problem."

Tadashi watches it all, while still scarce and sipping from his mug, until Jack jaunts over to join him.

Back on me are the twin's eyes of rage.

"Dude! I can't even look at you." Jed storms out of the café, leaving Jaxson in his wake.

To Jaxson, I offer, "I'm helping her research a paper for school."

All he gets out is, "Why?"

"Like I said, I was bored *and* you weren't supposed to be back from your family's vacation, for another three weeks. I thought, why not help her? It'll break up the monotony of my summer."

"You know how Jed feels about her," states Jaxson. "Any positive interaction with her is betrayal to him. You've left me with a lot of damage control, Ty."

"I know. I'll make it up to you."

"In the meantime," Jaxson stresses, "the body sprays? Throw those in the garbage. They're not doing you any favors. Use cologne, instead."

"Don't have any."

"What about your dad's? They were the bomb," states Jaxson, holding the collar of his shirt a moment. Though he tries on confidence, Jaxson's blush in response to a girl's smile is always the end result. Like now. With Gemma grinning at him.

"She threw them away." Although my mouth is bone-dry, I still try to gulp down the non-existent spit. "Actually, she broke the first one and drained it down the sink. Then, threw the rest away."

"Dude!" Jaxson's large, blue eyes blink at me.

"Doesn't matter." I squeeze my neck. "It was a year ago."

Sadness gone, Jaxson sports his gambler face: relaxed eyes and crooked grin. "Got a secret for you, Ty."

"What's that?"

"Jed stole one of his. Never worked up the nerve to give it back. After he …" Jaxson pauses. "Want me to steal it back for you? I can have it by next week."

"You're the best, Jax."

"I try." Before leaving, Jaxson fixates on the last croissant. "Mind if I…?" He glances at Gemma, again, his face flushing slightly pink.

"Go ahead." She motions.

Seizing the croissant, Jaxson gives his two-fingered wave and then leaves.

Gemma sits across from me. She plops her elbows down and cups her face with both hands. "That wasn't embarrassing at all." Pausing long enough for one breath, Gemma bursts out, "Tell my dad I'm in the car. Ready whenever both of you are."

From the booth, Gemma bounds out of the Morning Bliss and into the safety of her dad's black BMW; meanwhile, I'm left to finish my ice-cold cider in silence.

6

Into the Lion's Den

I approach their booth, as Jack Wayeland's voice fades into earshot, "You've still got the steel, Tadashi. Ginger will take a knife to that dragon painting, if she ever finds out."

"That's half the reward," states Tadashi. "The steep risk."

Clearing my throat, I lower my voice. "Mr. Galloway?"

Tadashi exclaims, "Tyler! Smooth things over with your friends?"

"Gemma's ready to go."

Tadashi's smile diminishes. "Where is she?"

"Car," is my abrupt reply.

Tadashi thinks a moment, while undoing the top button of his pale shirt. "Let's give her a few more minutes alone. Have a seat." With his leather jacket squeaking against the pleather booth, Tadashi moves over to let me slide in next to him.

Then Jack tilts his head, asking me, "How's your mom these days?"

I shrug. "Researching an eight-pointed star-stone thing, at the library."

Jack's eyes light up. "Like the one your dad entrusted me with two years ago?"

Pulse quickening, I ask, "He gave it to you?"

More solemn now, Jack nods. "It's why I wasn't at the funeral. I was in England. Taking it to his sister."

"That's why Miriam wasn't there," Tadashi scorns. "You were intercepting her in England? Couldn't that have waited, until after the funeral?"

Jack lifts his shoulders, in defense. "I admit my timing was bad, but Lance acted … odd when he gave it to me. Serious. Insistent. He said, 'Jack, if anything happens to me, make sure to give this star to my sister. Immediately.' His words were commanding, not requesting."

Tadashi leans back, his face as confused as my thoughts.

Why haven't I heard of this guy? I wonder. *Does he know more than he's letting on? Could he have left the note? How to find out?*

Tadashi's phone vibrates on the table. Lifting it into view, he frowns.

Stealing a glance at it, I see Gemma's texts popping onto the screen like rapid-fire bullets.

Waiting for like-

20 minutes!

Vibrating to sound like a quacking duck, Tadashi's phone receives more Gemma-Bullets.

Grab Tyler, so we can go

Please!

I'm not going back in there

Invite Tyler to dinner?

Molly wants to meet him

Show off her new French-cooking skills

Don't ask Tyler, while you're in there

Want to see his reaction

Jack's shoulders quake with stifled laughter. "Ginger or Kaida?"

"Neither. Gemma-Drama." Tadashi drums his fingers on the table, before glancing at his BMW outside. "What do you want to bet, she's watching?"

"Nothing," states Jack. "Because you win. Every time."

"Have to live up to the name," states Tadashi, with his gaze still on the car. He flashes me the text conversation, asking, "Tyler. Want to sample Molly's cooking tonight?"

I ask, "Who would ever turn down French-cooking?"

"Only fools," declares Jack.

The phone vibrates again.

Why would you show him?

Betrayal!

What'd he say?

"Better go, before her rage sets fire to the new car." Tadashi taps his knuckles on the table. "You're welcome to come too, Jack."

If I didn't know better, I'd think Gemma ... likes me? Nah. Can't be.

Jack slides a letter over to Tadashi, saying, "Another time."

"What were you saying about fools, Jack?" With a chuckle, Tadashi takes the letter.

"No fools here. Just don't want *her* putting the pieces together. Make sure *she* gets that?"

Catching the name scribbled on the letter—more importantly, the penmanship—my heart drops. *Molly Smith,* I muse. *Writing's nothing like the note on my bed. Who could've left that note. Tadashi? But why?*

They say goodbye, then Tadashi and I head for the BMW.

Easing into the driver's seat, Tadashi turns to Gemma. "Ask him yourself."

Plastered to the opposite side of the back seat, Gemma's discomfort bleeds through her makeup-mask. Not even two seconds after I click my seatbelt, she braves a quick look to ask, "Tyler, do you want to come over for dinner?"

Prolonging her misery with silence, I glimpse Tadashi's piercing eyes in the rearview mirror, and I flash my wicked grin. "I'll come for the food. Tolerate the company. I mean, it's French-cooking. Nuff said."

Too excited to notice my grin, she proclaims, "We'll have more time for the article."

"That too," I agree.

More like sabotaging the evidence of Awngeleik. Too many secrets floating around. Too risky to let someone see the pictures of her by Mirror Lake.

* * *

Tadashi unlocks the front door, thus initiating my first time in the Lion's Den. Over wine-red marble floors, it sways open without a sound. White panels wrap the large entrance perimeter and extend to the night sky ceiling. Then the panels fade into the sweeping staircase. As for the stairs, first are eight steps. Angled not quite ninety-degrees from them, thirteen more transition to end on the second floor. The rest are out of sight.

To the left, water flows down a wall of glass. Beyond the wall, black chairs and a large table wait to be filled.

On the marble pillars are swirls of white, gray, and black climbing upward. Two pillars greet all who enter or leave this den. Three—securing the second floor—outline the staircase wall. But every entry into another room is guarded by two. Eleven pillars in all.

"Don't be long, Gemma." Tadashi saunters to the far left corner doors, saying, "Molly should have dinner ready soon." With that, the double-doors click behind him.

When Gemma dashes upstairs, the first step cracks loudly. Yet, it's unbroken. Memorizing each stair, every creak, and all sighs, I follow her footsteps up two flights—thirty-four steps—to the third floor. On this level is a long hallway, French doors leading to the patio, and yet *another* flight of stairs.

The secret to staying rake-thin? Galloping up never-ending stairs.

As Gemma climbs the third flight, her backside calls for an audience. And I oblige, though conflicted, and ask myself, *To shake or not shake the habits of Jed Craven?*

The springing-hips stop, and my gaze races up to Gemma's downcast eyes, as she mutters, "I'm sorry."

"For what?" I ask, but think, *I should be the sorry one. Promised myself I wouldn't become him. Yet, here I am. Becoming the one and only Jed Craven.*

Mournfully, she replies, "Jed made me realize *today* that I haven't changed."

"You shouldn't be sorry. You told the truth."

"It's not … what I said." She wobbles her head. "It's what I did, after he left. The unending plotting? I can't shake it."

I nod. "Old habits die slowly?"

"And painfully," adds Gemma, now standing in front of the first door on the right. She shoves the door wide open. "Make yourself comfortable."

Upon entering, the deep-maroon furniture tries to calm the wrath of green. Green rug. Green walls. Green-striped curtains. But the pastel appalls the senses.

"Don't say it." She kicks her shoes off, into an adjoining room, exposing her painted purple and black toenails. "My mom still thinks I love pastel green."

I take the four steps to the only black in the room—a desk and computer chair. Together, they shield the window overlooking the Galloways' pool and colorful gardens.

Gemma waves at a corner of the ceiling. "Say hello to Kane Himura and Haru Maki."

Spotting the camera in the corner, I blurt out, "Someone's watching?"

"When my sister got caught sleeping with the chauffeur, my dad set up cameras. Only the bedrooms and bathrooms are safe. Have an alarm too. Stays off until after ten, because my mom hates putting in the code throughout the day."

Cameras everywhere? I muse. *Can kiss stealing the photos goodbye.*

My mouth goes dry, as I ask, "Can they hear us too?"

Filling the room, right then, is a masculine, Oriental-accented voice asking, "Everything all right, Miss Gemma?"

She jabs a button on the small intercom, next to her bedroom door. "Everything's fine, Kane. Meet Tyler Ravier."

Kane breathes his question right into the mic. "He agree to help with that paper?"

"Yes," replies Gemma.

Static distorts the accented words of Haru's perky greeting. "Hello, Tyler!"

A wave at the camera is all I muster. Never a good sign, when the shrugging turns to waving.

"Gemma." Haru taps the mic. "Do we get to see the photo of the Bear-Wolf?"

"Not until it's finished. Quiet, now, so we can work." Gemma scans Jack Wayeland's photo into her computer.

"What should I work on?"

"Transfer the files to this, for yourself?" She hands me a micro flash drive, then wakes up her computer and mistypes the password. During her re-type, I discreetly look. A 'V' is all I catch. The screen loads to a textured-purple wallpaper. On it, a quote in white reads:

Life's riches cannot be spent. Nor can they be burned. They soar in memories left behind, long after a life has lost its breath. –Bruce Parson

"Who's Bruce Parson?"

"Founder and head developer of Aviridian Corp." She points to a desktop folder. "That one."

"Ironic. That his quote's now on one of his devices." Dragging the folder 'Creature Sightings' to the flash drive, I ask, "That all?"

"For now. Wanna get started?"

I push away from the desk, asking, "After water?"

"Then off to the kitchen it is," states Gemma. As I stuff the flash drive in my pocket, she signals. "Camera-free elevator's this way."

Straight from the stairs, we make our way down a narrow corridor.

Of course they have an elevator for this monstrosity.

"Yet, we took the stairs?" I ask.

"Because I enjoy the exercise."

"Because"—I smirk—"you don't have chores?"

"That, and I hate elevators."

Gliding down to the first floor, the elevator ends our awkward glances swiftly with a ding and doors sliding open. We enter the kitchen, and it embraces us with its buttery spices and hint of seafood.

Also greeting us is a woman's rich, Southern accent. "Miss Gemma! Come for a peek at tonight's supper?"

"Just water," states Gemma.

"And an introduction." Stepping forward, I hold out my hand. "Molly Smith? Tyler Ravier."

Contrasting on her dark-brown skin are flecks of flour and dough, as Molly wipes her hands on the apron and then grips mine with her long piano fingers. "Good to meet you. Wash the hands. Don the apron. And

I'll put you to work," states Molly, while tucking some wispy black curls back into her loose braid.

"How about we set the table, instead?" suggests Gemma. Pulling out bottled water from the fridge, she gives it to me.

"I'll accept that," replies Molly, smiling. Her white teeth sparkle on her angular face.

In three gulps, I down half the water. Then spot them by the kitchen door: keys on a labeled holder.

Front and back door keys should be sufficient to get me in. But how to sneak them off the holder, without anyone noticing?

"Anyone, besides Tyler, joining us?" queries Gemma, before holding her breath.

"Meaning your sister's boyfriend? No," replies Molly.

"Good!" breathes Gemma.

Around the hospital-white kitchen—with burgundy tile floors and black granite counters—I glance with a sinking heart. *Cameras on all exits. Sneaking in? Impossible!*

Finishing my water, I follow Gemma through the double French doors and into the dining room bursting with art stills of flowers, birds, exotic fruits, and more. Next, we raid the china cabinet of square, white plates and arrange five place settings on the black table, but leave the deep-red runner gracing the middle.

Seating for twelve, I muse. Family of four. Must feel lonely.

Sweeping a hand over the glossy table finish, I ask to confirm my fear, "Who's the fifth setting for?"

"Kaida," Gemma mumbles. "Can't wait for her to graduate and move out next year." Not waiting for my response, Gemma calls out, "How many rooms can we tour before dinner, Molly?"

"Three!" she answers.

"I bet four." Gemma knocks, while opening the door adjacent to the dining archway and pokes her head in. "Mind if Tyler tours your office?"

Tadashi pauses his conversation, replying, "No, but be quiet. I'm on a business call."

At the door, Gemma stops me to say, "The goal is for you to see some of my mom's art collection, before dinner."

"Sure thing."

"Touring four rooms should get us up to twenty. That should satisfy her."

"Twenty?" I ask. "How many does she have?"

Searching for words, Gemma's mouth hangs open a moment. "Lost count at forty. That was two years ago. Probably double that, by now."

"As long as they're not all huge—"

Gemma cuts me off. "They're all *museum* size. Ulacious!"

"That's not a word."

"It is now. For my mom's art collection."

Sarcasm winning, I state, "Eighty's not excessive at all."

"If you only knew." Gemma pushes the door open all the way.

In front of the silky-white curtains, behind his desk, Tadashi paces with a phone in one hand and a Katana in the other. Rattling away in Japanese, he has not a hint of American touching his accent.

Like the entry, white panels refine the walls. Black tiles—flecked with copper and gold—sparkle beneath the spotlights shining down. The one simplifying feature is the all-black office furniture, in this room filled with Japanese metal-art of three bronze tigers, five dragon plaques, and eight tabletop Samurais.

When a slight grumble escapes Tadashi, he shoulders his phone to tug aside the curtains. Shielded by glass, the vibrant garden draws all attention. Its only competition in the room is the single painting: an Oriental watercolor of a dragon.

Unlike the terrifying Japanese-dragons—twisting round themselves, always ready for attack—it's suggestive of a noble English-dragon gazing, without a care in the world, over a vast landscape. His golden tiger-stripes paint across the scales of his black face, red sides, and magnificent wings. Atop a mound of golden relics, he sits like a cat wrapping its long tail around all four legs. Behind him, waves rise up to his head. Beneath the mound, a river of fire swirls. Yet, the great dragon does not care.

"What's the story behind this one, Gemma?"

"Family heirloom. Can never get the story right—" Gemma jumps, right then, as someone slams the front door.

High heels clack on the entry tile, and out comes a woman's shrill voice. "Tadashi! How was Jack Wayeland?"

Gemma bites her lower lip. "Dang! She's home early. Back to the elevator."

7

Vision of the Dragon

"Prosciutto and fig crostata, Tyler?" offers Molly, smiling.

"Yes. Thank you," I reply.

To Gemma, her parents, and me, Molly serves two thin pie slices each and then disappears back into the kitchen.

"Where's Kaida?" queries Tadashi, while eyeing the clean plate adjacent to Ginger's place setting.

"I haven't a clue, Tadashi," replies Ginger. "Gemma, do you know where your sister has gone?"

Gemma slightly shakes her head, while I bite into my crostata slice. Topped with cream cheese, fig, prosciutto, and thyme, it's a savory salty-sweetness promising of better things to come.

Flawless are Ginger Galloway's auburn waves framing her face, as she focuses on Tadashi like a lion stalking prey. "I went to an art auction today and bought new pieces. Should arrive tomorrow," she announces.

Tadashi dares to question the lioness. "When did you find time for that?"

"Early this morning. I was going to take Gemma, but she already went out." The lioness now stalks Gemma. "Remind me again, what were you doing?"

"Photography," is Gemma's quick reply.

"Summer's only started, Gemma." Ginger dabs a napkin to her red lips. "You'll have ample time for your camera later."

"She's getting a head start," defends Tadashi. "What's wrong with that?"

"Nothing," replies Ginger innocently. "Only, I don't understand what the fuss is about. She's not good enough to make a living at it."

Tadashi undoes another shirt button. His neck now free of the collar, but face unreadable, he says, "We did buy her that camera and several lens options. It would be wasteful, for her *not* to use them."

"Yes, yes, of course. So long as she doesn't let dreams go to her head." Petite nose wrinkling, Ginger picks off a piece of prosciutto and, to our dismay, continues, "Take Kaida, for example. Straight A's. Even in the advanced math and science classes."

Gemma's crushed expression shifts away from her mother, while she toys with her last crostata. "Only because she cheats," she whispers.

Neither parent responds to Gemma's remark, and I wonder, *Didn't they hear her?*

"Gemma, on the other hand," states Ginger, "is an A-B student. Occasional C's. Subjects? Math and science."

Gemma looks away, toward the French doors, to Molly standing hidden from the lioness. Lifting her head, Molly mouths the words 'chin up.' Then Gemma's dark eyes brighten. Shyly, she glances to me, then down at her plate.

Bullied by her own mom. How long? Her whole life?

"I wondered, Tadashi," continues the chorus of Ginger, still oblivious to Gemma's pain, "if you could move your Asian paintings to the office; it has so much wall space."

"*Why* would I need to move my *Asian* paintings?" queries Tadashi, his eyes angrily flickering.

"Weren't you listening? To make room for the pieces I bought at the auction. You'll love them. Some are by Vincenzo Giovannini. Should match our bedroom décor quite nicely."

I interrupt Ginger's chatter by saying, "Ms. Galloway?"

"Yes, Tyler? Finished your crostatas already? Molly should be out with the next course shortly." Her head turns back to Tadashi's simmering gaze.

Think fast! I tell myself. *Or Tadashi might explode.* Expecting frantic words to fly out, instead, my sharp composure speaks, "Why don't you think Gemma can make a career out of photography? She's no Ansel Adams, but she's won lots of awards."

All eyes are on me. That is, until Gemma's older sister—my former babysitter—picks that moment to burst into the dining room and take the seat next to Ginger. "Sorry I'm late!" exclaims Kaida. "I'm famished."

On cue, Molly brings out crostatas for Kaida and the next course for the rest of us. Like a promise fulfilled, buttery and smooth Lobster Bisque—topped with bits of chive—is set in front of us.

Weakly smiling at Molly, during her retreat, Tadashi addresses Kaida. "Where were you?"

Through a small mouthful of crostata, Kaida simply replies, "Doctor's appointment."

Tadashi sighs. "Another? You've had one every month, since January. You've not been sick, that I've noticed. Everything all right?"

Kaida nods. Finishing her crostatas, she shrills, "Molly! I'm ready for the bisque."

Tadashi fastens his hands together, in front of his hanging head, as if praying to some deity. Any deity. Perhaps, to strike Ginger and Kaida down with a bolt of lightning.

Like a server to the difficult customer, Molly delivers the bisque with a sweet smile plastered on her face. As she turns back to the kitchen, however, rage is in her dark eyes.

Sadly, that's when Kaida's malicious eyes notice me from across the table. "Little Tyler Ravier?" she croons. "Wouldn't have recognized you, if it weren't for the green eyes. No one said it was guest night. I would've invited Hunter."

"It's not guest night," states Ginger. "Gemma invited Tyler over for dinner."

"Oh! How sweet," teases Kaida, as Gemma's spoon clatters against her own bowl.

"He's helping me with an article, Kaida."

"And art analyzing," I add, now noticing the vein-popping forehead on

Tadashi. *Not good!*

"I forgot to ask." Ginger perks up. "Which of the paintings did you most admire, Tyler?"

Swallowing some bisque, I try recalling in detail just one of the twenty paintings Gemma made me study. First, the sunroom abounding in stills upon stills of … everything. Then the entertainment room sporting abstracts. We ended in the family room, splattered in a chaos of every art style imaginable. Gemma's words for it: an utter eyesore!

This should irritate her, I muse, before replying, "The dragon watercolor, in the office."

"Tadashi's heirloom?" Barely holding onto politeness, Ginger's fawn-brown eyes stare into my soul with disdain. "An interesting choice. You like dragons, then?"

"Guess so." I shrug. "What's the story behind it? A Japanese style, but an English-dragon. It's unusual."

"It is," agrees Tadashi, as Kaida pushes aside her half-finished bisque.

"Unusual," states Kaida, "like us having a Scottish surname, unusual?"

Right then, Molly comes to replace our soup bowls with chopped salads coated in vinaigrette.

Gemma adds, "We have our great-grandfather to thank, for the Scottish last name."

"Adair Galloway," states Tadashi proudly. "Adopted by a Scottish couple in 1923. As for the painting, it was the first of several art pieces painted by him, while he lived in Japan."

Gemma takes a sip of sparkling juice, before saying, "I always wondered how he ended up in Scotland."

"As do we all," murmurs Ginger.

"He wasn't *born* in Scotland?" I ask.

"We don't think so," replies Tadashi. "As the story goes, he moved to Hiroshima in 1945 to find his biological family and never left."

"Isn't that the year Japan was bombed?" I gulp down some water.

Munching on his salad, Tadashi responds with a nod. Then, wiping all past gloom away, Molly returns beaming, as she carries out a platter of braised pork topped with pearl onions, seared grapes, and sauce. By far, it's the best of the night.

"What do you think of Molly's cooking, Tyler?" Gemma cuts into her extra-smothered pork.

I think a moment, then say, "Indescribable, I guess. Words don't quite do it justice."

Everyone grins. Even the stuck-up Kaida smiles, before she's asking me, "Better than your mother's?"

I hold up a defensive hand, saying, "Plead the fifth."

"Smart boy," states Tadashi.

Kaida leaves her grapes and onions untouched, but finishes her pork, and shrills again, "Molly! Dessert, please!"

Vein-popping returns to Tadashi, but it's Gemma snapping out, "Kaida, stop shouting! You're giving us all a headache."

"I don't have a headache," soothes Ginger, while touching Tadashi's forearm. "Do you have a headache, dear?"

More like an aneurysm about to explode, I think, *if you and Kaida don't shut up.*

His eyes blinking blankly, Tadashi shakes his head. "Jet-lag. Tell Molly I'll take dessert in my office. Come get me, Tyler, when you need a ride home."

* * *

Sitting at his desk, Tadashi rubs at his temples. His mood, however, is eased by Gemma setting the floating island dessert in front of him and mustering a French accent to say, "Îles Flottantes. Bon Appétit."

He looks up to ask, "What flavor?" as she takes the seat opposite of the desk.

"Lemon Meringue," I reply. "Should help melt away the … jet-lag."

"Welcome"—Tadashi stifles a laugh—"to the Galloways, my burden to bear."

Stealing a glance at Gemma, I state, "At least they're not boring."

Recovering from a slight blush, Gemma says, "Never a dull moment, with

90

Kaida and Mother around."

"Or you," adds Tadashi. "Would love a no-girls day. Just me and the cat."

"You have a cat?" I ask, during my amble toward the dragon painting.

"Minksy. Didn't even get to name my own birthday present," grumbles Tadashi. "Ginger, Molly, and the girls voted on it. What can a man do, when he's out-numbered four-to-one?"

I shrug. "Go with it."

"Exactly." Tadashi takes his first bite, closing his eyes in ecstasy. "Paris trip was worth every penny."

When I glance from the painting, to the pair of them, Gemma has started munching on the sugar cage that protects the meringue. "Where's she going to next?" she queries.

"Hasn't yet decided." He takes another bite. "Where's yours, Tyler?"

"Finished it, while Ginger and Kaida discussed the latest fashions." By now, I'm looking into the mesmerizing eyes of the dragon. More importantly, its pupils. They reflect, as if life has been breathed into them.

"They would have gone on forever." Gemma exaggerates her eye-roll. "I suggested Kaida show Mom what she got today. That's why she was late. Shopping at the mall, after her *doctor's* appointment."

"Should I be worried?"

Tadashi scoops the remaining custard off the plate, as Gemma sets hers down to ask, "About how much she spent at the mall or the nature of the appointment?"

"Both."

Gemma cringes. "Yes, and maybe."

Tadashi sighs deeply, as if the weight of the world is crushing him. Meanwhile, I run my hand along the painting's black frame and little plaque labeled: *Vision of the Dragon.*

I try to stop them, but they persist. More numbers. *Twenty-two to slumber. Thirteen to conquer. Eight to rise.* It ends, and I wonder, *What do they mean?*

Tadashi jars me from my thoughts, saying, "Your dad loved that painting. First time seeing it, he insisted on knowing every detail of its history. Said if I ever wanted to part with it, he should be the first to know."

I whisper, "Don't know why I like it so much."

Tadashi fiddles with his cuff buttons, while admitting, "Neither did he. If you want it, Tyler, you can have it."

I whirl around. "I can't accept that. It's your family heirloom."

Tadashi chuckles. "Ginger can't stand that painting. Kaida's dislike of it is almost as bad. And Gemma isn't into dragons, are you?"

In a daze, Gemma shakes her head. "No, but—"

Tadashi cuts her off. "There you have it. *Vision of the Dragon* is yours."

I nod, not daring to refuse the gift a second time.

"Are you and Gemma going to work on that article tonight, or shall I take you home?"

"It's been a long day." Gemma yawns. "Mind if we work on it tomorrow, Tyler?"

"No. I'm tired too."

Tadashi stands, to cross the room. Rolling up his sleeves, he lifts the painting off the wall. "Then off we go."

* * *

Tadashi fires up the BMW, saying, "Tyler. Shotgun. Make the dragon sit in back."

After obeying, I click the seatbelt into place. Except for the quiet hum of the BMW, the ride is silent before we roll to a stop in the driveway absent of Mother's car.

Tadashi cuts the engine, while saying, "I'll get the painting."

I open the front door, to a dark house.

"Your mom's still in town this late?"

"Must be."

Tadashi taps two fingers on the frame. "Where do you want it?"

"Dad's study. This way." Taking the lead, I snap the lights on, and we wander in.

From the open bay window, a soft breeze sways the curtains back and forth. In my stride to close the window, the sight of strewn papers on the desk stops me mid-stride. Scattered across its surface are pictures, articles, and copies from books of the star-stone. Sifting through them, I state, "She must've come home. Then left again."

He leans the painting against the desk, asking, "These about that star she's researching?"

I break into a sweat, thinking, *What if something happened to her? It's almost eight. Why would she be out this late?* In a panic, the words fly out, "I need you to do something."

Tadashi looks up from the papers to ask, "Such as?"

"Don't think. Just write." I hand him a pen and motion to a notepad. "Forever at your service."

The words scratch into the paper. Then he clicks the pen and leaves it on the desk. "Is everything all right, Tyler?"

Penmanship doesn't match the note. Who could've written it? I shrug. "Must be Jack's story making me paranoid."

"Nothing a good night's sleep won't fix."

"Sleep sounds nice."

"Want help hanging the beast, before you do?"

I shake my head. "It'll take a while to pick a spot."

After one sweeping gaze around the study, Tadashi rips his penned words away from the pad, then folds and hands it to me, saying, "Even though I didn't say the words, they're true."

Accepting it, my battle against tears threatens a second debut in front of Tadashi.

"If you need anything." He grips my arm. "My doors are open. Except for the waking hours of morning."

"Thank you, Mr. Galloway."

Tadashi's weak smile diminishes. As he gently pulls, I take the invitation. Crushing the paper in one hand, my arms close around him and claw into his solid back. One arm wrapping around me, he grips my shoulders, while the fingertips of his other digs in between my shoulder blades.

My face buries into the nape of his neck. His pleasant cologne filling my lungs, I'm reminded of days my dad comforted me in the aftermath of bullying. Where classmates called me names like, The Little Terrorist; Son of the Al-Qaeda; and Prince of ISIS.

The sting of tears subsides. But Tadashi is the first to pull away, while I rasp out, "Almost as good as his epic bear hugs."

Tadashi clicks his tongue, saying, "Sorry. Can't compete with those. Things will get better in time."

"They already have."

"Good to hear."

"My mom ask you to speak with me?"

"She did say you're sharp." Tadashi taps a finger on the desk. "But yes, she asked. I agreed, on my terms. I figure, when you need to talk … you will. On your time. Not anyone else's."

"I'll take you up on that, someday," I reply.

"Look forward to it. Has to beat listening to Kaida call for Molly to feed her."

For a moment, we laugh together.

"So glad I don't have sisters." I shudder.

"Kaida and Gemma both wish they didn't."

"It's warranted," I state. "On Gemma's part."

"Agreed. I'll leave you to find my grandfather's beast a home."

"Have a good night, Mr. Galloway."

"I plan on it, Mr. Ravier. Have a new Katana to break in." With one wave, he leaves.

Panel by empty panel, I hold up the painting to them. Fighting my arch nemesis of indecision, the dragon at last finds its home, on the only panel right of the bay window, by a wall of bookcases.

Exhausted yet satisfied, I turn to leave. But a glint of red flickers. Glancing around, I lock onto the source. The dragon eyes now swirl with fire. I blink the image away, then look again. This time, its gaze of fire blinks back at me. Then the study lights brighten to blinding.

When they blow out, my heart jumps. Chills claw down my spine. And behind the painting, something clicks.

8

Demon in the Night

The wall panel gives way, as would a forgotten door. It crackles and creaks, dust falling, when I push against it. Something jams the panel, giving a mere sliver of space for me to wiggle through. After doing so, my feet scrape across dark splatters on the floorboards of this tiny room safeguarding a dust-covered shoebox and a single large painting. My stomach churns at the sight of what the splatters are: old blood. Originally smeared by boots, the prints are too small to be his.

Could this be the place of his fatal wound?

Discomfort departing to disturbance, I'm taken aback by the identical frame to Tadashi Galloway's heirloom. Even more disturbing is the portrait of two figures peering out. With eyes like Tadashi, the Oriental man stands in a fitted trench coat of black, white, and purple. Though more ornate, it's reminiscent of Ryco's dark uniform. On his left is a figure—leaning against a dark, etched door—in a similar coat of green, black, and white. Crooked red letters are painted over his blacked-out face, spelling the words: Thirteen. You're done!

Bending down, I pick up a bloodstained note resting on top of the shoebox. Blowing off the dust, I see that its penmanship is similar to the one left on my bed. Frantically, I read over the pen strokes.

Tyler, there's no time! He's dying. Wasn't meant to be this way. Wish I could do more, but it seems I've done enough. One day, I'll tell you everything. Hope you'll forgive me.

–Forever at Your Service

"Is this a confession of killing him? How could I ever forgive that?" I tuck the note in my pocket, then sweep my sleeve across the shoebox. Now matching the dusty box is my black shirt, as I open the lid. Set inside is a small children's book, called *The Dark Prince.* On its cover, a cartoon forest is situated behind a cloaked figure surrounded by six pillars—each one a color of the rainbow. Flipping through it, the story is ordinary in its telling of a prince who's lost his way—all alone—until a spunky, purple-haired girl helps him find the way again.

"Rather boring," I state. "Artwork is good, though." Getting to the end, I recognize my dad's scribbles on the inside of the back cover:

To Gemma,

May she one day find her perfect Dark Prince.

Your friend –Soren

Below that, in very dissimilar handwriting, Gemma's version of the poem is written word for word.

I slam it closed, almost exclaiming in this late hour, "She wasn't making it up. Why's he calling himself Soren? They can't be one and the same."

Just then, from the portrait painting, red flickers and then swirls with fire in the Oriental's eyes before fading back to brown.

Every nerve screams for me to leave this room. Yet I cannot. I must approach and read the small brass plaque, at the frame's bottom edge, labeled: *Adair Tamotsu Galloway & Soren of the Monel.*

"Who's Soren?" I ask, confused. "Why's he with Gemma's great-grandfather?"

Curiosity overcoming me, my trembling fingers inch toward the plaque. Mind aching to summon a slew of trickling numbers, my touch meets with the cold metal.

Numbers echo, *Twenty-two to rest. Thirteen pillars to end. Eight to light.*

Similar to the dragon painting. Maybe Talok will know what the numbers mean. At that moment, my heart leaps to my throat. I remember Awngeleik and exclaim, "Haven't checked on her all day!"

* * *

Lit by the dim lights overhead, the search in every stall reveals nothing of Awngeleik. One more time, I decide to check Ginger Snap's stall. While rasping, "Awngeleik?" I climb Snap's gate. Something weasels its way between my legs. I'm lunged to the other side, my flailing arms thudding into the scratchy straw first.

Awngeleik gawks over the gate, her snake-eyes amused.

I scowl up at her. "Walking Terror strikes again."

With a few flaps of her wings, she glides over. Shaking off the rest of the cloak, she saunters toward me. I rise, patting off the straw. "You missed a delicious dinner. Brought you Baklava, to soothe away my neglect."

In her characteristic way, she gobbles it down.

Reaching down for the now-visible cloak, I state, "Too bad you can't sneak in there with *this* and get all the pictures."

There's a thought! I muse. Before I can think more on it, she yanks the cloak away; thus, reeling me into the gate.

Holding my bruised side, I speak, "Awngeleik! Stop being selfish! I'll bring it back."

Three flaps, and she's back on the barn walkway to wave the cloak like a proud flag.

The gate latch slides open, but I stop mid-step. *She wants me to chase her. What happens if I don't?*

Back and forth, she clops down the cobblestone—goading me—but during every pass she makes, I stand firm and stare her down. Snapping my fingers, I point to the spot in front of me, six times for six passes. At last, she slows to staggering and drops the cloak at my feet.

"Was that so hard?" I complain. Wrapping up in it, I peer into the trough water's reflection. "Not invisible. Wonder why?" Tapping the metal trough, I glance at Awngeleik in the shadowy corner of the stall. "Special physiology, maybe?" *Which one?* I muse. *Hair-Feathers-Scales. Better not be the scales.*

I wince. "Hope I don't have to take you with me."

Ignoring me, Awngeleik curls up in the corner and pouts like a scolded dog.

"You know why it's not working?"

Her response to me? To turn her head away.

Have it your way. Pulling out a mini multi-tool from one of my many pockets, I stroke the downy hair on her neck. Then I twist a lock of Awngeleik's silver-smooth mane round one finger, like Gemma's Strand-Twirl, and think, *Strong like horsehair with the silkiness of down feathers. Interesting. Well, here it goes.*

Suspicious like a cat, her ears go back.

Swiftly, the blade slices off the lock. "That wasn't so bad. Was it?" I soothe.

She leaps to her feet, raging out screeches. I scrunch the strand under the cloak, scrambling away to peer again at the unchanged reflection. Meanwhile, as a predator about to pounce on prey, Awngeleik approaches. With her body darkening to a silvery-black, the undersides of her feathered wings glow a brilliant white.

Is this her throwing a real temper tantrum?

When her pupils alter to sharp-white, the rest of both eyes morph to an unreflecting black. I try to gulp back my fear, but staring into her eyes is like staring into death itself. Then, like when the star-creature was dying, his voice echoes inside my head, "When the time is right, tell him everything."

Utterly afraid, I slam the gate shut behind me, shouting, "Awngeleik, what's happening? You're freaking me out!" Though I try, my gaze cannot tear away from her demonic face.

She fades back to her usual shelf, and I stroke her cheek. Trying to purge my mind of the demon, I attempt to slow my racing heart. But, in a flash, the demon-horse is back. All around, distorted voices hum and chatter. Then, from her face, electricity emits to shock through my left hand. The force of it hurls me to the opposite side of the walkway.

Nauseous and dizzy, I labor to sit up and massage the burn of my left arm. Slowly, my hands start trembling. In horror, I watch it: black murkiness creeping from fingertips up to my elbow. Fingernails start glowing white, while prismatic colors course over my palm creases. "What did you do?" I shout, while gripping one of the stall slats. Almost catching fire, the wood smokes. My grip frightens off the slat.

Now burned into the wood is my left handprint.

Air catches in my throat, threatening to strangle me to a blackout. Right then, my dark-olive tone replaces the black. No more glowing fingernails or colorful palms, either.

Calmer now, I rasp, "You'll be the death of me, Walking Demon. If not you, then my mom. I can't imagine what would happen if the barn, suddenly, erupted in flames. You owe me an apology, Awngeleik. All I want is to keep you safe."

The guilt tactic works.

Using her teeth, Awngeleik plucks one of her wing feathers. Then she snatches up the cut strands from the floor and shoves both into my left hand. When she drops the cloak over my fist, it disappears under the fabric.

"Apology accepted." I grin. "I'll be back before you miss me."

* * *

Rain pours down, as I hold tight to the shielding cloak. By the stone exterior wall of the Galloways' kitchen, I stand staring at the place where the keys rest on the other side, taunting me.

So close, I muse. *Yet so far away.*

At 9:36 PM, the watch twists round.

No alarm to worry about ... yet. Dad must've used magic, all this time. Maybe I can too.

Right hand clutching *The Dark Prince,* I rest my left on the slick wall and whisper, "Black hand, don't fail me now."

I focus on words. Any to help access what might've been dormant all along.

When the time is right, tell him everything. It echoes, and I return with, *Tell me what?*

Body still shielded by the cloak, my hand turns ice-cold. Then the nails go white and fingertips stain black, continuing up to my elbow.

I have the answers to what you seek. Forgive that all I have is how much he loved you. Enough to die for you. Its echo stops, and *Why?* is my echoing reply.

Ragged breaths suffocate me. Right then, the wall shifts to be as thick dough under my hand. Pushing through, my fingers bump the keys. Counting to the back-door key, deciding that it's all I need to get in, I work it off. Slowly, with my fist clenched, I pull back. When I'm almost free of the wall, lightning flashes and booms.

Something snags me. And the black stain starts disappearing.

Panicking, my shoulder digs into the wall. Teeth clenching. Arm shaking. Muscles throbbing. I heave and thrash. Still. I'm stuck, as mocking thunder rolls in the distance.

Searching for something to free me—the password to release me—the painting's blacked-out face seeps into focus. I speak, barely above a whisper, to the wall, "Thirteen. You're done."

The wall surrenders my hand to freedom, but—as if struck by a hammer—a bit of stone crumbles away. Shrugging it off, I open the kitchen door, hurry in, and click the door shut.

Pulse calming, I untie my boots. *Can't have muddy prints or squeaky soles giving me away.* Boots in hand, the elevator doors open. Stepping in, I punch the button to Gemma's level. During the elevator's glide to my destination, I drop the boots in a corner. *Going to gamble that no one uses the elevator this late.*

Shaking the cloak free of rain droplets, I ready myself. When the doors open, I rush out. At Gemma's study door, I weigh my options. With a camera angled at this one, the left door bids me to enter.

Do I want to go into what most likely is her bedroom? No! But what choice have I? Hope her door doesn't squeak like mine.

To my relief, it opens without a sound.

Gemma—in pajama shorts and a cami—is sprawled on her back as if someone broke her bones then threw her atop the naked bed. In a heap on the floor are the blankets—the sheets, as well—all of it lies in front of the adjoining study door.

I stifle a groan. *Why has nothing been easy this day?*

On her nightstand, I set *The Dark Prince* and wish I could see her reaction to it when she wakes up. While I gather the pile of bedding, Gemma's body contorts further. Stopping to gawk at her, I think, *Does she even have a back?*

In opposite directions, while she sleeps, her torso and legs are twisted. My own neck twinges at the sight of her, as I set the bedding aside and open the adjoining door.

An escaping grumble from Gemma freezes me in place. After she rolls into a more natural position, I close the door.

The watch beneath the cloak reads: 9:50 PM. *No time to pick through everything.* Stuffing all hard copies into an empty folder from her drawer, I sit in the black chair facing the chief enemy of the night: the computer password.

Favorite crush at school, I muse. *Tons have a 'V.' Which one could it be?*

Like the ticking of a clock—one by one—the five lead candidates are eliminated.

Fingers drum on the desk.

No time for this! Maybe it's me, but doubtful.

When entrance is still denied, I'm confirmed right.

Maybe her nickname for me, in elementary, before her witch days?

The keystrokes spell out: T-R-A-V-I-E-R.

The screen loads her desktop. Then the mouse hovers over 'delete.' A pang of guilt rises, but I push it down. *No one must know about Awngeleik.* Without further hesitation, I delete all the research files and ensure that recovery's not an option.

I skirt around Gemma's bed, and clutch the folder to my chest, my thoughts commanding, *Do-not-drop-this!*

Gemma, in the fetal position and hugging her pillow, is now the picture of cute tranquility.

Favorite crush at school, huh, Rich Witch? You have a funny way of showing it.

Door silently closing behind, I head for the elevator but stop at the sound of plodding footsteps traveling down the narrow passage. Back pressed against the wall, I wait.

Approaching from the corridor is Kane's voice, asking, "Haru, these your boots?"

Now what will I do? Walk all the way home in my socks?

Slightly taller than Tadashi, Kane strolls into view holding my muddy military-boots.

Meanwhile, Haru tiptoes up the remaining stairs. His smaller frame is almost engulfed by the giant painting in his hands. He glances from the boots to Kane, rasping, "No. But they might be Hunter Mason's size."

His longer face contorting, Kane questions Haru, "What *is* that?"

"A painting, what else?" proclaims Haru, with frenzied eyes searching the hallways.

"I see it's a painting. What're you doing with it?"

Haru huffs. "Tadashi business. Meaning? None of yours."

Breaking into a smile, Kane states, "I forgot about his other pastime. Continue, Haru."

With my boots in tow, Kane gallops down the stairs. But Haru rushes to the elevator, as if an invisible monster is chasing him the whole way.

Boots or elevator? When the elevator doors close in my face, the choice is made for me. To the balcony—between the second and third floor—I follow Kane, hoping he will set the boots down for one second; it's all I need. *One.*

"Tadashi?" he calls down, holding up the boots. "These were in the elevator. They yours?"

Out of his office, Tadashi saunters. With one headshake, his expression darkens to match the black samurai-like robes he wears. Kane continues on downstairs. Right behind him, I lurk and avoid all creaking Gemma-Steps of earlier.

Around the entryway, several ballistic dummies have been dispersed, and I wonder, *Is this how he breaks in a new Katana?*

Kane offers the boots to Tadashi, saying, "Haru thinks they're Hunter's size."

Finishing off Tadashi's shaded face are his flashing angry eyes, as he tosses my boots into the dining room. "Go wake up Kaida," he commands.

Kane starts, "Shouldn't it be you—"

Tadashi, raising a hand to cut off Kane, points two fingers at him and says, "If he's in there, I will kill him. Then her. She *knew* about the new Katana. Must've figured out I don't like being on camera. That. Conniving. Little. Dragon." Ending with that, Tadashi unsheathes the Katana.

They were off the whole time? Feeling like a fool, I watch as Kane flies past on the stairs. Steps now on the marble, I skulk.

Then begins Tadashi's slashing of the dummies.Across their chests, necks, and abs, he vanquishes three. Halfway to the goal are my steps, during Tadashi's gutting of another.

There goes Kaida.

In seconds, he beheads the dummy facing where I loiter by the front door. My back almost slamming against the door, I sink out of the Katana's reach. When a head rolls, I smile to myself. *Off with Ginger's head. Glad it wasn't mine.*

Upstairs, Kaida's scream resounds. Then the shouting arguments begin.

Tadashi stops mid-swing—pained—and his face crumples. "Kaida, why?" Readying for the slaughter of another dummy, he tightens his grip on the Katana and whirls to the one by the dining room archway.

At that moment, a black streak bolts down the stairs, across the marble, and straight for the dining room. It crosses Tadashi's path, as he swings and then trips to falling. The Katana nicks across my cheek, before Tadashi lands with a clanking thud.

Touching fingers to the wound, I smear sticky blood and muse, *Razor sharp. Didn't feel a thing.*

"Minksy!" Tadashi hollers. "You little assassin! Do you have a death wish like Kaida?"

When Tadashi stands, the fluffy black cat weaves around his feet and yowls long, happy cries in between rumbling purrs.

"What a day." Tadashi sighs. "Want to kill my eldest child. Almost kill my cat."

While I fight the cackling, Minksy must hear me. His big golden-green eyes lock onto where I crouch, hidden. To my dismay, he advances to prancing like an adorable fluff ball. Mid-prance, Tadashi picks him up. As the fluffy little assassin is lifted, his claws snag on the cloak. Reacting quickly, I grab Minksy's outstretched paw. He wails and hisses. Just as I manage to free the cloak of claws, Minksy makes his escaping leap off Tadashi's chest and bolts for the study.

Fist clenching his wounded chest, Tadashi gripes, "What's gotten into you, cat? Too much catnip from Kaida? Or was it Ginger enabling your addiction?"

"Mr. Tadashi." Kane leans over the balcony.

When their eyes meet, Kane signals with a nod.

"I'll take care of it," states Tadashi. "See that Mr. Mason doesn't leave." Retreating into his study, Tadashi closes the doors.

In his absence, the battlefield of slaughter oozes green and blue goo. Now safe in the dining room, I tighten my bootlaces. Then three knocks sound on the front door, and I groan inside. *Now what?*

Robes gone, Tadashi jogs out in a white tee and plaid flannel pants. Shouldering his phone, he swings the front door open. Standing on the terrace is Mother, a sweaty mess with her frazzled hair, blood-shot eyes, and a look set to kill anyone in her way.

Tadashi almost drops his phone. "Amira?"

One-two-three. I leave the dining room.

"Where's Tyler?" questions the icy voice of Mother.

"Call you back." Tadashi hangs up, confessing, "Dropped him off two hours ago."

"Mirror Lake again," she seethes.

"There are worse places he could be."

Four-five-then six. Halfway there.

"It's the principle of it. I asked him not to. Yet, he still does it. I even told him about that large thing I caught a glimpse of the other night. Clearly, he didn't believe me."

Tadashi's skeptical, asking, "Are you sure you actually saw it run away? It could've been your mind filling in, for what you heard. It was probably just some stray dog."

"So, you don't believe Jack's story about his Bear-Wolf?"

Seven-eight-put nine to the test.

Sighing, Tadashi replies, "If there's one thing I know about Jack, it's that he blows things out of proportion. He wouldn't even show me, two years ago, what he's now relinquished to Gemma. I'm certain something happened to him that day, but a Bear-Wolf? I'll believe it when I see it." Right then, he glances past her stiff shoulders, asking, "You drive here?"

"No. Wanted to be tired, in case he was here."

"Not sure I follow."

"Didn't want any energy left to wring his neck."

Tadashi tries, but fails, hiding a smile. "You don't look tired, to me."

"I'm not," admits Mother, while eyeing the dummies. "And it appears, neither are you."

His shirt void of buttons, Tadashi just scratches his neck.

"What does … Ginger think of this?"

Ten-eleven. To confession.

"She doesn't know," replies Tadashi.

"How do you manage that?"

"I ensure she sleeps like the dead."

"Do I want to know?"

Tadashi looks to the running shoes by the door, saying, "It wouldn't take much, to make an educated guess."

"Mr. Tadashi." Haru squeaks, "I finished that … errand. Now, Kane's asking what to do about … the situation."

"Situation?" Mother cocks an eyebrow. "Have I walked into a bloodbath?"

"Whatever it is might end in one." Tadashi slips on the running shoes, replying, "You and Kane handle it. I'm taking Amira home. Shall we?"

"Definitely," replies Mother, stepping back to let Tadashi pass. "You can recount how the Tyler-Talk went."

Tadashi groans. "I was afraid you might say that."

Twelve and thirteen. To freedom. Slipping out ahead of them, I run the whole way home like a demon in the night.

9

The Trouble with Truth

Knocking on the matte-black surface, I speak, "Thirteen. You're done."

Comb in hand, I set it down on my dresser. But something's different. A small book rests there, face down. It was absent, before my shower. Cocking my head, I flip the book over. Sent through me is a bolting shock, as *The Dark Prince* gapes at me.

Heart stopping, my thoughts race, *Someone followed me last night. Then went to the trouble of bringing the book back? Why?* I scan the room for anything else amiss. Then I spot it on my pillow: another note. I snatch it up, to scan it. Plainly, it's written in the phantom's writing.

Perhaps, not a good idea to include Miss Gemma Galloway in all this. Here's a second chance to rethink your decision.

—Forever Your Servant

More confused than ever, I stroll to the stairs and hear Gemma's excited voice traveling from the front door. *Found my surprise for you this morning?* I reason, while taking every step of the squeaking six and silent seven. *Have to face her some time. Might as well be now.*

To the pit of my stomach, guilt from the dirty deed sinks to sickness and provokes more musing. *Was it a mistake to burn all of Gemma's resources last night—at Mirror Lake, in the dead of night—while Mother slept in her bed? Maybe. But it's too late to save anything now. Should've burned Ryco's note, while I was at it.*

Gemma spots me, exclaiming, "Tyler! You won't believe what happened."

Feigning ignorance, I just shrug. *Oh! But I will. Saw more than you did. For once.*

"Tyler." Mother's hawk eyes glare at me. "Where were you last night?"

My reply is simply, "The attic."

"I called and called for you. Why didn't you answer?"

"Fell asleep. When I woke up, you were still gone or asleep. So, I went to bed."

"A likely story." Mother flashes the Assassin-Smile. "Breakfast will be ready soon." With that, she goes back to the kitchen.

Gemma—her eyes puffy and face free of makeup—centers on me, saying, "All the research for that paper's gone. Computer files. Articles. Pictures. Everything! Tried a computer reset. Since that didn't work, I came for the flash drive. It'll save me hours."

Burned that too, I muse, but—with a voice calmer than I expect—I lie, "Went to upload it last night, but found a hole in my pocket. It's probably somewhere in your driveway or mine."

Like a hurt little girl, her sad gaze sinks to the floor.

The words fly out of me, asking, "Want help looking for it?" Cringing inside, I silently continue saying, *I mean, it's gone, but I can still pretend to search for what is now ash on the rocks.*

"I'll start over." Gemma shakes her head. "Bet it was Kaida retaliating after her bereavement from last night. Never thought she'd guess my password, though. She's not that tech-savvy for hacking, either."

Absentminded, I wonder, *Why would she guess your favorite crush at school?* Startling, I look away. Trying to process if she meant it or not. *Was it one of those antonym passwords? One that's not true, at all, so no one will ever be able to guess it?*

"You all right, Tyler?" queries Gemma, with concern.

Ignoring the question, I ask, "Want help starting over?"

"Of course!" She smiles.

"How about having breakfast here, before we start?"

"I would love to, but I need to get going. Have a lot of work to do. Come over, after breakfast?" Gemma's eyes plead.

I give in, saying, "Sure thing." Waving goodbye, I close the door. *I did have good reasons for doing what I did.*

I think.

* * *

Mother—her tight grip on the wheel—turns to me, saying, "I have a house call to make. Under no circumstance will you leave here, unless it relates to Gemma's paper. Understood?"

"Yes, ma'am," is my simple answer. Any more might be dangerous, with the current mood of Emerald-Fury.

I exit the car, and she drives off the Galloways' gravel driveway. The wheels scatter up pebbles, before the car starts its journey to wherever Mother is in such a hurry to get to.

Feet weighed down by dread, I approach the front door of the Galloway mansion. Shielded by a paper bag is Soren's gift to Gemma—now clutched in my hand—as I ring the doorbell. Then I wait. And listen. And twist the watch round.

To my horror, it's Kaida swinging the door open and smiling like a devil. "Tyler Ravier!" she coos. "Here to console the baby sister, while she pines for the loss of her dear, sweet paper?"

"Sure." I shrug.

"So sweet! Too bad you're not older." She sighs. "I'd steal you away."

Shivering inside, and hating the Little Dragon more, I ask, "What about Hunter Mason?"

"You mean my ex-boyfriend?" Kaida strokes her arm with manicured nails, before saying, "He spent the night in jail, for trespassing. That wasn't a bother to me, but his theft of my mother's favorite painting was. Daddy's pressing charges, and I'm on house arrest. Until further notice."

I can't help but wonder, *Was that Haru's errand? Framing Hunter for theft. Would Tadashi do that?*

Kaida wets her lips, saying, "You get bored with little Gemma, let me know."

"Jed Craven might take you up on that. But not me."

Her nose wrinkles, in distaste. "Jed Craven? Uh, no."

"Too bad, then. Gemma in her room?"

"Upstairs. Crying her little eyes out." Kaida saunters into the dining room, hollering, "Molly! Breakfast finished, yet?"

Too bad somebody can't light that straight black hair on fire.

Steps on stairs turn to strides down halls. Uncertainty shifts to agony. Before I'm ready, I arrive in front of Gemma's study door to face my dilemma of the day: the trouble with truth. Today, it's worse than the longing for the lake. Worse than hatred for the surfer-hair. Worse than the sting of hot water on my back. Almost as bad as missing him. At last, my thoughts clear. *Tell her what I know, or give her the book and just go? He or Soren went to the trouble of including her family in this. Whatever this is. And what about this Phantom of Muraine? Why care if Gemma's included or not?*

Mustering up courage, I knock three times.

The door opens.

"Tyler!" Gemma perks up. "How was breakfast?"

I follow her in, calmly lying, "Good, but it wasn't Molly's cooking." The truth is, I was too sick to eat—too anxious for this moment—yet, here I am in this moment of my own making.

Gemma cutely lifts her shoulders, asking, "Have we ruined you?"

"Give it a few months and maybe." I ease down into the black confession-chair.

"Since you're in the hot seat," Gemma says with a grin, "You can look for—"

"Don't get mad," I cut her off. "You have every right, but I'm asking you not to."

Like waves on a dry beach, her joy washes away to wrench my heart. But I press on, "I'm not here to help you—"

"Then why?" she bursts out, her lower lip quivering. "To bully me as I did to you?"

When Gemma bolts, I spring out of the confession-chair to block her escape. "No!" I tear open the paper bag and hand her the book. "I'm here to confess what little I know. It's more than my dad gave me."

Astonished, she pulls it from my grasp. "Where'd you find this?"

"Hidden room in his study. Along with a painting of your great-grandfather and Soren."

Gemma scoffs. "Very funny, Tyler."

"Who's laughing? I took your resources—burned them too—because I'm afraid of someone finding her."

"Her? You don't mean…?"

"The winged-horse. Who else?"

"Where'd she come from?"

I smile the wicked grin, and reply, "Muraine."

"From that story I told you?" Her eyes grow big. "It's real?"

"Are you mad?"

"Depends." She rests her hands on her hips.

Wincing, I ask, "On?"

"If you'll do me a favor or not."

"You want to see her. The Walking Terror, as I like to call her."

Gemma's mouth drops open. "That's a mean name. From what I could tell, she's gorgeous."

"She is," I agree. "Until you see her in motion."

Gemma reaches out, to brush my forearm. But Haru's voice comes out of nowhere, loudly crackling, "No touching!"

Gemma stomps to the intercom, complaining, "What are you going to do about it, sissy Haru? Kane's the one to fear."

"More like your dad's the one to fear—in his Kendo robes—slaying a battlefield of dummies with his new Katana."

Perturbed, Gemma double-takes my way. "Care to illuminate?"

"Will on the way."

She jabs the button, saying, "Tyler and I are leaving."

"Where are you going?" demands Kane.

"Horse ride," replies Gemma, "to get pictures of the lake."

"We will inform your father," proclaims Haru, provoking Gemma to stick her tongue out at the camera.

"They're the rules, Gemma," offers Kane. "Especially after last night."

"Privacy?" She rolls her eyes. "Nonexistent in this giant house."

We head for the stairs. But I long for the elevator, while saying, "For once, I don't envy you."

She laughs. "No one should envy me. By the way, Tyler, I forgot to thank you."

"For?"

"Defending my photography skills. It dampens the image of your sabotage."

"Now I'm the one who's sorry."

"You should be. It was mean—Kaida mean. Bad Tyler Malik Ravier! You've made me compare you to my rotten sister."

"Ouch!" I grimace. "Wait! How do you know my middle name?"

"Your mom. She loves bringing out the full name, when she's mad at you."

Now at the bottom of the stairs, Gemma heads for the dining room, hollering, "Molly! Want to help make sandwiches?"

Does Molly ever have a moment's peace?

Tadashi strolls out of his office, asking, "You and Gemma going out?"

My heart stops. *Does he mean dating?* The words tumble out. "What? No! I mean—I don't know." I rub my neck, remembering the beheaded dummy of last night.

"You don't know"—Tadashi scratches his temple—"if you and Gemma are going out to take pictures?"

"In my defense," I begin, while holding up a finger, "it was a leading question."

Tadashi cracks up. "And you fell for it."

Right then, it feels like my dad's teasing. Instead of *his* gaze of life's passion looking at me, however, it's Tadashi's that are filled with the same kindness and wisdom I saw that day after pummeling on his chest. Again, I remember what I've lost: a dad. My dad.

Like a mind reader, Tadashi offers, "If you ever need a punching bag, let me know."

"I will, Mr. Tadashi."

From my boots to my face, he glances with a smile. "I think your mom worries too much. Your dad would've liked this dark style you've taken to."

Glad I chose different boots today. Inside, I sigh, but say, "You think so?"

After nodding, Tadashi taps a finger to his cheek. "You didn't have that cut yesterday."

I brush at the wound, replying, "Face found a sharp edge, while hanging the beast."

"Hate it when that happens. Don't you and Gemma have too much fun."

"That will be up to Gemma."

"If she talks too much"—Tadashi leans closer, whispering—"tell her to listen to nature. That's my cue for her to shut up."

"Thanks." I chuckle. "I'm sure I'll use it, at some point."

"I wish you better results than me."

My smile fading, I have to know. "Mr. Tadashi?" I clear my throat.

"You're not Kane or Haru," he states, undoing his top button. "Plain Tadashi is fine."

"How well did you know my dad?"

"We spent much time together, in college. Then my little sister died. Both of us married. Focused on careers. Our families. I *will* always regret drifting apart from your parents, Jack Wayeland, and the others. Lance was a good friend. But my loss doesn't compare to yours." He hesitates, finishing with, "I see you're not ready for that talk. Another time?"

I manage to rasp out, "Agreed."

He gives my arm an encouraging squeeze, then retreats to his office and, I swear, he wipes at a lone tear.

* * *

"She's exquisite!" exclaims Gemma. "When can I ride her?"

Cloak in hand, I tease, "When it's dark enough to take low-light shots."

Her arms hanging over Ginger Snap's gate, Gemma lifts a counting hand. "Let's see how much I remember. King Talok; Ryco, the sadist; Soren, your dad, and the poem; Awngeleik and her cloak, which"—she points accusingly—"you used to sneak into my house like a demon in the night."

"Sounds about right."

She continues, "The star-rock, journals, and ninja-star. Thirteen items, but you haven't found any?"

"You forgot the dragon's fiery eyes, and your great-grandfather's portrait with Soren."

"Still don't believe that one," states Gemma.

"You believe everything else, except that a painting of your ancestor is hidden in my dad's study. You don't make any sense." To the gate, Gemma still clings—with her gaze transfixed on the slumbering Awngeleik—as I swing it open and ask, "Want to pet her or not?"

Before I finish, Gemma leaps off the gate like a racehorse at the start. Nearing, she slows her step and kneels down to stretch out a trembling hand. When touching Awngeleik's shoulder, the trembling stops.

Awngeleik's eyes crack open, then sleepily close again.

"Come on." I slip the cloak over the slumbering dragon-horse. "I'll show you the painting."

Closing up the barn, I lead the way inside. Then to the study. Pushing on the panel, which gives way a little easier than before, I ask, "Believe me now?"

"Was this here before?" queries Gemma, while snatching something tucked between the frame and painting. She gives it to me, asking, "Who would've thought our families might go way back?"

Fingers raking through my tiresome hair, I read the phantom's words:

Since you insist on finding LanSoren's things with your friend, Gemma Galloway, you'll be needing this number map I stole the other night.

–The Phantom of Muraine

Gemma peers over my shoulder, asking, "Phantom? Can he read your mind?"

"Probably," I whisper, as a shiver runs up my spine.

On the map, there are no buildings—no locations—only lines, shapes, numbers, and a few symbols. One appears to be a sun on the horizon. Another is like a curved 'X' with a plus sign crossing its center. But the third resembles an umbrella, surrounded by triangles and numbers within a circle. In no particular order, the numbers—one through thirteen—are sprinkled on the parchment. Some are grouped together, while others are not, but all are encased in different triangular-shapes.

Gemma, starting her typical Strand-Twirl, says, "Might be some weird geometry puzzle. Or the numbers are items."

"Could be," I agree. "Remember any places you encountered Soren as a child?"

"Still pass them, on rides," replies Gemma.

"Then we should go to one," I suggest. "Might find something to help make sense of this map."

<h1 style="text-align:center">10</h1>

Phantom of the Forest

From her house to mine, then into the forest, we rode. Gemma, on Goliath. Me, on Cosmo. Mirror Lake passes by on the left. Farther, still, we wander below the chorus of chatter: the forest creatures chittering, chirping, and pecking too.

"Are we feeding an army?" I ask. "What's with the massive bag?"

Gemma's lap is engulfed by it, as she sifts through the supplies. She explains, "Skipped breakfast—was too upset—plus, I get hungry on rides. Packed a first-aid kit too."

"Are you accident-prone or something?"

"Don't think so. Maybe it's in case karma rewards you for the evil sabotaging, by smacking your face with a branch." She leers.

I point to the Katana cut, saying, "Karma and your dad already got me."

"Serves you right, for sneaking into my room."

When Gemma begins crunching on chips, I tug Cosmo close enough to snatch her Doritos.

"Rude!" She gapes a moment, then digs out a different flavor.

"Yet, you let me have it."

"Want a sandwich too? Molly helped."

I take the bag filled to the brim with six of everything: sandwiches, waters, Gatorades, baggies of carrots, and a plethora of single-serve chips. At the top of it all, however, is a lonesome container of raspberries. I glance at

Gemma, asking, "Do we have an imaginary friend today?"

"We might, if the Phantom of Muraine continues to follow you." Amused, Gemma bites her lower lip—stained Dorito-orange—before finishing her chips and munching on a sandwich.

Choosing my sandwich, I surrender the bag. "At least he doesn't seem dangerous."

"Think your dad and Soren are somehow connected?"

"No idea." I shrug, before crunching into the sandwich. But the *crunch* is not lettuce. Indignant, I lift the top bread slice and ask, "Are these barbeque chips?"

"No, Tyler. It's fried chicken. Haven't you experimented with flavored chips on sandwiches?"

"Plain potato chips."

"That's not experimenting."

While she grins, I just blink at her. Then she asks, "Want something to wash away the barbeque? Perhaps some lovely, plain water?" She tosses a bottle, and I catch it.

"So I like water. That okay?" I gulp down half of it.

"It better be, since I brought it for you." Finishing her sandwich and wiping her mouth, she cracks open a Gatorade.

"How much farther?" I ask, while bending forward to scratch Cosmo's neck. At my touch, he relaxes. Lowering his head, he lets it lazily sway side to side with each plodding step.

She points. "To the top of that hill."

"That where you shot the pictures?"

"Yep!" She puts away the Gatorade.

Impatience overcoming me, I nudge Cosmo into an alert trot. His head jerks up, cuing Goliath to pursue.

"What made you decide to redeem yourself?"

"My dad taking a belt to me."

I cough. "He did what?"

"That day, the stable master told my dad about the purple-dyed horse. My friends agreed to take the blame, so I could claim innocence. When he threatened to call their parents, one of them turned and told the truth—my whole plan. Said he'd deal with me later, then stormed off in his car. Not sure where he went."

"To find me."

"Should've guessed." Gemma sighs. "When he got back, he hunted me down, dragged me to his office, and cracked his suit belt on my back three times. All while *Vision of the Dragon* stared with its beady eyes. When it was over, he said he's never been so ashamed of anyone in his life. Had to muck out stalls and groom horses the whole summer. No friend privileges."

I squirm in the saddle, unsure of what else to say except one word: "Brutal."

"We can agree, I deserved it."

"Both of you get along, though. I'd think after—"

She interrupts, "He apologized the next day. While I was grooming Cosmo, actually. That's when he told me your dad died. Never felt so wicked in my life." She hesitates, before asking, "You think of that third favor from the witch?"

"After what I did, you're still going to give it to me?"

"Your sabotage almost makes us even, but not quite."

I reply, "Been too busy, with lies and sneaking."

Nodding, Gemma pulls back on Goliath's reins, announcing, "Here we are."

Into a serene meadow, we wander among the colorful wildflowers scattered around and warmed by the afternoon sun.

"This is where Soren and I first played hide-and-seek."

"Better start the seeking, then."

Both of us dismounting, Gemma takes the bridles off Goliath and Cosmo to let them munch on lush grass.

For what feels like hours, we search the meadow's perimeter.

Then Gemma jogs toward me, asking, "You good at climbing trees?"

"Who isn't?"

"Me," she admits, while tugging on my arm. "I finally found the tree he hid in for hours one time. There's something high in the branches."

Within minutes, I'm two-thirds of the way. With one more hoist up, I'll have a hold of a dark wooden box tied to a branch. Pulse flooding my veins, I untie the cord and call down, "Get ready to catch."

"Ready!" she answers.

The cord unwinds, releasing its hold, and I let go of it.

"Wait!" she shouts. "Not ready."

I yell, "Too late!"

During its descent, the box strikes and tears something. Rushing down, I hurry over to Gemma, now lying on the ground. Goliath sniffs her head, but prances off as she smacks his head away from her face. She points to the box. "Would've caught it, if Goliath's fat-head didn't get in the way."

"At least it didn't knock you into comatose, or I'd be dragging the body home."

"You could've draped me over Goliath, instead. No need to drag."

"But dragging would be more fun."

"Rude!" She sits up, with a deep scowl.

Glancing around, I state, "Thought I heard something tear."

"My pants." Gemma stands. "How bad is it?"

Eyeing the five-inch, bloodstained rip—halfway up the back of her thigh—I lie to her, saying, "It's not too bad. Bleeding, though."

"Figures!" she gripes, while dusting off the box and kneeling in front of it. "It's the third pair I've ruined this year. From really stupid things too."

"That sounds accident-prone to me." I nudge her shoulder, on the way down.

"Nobody"—Gemma nudges back—"who's accident-prone is going to admit it, Tyler."

"Until they're caught in the act of being klutzy?" I inspect the box, but ignore Gemma's witch-glare.

"Fine!" She shoves the box toward me. "My all-time record was twelve pants in a single year. One for each month, as my mother constantly reminded me. Satisfied? I admitted to it."

"Would never peg you for the school klutz. What changed?" I turn the box over.

"My mother insisted I stop playing like a boy and act more lady-like."

Seeing a lock on the box's underside, I clench my jaw. *No key? No open box.* Gripping its handle, I stand and then say, "I think she meant act more like her: a full-fledged bully."

Gemma follows, asking, "Where are you going?"

"Not getting in this without the key." I tap on the bottom. "Ninja-star's still in the barn."

Gemma falls in step with me. "You think my mom's a bully?"

"The worst kind," I reply. "One who bullies her own flesh and blood."

"She's only voicing her strong opinion."

I stop to look Gemma square in the face, asking, "By crushing your love of photography?"

"She doesn't mean to. That's what my dad tells me."

I shake my head. "Your family is your deal. But you should see them for who they really are. Not who you want them to be."

Tension fills the air, as Gemma slips the bridles back on Goliath and Cosmo, asking, "Who do you want your dad to be?"

"Don't know. Not after the recently discovered lies." I hand the box to Gemma. "Still, I can't help but think: who was he really, if not my dad?" Mounting Cosmo, I reach for the box.

Lifting it to me, then mounting Goliath, Gemma leads the way back to my house.

I ask, "Where to next?"

Gemma starts to open the cooler bag, replying, "The tree Soren carved into, the first time I saw—" Terror in her eyes, she stops mid-sentence.

"What's wrong?"

"Did you raid all the food, while we were searching?"

"No. Why?"

"Only drinks and raspberries are left," she grumbles.

A cold sadness, like when the star-creature died, sinks down into the pit of my stomach. I start to say, "Gemma, we should hurry—"

Cutting my words short, Goliath bolts into a run. Bag flying from her grip, Gemma screams. She tightly hangs onto the saddle. Box secured in my grip, I dig my heels into Cosmo's sides. Compared to Awngeleik, these horses are prancing, not running, away from whatever invisible phantom in the forest is chasing us.

Without incident, we reach the forest edge. And I muse, *No carved-tree visit today.*

* * *

A while later, I ask, "What are you doing?"

Gemma holds her phone to her ear, replying, "Ordering pizza."

"Who's going to pay?"

"Debit card." She holds it up.

"We've been gone a while. Won't someone come looking for us?"

She shakes her head. "While you were in the barn, I texted Kane. He'll cover for us. Mind finding a game to play? I'm still too jittery to go outside."

As she begins the order, I amble to the study with the box and ninja-star in tow. Over and again, I tinker with the star-key until, finally, I shake it and complain, "I have the key to the box, but can't open the *said* key, to open the *said* box. Why so complicated?"

I toss both aside, as Gemma waltzes in, asking, "Any luck?"

"With?"

"Opening the box or picking a game?"

I purse my lips, before asking, "How does Chess sound?"

"Boring."

"It's a classic."

She cocks her head. "Still boring, though."

"Then Clue?"

Her eyes light up. "Scarlet, with the Hall facing me."

"Anything else, Highness?"

"How good are you at losing?"

I ask, "You're *that* confident you're going to win?"

"I'm positive I'm going to win."

"There she is." I summon my wicked grin. "The Rich Witch. Bring it!"

"I will, Demon in the Night."

Easing into the leather chairs, like negotiators before a war, we set up the game on the table by the bay window. Fifteen minutes pass, before Gemma is announcing the hidden cards.

Indignant, I throw the cards on the board. "A lucky guess."

"It's a Galloway thing. Another?" Gemma motions.

"If we deal out a hand for the phantom," I suggest.

"By all means."

With everything reset, I organize my cards and say, "You're not winning so easily, this time."

Gemma giggles. "Sure, Ty-Ty."

"Now," I seethe, "you're definitely going down."

Another fifteen minutes pass. Then Gemma fakes a cough.

"No!" I shout. "You can't possibly know. We've hardly done anything."

Gemma announces, "Mrs. Peacock. Candlestick. Study," then starts a drumroll.

Opening the envelope and groaning, I let the cards fall to the board. "Right again."

"Knew it!" she exclaims.

"Somehow, someway"—I point at her—"you *are* cheating."

Just then, a loud banging knock interrupts me.

"I'll get it." Gemma races out of the study.

Like a whipped dog, I follow.

When Gemma opens the front door, her head jerks back. "Haru? What are you—"

Haru thrusts two pizza boxes at her. "Pizza guy assumed you were at home."

"Oops!" She grimaces. "Forgot to say they should bring it here."

Strolling into view, I wave at Haru.

At the sight of me, his eyes widen to bulging. "Gemma! What's Tyler doing here?"

"He lives here."

"Kane said you were here with a girlfriend."

Silently, I complain, *I've been reduced to Gemma's girlfriend? Fabulous!*

"But he knows Tyler lives here."

Haru starts to say, "As long as Amira is here, there shouldn't be any—"

Gemma blurts, "She's not here. Went on a house call." Then, in realization, she claps her hands over her mouth.

"Bravo, Gemma." I applaud. "Announce it to the world."

"Kane's covering for you." Haru's black eyebrows furrow into one thick line. "Because he vouched to Mr. Tadashi that he saw you and Tyler come back. Then Tyler left, and you went to a girlfriend's house. Your father must be informed immediately."

"Please, Haru!" Gemma begs. "My dad will ground me for, like, ever! Might even fire Kane. It can be our secret. Kane's cool enough to cover for me. Plus, we've only been playing Clue to relax, after something chased us in the forest."

"Chased you?" Squeezing his eyes shut, Haru waves his hand. "Don't want to know. The less, the better. Come home soon, or else." He points.

Victoriously, Gemma says, "Pizza. One more game of Clue. Then home. I promise."

Haru folds his arms, grumbling, "Fine."

"Thank you!" Gemma pecks his cheek, takes the pizzas, and dashes for the kitchen.

Left blushing on my doorstep is Haru, turning his fuming gaze to me. "Still helping Gemma with the paper, Tyler?"

"Yep!"

"Right. Bye, Gemma!" calls out Haru. "Farewell, Tyler. If you never hear from me again, it's because Tadashi Galloway has killed me with his new Katana and burned my body to ash. All for leaving you alone with his daughter."

"Drama king, Haru!" Gemma shouts from the kitchen. "He would do no such thing."

"That's what you think," Haru mutters, plodding back to the silver car in my driveway.

Joining Gemma in the kitchen, I ask, "Why two pizzas?"

"Because I eat a whole medium by myself.   Barbeque chicken or pepperoni?"

"Pepperoni."

"Thought so, after the barbeque chips." Gemma devours her third piece.

As I finish my first, crashing and wood splitting sounds from outside. Then out rings a loud screech. Knowing that shriek, I race for the back door—hoping with all hope that Awngeleik is safe in the barn.

* * *

"She's not here, Tyler," states Gemma.

Out of the barn, then into the pouring rain, I sprint to the forest. Toward Mirror Lake. But Gemma's grasp pulls me back.

"Tyler!" she shouts over the rain and thunder. "There are wolf tracks by the barn. Huge tracks!" Fear floods her eyes.

"Then we need to find her. Now! What if it's Jack Wayeland's beast after her? I was supposed to take care of her. Look at how I'm failing! A last piece of my dad. Gone!"

"Is she worth dying for?" Gemma digs her fingernails into my left wrist. "What if the Bear-Wolf kills us?"

"The phantom claims he's forever at my service."

"Sure he'll protect you *and* me, when he's too afraid to even show his face?"

Though confusion has consumed me up to this point, something in my heart summons confidence in my unseen protector, and I speak, "Yes."

"Then let's go." She releases me.

We tear through the forest, stopping when we come to where the lonesome clawed tree was lying on the path to Mirror Lake. Now shattered, the tree has been relegated to dozens of splinters. Scattered with the wreckage are some of Awngeleik's feathers, but no Awngeleik.

Off the path, I pull Gemma to a tall oak tree and shielding patch of shrubs. "No blood." I turn to her. "That's a good sign, right?"

Gemma agrees. "Think she has her cloak?"

123

Just then, a deep growl makes my heart freeze like ice, and Gemma trembles at the steps of the advancing beast.

That's when I know my mother wasn't trying to scare me. Or that Jack Wayeland wasn't exaggerating. The growl leaches through the air, seeming to search for victims to feed its master. How my mother was even able to take one step and *startle* this beast away is a mystery to me. Right now, I can't move at all. I'm literally frozen in fear.

Overhead—too far away to be the growling beast—branches rustle and creak. Though a chill sinks in from rain and fear, each step of the beast starts to warm my veins. For one breath, droplets of rain freeze to specks of ice, then melt on my hot skin.

Twigs, leaves, and pine needles crunch under its footsteps. Anticipating the beast, I hold my breath. Longing for it. Craving the warmth it gives. But then a splitting branch overhead pulls me from the longing and crashes down in front of us. Out of the way, we scramble to uncertainty of where to go.

Then, echoing from the lake is Awngeleik's screeching. The beast's breath quickens. It sprints from the scene, heading for Mirror Lake and Awngeleik. Without thinking, I take off down the path. Ahead, the unseen beast howls. Then snarls.

Awngeleik's screams erupt.

"Tyler!" Gemma pulls on my arm. "It's going to kill you!"

Don't think, my thoughts scream. *Just run.*

During my efforts to shake her off, invisible hands whirl us around to toss us on the path home. In seconds, the phantom's bipedal footsteps are gone. Scrambling up, we search for a way out. All around, we press our palms on the confining five-foot invisible cage.

Seeming to echo in my head are Awngeleik's cries of pain. While the beast's snarls—akin to sordid laughter—deepen to murder, my body shakes. Driven to a fear I've never known, I'm unable to get to her. To see her. Nor save her. I just close my eyes.

To my torment and relief, the beast's howls cut out.

The forest is left quiet.

Too quiet.

Hoof-beats pound on the path. I open my eyes to the sight of Awngeleik leaping through our prison. It shatters into visible shards of glass. When they hit the ground, they're gone. Without looking back, Awngeleik gallops for home. Now free, Gemma and I run after her. We spot the fresh trail of blood. At the forest edge, Awngeleik circles around us like a dog herding sheep. As her shoulder continues to bleed, she waves her head.

"Yes! I see you're hurt." I grab her muzzle, then say, "Hold still."

Awngeleik paws in a muddy pit, oozing muck over her hooves. Trying to soothe the dragon-horse is Gemma, petting her neck, stating, "Shoulder isn't too bad."

At that moment, Awngeleik bolts forward to the barn. Thrown off balance, Gemma thrashes out her arms on the way into the mud. Like a splattering egg in a pan, she lands spitting and sputtering. Attempting to find her footing—and failing—she grips my hand. I end up dragging her from the mire. Sludge covering her head to toe, Gemma manages to smear enough away from her eyes to see. Then she races for the barn like a giant glob of mud.

My heart calming an inch, I sweep one last gaze over the trees, whispering, "Safe. For now." Reaching the barn, I assess the damage. Though bent, the barn lock's still usable. Then before me is Gemma, the mud creature. I hold back a laugh, stating, "Cracked the wood a bit. Overall, it's repairable. More importantly: hardly noticeable."

Unlike you, I silently say.

"Good!" Gemma glances from the loft to me. "She's up there with her cloak. Should be the safest place, right now. How much longer, until someone comes to check on you?"

"A week, maybe."

"That can't come soon enough."

"Agreed." I smile.

Gemma wipes more mud off her face, saying, "Look at me! I'm a mess!"

"Again. Agreed." I laugh.

"Want some?"

I try stopping her hands, but she succeeds in smearing sludge on my face. As I rid myself of it—only to make it worse—on and on, Gemma giggles, and I grumble, "Thanks, Rich Witch."

"You're welcome," sings Gemma, before squeezing grimy water out of her hair. Turning serious, she states, "Can't go back like this. With Kaida home all day, she'd love nothing better than to take a picture of me like *this* to post on social media."

"Then wash up here," I suggest, but think, *The phantom and beast are probably gone. But what if they're not? I don't want to be alone.*

"Your mom won't mind too much?"

"What she doesn't know won't hurt her."

Closing the barn up, we head for the house.

I open the kitchen door, saying, "See? Dragging the body *was* more fun."

"For you," seethes Gemma. "Not for me." Through the mud mask, she scowls while stomping past me to the sink.

Turning to press the door shut, I snicker as the faucet turns on. Right then, Gemma screams. Something muffles her. At the same time someone pushes hard on my back, a hot hand wraps around the front of my neck.

The point of a dagger presses to my throat, and a guttural voice jeers in my ear, "Who are you, and what've you done with the dragon-horse, Awngeleik?"

11

Dual Edge of a Sunset

The hot hand holds tight on my neck, and the dagger's sharp tip pricks along my skin.

The room spins, as I'm pressed harder against the kitchen door. But I manage to say, "Don't know who you mean."

My captor scoffs. "Awngeleik's a bit hard to miss."

I look over my shoulder. Gemma's captor is younger, close to our age. He has her arms immobilized behind her. And, from below his choppy, espresso-brown hair, his eyes study me.

Afraid to misspeak one word, my jaw clenches, while I muse, *Refusing to answer could mean the end of me.*

My captor starts to say, "Ben, you're sure—"

That's when recognition lights in the russet-brown eyes of Gemma's captor. He releases her, exclaiming, "Stop, Musgrae! That's Tyler Ravier!" His accent is flowing, yet harsh. Akin to something between Russian, German, and French.

The dagger flicks away from my throat. Yet, when my captor grips my shoulders and whirls me around to face his bloodshot, hazel gaze, *all* relief is gone. Adding to the spectacle of a sleep-deprived soul are the locks of his wet mahogany-colored undercut clinging to his face—the face of a tank on two legs. Even beneath the matte-black trench coat, his muscles bulge.

"So he is." Musgrae's gaze sinks down to my feet, then up to my face.

127

"Couldn't mistake those emerald eyes. I thought you'd be shorter, though, by Ryco's estimation."

Blood pressure rising, I ask, "Ryco sent you?"

"Not a chance!" replies Musgrae, slipping the dagger into his armband sheath. "'Twas First of the King's Guard: Quall."

"And King Talok," adds Gemma's captor, stepping forward. His unreflecting black trench coat is splotched with mud, but catching the light are his swaying coat-tails with irregular stripes of satin-black.

Musgrae states, "Needed to ensure that you're still in one piece. Which you are. So congrats on surviving the dragon-horse. You didn't lose her, did you?"

Before I can answer, Gemma's captor is offering me a handshake of introduction. "Ben-Yharss. Newest addition to the guard."

"Hence, the new coat design I envy." Musgrae adjusts his plain one, before pinching at the front of his neck.

I shake Ben's hand. As I do, my veins heat pleasantly to warm.

In nervousness, Ben pulls away. "Musgrae, didn't King Talok say Tyler was without magic, when last they came?"

Jealousy shifting to an absentminded nod, Musgrae points to Gemma. "What's with the mud fiend? Did we interrupt some sort of Earth game?" He glances to Ben, then me. "If so, can we join? Feels like I haven't had a stroke of fun in three years."

"Not according to Ryco," Ben mutters.

In response, Musgrae just leers at him.

Ben turns to Gemma, asking, "You're a friend of Tyler Ravier's?"

"Guess so. I'm Gemma Galloway."

"A pleasure to meet you." Ben bows his head a moment.

"Musgrae of Bethsaide," he announces, beating a fist to his opposite shoulder, then lowering it. "Promoted to Fourth of the Guard."

I turn off the faucet, confirming, "Three years ago?"

"You got it." Musgrae grins.

No pointy teeth, I muse. *Must not be a consistent trait.*

Interrupting my thoughts, Gemma asks, "Tyler, mind if I have that shower now? Rid myself of all these nerves?"

Chuckling, Musgrae says, "You mean, de-muckify?"

"That too," she agrees, folding her mud-crusted arms across her chest.

Musgrae, striding over to the table, scrutinizes the two cold pizzas, before asking. "What are these triangular bread-entities?"

Covering a laugh, Gemma coughs, "Pizza. Have all you want." She motions to me.

"Want some, Ben? It's Earth food." Musgrae offers him the barbeque chicken. "Looks to have some meat on it. Come on, try it."

I lead Gemma to the spare bathroom, across from the study, as Ben's voice travels from the kitchen, proclaiming, "I ate, before we came."

"Ben of Yharss," utters Musgrae. "Tsk-tsk. Ever the food purist."

Her eyes uneasy, Gemma stands in the bathroom doorway, asking, "What do you make of them? Think they're really from Paragon?"

"Too soon to tell. But Musgrae didn't cut my throat *and* Ben didn't break your neck. If they're on an opposing side of Paragon, they'd have no reason to spare us."

"True," states Gemma, rubbing at the dried mud on her throat.

Not knowing what else to say, I mutter, "I'll leave you to it."

Smiling gratefully, she closes the door.

I retrieve the box and key from the study, and pace back into the kitchen to the sight of *both* Paragonians sitting at the table and eating pizza. His closed eyes, Musgrae savors every bite. Meanwhile, Ben sits on the edge of his seat, picking off the chicken—as if it's rancid—before braving a taste of his slice.

"Technically"—I clear my throat—"I did lose her. But found her again."

They look my way, while I hand Musgrae the box and set the star-key on the table.

Musgrae swallows his last bite, saying, "That's better than the other caretakers who came after your father's passing."

Ben, giving up on the barbeque, peels pepperoni off a slice. "She has a bad habit of running away," he mumbles. "Among other things."

"You mean her demon form?"

With surprise, Ben says, "That's a new one."

"What do you mean by … demon?" Musgrae glances up from the box, then leans forward to grab the star.

"Black body," I reply. "Freaky white eyes. Shocks you, when touched."

Musgrae lifts a shoulder, saying, "She's never done that before."

When Ben abandons his second slice, Musgrae thrusts the star at him. "You're good with these. You open it."

Confused, Ben accepts it. "You don't know how to open Vardiya Enigma Stars?"

"Of course I do." Musgrae drops the box on the table. "But it requires effort. Needlessly wasted, when there's an eager rookie around to do it."

Ignoring Musgrae, Ben chews on his lower lip and fiddles with the star.

"Why'd Talok send you both so early?"

"Early?" Musgrae gawks. "The portal's been broken for six months."

Ben looks up to add, "A day or two after King Talok and Ryco came here, something broke the portal. We were afraid something happened to you. That's why we sort of … attacked you and your friend, Gemma Galloway."

Musgrae circles a hand around his face, saying, "Didn't recognize you with all the mud. Then, we heard something about a body being dragged?"

I blurt, "Gemma's body … from the mire. She was all mud. No legs. Did Awngeleik's cloaking spell get finished?" For once, I'm thankful for my darker skin, now hiding the flush of heat to my face. Otherwise, there'd be no hiding it from these two in front of me.

"Weeks ago," replies Musgrae with amusement.

Falling away are the Enigma Star's points to the table. "Easy," states Ben, flexing his fingers. "A question, Tyler? How long has it been on Earth, since King Talok and Ryco visited?"

"Three days," is my reply.

Musgrae flies out of his chair, exclaiming, "You're joking! LanSoren said, it's double time on Muraine at most."

"Meaning: a day on Earth is—" I start.

"Two days on Muraine," Ben finishes. "Just shy of forty-eight hours. Intro to Earth Horology."

Musgrae digs at his throat, asking, "How long, since your father passed?"

"A year and a few days."

Ben lowers his head. "Two and a half years, for us."

Staring at the Windmill painting, expressionless, Musgrae says, "Lines up, except for the six months. Time shouldn't be that far off. Unless … something unusual happened."

Expecting an answer, both focus on me. Silently, I recount the events since last seeing Talok. Above the rest, the star-creature stands out.

"A day after they came, my mom and I caught a star-creature at the lake. Wind rippled over the waters. Time reverted a few minutes. Then, it … died."

Musgrae's chest heaves, while Ben's doesn't move at all.

Finally, Musgrae cuts the tension by asking, "A living Vardiya. Died. At the lake? Is it still there? We didn't see anything, after coming through."

"Don't know where my mom put it."

Musgrae presses, "Where *might* she put it?"

"Bedroom, most likely."

"You comfortable snooping in there?"

"Uh! No," is my curt reply.

"Didn't think so." He sighs. "I'll search upstairs for anything giving off a *magical* vibe. Ben, check down here with Tyler." With that, Musgrae charges up the thirteen stairs like a bull.

"We'll start with this box, before searching," states Ben. With a flick of his fingers, the key-points perfectly align themselves. Taken aback, Ben remarks, "Ryco's right. Magic's different here. More resistance. More draining."

I begin the task of testing each key on the box, asking Ben, "Earlier, you implied I have magic now, but I didn't when Talok and Ryco came? How's that possible?"

When *key one* does nothing, Ben hands me another and replies, "I'm not sure. Quall or Ryco could answer better than I. Still learning of human physiology."

Second, third, and fourth key lead to nowhere, and I ask, "You study human physiology?" What other things do you study?"

"Whatever texts are approved by the Pawv'Ragaenen Sovereignty."

"Pawv-what?"

Fifth key trades for the sixth, as Ben wobbles his head. "Sorry! I mean, Paragonian. Maybe we wait for Musgrae to explain. My English could be better." Embarrassed, Ben looks down and flicks mud spots off his coat.

"It's fine. Occasionally, my mom relapses to her old accent. Trips me up every time." I shrug. "Old habits linger, I guess."

Clasping his hands nervously in his lap, Ben states. "But I'm not old enough, to have old habits."

"Good point. How old are you?"

Seventh key is frustrating to no end, while Ben squirms. He struggles to find the right words, finally saying, "Between my fifteenth and sixteenth birthday."

"We say fifteen and a half, almost sixteen, or barely fifteen. Depending on how—"

Ben interrupts. "Fifteen I am?"

"Close enough." I drop the seventh, to scratch the twitching itch on top of my nose.

Then Ben hands me the eighth and last key, confidently saying, "Fifteen and a half."

When the last key fails, as well, I state, "None of these work. Think we can break it open?"

Ben inspects the box. "Not enchanted. But anything fragile in it … might get broken."

"Can you use magic, to see what's inside?"

Over the box, Ben skims his palms, stating, "Metal lining. I'm not *that* good with Gendras, to see past it." He recoils his hands, correcting, "I mean, Green Magic."

"That's okay." I pull out the number map. from my pocket. "Maybe you can help with this. I think it's for the thirteen items."

He unfolds it. "A numerical guide? But there's no number on this box. Have you found anything with numbers on it?"

Should I tell him about my weird number obsession?

Ben jerks a hand to his chin, and I cringe. "You heard, didn't you?"

"Stopped listening at, 'him.'" Ben stands. Giving the map back to me, he continues, "Once we find a numbered one, this guide will help. Until then, perhaps we take a look around?"

A pain-stricken yell, coming from upstairs suddenly, startles us. Ben's at the bottom of the thirteen steps before me, while Musgrae stumbles down pressing his hand to his forehead.

Ben demands to know, "What happened?"

Now at the bottom, Musgrae gripes, "Ryco's writing enchantment happened. That's what! Haven't fallen for it in years. Ben, have you an envelope or spare pouch to contain it?"

"Is that all I am to you? Your supply store?" Ben scowls, but hands him a pouch anyway.

"It's in the job description, as healer of Ryco's Triad. Didn't he tell you?"

"No." Ben huffs.

"Classic Ryco." Musgrae grins. "Leaves out the details, any chance he gets."

Indignantly, Ben is asking, "I suppose you want a potion for your head too?"

"That will be lovely," croons Musgrae. "Give Tyler one too. Bet you got a few nasties."

"Yes," I reply. "But they're gone now."

Onto a tiny cloth square, Ben pours a runny liquid. Meanwhile, Musgrae starts unfolding the letter. Glancing up, Ben clamps a hand onto Musgrae's wrist. "Musgrae! That *is* a letter from Ryco to Tyler."

Musgrae holds the letter out of Ben's reach, asking, "Your point?"

"Shouldn't you ask permission?"

"Tyler? Mind if I read the words from"—mockingly, Musgrae continues in Ben's accent, saying—"Ryco'el de Pawv'Ragaen?"

Ben turns on his heel and leaves for the kitchen.

"By all means." I motion, before following Ben.

Inspecting the windmill painting, Ben queries, "Was this your father's?"

Mill? Windmill? I muse. *How's that supposed to be obvious?* Lifting it off the wall, I reply, "It was his gift to my mom."

Musgrae paces around the living room, and exclaims such words as: *vicious* or *nasty*. Next, he is roaring, "You called him the Sadist?" He rushes to us—me, specifically. "Tyler Ravier! We're going to get along fabulously. What's that?" He points to the facedown painting.

"LanSoren's gift to Tyler's mother," replies Ben.

Tucking letter into pouch, Musgrae adds, "And a hidden gift for Tyler."

From one of his pouches, Ben takes a scalpel and cuts the paper backing along three sides. He flips it away—as one would with brittle paper—proceeding to tap his fingers on the wooden backside like a pianist playing a soft melody. Screws unwind from the wood and drop to the table, as Ben stands aside. "Tyler, it should be you."

Heart pounding, I lift off the thin wood.

"A skinny box within a painting," states Musgrae. "Definitely LanSoren-esque."

I turn the two-inch-thick box over, revealing four more screws waiting for release. Ben works his magic, then stands aside again. Straight up, I lift the loose panel and hand it to Musgrae. Inside the shallow box lies one key, a pair of fingerless gloves, and a note, written in the phantom's handwriting.

Musgrae reads aloud, "Put these on first."

Confusion crosses our faces. Then Musgrae flips the panel to show the prize of the day. Secured in place by tiny leather belts, which are riveted to the panel, are two short, sheathed daggers.

"Weight reduction spell," states Musgrae. "Not heavy at all."

Ben stops me from putting on the black gloves, saying, "Try gripping without them, first."

"Bet LanSoren was accounting for your lack of magic," adds Musgrae.

Straps undone, the blades beckon for a new master, and I oblige. The twin-daggers are weightless, in my grasp. Curved and conforming hilts—with hooked pommels reminiscent to heads of hens, yet more elegant—lock my grip in place.

"Odd," states Ben. "No numbers."

Starting to burn from within are my hands and arms. While sweat beads on my face, Musgrae's face contorts. Then Ben gives him the numerical guide.

Musgrae takes it, asking, "You ever used one of these?"

"Not without help," replies Ben, now noticing my discomfort.

"This circle," states Musgrae, "is a zoomed-in view, because multiple items are in a small space. Either it's the barn, or the house. Barn? Doubtful. Three items in the painting could be the one-two-three by itself, but I'm betting it's the four-five-six below the Rentwar symbol."

Musgrae points to the rising-sun mark. And Ben offers the gloves, while asking, "Does it burn?"

I nod in reply, setting the daggers down to put on the gloves.

"This other symbol, Ben," continues Musgrae, "here in the center? Isn't that one of the Sorsrynian figures for a Vardiya?"

He taps the eight-point symbol and, once again, I grip the daggers.

Ben scratches at his wrist in frustration, mumbling, "I shouldn't have missed that."

"Don't sweat it, Rookie."

"Bet it's the lake," is my suggestion, as the dagger sheaths wither to nothing. Exposed are two curved, asymmetrical Damascus-blades. There's a minor 'S' shape, on one side, while the other gently curves in line with the handle, then—almost halfway down—transitions in the opposite direction. From their eight-inch blade length—retaining the same contours—the daggers grow to fourteen-inches.

Ben leans closer, to scrutinize the blades.

Meanwhile, oblivious and still holding the map, Musgrae mutters, "This other one. What is it? A parasol?" He tilts his head, rotating the map. "Monel! He wrote it upside down."

In my hands, the daggers become heavier. Then I swing one around. *Lighter than an ax, but tip-heavy. Wait! Did he say Monel?*

I ask, "Soren of the Monel mean anything to you?"

Musgrae looks up. "Where'd you hear that name? Hey! Wicked blades! I like."

I reply, "It's etched on a hidden painting in my dad's study."

"Ben." Musgrae turns to him. "You know that name?"

"Why would I know it?"

"Because it hasn't been years since you took Paragon's series on Sorsrynian Ancestry."

Ben huffs, "Monel was home to Withrasyns."

Musgrae folds the numerical guide, correcting, "He means White Sorsryns. Continue."

"That's all I know," replies Ben. "Sorry, Tyler."

I just shrug, examining the daggers further. One blade fades from dark-blue, to copper, then dull-yellow. Its twin, however, transitions from metallic-red, to the same yellow, then white. On the blade with blue is a black handle, streaked with white. Around the bird's closed eyes are white crescents. The other handle is white, streaked with black; but the eyes are open and identical to Awngeleik's demon form. Snake-eyes and all, they are black with white pupils.

"Together," states Ben, "they're like a vanishing sunset."

"Think they represent night and day?"

"Could be," replies Ben. "Rentwaramein *is* our solar star's name. Informally called, Rentwar."

"Informally?"

Ben clarifies, "When it's not used in spells or rituals."

Musgrae reaches for the darker dagger. "May I?"

Relinquishing daggers to both Paragonians, I rub my gloved palms together, then clench and unclench my fists. Though they're strong like leather, the gloves stretch like spandex. Toward the fingers are 'V' cutouts, while black studs rivet three straps across the back of each glove. Altogether? They're simple. I slip them off.

After reassembling everything, Ben smooths out the backing's paper. Next, his fingertips flicker with green light and seal the cut edges. "There!" He smiles. "Back to undisturbed."

In slight alarm, Musgrae sets the dagger on the table, asking, "What happened to Mud Fiend? Should we make sure she hasn't drowned in her own muck?"

"I'll see if she's done." With that, I head for the hallway.

Door wide open, the spare bathroom's light is off and—except for dried mud flecking the floor—there's no sign of Gemma. I grow uneasy, as one thought creeps to the surface. *Would the phantom kidnap her right under our noses?*

12

Ticking Through an Era

I call out Gemma's name, before starting to open the study doors. Hands still on handles, the doors fly open and knock me to the ground. Then out comes Gemma in her soggy clothes, tripping over me and screaming as she falls on top of my chest.

"Found her!" I yell, as Gemma scrambles off me like smoke in the wind.

"Mud Fiend!" Musgrae smiles, holding the box against his side. "You do have a face. A cute one too." He nudges Ben. "Should Khyra be worried?"

Gemma blushes—running fingers through damp, stringy hair—then retreats to safety in the study.

Ben scoffs, "To Khyra, only King Talok and Ryco exist for flirting with."

"She flirts with Talok too?"

"Not intentionally," replies Ben to Musgrae, while handing me the gloves and daggers.

All now in the study, it's Gemma asking, "Where'd the key come from?"

"Windmill painting. Found these too." I hand her the daggers. When they leave my grasp, their protecting sheaths reform.

She turns them side to side. "Wonder what he wants you to do with them."

Right then, Musgrae rattles the key in the lock, saying, "Opening this is like my first time."

"First time?" Gemma looks up.

"No!" huffs Ben. "Do not answer that, Musgrae of Bethsaide."

"Sure thing, Rookie. How about the second time?"

"No!" shouts Ben, in a rage. "I'll not hear of it, or the third or seventh or however many. How you keep track? Use a stick? No! I bet it's a staff. A long Arkiveis staff Eli stole for you."

Silently laughing, Musgrae patronizes Ben more. "Sharing my escapade stories with Ben of Yharss? No more. Got it! Anything else, Rookie?"

"No!" Ben seethes.

Meanwhile, I peer at the winning Clue cards on the board. *Mrs. Peacock-candlestick-study. Why's that familiar?* Glancing, first, to the secondary desk, I spot the peacock lamp. Next, a candleholder. Then two and three more on the wall. The six peacock-feather holders are of a flowing metal design.

Daggers still in Gemma's grasp, I look to their bird-head pommels. *Not a hen, a peacock! Feathers like eyes.* Then I whisper, "Fading light of my eyes."

Now calmer, Ben queries, "That a line from LanSoren's Last?"

"Can you light those with magic?" I point to the candles. "Some are too hard to reach."

Spotting them—and rubbing palms together—Ben snaps his fingers and claps once. His hands part, and a puff of fire forms between. Then, like a puppeteer, he flicks flames to wicks.

We wait, but nothing happens, and I shrug. "Was worth a shot."

With a wave of his hand, Ben snuffs out the wicks. "Six is odd," he says. "I'd expect LanSoren to have eight or thirteen candles. Musgrae?"

Now ignoring the box, Musgrae pinches at his throat. "With his tendency toward precision, it should be eight or thirteen. Maybe some are hidden."

During Musgrae and Ben's exchange, Gemma searches the bookcases. At the tall case—next to the grandfather clock—she grabs a book off, to flip through it. "This one's all in German," she comments.

I ask, "What is?"

"Ever-Present Origin," she says.

Ben—ambling over to peruse the book with her—bumps his shoulder against hers, provoking a second blush to her cheeks.

That's when Musgrae quotes, "Ever-present fading light of the sun-eclipse."

I ask, "How do you know that line?"

"Everyone, who's anyone, knows LanSoren's Last Poem," states Musgrae, peeking at the sliver of empty space on the shelf.

Brow furrowing, Ben states, "Don't know *that* language."

Gemma closes the book, pouting. "Back to square one."

A sly smile crosses Musgrae's face, as his hand glides to the shelf's backing. "Found it," he declares.

A soft click sounds. Then panels rotate around, adding seven more candleholders to the room. When a ceiling panel opens, a candelabrum lowers itself. Its center boasts of a metal indigo-peacock. Nine holders drape away from it, fashioned as a tranquil feathered-tail.

"Definitely his craftsmanship. I'll leave you kids to it." Excitedly, Musgrae rubs his hands together. "Going to see what I can find, using this guide, while there's still daylight. Back in a Dragon's Spout."

After waving once to Musgrae, Ben snaps his fingers. All wicks burst to flames, crackling like a fireplace. With a loud spark, they go out.

Windows darken to pitch-black. The room's now cloaked like night, with warm light floating out from the candelabrum center. Made visible on the walls are illuminated symbols and scrollwork. Painted animals in motion are confined to those same walls. Deer. Horses. Foxes. Birds. Yet, somehow, different. Harder and faster, they run: across panels, bookcases, and swaying curtains.

Wolves howl. Horses whinny. Birds call. Other indistinguishable cries fill the room too. As fast as the animals began, they stop to listen. Chills prick my skin, then out from the room comes the sound of an eerie creature's moans and screeches vibrating everything.

At full speed, the paint-animals scatter.

Then, gone are the reverberating echoes.

"That sound was of a massive dragon," states Ben. "The larger? The louder their cries."

Still clinging to its new home, *Vision of the Dragon* watches over the room. But the dragon is missing.

Before I can say anything about it, Gemma points. "Tyler, your watch. It's glowing!"

Sure enough, the diver-watch glows blue, first, then green. In their upward travel, the lighted-colors fan out. Staring up at the ceiling, I state, "Number pad. Any combination ideas?"

When I tap the watch-face and nothing happens, Ben suggests, "Aim it on the wall."

As I do, Gemma presses one of the buttons. Like a lock pad, it beeps. She presses five more times, until it bleeps and resets.

"Six numbers," states Ben.

"A date?" Gemma lifts her shoulders. "Birthday? Anniversary?"

After I try a few, nothing changes.

"For laughs, let's try my birthday," suggests Gemma, while inputting all six digits.

Instead of beeping, it clicks, and the Grandfather clock-front swings open. There first, Ben says, "Don't detect any traps. Go ahead, Tyler."

I peer inside, to the blackish-blue diving armor nestled at the bottom. Leaf-shaped scales cover the entire piece. Weighing little more than tissue, its shape is similar to a wet suit. When I pull it out, something else falls to the floor, and Ben picks it up. "This one must be for you." He gives it to Gemma.

Confused, she accepts it. "How could your dad know I'd be helping you?"

"At this point?" I shrug. "Who knows?"

"I'm sure LanSoren will reveal more," states Ben, clasping his hands in front of him.

"Hope so," I reply, while closing the clock case. After it clicks shut, something triggers a conversing pair of masculine voices behind the three of us. We spin around, to see the realistic projection of my dad—sitting at an antique desk—writing with a quill.

Thrown off guard, I think, *He's so lifelike. Is he here now?* When I start to approach, a presence stops me.

Fading into view is another man—in a modern-day suit—inspecting the grandfather clock and saying, "Fine piece, Lance. You're sure it was worth the money?"

In an English accent, my dad replies, "Certainly." Suggestive of pre-Colonial times, his clothing is frillier than that of the 1800s. Absent of lace, his bright-red coat resembles the British military.

Gemma frantically points to the man in the suit, whispering, "Tyler. That's Soren."

Arrogantly, Soren is asking, "You find a way to save your son yet, Lance?"

"What son?" My dad looks up. "I'm not supposed to have a son."

"Right!" Soren startles. "It hasn't happened. Silly me. Plenty of time to learn what I mean. After all, it's only 1656."

Into my eyes, Soren stares with a murderous gleam.

The scene changes out.

I ask Ben, "How do you explain that time gap?"

"Perhaps we keep watching. Maybe it explains."

This time, my dad's dressed like the classic British Redcoat of the Revolutionary War.

Soren, still in the suit, inspects the grandfather clock yet again. "Nice updates on the clock. Bigger and better." He steps away from it, asking, "What's that you're writing, Lance?"

"Journal … for my son? Me? Not sure, yet." My dad shrugs, while desperately continuing to scratch the quill to journal pages.

"You know the rules. Sure you can write that?"

"Yes! Given it much thought."

"This one in English?"

"Murainian," replies my dad.

Soren gazes back at me, saying, "Want me to tell you who Tyler Ravier is? What he is?"

"I think," whispers Ben, "that Soren can see us."

"And it's freaky," hisses Gemma.

"No, thank you," states my dad.

Jaggedly smiling, Soren counts three on his fingers like a ticking clock.

That smile? I've seen it before, but where? Except for his lighter skin, staring at Soren is like watching some twisted version of me. Then it dawns on me—where I've seen the smile—and all sound fades to static. It's *my* wicked grin, stripped of playfulness. It's now malicious, dark, and evil.

Sounds reemerge to Soren waltzing near us, speaking the Count of Despairion, "One-two-three. The count goes."

"Goes to where?" my dad queries.

"Wouldn't you like to know? Four-five-then six." Soren laughs and waltzes away.

Weary, my dad finishes, "Why stop there?"

Like a predator, Soren approaches Gemma and hisses, "Seven-eight!" Now in front of her face, he croons, "But nine *is* best."

"Best of what?" My dad looks up. "Is someone coming, Soren?"

His hand wagging twice, Soren backs away from Gemma and then continues, "Ten-eleven!"

"To confession." My dad sighs. "Don't you ever tire of the numbers?"

"Never!" shouts Soren. "Twelve! Thirteen!" His voice deepens to that of a monster, speaking, "Beginning. End. And all in between."

The room quivers with each word of the last bit, as if even the walls fear Soren's voice.

Mood brightening, Soren mimics a child's voice, saying, "Thirteen. You're done."

The quill tip breaks off. And my dad glances up, with fear engulfing his eyes.

Soren pets the crown of my dad's head. "There's the look I've been waiting for. At last, you've realized Tyler Ravier will die." Soren shrugs at me. "Whoever he is."

"If you don't mind, Soren." My dad smacks the petting hand. "Go away!"

To me, Soren makes his way to bow. "As you wish," he says.

Reaching up, and shifting from the realistic projection to a ghost-like figure, Soren's fingers brush down my cheek. His chilling touch takes hold for a moment, then passes through my face.

Onward, the scene switches to my dad—now dressed to match Soren—staring out the study window, with a gaze that sees anything but what lies beyond the glass. In contrast, Soren hums some eerie tune, while fiddling with the candles and such around the room.

"Stop touching those, you filth!" my dad shouts.

The child-mimic says, "So touchy these days, Lance. Sure you're all right?"

"I would've been, if it hadn't been for—" Pained, my dad faces Soren.

At the sight of my dad's glowing-red eyes, Ben recoils. "Vitiosyn-eyes. He has Vitiosyn-eyes. He couldn't have been one. He was too good."

Moments later, in the scene, I stroll in at age twelve, saying, "Thought I heard you. Who were you shouting at?"

"Old acquaintance on the phone," states my dad. "Said something that got on my nerves."

During the whole sequence, my dad hasn't aged at all. And neither has Soren, now pacing in circles around the younger me. My mind whirls, *What is he? What am I? Soren. He can't be me.*

My dad lays the windmill painting down on the desk-top, saying, "I have something to show you, Tyler. It's for your mom. Been putting money aside for that kitchen remodel she's always talking about. Thought this would go nicely in there. What do you think?"

Soren leans down, whispering to the younger me: "I think he would like it more, Lance, if he knew what's held within."

In response, my dad's eyes deaden.

"She'll love it, Dad." The younger me glances up, asking, "You okay?"

"Tired. Feel old today."

Again, the scene shifts.

This time, my dad faces the clock's projection, saying, "If you're watching this, Tyler, it means I'm dead." Tears pool in his copper-colored eyes. "I'm sorry I couldn't change that."

Battling my own tears, my chest clenches.

My dad continues, "With the diving armor, daggers, and Gemma, you have everything you need to get the English journal. It's below Mirror Lake. Inserts for the daggers rest underwater. Once inserted, they open a hidden chamber under the lakebed. The Enigma Star Talok gave you will open the door after the tunnel, and the black chest beyond that."

Gemma says, "Maybe he'll finally explain where I fit."

"There *is* a catch." My dad folds his arms. "Not sure when you'll be watching this, but an eclipse will occur one to three days from now. You must wait for it. Once it's full, set your watch. My watch. To twenty-two minutes and thirteen seconds."

Twenty-two and thirteen? I muse. *Why are they so important?*

Nervously, Ben shuffles away from the wall. "He's going to stop time. I've never heard of someone being able to cast a spell after they're gone."

He continues, "Don't worry about breathing. You won't need to, because time will have stopped. Be sure you're above the surface, though, before the timer's up. You'll drown, otherwise. Gemma will cut the task-time in half. In case you're wondering, 'Why Gemma?' I can't tell you. Doing so would change everything. Utterly disastrous. Please. Trust. Me." Tears pooling again, they threaten to spill over his long face. "We'll save the goodbyes, for when you get to Muraine. Under no circumstances are you to leave Gemma Galloway behind. Not those two diving armors, either. They're meant to help your bodies adapt to a new environment. To magic. One day, all this will make sense. I hope."

That's it? This will make sense, one day? That's not enough.

The scene fades to nothing.

Just when we think it's over, the room shakes.

Projections start again.

Standing next to my father, who's pulling on his own hair, Soren digs his fingernails into my dad's face. He spews out, "This time, you won't stand in our way, Lance Ravier. Again, we are strong. Do what you want with the Vardiya. His end will come, before he can deliver your message to Tyler."

Projections vanishing, my dad's study reverts to normal.

Battle Against Tears turning to Black-Absence, I ask, "What do you make of it?"

Eyes closed, Ben massages his temples. "It's all so confusing," he mumbles.

"What's confusing?" booms a deep voice, and all three of us jump.

From the study doorway, Musgrae smiles. He holds up a journal. "Number seven. Took some mining skills, but I got it."

I take the leather journal from him. On the navy cover, a multi-shaded figure of turquoise stands like a statue. Although it has fish or dragon-like features, it appears to be humanoid. The other figure's taller, cloaked in white, with no other distinguishable traits. When the journal's tilted, a dark-gray outline fades in and out.

Spotting it, as well, Gemma says, "Looks like the mouth of a beast."

"Good luck reading it," states Musgrae, leaning against the wall.

I flip it open. "You don't know what language this is?"

Unconcerned with my question, Gemma sweeps her hand over a page. "Flowing, but sharp in places. Reminds me of Arabic."

Musgrae examines the armor, replying, "Not a clue. Ben, you?"

"It's unfamiliar to me."

"Worry about the journal later." Musgrae pulls out the guide. "Only the two armors? They must be ten and eleven. I found seven. Painting was four-five-six. Where did you and Gemma find the box?"

I reply, "Well past the lake."

"Then it must be one-two-three, according to this guide. Twelve and thirteen should be around the lake, where the Vardiya … died. That leaves eight and nine. Not too bad, for a day's work."

Remembering Soren's interest in Gemma, I clear my throat to say, "I think I already found nine."

"Wonderful!" Musgrae claps his hands.

But Gemma asks, "When?"

"The Dark Prince."

"Right!" She squirms in her stiff, stained clothes.

That's when I ask her, "Weren't you supposed to go home, like, hours ago?"

"Texted a friend who owed me one. She'll be a good cover."

"What about the horses?"

"Forgot about them." Gemma cringes.

Musgrae—staring at the guide—says, "In the barn?" Then hands me the guide. "Number eight is close to the house. Should be in there."

Indignant again, Ben is asking, "Didn't you look?"

"I tried. But, it would seem, the only person Awngeleik likes less than me is Ryco. She loves you, though, Ben. Guess who's going to retrieve number eight?"

"The rookie," Ben grumbles.

Turning serious, Musgrae looks to me. "Almost forgot to ask. Do you have giant wolves round these parts?"

"Don't think so. Why?"

Neck-pinching once again, Musgrae says, "Found a horrific bloodbath and feather mess at the lake. Prints and claw gouges everywhere. Tree demolished to splinters, on the way there. You and Gemma get chased by something?"

Gemma tells him, "More like hunted, then trapped by an invisible cage."

"Was that today?" queries Ben.

"Right before we got to the house," I reply.

Musgrae cocks his head, asking, "How'd we miss you?"

"Because," states Ben, "you didn't know where we were going. Did you even hear Ryco's directions?"

"I make it a habit to listen to Ryco as little as possible."

Ben nods. "Hence, why we took the scenic route to Tyler's. Were you even sure this was his house?"

"So I took a gamble," Musgrae confesses.

Ben's face reddens to rage. "You told me to subdue Gemma Galloway, when you weren't even sure Tyler Ravier lived here?"

"She looked suspicious, covered in muck." Musgrae smiles. "I wasn't even sure she was a girl, until she screamed. Before that, there was mention of a body being dragged too."

"I'm fine," says Gemma. "So no harm done."

"That's not the point." Ben glares at Musgrae.

"What *is* the point, Rookie?"

"You're reckless. If you're not careful, we're going to get suspended."

Musgrae sucks in a breath. "Fine. Here's what we're going to do—"

But Ben interrupts, "I'm done listening to you. I want to hear what Tyler wants us to do."

Searching the room, I collect my thoughts before saying, "Ben, search the barn for number eight. I'll use the key we found with the daggers. See if I can get that box open. Gemma, you *really* should go home. Musgrae, help her take the horses back. After that, I don't know."

"Good plan." Musgrae holds up the Jed-finger, stating, "After dropping off Gemma, I need to go back to Muraine. Make sure we have a sizable escort, to meet us on the other side of the portal in a few days. It's not as safe as we thought. Not after seeing the wreckage at the lake."

Gemma brushes her hand on my forearm. "Meet you tomorrow morning at the lake, for eclipse watching?"

"Might be a long watch." I hand her a diving armor and say, "Pack your weight in food."

Musgrae shakes my hand. "Until tomorrow, Tyler Ravier." Without another word, he and Gemma leave.

Sweeping some dust off my dad's desk, Ben says, "We forgot to tell him about LanSoren's memories."

"No, we didn't." I smile. "Gemma loves to talk. She'll fill him in on everything and then some, trust me. I call it *the Barrage of Gemma*."

Looking down at the floor, Ben can't help but smile. "I'd take that, over spending a day-off with Musgrae."

"He doesn't seem that bad."

"You only say that, because you've not had to spend an entire day-off going on *five* separate expeditions with him."

"What do you mean by, expeditions?"

Hesitating a moment, Ben replies, "Chasing a pretty face or two. Or five, if you're Musgrae. But they have to be close to his age."

"Five?" I choke out, before laughing. "That's ambitious."

"I see how it's funny to you. But next time Musgrae wants to go for expeditions, if you're on Muraine, you can go with him."

"Deal! Should we call it a night?"

"After looking in the barn, yes," replies Ben. "I'll sleep in there too. Make sure Awngeleik doesn't get lonely."

"I'll bring breakfast, in the morning."

"I thank you, Tyler. Goodnight."

With everyone gone, I rush to look at *Vision of the Dragon*. Still resting on its panel, the dragon mocks me to exhausted paranoia. Part of me wonders if I imagined it, and the lights blowing out the other night too.

13

To Outrace Twenty-two

In my favorite patch of grass by the lake, Gemma sits. As morning light touches her face free of the makeup-mask, she looks up at me to ask, "What's in the big black bag?"

After dropping the military duffle at the base of a nearby tree, I pull at the diving armor's tight neckline. On my way down to join her among the green blades of grass, I nudge her shoulder and simply reply, "Stuff."

"Keep your secrets," teases Gemma, with her eyes sparkling in golden light. "See if I care."

Grinning briefly, I state, "Has everything we've found so far. Except the locked box. Packed a picture of my seven-year-old cousin Alec too." I pause. "He sort of looks like Talok."

"You think King Talok of Paragon is your cousin?"

"Only one way to find out. Knowing time passes on Muraine twice as fast, means fifteen-year-old *Talok* could be a seven-year-old *Alec*."

"Why not ask Ben? Or Musgrae, when he gets back?"

I shake my head. "If it's true, I want to give Talok the chance to tell me himself."

Gemma squirms, asking, "Wouldn't that be the first thing he told you?"

"Not if he was distracted. Visiting a new planet; fence inflicting wounds to Awngeleik; not to mention, the company of a sadist—all of it would be enough to unnerve anyone."

"Any luck with the box last night?"

"Key got stuck. Lock's too rusted … or something. Ben's still in the barn with it. Grumbled over Musgrae's brute force being more of a hindrance than a help."

"What about number eight?"

I chuckle. "Apparently, Ben needed sleep, more than number eight needed to be found. He'll be here in a bit."

"Awngeleik coming with him?" Her voice strains, while she claws at her forearm.

"Yep! Said he's not going to let her out of his sight."

Ignoring me, she continues the clawing.

Nudging her again, I ask, "What do you think of the diving gear?"

The clawing stops, but Gemma groans, "With all of these annoying bumps on the inside, it's going to look like I have the chicken pox." Sighing forlornly, she adds, "Did discover something interesting about it, though."

"Which is?"

Unzipping her jacket, she grips a little black-leaf tab at her center-front neckline and says, "The fabric relaxes, when I pull this leaf tab and run my fingertips down the armor core."

"Wish I'd known that this morning. It was like putting on an itchy second skin."

Gemma's smile turns serious. "Your dad's memories last night. What do you make of them?"

"Not sure what to think." I wet my lips. "One thing's certain. Whoever he is, Soren of the Monel's unhinged. He ever do anything to you?"

"No!" exclaims Gemma. "Although, I never *actually* believed he was real, until last night. Turns out he was, or still is, psychotic. But I don't remember him being that way." Seeming to shiver away whatever haunts her, Gemma changes the subject. "What do you think you'll get, once you know what all the journals say?"

"Answers for why he lied to me all these—"

Just then, cutting me short, is a shadow spreading from overhead. It shades the lake waters and, through the trees' protection, we glance at the imminent eclipse. Gemma grabs one glove and the waking-dagger, while I set my watch.

"Twenty-two and thirteen. You ready?" I ask, glancing up to Gemma.

Already stripped to just armor, she's jogging into the lake and hollering, "Hurry up, Tyler!"

"Well," I whine, "turn around. I'm not Jed. Don't like the idea of stripping in front of you."

Irked with me, Gemma harshly motions. "You have armor, under it all. So, what does it matter? You know, all this time, I've wondered what's so different about you, Tyler. Now I know. It's because you're an alien-wizard-thing."

I gape at her, with absolutely no comeback for the Barrage of Gemma.

"Sorry!" She cringes, folding her arms. She reluctantly turns around.

Stripping down to armor, I stride knee-deep into freezing water and defend myself with, "If you want to get technical, I'm half-alien. Although, I hadn't thought about it, until—"

Once again, I'm cut off. This time, by Gemma excitedly saying, "Don't think about it now! We have a mission. No distractions."

Slightly aggravated, yet anxious, I strap the sleeping-dagger and Enigma Star to my waist. Dramatically, I roll my eyes at Gemma. "I take left. You take right?"

Her mouth clamped shut, Gemma gives a thumbs-up.

With our backs to it, we wait for the eclipse to complete. Spilling through the swaying tree leaves all around are countless shadows of light-crescents dancing on the ground. Finger hovering over the timer-button, I press it the very moment everything darkens. All at once, I feel a warmth and chill—when sloshing forward—as Gemma and I dive into the now-pleasantly warm water and swim down and farther into its depths.

Going our separate ways, fins start forming on my armor's forearms. The material stretches up toward my fingers, to web my hands. Fins, on the calves, do the same to my feet. Even with the added speed from the armor, five minutes tick by. Then a white object blurs by, making my heart palpitate to exploding.

The object slows, and I realize it's Awngeleik approaching me. Instead of four legs, however, a mermaid-like tail has replaced her back two. Seamlessly, it blends with her body, whipping side to side and propelling her through the water with ease. Replacing her front hooves are clawed, webbed hands splayed out, paddling like a dog. Then comes her head-flail.

Flailing equals: follow, dumb-head.

Gemma coasts by, with a dagger in one hand. She pats my shoulder with her free hand, then gives another thumbs-up. Together, we swim deeper than I've ever gone. Expecting the water pressure to tighten around me, when it doesn't, surprise hits at the contradiction of it.

For one solid year, this is where my heart has longed to go. But my mind has feared to tread. To the bottom of the lake. Not to live, but to die. *Ironic, I muse, that I'm here now, with Gemma and a mermaid-dragon-horse—trying to outrace twenty-two—so I can live long enough to learn the truth.*

Below where Gemma and Awngeleik are waiting for me, the dagger's insert spews flames the color of the blade: blue, copper, and yellow. When the sharp tip closes in on its mark, the blade bends to a tri-edge. When I rotate the inserted dagger, something gives way. I pull the dagger free of the insert, and they shift to normal. No more spewing insert. No more tri-edge.

A current tugs the three of us toward the lake's center. And, down, we travel to the lakebed, where my longing turns to obsession, though I know not why. Looking at the watch, it reads, thirteen minutes and eight seconds. That's when I see it hovering over the sediment.

Paper now gone, my discarded poem glows the blue words of 'I know you, but I have never spoken to you. Familiar as my own face staring back at me. How can that be?'

From Awngeleik's mane and tail, light begins emitting to illuminate the dark hole in the lakebed's center. As we pass the glowing words—but before the black hole swallows us—I spot the Vardiya's two tentacles. Both petrified and clinging to the water-sodden poem, they remind me of Soren's words. *He said the Vardiya's message would never be delivered. What message?*

Down and through a winding tunnel, we're swallowed up.

On the way through, I remember the hidden painting with Soren's blacked-out face and the Vardiya's answer to who killed my dad. *They are near the same. Thirteen. Done. Soren killed my dad. It all points to him.*

Nearing the tunnel's end, a soft light twinkles from above the surface. Then we burst from the water to climb onto a dirt-floor. Straight ahead is a door. Above it, a flaming sphere illuminates the small room, and I force myself to focus.

In Gemma's words: *No distractions.*

Advancing to the door, I untie the Enigma Star from my waist and follow the motions of Talok and Ben. On and on, I fiddle without success.

Impatiently, Gemma grabs it. "You're taking too long."

In seconds, the keys fall to the floor.

"What do you know?" I tease. "You *are* good for something."

She just flicks my arm, in retaliation. And I help collect keys off the floor, asking, "How'd you find the dagger-insert that fast?"

"I didn't." Gemma ruffles Awngeleik's mane. "The Water Angel showed up to help."

Awngeleik—still floating in the exiting pool of water—leans into Gemma's hand.

"Careful," I warn. "Don't let her snot slime you. It reeks."

Chuckling, Gemma comes to help put all keys in the metal door. Into slots, I slip the daggers. Every piece now in place, keys and daggers turn themselves. The door grinds open. We collect the keys, then rush into the even tinier room with a single black chest in its center.

I insert my keys into the chest, stating, "No time to waste."

Agreeing, Gemma puts in the last of hers.

The chest opens to a moderately sized black satchel resting on the base. On top of it is a note. Smoothing it out, I read aloud, "Take bag and daggers. Leave chest and keys, if short on time. Best of luck. –Dad."

Awngeleik screeches an echoing cry, as her mane forms into one long, flimsy dorsal fin.

Gemma glances at my watch. "Less than two minutes. Time to go." She rushes out to pull the daggers from the door and joins me on Awngeleik's back.

I clutch the bag, sandwiching it between Gemma's back and my chest. Then down dives Awngeleik beneath the surface—shivering her body a moment—as an iridescent sphere encases Gemma and me. Forward, then up, Awngeleik propels like a speeding sailfish, clearing the tunnel in seconds. Faster still, her mermaid tail ripples through the water.

On the surface above, light scatters. Then—creaking like an icy-lake in winter—spiny cracks form on the sphere.

Eight seconds left.

Gemma holds her throat, gasping, and I begin to choke. Lungs longing for air, we need to breathe. When time hits to one, we break the surface. Sure to not look at the unchanged eclipse—while our surroundings spin—the eclipse quickly shifts. Sunlight races over Mirror Lake's waters. And for a breath, time speeds up.

Awngeleik rushes to shore. Stomping her scaly-hands, they turn back into hooves. And her mermaid tail writhes on the rocks, before it, too, shifts back to what is normal for a dragon-horse. All signs of the Water Angel now gone, Awngeleik gallops to the unsuspecting Ben sitting on a rock and digging through Gemma's lunch bag.

Noticing her, Ben jumps up to shout, "No, Awngeleik!"

His hands flash, raising a glass-like barrier for protection. Yet, that doesn't stop the dragon-horse from forming white light at her forehead and breaking through the barrier. Stunned, he holds his casting wrist. Then Awngeleik knocks him off the rock.

Shrieking once, and limbs flailing, Ben splashes in.

We swim to shore, then climb out of the water.

Glancing at Gemma, I mutter, "Glad I'm not her only victim."

She holds back giggles, and starts dressing. Then, lifting a brow, she watches me gather discarded clothes like all my joints are suddenly stiff and frozen. "Do you sanction me seeing you dress? Or do I need to avert my eyes again?"

The clothes in hand fall to the ground, and I cross my arms. "I can't help that I don't like you watching. It's weird."

Eyes narrowing, Gemma puts her hands on her hips. "Like you watching me sleep?"

"That was out of necessity. Besides, I didn't stare at you. Well, actually, that's not true. You sleeping in a contorted doll pose *was* a bit freaky. So disturbing, I had to force myself to look away."

She frowns. "I sleep like a contorted doll?"

"I was going to say *dead doll*. Contorted sounded better. Nicer, even." I shrug, smiling my wicked grin.

Gemma huffs. "I don't believe you."

That's when someone nearby clears their throat to ask, "What's a doll?"

Startling, Gemma and I gawk at Ben.

"Sorry!" He grimaces. "Didn't mean to eavesdrop, but you're kind of hard not to hear. Find anything in the lake?"

"Just that." I point to the satchel. "Had to leave the Enigma and a chest behind, though."

"I'll attempt to retrieve them," states Ben. Struggling his coat off, to wring out water, he drops it. Then he rests one hand on Awngeleik's forehead and whispers, "Awngeleik, show me the way you took?"

Deeply, Awngeleik inhales and then closes her eyes. When they open, Ben smiles and says, "Thank you, Equidyn." Sweeping his gaze over the lake, Ben softly runs one ring finger down the center of his forehead. Then, toward the lake, he waves that same hand out and snaps his fingers.

With keys still in it, the chest appears between us three with a loud *pop!*

Surprised, I state, "You made that look too easy. Could've spared us a trip down there."

Ben shakes his head. "I still have to see most of the way. The path. Others only have to see the destination. Like Eli of Kirja. We're both Object Retrievers," states Ben, wiggling back into the coat. "He's better, but I'm good at getting the hard-to-reach things and detecting the hidden. It's one reason why King Talok sent me. In case you hadn't found everything."

"Glad he did," I state.

Gemma adds, "You seem nice."

Clasping his hands in front of him, Ben blushes. "I try, but Musgrae tends to bring out my temper."

"He's not that bad." Gemma lifts a shoulder.

Ben narrows his eyes at the forest. "Wait until you see him on Muraine. You will change your mind. He and Eli drive everyone to madness, possibly even each other."

"On his best behavior away from home?" I ask.

"Precisely," replies Ben.

"Find anything in the barn?" queries Gemma.

Blush fading, Ben announces, "Found journal in loft. Couldn't open box, though."

Ben leads us toward the items, while searching inside the black satchel.

I take up the journal Ben found. On its black-leather cover is an etched sunrise. Toward the top, a red-and-copper dragon flies downward. Below the sun-crest, a gray wolf, with green eyes staring up at the dragon above, stands howling.

"Look through it, already?" I ask.

"Thought you'd want to be first," replies Ben, removing a jade-colored journal from the satchel.

Crowding next to Ben, Gemma says, "It looks like a family crest … with *a lot* going on."

Peeking inside the black journal, I scowl at its unrecognizable language.

Then Gemma bursts out, "Tyler, this one's in English."

I trade journals with Ben, then say, "See if this makes sense to you."

On the cover of the jade-leather journal is an ornate family-crest etched on a white-shield outlined in black. At the top, the shield curves into three points. Below the left point is a white tree; a black tree is below the right; and a withered or sprouting tree is beneath the center one. Purple lines, black ones, and some white lines—encased by parallel black or purple—draw downward from the trunks of the trees.

"So. Many. Lines," I complain.

"Right?" Gemma chuckles.

The lines are vertical—on the upper-third of the crest—before angling to the shield's base. Two-thirds of the way down the shield, my focus stops on the diamond. Half black. Half white. The Vardiya's Mark is etched on it: the plus-symbol overlaid with a curved 'X.' While the rest of the lines are chaotic, the diamond is not; the only connection it has to the crest is at its top and bottom. Above, lines draw together, then angle downward into an arrow meeting the diamond. Then, from the diamond's base, one purple line travels to the shield's very bottom tip.

"Kind of looks like it has a face," states Gemma. "See the large arrow encasing the smaller one and that diamond?"

To the two dots—almost in horizontal alignment with the diamond—I point. "These purple dots, with the curving lines—"

Gemma finishes, "Could be eyes with lashes."

Flipping it open, I skim its pages and say, "Aside from that, I've no idea what this is."

Impatiently, Gemma is asking, "What's it say?"

"It's a personal journal about his life after marrying my mom. Details almost every day."

Ben closes the dragon-wolf journal, announcing, "This is in at least three Murainian languages. Mentions ReNovamen and Siveyra Sorsryns in places too."

Gemma makes her request of, "In English?"

Ben takes a deep breath, before starting his recital. "ReNovamen is a process only Sorsryns can perform. A type of rebirth, to put it simply. Siveyra Sorsryns are the most revered beings of Muraine. Next to Vardiyas."

"Which I've already seen," I interrupt.

Then Gemma adds, "And Sorsryns are ancestors of Paragonians."

"White Sorsryns, specifically." Ben continues, "To earn title of Siveyra, a Sorsryn must reach a thousand years. They gain more abilities and are harder to kill, after that."

"One-thousand years old," I rasp out. "Hard to imagine."

Gemma's eyes grow to anime proportions. "Think of the candles covering their birthday cakes."

Confused, Ben queries, "On Earth, you celebrate the day you're born?"

Closing the jade-journal, I nod. "You don't?"

He just grins, nervously saying, "Should be interesting. Getting used to each other's cultural differences." Swallowing hard, he looks to Gemma. "I see Tyler has packed a bag. But what of you, Gemma Galloway?"

She hangs her head. "Packed one, but forgot it at home."

Ben holds out a hand. "Object Retriever. Remember? Try to think about where it is. And only that. Then take my hand."

"You don't have to touch my forehead, like you did with Awngeleik?"

"That might be dangerous, as that connection is stronger. And I've not practiced magic with you. But I have with Awngeleik. She's good at visualizing things." Smilingly brighter, Ben wiggles the fingers of his outstretched hand. Then Gemma awkwardly takes it, and Ben starts to chuckle.

Gemma squirms, then laughs, and says, "It tickles."

Ben, turning serious for a moment, snaps the fingers of his other hand, and a neon-green wheelie case thuds on the ground in front of Gemma. Along with everything else, but Gemma's case and my bag, he sets the stingy locked box into the black chest. "Have everything you need, before we go?"

I ask, "Won't people notice we're gone?"

"I brought a functional Vardiya-Stone. It'll stop time on Earth, once we pass through the portal. Magic should last about a month, two to three months Murainian time. Still never figured out why they won't work, until *after* someone goes through the portal." Ben shrugs much like me, before perking up to ask, "Ready?"

"More than," I reply. "But what about Musgrae?"

"Came back last night," states Ben. "Found that star you and your mother caught. Said he made preparations. And that we should come through, as soon as we have everything."

Her eyes sparkling, Gemma grips the wheelie suitcase. "Then let's go."

To the water's edge, Ben takes a few steps and pulls out the Vardiya-Stone—smaller than the one that died—and drops it. Hitting the water, it takes on life. Three limbs wrap around one, while its other four construct webbing between each other. The final result is a star-fox-jellyfish half the size of the other Vardiya. Adorable, in its own way, it patters farther into the lake and leaves a wake of ice. Rushing over this ice-wake, wind freezes the entire lake surface in seconds.

Ben carefully strolls to the frozen center, then stops. Pushing aside the unbuttoned front of his trench coat, he pulls out a mini Katana. Like my dad's daggers, the blade grows to full length. Then he slashes in the air. Turning it this way, then that. Motions complete, a glowing-red symbol has been created by his blade-strokes.

"Pawv'Ragaen-el-Muraine!" Ben speaks, thrusting the Katana tip forward then through the symbol. Sharp red lines swirl and form a doorway into another world.

"Guests first," says Ben, while Awngeleik starts running forward at full speed. Wings tucked tight against her sides, she's already through the entrance, as Ben hollers, "You're not a guest. You bad horse! No manners. That one. Only behaved for LanSoren. Stubborn beast."

Hanging back with her wheelie case, Gemma waits for me to go. Silently, I volunteer. Death grip on my duffel, apprehension overcomes me. But I push it aside, and step through the doorway leading into Muraine, anxiously anticipating what waits on the other side.

II

Misgivings & Magic

Darkness?
Is it terrifying,
Or is it beautiful?

14

The Vacancy of Crimson

Red flames surround me. Then the burning starts. Through my veins, it courses before diminishing to pleasant warmth. My chest. My arms. They should be lit with the same red flames. Yet, they are not. When the fire subsides, silky blades of lush golden-grass soften the landing on my hands and knees. Flowing through the forest, a misting breeze carries the scent of pinesap and sweetness of white flowers embellishing the grass.

Giant trees, with a constitution like old sequoias, soar over their cousins of common magnitude that fill in the vast spaces between the colossals. Further adding to their splendor, skins of the giants paint a new canvas. Burnt umber. Rust. Yellow ochre. Ash. And coal. Rustling in the breeze, the brighter skins flaunt wispy malachite-colored leaves. While long, red quills protect the branches of coal, ash is armed with citrine thorns.

"Tyler"—Ben crouches down by my side—"want a healing spell? To help with the burning?"

Before I can answer, a man's low voice calls outs, "Ben! Let his body acclimate to the environment. I presume the girl is Gemma Galloway. Mud Fiend, as Musgrae calls her?"

Ben replies, "Yes, Quall."

When I stand on wobbly legs, strong hands steady me. I gaze up to the towering man Ben calls Quall, musing, *Taller than Jack Wayeland. Much*

163

taller.

Eight others—clad in brown robes, black cloaks, and dull yet tailored clothes—are of average size. Set apart from them are the three men standing around, in hooded white-coats similar to Talok and Quall's, staring out into the forest as if searching for the unseen.

Across Gemma's cheek, Ben sweeps the back of his hand. "She's out cold," he says.

Quall commands, "Someone corral Awngeleik. Before she runs off like a menace."

After calling for Awngeleik, she comes to me, with her head flailing, hooves prancing, and all.

Betraying his surprise, Quall's amber-colored eyes widen. "Glad she'll come for someone. The *first* time."

"We had to work up to that," I state, while petting Awngeleik's forehead.

Quall grins, motioning to the youngest in white. "Eli, the cloak."

With his head snapping to attentiveness in my direction, Eli begins the proud and happy strut to me. Each step taken makes his swept hair strands colored of strawberry-champagne bob up and down. Standing no taller than Ben, he proclaims, "They call me, Eli of Kirja." Grinning with perfect vampire teeth, he thrusts his hand out. "Here's a better cloak for Awngeleik."

"Tyler Ravier," I state. "But I'm sure you already knew that."

In response, Eli's head bobbles.

After taking the cloak, I unfold it. As I toss it over Awngeleik, a man with mocha-colored skin scoffs at Eli. "And I'm the Kyanite specimen," says the man, with a physique an athlete would envy. "Eli, can't you cut the dramatics for two seconds?"

Eli defends, "Drama's my lifeblood, Warren."

Quall's face reddens like a pimple about to burst. Then the last of the Whitecoats blushes to the same shade as his ginger hair. When his azure gaze flits my way, I shrug in amusement.

The azure eyes now watch Warren, and the ginger's blush fades. Shoulders press back. His hands clasp behind him. From his smooth voice, confidence exudes: "If you wish to die by Quall's hand today, rather than a

Vitiosyn's, I suggest both of you continue."

Cobalt-blue eyes blazing, Warren's deep voice booms, "Don't patronize me, Siege!"

Pinching the bridge of his nose, Quall mutters, "I knew Ryco should have come with us." He looks down at me. "Welcome to Muraine, Tyler. Where the King's Guard of Paragon is in upheaval. Due to three of us being offed over the past five years. I don't want to add five to that." He glares at the two offenders. "Do you?"

"No, Master Quall," the offenders reply, then clamp their mouths shut.

"Tyler?" Quall sighs. "Ride Awngeleik for us? She's better behaved with a rider."

"Sure thing." I pull back the cloak and hoist myself up onto her back.

Quall's eyes sadden, while he picks up Gemma's limp body and drapes her in front of my lap. "We made the new cloak big enough for a rider to hide beneath. It should shield you from the Vitiosyn's attention. You and your friend ought to go home this minute, but the decision is not mine."

Pressing my hand onto the middle of Gemma's back, I hold onto one of her dead arms with the other, before asking Quall, "I get a day?"

Affirming with one nod, he trails to the front of the company and motions his instructions, stating, "Scouts, to trees. My triad, in back. Ben, beside cargo."

To the back, Eli and Siege trek before the scowling Warren slings my duffle over one shoulder and follows. Ben, meanwhile, falls in step with Awngeleik, and positions Gemma's wheelie case behind me.

I whisper to him, "Where'd the boxes go?"

Sliding back his coat front, Ben pats the black satchel resting against his hip. "Miniaturizing spell. Should be safe in here."

After Ben finishes covering the three of us with the enormous cloak, and the Whitecoats are in position, the eight scouts scurry up the trees.

Quall holds up a finger, demanding, "I want absolute silence, the rest of the way."

* * *

Through the forest, we drift on a beaten path in a Quall-induced silence. That is, until Ben's whispers fracture it with the question, "Why are we going this slow, Quall?"

"Fear factor," he replies. "Vitiosyns were seen near here, early this morning. We can't look like we're in any hurry. Can't give the impression that something's wrong. If they smell fear, they're more likely to attack without provocation."

"They don't need provocation," Warren seethes. "Look what happened to Yharss and Dysarda."

Ben's step quickens. "Something happened to my home city?"

Quall sighs out, "Quiet your thoughts, Ben of Yharss. You will be informed, when we get to the Eye of Paragon."

Silently descending from the colorful tree canopy, while Quall is still talking, is a tall figure masked in all black. As it lands next to Quall, I call out a warning a breath too late. Over Quall's mouth, the figure clamps one hand and restrains him with the other. When Quall thrashes, the figure holds tight. Overhead are muffled screams, doubtless from the scouts.

In one swift motion, a bow and arrow appear in Ben's grasp. Preparing to fire at the masked figure, he draws the string back. Also drawing their weapons are Quall's Whitecoats. Stances showing readiness for attack, their eyes lock onto the figure.

When Quall starts to yell, the figure releases him and hushes with, "Quall, it's me."

"Siveyra Gyronawv?" Quall pants. "Paragonians, stand down."

Descending from the tree canopy, the eight scouts slither. As sweat drips from their faces, the crazed gleam in their eyes settles. Then everyone breathes in relief. Except, that is, for Gemma, still passed out. And Awngeleik, pawing at the grass.

"There's not much time," states Gyronawv. "But I must know, has war been declared between Pawv'Ragaen and the Vitiosyns?"

"Not yet," replies Quall. "Presently, King Talok is discussing it with the Advisers and Ryco's Triad. Although … he wishes to hold off, until a precious cargo can be returned home." Briefly, Quall glances to where I'm hidden.

In surprise, Gyronawv snatches off his hood, asking, "You have Awngeleik out in the open?"

Warren states, "We only got her back today, Siveyra Gyron."

Eyes widening, Quall asks Gyron, "You can see her?"

"Not see—sense. Save for the Greyvons, she gives off an aura and smell unlike anything."

Remembering her rancid-fish sneeze and needing to hold back a gag at the memory, I can fully agree with him, before wondering, *Can he sense me too?*

"Who was that?" calls out Gyron, his gaze skimming the area in alarm.

If he couldn't before, he can sense me now.

"LanSoren?" Gyronawv flinches. "Is that you?"

Unfurling from under the cloak, I stare into Gyronawv's face.

His footfalls absent of sound, Gyronawv edges toward me. Watching as if looking away will make me vanish into nothing, he says, "Tyler Ravier? Has anyone ever told you, that while you look nothing like your father, you have the countenance of his magic? Soon. It will serve us well."

From Awngeleik's back, I'm now almost eye-to-eye with him. "Want to know a secret?" I frown. "Until a few days ago, I had no idea any of this existed."

Gyron is the first to look away. While running two of his fingers over his mouth, his thoughts are far from here.

I ask, "Why will it serve us well?"

Gyron's gaze startles, while still on the stretch of forest behind us. "Vitiosyns approach," he whispers. "Onyx Warriors, ready yourselves. Paragonians, group together. Quickly. They can sense us in. Three. Two. One." He counts on his fingers.

Overhead, leaves rustle in the warriors' haste to reposition. Meanwhile, on the ground, the Paragonians rush to obey his orders.

"Paragonians," Gyron warns, "it is paramount that you act as if we've been scouting with you the whole time. No slip-ups."

I snap my fingers. "Warren. My duffle." I reach for it.

Tugging it off his shoulder, he proceeds to drop it on Gemma's back.

"Ow!" she cries out. "Can't breathe."

Gyron holds out a desperate hand. "Quiet her!" he commands. "Cover them!"

I pull the duffle off Gemma and hug it to my chest, as she catches her breath.

"They'll see us in three," Gyron counts.

While I help Gemma resituate on Awngeleik, Warren and Ben fumble with the cloak.

"Two!" The count continues.

Gyron's olive-toned skin glistens, as the cloak is smoothed out and the remaining Paragonians step to their positions.

"One." Gyron's face erases any trace of fear, and he takes the lead with Quall.

Like a bird with no place to land, Gemma glances around, asking, "What's happening? Why's everyone so tense?"

"Vitiosyns," I reply. "Need to be quiet."

Gyron interrupts, "Paragonians, whatever you do, don't hold their gaze. They'll see it as a challenge and attack. If you challenge them, we will be forced to leave you. I am sorry. But it is the way of the Onyx Warriors. Once war is declared, we will take our leave. Entirely."

"But you are a Siveyra," states Ben.

"Even Siveyras are bound to rules. To a chain of command. My King ReNovak has not permitted a war with Zymarc of Vitiosus. It does not help matters that you have lost five—one for every year—among the Paragonian Sovereignty."

"This year," states Quall, "that changes."

"You must ensure," Gyron continues, "that not another soul of the Paragonian Sovereignty perishes."

As Gyron repositions the long blade strapped to his belt, Quall dares to ask, "What happens, if we lose one more?"

"It will prove that Paragon is unworthy of being saved. That you are weak and inferior. By Onyx law, we are not permitted to save the unworthy. You will be beyond the help of the Nyxane."

"Hear that, King's Guard?" Quall momentarily turns to face us. "No dying."

"They're almost within earshot," states Gyron. "Whatever you must say or think, do it now. Before erasing fear from your minds. They hear us in three," he counts.

Gemma, tensing, pushes back against my duffle, and her fists scrunch some of Awngeleik's mane.

"Two," Gyron continues.

Like the unseen beast by Mirror Lake, numbing my lungs yet warming my veins, I feel their steps and think, *Could it have been a Vitiosyn, back home?*

"One." The count finishes.

Scuffling footsteps crunch over fallen leaves and twigs. The red quills and citrine thorns too.

Then they scamper into view. Tall and lanky. Pallid-gray skin. Short hair. But the worst? Their piercing scarlet eyes. All female, with wide-contoured belts across their chests. The only solid piece on each are their black, brown, or blue leggings. Hanging around their arms, legs, and cores—as snakes do when crushing prey—are straps, chains, and leather cords. Peering out from the bonds, blackish-blue tattoos are carved on any exposed skin.

Curved and bloodied blades, they swing. And the metal reverberates, though it touches nothing but air. On and on. These Vitiosyns run. And hiss. And laugh. As if they have been loosed from a tormenting prison. But one woman is stripped of bonds. As tall as Quall, she stands composed. Her midnight-blue chest plate rises and falls with every breath, while a haunting smile tugs at her mouth.

Toward Gyron, holding his head high, she saunters. And he narrows the distance.

On the composed one, living black snakes are wrapped. One on each arm. Their heads rest on her shoulders, with unblinking crimson eyes.

"Belzara, you get around," says Gyron. "Don't you?"

Her haunting smile deepens. "Gyronawv. Great Warrior of the Onyx.

King ReNovak's errand boy. What brings you to Pawv'Ragaen … this lovely morning? Come to watch the death of Muraine's child-king?"

Anger etching into their faces, Warren and Siege grip their weapon hilts. Ben discreetly buttons his coat, then rests his arm against the concealed satchel.

Gyron smirks. "Has war been declared already?"

Thinking a moment, Belzara states, "Not yet."

Slowly, the snakes lift their heads from Belzara's shoulders. Fanning out their hoods, their vacant eyes glance at Gyron. Left and right, their noses sway. When their crimson gaze lingers in my direction, the snakes yawn then hiss and spit.

In front of me, though the air's warm, Gemma shivers. Resting my left hand on her arm, I try to stifle my own fear and hers.

Away from Belzara, the other Vitiosyns steal a few steps back. Quickening their breaths. Steadying their hands. Diminishing their sneers. It seems, this day, even they have something to fear.

Still gripping Gemma's arm, my hand cools to ice the way it did that night at her house. My fingertips stain black, and nails turn white.

Fangs bared, the snakes latch onto Belzara's neck. Closing her eyes, she winces. The Vitiosyns widen the distance. When the snakes' eyes of crimson go black, Belzara opens hers. No longer bright scarlet, they are the same dark-crimson of the snakes'.

Belzara's countenance darkens. Her voice is stripped away. Replacing it is a masculine demon's. With a voice like silk, he begins, "Ben of Yharss. Many fond memories they had of you. Before you went away to the Eye of Paragon. Never to return. Only to visit."

As if strolling through a park, Belzara ambles to Ben. The closer she gets, the more Ben's eyelids flicker in fury, like flames to a breeze.

In front of him, she stops. But the demon whispers, "What are you hiding?"

"Perhaps," replies Ben, "a little fear. For I have never seen living Vitiosyns this close before."

The demon laughs. "But you've seen dead ones? Was it Ryco of Paragon who showed you?" Though Ben remains silent, the demon goes on, "Of course it was that Sylvadyn Parasogyn."

When the Prismatic of Magic dims to gray on my hand, Awngeleik leans her neck forward to pull her mane free of Gemma's grasp.

When she does, the demon sucks in a breath of elation. "Awngeleik. She is near. I can almost feel her." Belzara's body takes the demon to Gyron and Quall. "If I find her here, King's Guard, I will level Paragon this very day. You're sure, little Paragonians, that you do not have her here? Now. In our very presence?"

His face a blank slate, Quall says, "If you can find her, Zymarc, you can have her."

Twice, Zymarc calls for Awngeleik. While he paces around, in Belzara's body, Gemma curls her shoulders and hugs herself. My hand tightens on her arm, as fear of Awngeleik giving us away starts surfacing. However … luck is on our side, and Awngeleik stays frozen in place.

Belzara's face contorts. "What did LanSoren do to her? That she will not come to the call of her master?"

Skin warming, the gray-tinge leaves my left hand. Yet, the dim-white nails remain.

"Perchance, Gyronawv of the Nyxane knows." Belzara strides to him, then continues, "Knows what magic the Great LanSoren used. The only magic to contend with my own."

Quall states, "*Those* are LanSoren's secrets to keep."

Now a greater distance from the demon, Gemma lets her shoulders relax. And I let go of her. Though questions beg for the stage of my thoughts, I push them away, unwilling to allow mere thought betray us: the precious cargo.

Gyron's broad chest hammers out his breaths. Belzara places her hand there, and runs her fingers up to his neck. Then his face. But she stops on his forehead.

Crimson eyes ablaze, Zymarc scoffs. "What good are you, little Onyx? You know nothing of her physiology. Nor where she might be." Her palm beating Gyron's chest once, Belzara plods away and leaves him to cough for several breaths.

Belzara snaps her fingers, commanding, "Down. Little Onyx Warriors. I want to look at you."

From the canopy, twelve men and teenagers drop. In solid black coats—with only buckles, rivets, and buttons of chrome to break up the monotony—they stand at attention and refuse to acknowledge Belzara with as much as a pause in their calm breathing.

"All useless," hisses Zymarc. "You know nothing. Then again, you *are* Onyx. You dance both sides. When it suits your King ReNovak. If I learn that Awngeleik was hiding right within my grasp this day, I will level Paragon that very moment."

Quall states, "We'll be ready for a fight."

"You mean war?" Belzara, ambling back, looks to Quall. But she lingers on Gyron. "That is my greatest hope."

Unflinching, the two stare at each other. The demon and the Siveyra. Zymarc of Vitiosus and Gyronawv of the Nyxane. The first to move, however, is Gyron. Stiffening his neck, something he does or thinks provokes Belzara's haunting smile to the surface.

"You can't remember my face?" Zymarc mocks. "Can you, Siveyra Gyron? No matter how hard you try, you cannot remember the Onyx pet you trained all those centuries ago."

Gyron's dark-colored eyes water, as if they burn, but he manages to hold Zymarc's gaze.

On again, Zymarc rants, "The favored warrior of ReNovak. *Zymarc.* No one, not even the Siveyras, can remember what I looked like before Vitiosus. All they see, in place of their memories, is a shadowed figure. No face. Just black. Even if I were to walk in my true form,among the Onyx of the Nyxane, no one would bat an eye to me. For they do not know my face. There was one permitted to remember. And. He. Is. Dead."

Gyron's eyes light in wrath, and he spews out, "You will not mock the memory of the dead. Certainly not LanSoren of Trauvo! To mock the dead, is to mock an Onyx. I am Onyx. I will not be intimidated or mocked. Nor will I allow such treatment toward those in my care. King Zymarc of

Vitiosus. Stand. Down. Now!"

"Forgive my insolence." Belzara bows her head and waves a hand out toward the other Vitiosyns, while Zymarc is saying, "Pick one, to restore the Neutrality of the Onyx."

His eyes fixed on Belzara, Gyron snaps his fingers and commands, "That one, on the end. She's wanted to attack us the whole time. Onyx Warriors, kill her now."

The smallest Vitiosyn startles and starts to run away. But Zymarc's shout of, "Stay where you stand, Vitiosyn!" stops her in her tracks.

With a great blade in his hand, one of the older Onyx approaches the one about to meet her end.

As she whimpers, Zymarc hisses, "Stop your crying or I'll kill you myself. We have insulted an Onyx today. Therefore, you must die a Dishonorable Death."

Just before the Onyx cuts her down, I can't help but look away. Gemma silently sobs, and her shoulders quiver.

"Another?" Belzara holds her hand out again. "For good measure?"

Gyron points to the one nearest the dead Vitiosyn. "Her! She wants revenge for her fallen sister. Kill her."

When she's cut down, as well, the other Vitiosyns back farther away. Their scarlet eyes watching the back of Belzara's head, fear engulfs their faces. But Gyron is as an unfeeling statue. His gaze never leaves Belzara's crimson eyes, even as she runs a finger along his coat-collar.

Again, Zymarc speaks out, "I think one should pay for my intimidation of Ben'el Yharss-Rawshuen. Don't you?"

With a snap of his fingers, Gyron commands the fall of another.

Reason after reason. Vitiosyn by Vitiosyn. They are cut down. Until none are left but the possessed Belzara.

"One more. For—" Zymarc starts to say, but stops and spins around. "What do you know? They're all dead."

Though Paragonian Scouts try to hide their trembling, Quall and his Whitecoats remain resolute in guarding Ben of Yharss next to the invisible cargo. In contrast, the Onyx stand at attention, callous toward the now lifeless and bleeding Vitiosyns in front of them.

Belzara's hand extends to Gyron, as Zymarc states, "Dear Gyron, I thank you. Belzara has been a bit wild of late. Couldn't think of a proper punishment for her. This should do quite nicely."

His laugh chilling me to the core, Zymarc ambles away. Forcing Belzara's fingers to brush at the snakes, still latched to her throat, he speaks, "Come home, Belzara. Let the Paragonians have one last festival. Before the death of all. I have new warriors for you to lead."

The snakes' fangs release Belzara's neck. And the crimson eyes turn to scarlet.

To her fallen Vitiosyns, Belzara rushes, begging, "Zymarc! Please. Bring them back. Bring her back!" To the first fallen Vitiosyn, Belzara holds a shaking hand to the slit throat of her beloved one. She caresses her like a mother clinging to her dead child. As spewing blood darkens to dirty oil, the scarlet eyes of the smallest Vitiosyn go black. And Belzara wails like a tormented animal.

Grief softening Gyron's eyes, he whispers, "Was she your daughter?"

"She might as well have been." Belzara sniffles.

With each passing minute, the blood of the fallen Vitiosyns darkens like Belzara's Beloved.

When Gyron steps forward, Belzara snaps at him, "Don't you take another step toward me, Onyx!" She scrambles to her feet and points at the Siveyra, spitting out, "Zymarc used you to punish me. The day the Onyx join Paragon, I will hunt you down and cut that attractive head from your magnificent form. Then adorn my bed with your skin."

Belzara whirls around and strides away from us. Her screams fading, her figure diminishes from view.

Gripping his head, Gyron sinks to his knees.

Then one of his warriors addresses him, "Did we kill them by your orders or King Zymarc's?"

"Mine," whispers Gyron. "I wish it had been by his, but it was by mine. My hatred of them clouded observation."

The warrior continues, "You need the presence of King ReNovak. It has been too long, since last you saw each other."

Another warrior interrupts to add, "Siveyra Gyronawv, do not make us drag you to the Nyxane. We will, if we must."

Gyron scoffs. "A prisoner to my own Onyx Warriors? Do not worry for me, Quall. My King ReNovak will defend my actions of this day." Starting to follow his leading warriors away, Gyron stops in front of the first fallen one. Looking to me, then down to her, he says, "It's safe now, Tyler Ravier. Come down from Awngeleik."

I slide down to approach Gyron, now crouching next to Belzara's Beloved.

Over her face, he sweeps his hand, saying, "I wonder … can the love for a fallen sister touch the heart of even the cruelest Vitiosyn?"

I mull over his words, searching for an answer, even while the gray complexion of Belzara's Beloved darkens to charcoal. Like cracks in ceramic, black veins paint across her skin's canvas. Then I find the words and say, "I want to believe that the darkest hearts are capable of love. Even if it's a twisted love."

"An insightful answer." Gyron nods. "Warriors, we'll take this one to the Nyxane."

Gemma picks that moment to find her voice. "Can someone help me down?"

Though Warren rips off the cloak, he allows Eli to help her.

Smiling a contagious smile, to dampen the fear heavy in the air, Eli gives his proclamation. "I agree with Musgrae. You *do* have a cute face. When you're not passed out or covered in muck."

Slinking to me while shivering, Gemma blushes. "Never going to live that down."

"Do you want to go home, Gemma?" I ask. "There's still time to take you back."

Tears washing over her brown eyes, Gemma looks around. "You think I would abandon you, to this place? It would be more tormenting sitting at home, wondering every day if you're dead, than to be cut down beside you. Like one of them." She points to the Vitiosyns.

I state, "It was just a question."

While looking to the fallen ones, the image burns into my memory. *If I lose Gemma to this place, how could I ever forgive myself or face Tadashi again?*

That's when Gemma says, "I'm not leaving without you. But I have a feeling, you're not leaving without answers. Without truth."

Avoiding her eyes' intensity, a pathetic nod is the only response I can manage before Quall asks Gyron, "When did Zymarc find a way to see through his Vitiosyns' eyes?"

"I'm unsure. It goes without saying, though, he's stronger than he's ever been. We must relay this new turn of events to King ReNovak, along with Belzara's Beloved. Nevertheless, we will be back this night, for the festival. From here on, I wish you an uneventful journey to the Eye of Paragon."

15

The Eye of Paragon

A while later, we arrive in front of a wall of crowded black trees. Upward, they soar, for several hundred feet. Their weeping-willow vines of cardinal drape at their sides. The vines, the leaves, they sway hypnotically. Akin to flames, but without the heat and light.

Although we're on a beaten path—headed straight for the wall of colossals—there's no gate for admittance.

Quall points his Katana to the black wall, stabbing forward and up, shouting, "Dismoveo!"

Green lightning hurls from the blade tip and shocks two of the trees. The two colossals groan, then crack, in retaliation. Starting from the ground, their black bark and cardinal vines peel away. Stopping one-hundred feet up, the black skins flatten to a canvas. Revealed is the charcoal layer underneath. After Quall repeats the Katana process, the now-pliable charcoal twists with the vines. To the right and left, it spreads scrollwork upward and across the canvas. Hardening once more, it concludes at an upward ninety-degree angle. The next layer of gray repeats the process, but completes a one-eighty. The last and third pallid layer ends at a downward ninety.

All that remain of the shocked trees are two snow-white heartwoods. Even with the thick forest canopy shading the space below, the adjacent heartwoods collect every particle of light near them. Soaring high, at one-hundred feet, they reflect like sanded mirrors encased by unaltered, neighboring bark. The heartwoods twist into pillars, stopping where the two trunks remain unchanged up top. Now promising a different sight—beyond the wall—are slivers of green peering from the pillars' sides.

As Quall sheathes his Katana, Warren takes his place on the road. Clapping hands in front of chest, Warren domes them forward until only his fingertips are touching. Between his lighter palms, blue sparks swirl. Then, buzzing and crackling are the pillars, distorting and warping with the motions of Warren's hands like reflections of trees in disturbed water. Yet they stand, stubbornly refusing to break.

Then, slowly, the heartwoods begin moving apart. But needing to have the last word, they blast a gust at us. Stopping it, Quall raises his hand. With it? An iridescent shielding wall.

To the pillars now spread far apart, Siege steps between, then into the distortion first. Sputtering from his hands is green electricity, as Eli draws out two side-handled Tonfa blades. Into the space with Siege, Eli struts to face the ginger, and touch the blade tips to sputtering-green.

After Eli's blades have collected his magic, Siege exits the distortion. Breathing hard, he says, "What takes four of us to do, Ryco does in one swift motion."

"Don't be hard on yourself," states Quall. "Ryco's a near master of Gendras. Has been for some time."

"Only ones better," grumbles Warren, "are Siveyras and Emerald Sorsryns."

Gemma nervously wrings her hands, asking, "Not the Vitiosyns?"

"Their expertise," replies Quall, "is in Vitiosus and Death Magic, not Green."

"Thank the Vardiyas," states Warren. "We would've died long ago."

Siege, approaching the precious cargo, looks up at me. "LanSoren was a master of Gendras. The only one in Paragon to contend with Ryco's flair for it. You would've loved watching him."

"I definitely would have," is my response, before I let Ben take Gemma's wheelie case off Awngeleik's back.

"With any luck," says Quall, "the Arkiveis may be able to grant you that, tonight."

Siege perks his head up first, inquiring, "What do you mean?"

Ben pipes in, asking, "They found a way? To create an artificial Arkivara heart, without LanSoren?"

"It's a surprise for Paragon, but yes," replies Quall.

Patience ending, Warren booms, "We're waiting, Eli! Any day now."

"Shut up, Warren!" Eli glares. "I've only opened this *twice* before."

Warren scoffs. "I thought you were supposed to get faster, after each time. Not slower. Hurry up. Before Vitiosyns come back and kill us all."

"And you say I'm dramatic." Eli lowers the Tonfas. "You want to do it, Warren? Be my guest." He stomps out of the distortion.

"I would." Warren grins. "But Blue Magic is my forte. Remember? Not Green."

Siege frowns. "I'd do it myself, Quall, but I'm a bit drained from this morning."

Rubbing his face, Quall yanks away the Tonfas from Eli. "I understand we're all tense after what happened. But we are the King's Guard. We have standards to uphold. This is not the time for bickering. Siege understands this. Why can't the two of you?"

Warren and Eli look to the ground in shame, while Siege silently pities them.

Quall, unsheathing his Katana, scrapes its edge on Eli's electrified blades. At the squealing of metal on metal, everyone winces. Except Quall, that is. And Awngeleik, now chewing the hem of her cloak. Ignoring everything else, on and on she chews, living up to the name I gave her—Walking Terror.

Tossing shorter blades aside, Quall thrusts his Katana into the ground between the pillars. Green sparks radiate out, to race up the heartwoods. When they hit where the two trees meet, Quall raises the Katana. A green lightning bolt cracks down to the blade tip. Then he gently lowers the charged Katana, swinging two full rotations. The distortion fills with erratic sparks. They flash, as the blade tip touches the ground. That's when Quall stops.

Gone is the distortion, now replaced by a wide entrance leading into the city. To the Eye of Paragon. The first to enter is Awngeleik. She runs, screeching, bucking, and then rolling in the shamrock-grass. The scouts take a moment to watch her, before heading off to wherever. The four Whitecoats linger, however, as Awngeleik loops around—flailing her head—trotting like some sort of confused herding dog.

I readjust my duffle strap, saying, "Somebody missed home."

Gemma proclaims, "Never saw a happier horse-thing."

To both sides of the road are large clearings of vibrant wildflowers stretching out for miles: blanketing rolling hills, along riverbanks, and shamrock-grass pastures. Giant horses graze among them. Some winged. Others not. Dotting the clearings absent of horses, mounds of soot rest undisturbed.

In the distance—on the road ahead—even greater trees dwarf the colossals of the black wall. Massive are their green leaves rustling in the warmer, city breeze. And glistening are their skins of rust, in full light. Away from them is the tallest tree, unmatched in uniqueness. Its tree bark is white mixed with black. And its wide, turquoise leaves defy the wind, to dance to their own rhythm.

My hypnosis breaks, when Awngeleik shrieks that nails-on-chalkboard screech. Glancing up are the other horses, just snorting at the dragon-horse before they return to grazing.

Gemma points to three soot mounds, asking, "What're those?"

Wings grow out from the mounds. Emerging next are dragon faces. I gaze at them, in wonder, replying, "Dragons. What else?"

Off, they shudder soot to reveal metallic-black scales catching streaks of light like dull mirrors. They spew fire onto each other—more soot falling away—as they surge up toward the treetops. Nipping at one another's clawed-feet, the dragons goad each other into a faster ascent. Then Awngeleik prances, before taking off after the three dragons.

"Where are the homes?" queries Gemma.

Ben—with Gemma's wheelie case resting on his shoulder—points to the structures in the tree canopies. Grafted in to be part of the trunks and branches, they add subtle beauty to the forest. Altogether? It's a city-made-of-trees.

From the road ahead, Musgrae is waltzing our way. "Mud Fiend!" he hollers. "You made it. And Tyler too. What do you think of the gang, so far?"

I shrug. "She was out most of the way."

"When I woke up—"

Siege interrupts her, whispering, "We had a Vitiosyn greeting."

"Vitiosyns!" Musgrae's eyes pop wide open. "Did they attack again?" He looks to Quall.

Ignoring Musgrae, Quall just rubs his forehead, then bursts out, "Warren! Eli! Wrangle Awngeleik. We needed that spell done yesterday. Musgrae. Siege. You will help them."

"If we were to cloak her right away"—Musgrae points a hand at Ben—"why'd you let her fly off? She spends hours, trying to play with the dyns."

Ben shrugs. "Didn't think about it. Was distracted."

"Drop it, you two." Quall holds up a referee hand. "Before it starts. Once the spell's complete, deliver Tyler and Gemma's things to the castle, unless otherwise instructed. Go now. Before I lose my temper."

Musgrae tugs Gemma's case from Ben, while Warren takes my duffle. With Whitecoats trailing after him, Musgrae treads to a great ebony dragon resting in a bed of hot embers.

Ben stares at his feet, swallowing hard, before asking, "Where am I to go, Master Quall?"

"Stay with me. Or King Talok, if he requires you later."

"Reign!" Musgrae's shout carries over the distance. "Call for Awngeleik."

"Please," adds Siege, giving a bow of respect to Reign.

Up from his nap, Reign raises his rugged face of battle-scarred scales. To the sky, he looks. Then to Quall. Seeming to catch a signal from Reign, Quall says, "Best we clear some distance. Reign's Roar has a tendency of knocking your legs out from under you."

"Or rattling heart from chest," adds Ben.

"That too," agrees Quall, now sprinting on the beaten road.

In pursuit, Gemma and Ben race. But I stand, watching Reign lift his head higher. From his barbed forehead, a silver glint runs down his spiked neck and continues over his smooth back to veil the ridge of his spine.

His erupting roar vibrates everything: the ground, my chest, the air. The rumble of breath. The hum of inhales. Together, they steal away *my* breath. Only when Reign breathes a deep hum, can I take a ragged breath in unison. The rumble and hum shake the ground with more violence. Threatening to tear it open. Then it ceases, and Reign lowers his head back to the ground for another nap. Like a giant, sleepy cat, he curls up in an ember bed too small for him.

The Whitecoats and Musgrae uncover their ears and talk among themselves, until Siege points back at me.

Musgrae turns, to call out, "Better hurry, Tyler! King Talok will be out of his meeting soon. Who knows where he'll be after that."

Waving once, I continue on the road, meandering, in no mood to miss anything.

Down a hill, and to the right, a white-dragon fountain rests in the center of a small lake. In all shapes, sizes, and colors, an array of waterfowl paint themselves across its waters. Splashing and playing with several winged-horses flapping and wading through the water, together, the birds and horses croon a loud chorus of erratic and chatty racket, yet somehow pleasant.

Catching up to the others, I fall in step with Gemma.

She nudges my shoulder, asking, "Did it knock you to your feet?"

"Not quite. Ben, are all dragons like Reign?"

"No," he replies. "Reign is a BlacKaidyn."

"Black Dragon," Quall corrects. "The largest species of dyn on Muraine."

"Dyn meaning dragon?" queries Gemma.

"Yes," replies Quall. "Only ones larger and stronger are Zymarc's Vitasadyns. They were once noble BlacKaidyns. But now they're corrupted by Vitiosus."

Before traveling beneath the underpass of the city-made-of-trees, we approach small buildings. Smooth are their exteriors, matching the colossal tree layers of black, gray, and white. Outside one building, a sun-weathered man hammers out metal on an anvil. With fire emitting from his free hand, he reheats his piece and then pounds a rhythmic song of metal on steel.

Waving at the man, Ben calls out, "Yigoshi!"

Leaning down, Quall whispers, "Our head blacksmith. Presumably, preparing weapons."

"Ben-Yharss." Yigoshi waves the hammer side to side. "We'll talk weapons later. I'm swamped with orders. Straight from the Paragonian Sovereignty. First time for everything, I suppose. If Siege has a moment, ask him to stop by. Could really use some extra hands." Looking back down, Yigoshi continues his song.

Beside Yigoshi's forge are several glass storefronts boasting of battleaxes, shields, daggers, long-blades, and weapons I've never seen. Next are the burgundy-brick sweet shops, with white-trim around the windows. Instead of being stocked with candy, inside, they hold potions, herbs, and flowers. Then we pass several white-brick infirmaries. After those, there are countless campfires and stoves, where children watch adults chop, slice, and cook who knows what. All are dressed to the appearance of a renaissance faire.

Tucked farther away from the rest is a tall shop bursting with pots. So. Many. Pots. From tiny pots with flowers, all the way to monstrous ones suppressing their host of trees.

Leaning closer to Gemma, I state, "If those pots were paintings, your mom would be jealous."

Gemma laughs. "I was thinking the same."

I turn to Ben. "Was she, really?"

"Among other things," replies Ben, clasping his hands.

Gemma turns anime-eyes on him, exclaiming, "You were reading my mind?"

"And now," says Quall, "you've been caught, so stop."

"Yes, Master Quall," replies Ben, while distracted. Licking his lips once, he shyly lingers his gaze in the general direction of a girl not much older than Gemma.

On an overturned pot, the girl sits. First, she adjusts her walnut-colored peasant dress. Next, the hair of long black waves stopping at her hips. Then, up, she rolls her dull-white sleeves, before spinning a sapling on a wide turntable. At the touch of her palm—emitting a pastel-green glow—it grows. Shifting and twisting, the wood forms into an elegant chair. Like twisted yards of fabric—fanning out at the bottom—are its wooden legs. But the backrest and seat have ruffled ribbon-like edges. Behind her is comparable furniture, stained to the richness of cherry-wood.

All of it is unlike anything I've ever seen.

Quall whispers to Ben, "Are you going to ask the beautiful Khyra to go on a Dragon Ride or not, Ben?"

He wags his head side to side, looking at his feet. "I was. But not now. Not with everything that's happened."

Quall straightens in alarm. "What if she were to die tomorrow, having never gone on a Dragon Ride?"

"She would rather go with King Talok," replies Ben, crossing his arms.

"Don't be too sure of that."

"What are you saying? That she would go with me now?"

Perplexed, Quall traces his jaw-line. "What do you mean, *now*?" he queries.

Brown eyes scowling, Ben states, "I have asked her seven times. Her reply is always a variation of the same answer."

Looking at Gemma, I mouth one word, 'Ouch!' and she grimaces in reply.

Face flushing to irritation, Ben continues, "It's always: I'm too busy. I'm tired. I need to practice Gendras and I can't do that on the back of a dragon. Why don't you go with King Talok? Or Eli? Or Warren?"

Quall covers a laugh.

Ben glares at him. "You think it funny?"

"I've never seen you complain," Quall defends. "I didn't know you were capable of the deed. It only means you've been alone with Musgrae too much. Next time I send you somewhere, Kent will partner with you."

Ben sighs out a relieved, "Thank you."

Out of nowhere, a girl's cheerful voice chatters, "Good day, Master Quall! I had to come over and meet Musgrae's Mud Fiend. Find out her real name. He refused to tell any of us."

To Ben's chagrin, it's Khyra standing within reach of him, extending her elegant hand to Gemma. Accepting the handshake, Gemma grins in introduction, "Gemma Galloway."

Khyra's violet eyes brighten. "A beautiful name, and a face to match. May I call you Gigi?"

"It's a step up from Mud Fiend," I tease.

"And witch," adds Gemma, before replying, "Of course you may, Khyra."

"Musgrae should be scolded, for his estimation of you," says Khyra.

"Musgrae," Ben mumbles, under his breath, "should be scolded for many things."

Eyes saddening, Khyra touches Ben's arm. "Ben-Yharss, I'm very sorry for your home city. I'm sure you're devastated."

Ben absently nods, asking, "Did Arkivy Nyrim escape bloodshed?"

"I don't know." Khyra turns from Ben to Gemma, then to me. "You must be Tyler Ravier?" She shakes my hand, declaring, "Khyra of Paragon. Ever since hearing LanSoren talk of you and your mother, I've longed to meet you."

"I would say the same, but it would be a lie."

"Musgrae told us that LanSoren never said a thing to you about Muraine. He was so meticulous. It's hard to believe he would hide that from you. Master Quall? You grew up with LanSoren. Did he ever give reasons for keeping Tyler in the dark?" queries Khyra.

"Nothing concrete. For a while, he dabbled in a bit of Time Magic with a Metimora. He said, what he saw was the reason he knew he must hide the truth. When I finally made some headway and convinced him to tell Tyler and Amira the truth …" Quall trails off, letting a deep frown form.

I finish for Quall, saying, "He died soon after."

"Two months after," states Quall, before wincing. "I shouldn't have said that here. Forgive me! We should hurry the rest of the way, before my mouth prattles away more." He strides on the road.

"A good day to you, Khyra," states Ben, bowing from the waist—briefly the picture of a traditional gentleman—before he hurries after Quall.

Smoothing out her dress, Khyra says, "If I know King Talok, he'll be famished after the Sovereignty meeting."

"Knowing Gemma," I add, "she's already famished."

"How can you *not* be?" Gemma gripes.

"Have him meet me for lunch, in the Fermata Canopy"—Khyra starts walking back to her pots—"Zima's Kitchen should be prompt enough for him. See you there."

After waving goodbye, we catch up to Quall and Ben in their approach to a four-story castle. Around each fused pillar, cardinal metal-vines criss-cross on the Blackwood pillars shaping the exterior. And carved into these pillars are white-Faberge veins.

Quall stands at the stair base, grinning a fatherly smile. "The Castle of Sosha," he says. "The one place, above all else, that your father yearned to show you. Tyler, you should enter first."

Looking to the thirteen steps, then to the soaring double-doors of cardinal and black, I wonder, *Do they lead to King Talok? To his answers? To my truth?*

I take the first step, and unexpected familiarity comforts me like an embrace from my dad.

Akin to the rhythm of a wound watch, the count starts. *One-two. Three-four.* It echoes from far away.

A shiver runs down my spine, as it approaches, echoing again, *Five-six. Seven-eight.*

Hand drifting along the stair railing, I echo back, *I want you here. For your truth. In your words. Not anyone else's. Why would you rob me of that?*

A deep hush whispers, as though next to me, "Tyler Ravier. Son of LanSoren. I welcome you, in his stead."

I stumble up steps nine and ten.

The doors open to me.

Eleven-twelve, it echoes.

"Did he speak to you, Tyler?" queries Quall.

Frozen between the last two steps, I stop to gawk at Quall. "The castle's alive?"

Gemma's mouth drops open. "I want a talking castle."

"With Kane and Haru on the intercoms, you already have one."

"That's different. They're people. Not a sentient castle made of trees."

Quall states, "While we have Siveyra Dezarin and the Emerald Sorsryns to thank for building the castle of our capital, it was your father who gave it personality. Strength. A voice. An identity."

Taking the last step, I ask, "How's that possible?"

Wandering inside with me is Gemma, her eyes filling with wonder. Apparently, the interior beauty is striking enough to silence her. Behind us, Quall and Ben close the doors.

Quall says, "While he and I trained together as children, LanSoren was years ahead of everyone; obsessed with mastering Gendras. Because his mother wasn't especially gifted, everyone assumed his father was a soul of great power."

"Not a Paragonian?" I ask.

Two steps at a time, Ben takes to the soaring Blackwood staircase—embedded with golden flecks—leading to the second floor.

"When we were searching," replies Quall, "for what ailed LanSoren, his blood samples came back with only Paragonian markers. No curse or anything unusual. But that was when he was dying, then dead."

Galloping up the stairs—in her characteristic way—Gemma follows Ben, but shrieks when cardinal vines start unwinding from the stair railings. Before she tumbles down the stairs, Ben catches her by the hand.

Then, like two long snakes, the vines are thudding onto the stairs. Down, they slither to the floor in front of me. Lifting and twisting into two S's, they explode up with a loud *bang!* of a cannon. Banging with it is my heart, as if shocked by an eel, ramming me into action. The action? My backside slamming against the doors. The ram? A door's handle now digging into my spine, sure to leave behind a bruise.

Leaves drift from above as falling red-snow, unapologetic of anything, not even their beauty born out of havoc.

Heartbeat quieting, I ask, "What if his father was Withrasyn?"

"Pure. Male. Withrasyn," states Quall. "Not possible."

I push away from the ram, to follow Quall up the stairs, and ask, "Because?"

Following a distance behind Gemma and Ben, we stride down an endless corridor and past painted animals gracing the high walls like murals. Though quiet and lifeless, they're similar to the ones in my dad's study.

"Ask Talok," replies Quall. "He needs a good distraction. Recounting history and memories should do the trick."

"How is he? After the attacks on Yharss and Dysarda?"

Quall blows out a breath. "All I can say is, your arrival has been greatly anticipated by him. He's talked of little else."

He has to be Alec, I muse. *Why else single me out, unless we're family. Cousins?*

Every few minutes, far ahead, Ben smiles at the Barrage of Gemma. Shoving hands in his pockets, he gives inaudible short-answers. Meanwhile, Gemma hooks her arm with his, and the indistinguishable barrage quickens. That is, until Ben points up. Gemma looks to the ceiling of interwoven vines. Though the ceiling blocks view of the outside sky, natural light fills the castle. Again, Gemma is struck silent.

Quickly, Quall's stride lengthens, and he cuts in front of Ben. Meanwhile, not far ahead, muffled masculine voices argue. Chairs scrape across a wooden floor. Then shouting commences. Quall motions for a stop beside a partly open door, where the shouts are free to drift into the corridor.

Talok, his voice deeper than before, states, "We don't have enough trained Paragonians to fight them off. What would you have us do, Zepharre?"

"We will not entangle ourselves with the Rubidyns. It's bad enough we have partnered with dogs," scoffs Zepharre.

Firmly, Talok says, "You may insult my suggestions however you wish, Zepharre. But do not speak of Jasper, nor his Greyvons, as if they are beneath us. All other alliances are beginning to fall away. Except theirs. We need them, to win this war."

"Understood," states Zepharre. "But no negotiating with Rubidyns. Ever."

Another man adds, "We don't trust those red dragons."

"Yes, EmiKal!" Talok snaps. "You have been abundantly clear on that."

"To other matters," interrupts Zepharre, "LanSoren's Tyler Ravier: you're sure it wise to let him come here?"

"It's only for the festival," replies Talok. "He has many questions. Both spoken and silent. We can all agree that LanSoren was closest to me. If I die in this war, much of his father dies with me. Wouldn't it be better for Tyler Ravier to die knowing the truth, rather than wonder forever?"

"When will he be here?" queries EmiKal.

"If I may?" interrupts Ryco. "The scouts and Quall's Triad arrived some time ago. They should've been here by now."

Right then, Quall saunters the rest of the way and knocks on the doorframe.

Zepharre yells, "Enter!"

We spill into the room, containing a long Khyra-styled table, to be greeted by the ogling of twelve men in gray. In a straight-shot view from us is Talok, sitting at the table's head alone. He tiredly cups his face. Behind him, a bay window leaches in more light than does the rest of the castle.

Though I can't place it, I know something's different about him … but what?

Except for Talok, lost in his thoughts, all eyes are on us.

Breaking the silence is Ben, saying two words: "King Talok?"

"Ben!" Talok's attention jerks up. "You're back."

When his icy-blue eyes see me, Talok smiles as if we're the only ones in the room. It's then, that I realize what's different. He's older. Six months older, with a slight, blond beard now on his face. He's thinner too, and I wonder, *Maybe he forgets to eat like I do.*

Chair clattering to the floor, Talok paces to me, exclaiming, "Tyler!" He grips my hand, crushing it to numbness. "You're finally here. The six months felt like the two years since LanSoren died. Is it true? That you only saw us a few days ago?" He releases me.

"With Awngeleik's antics," I reply, "it felt like two weeks. But, it's true."

Talok rubs his neck. "So much has happened. I trust you had a safe journey?"

I shrug. "If almost being attacked by Vitiosyns *is* safe, then yes."

Ryco, leaning against a wall—but straightening from it now—says, "Quall, if you sensed Vitiosyns, why didn't you take them back?"

"We were already halfway, when they showed."

"Halfway," I add, "is as far as we would've gone, if it hadn't been for Siveyra Gyron."

Hatred in his citrine-yellow eyes, Ryco slumps back against the wall and just grips his blade hilt.

Dipping his head down once, Zepharre says, "We are happy you made it here, Tyler."

"Are you? Or do you wish I'd never come? That I'd give you my father's things, then leave?"

Zepharre eases out of his chair, saying, "You are the only child of LanSoren. If you die here, in this war we fight, we will have dishonored him. Would you ask that of us?"

"It's *my* life. I ask that you let me choose what I do with it."

"You have your father's cadence." Zepharre grins. "Who are we to argue against you? However, you and your friend will return to Earth in two days' time. After the conclusion of the Withrasyn-Vaegon Festival. If you refuse to return, I will tie then drag you to the portal myself. Understood?"

"Glad I brought my phone," says Gemma. "Jed will pay good money to see that."

"There's the Rich Witch, again. When we get home, I'm signing you up for Bullies Anonymous. Do you want group therapy or one-on-one?"

"But I wasn't being mean," Gemma defends.

"You were planning to profit. At my expense."

"It's called making use of available resources," she prattles, then flinches.

"*Now* I'm a resource?" I seethe.

"I didn't mean it like that."

I retort, "Glad I burned yours."

Gasping, Gemma says, "But you were remorseful."

"Not now."

"In my defense!" she shouts. "I'm starving. Have been since Warren squashed me with your duffle. What did I get, upon waking? Red-eyed Vitiosyns staring at me. Like they want to eat me. Even though they can't see me."

Rage relaxing to amusement, I smile. "It was just a statement, Gemma."

She points at my face. "I'll give you a statement, Tyler. Malik. Ravier."

"What would that be?"

Shoulders relaxing, she replies, "Tell you, after we eat."

"Speaking of appetites." I look to Talok. "Khyra said to meet her at Zima's Kitchen."

"What for?" queries Talok.

"I assume to eat. But she didn't say, for sure."

That's when a man dressed like Ryco and Musgrae steps forward to say, "Better get there before her, King Talok. Khyra's boredom is notorious for planning surprise parties to cheer everyone."

Ryco straightens again, asking, "You would know this, how, Kent?"

Chestnut waves brightening Kent's amusement, he replies, "Who do you think gets roped into helping her plan surprise parties for you and everyone else? Me, to appease her boredom."

"If she's so bored," states Ryco. "Have King Talok assign more work for her. After all, she's the City Architect of Paragon."

"And your ward," adds Kent.

"Shut up, about that. I get enough from Musgrae," states Ryco, briefly eyeing Gemma.

"Yes!" huffs Gemma. "I was covered head to toe, in mud. Hence, Mud-Fiend-Forever."

Ryco starts, "Wasn't going to say anything about that—"

But Gemma cuts him off, saying, "Didn't need to. Your eyes said enough."

"Maybe." Ryco nods in agreement, before looking to Ben. "I've had a full report from Musgrae. I expect yours, Ben, after lunch."

"Yes, Master Ryco."

"Unofficially, how was it?" queries Ryco, with a very intent look on his face.

"Fine." Ben shrugs.

"Specifically, Musgrae."

"He was"—Ben pauses, then continues—"enthusiastic."

The Advisers and King's Guard share knowing looks, except for Talok, staring down and fiddling with his front buttons—the same odd ones as his old coat. This new one, however, is fitted to perfection. Far more elegant in its boasting of white-scales and black-trim between the seams.

Ryco saunters to Ben, and continues the interrogation. "Both of you were together the whole time?"

"I stayed with Tyler and Gemma. In LanSoren's study …" Ben hesitates, wobbling his head.

"While Musgrae was following the numerical guide. Yes. That's what he said." Ryco drums his fingers on the hilt, asking, "Not once. Did you go and clean up the mess at the lake?"

"Mess?" sputters Ben.

"The blood. The splinters. The feathers," states Zepharre. "Were you the one who washed the scene of everything?"

Calmly, Ryco says, "Didn't you notice that it was all gone, before you came back through the portal?"

"Yes." Ben bobs his head. "But I thought Musgrae cleared it, on one of his trips from the portal."

"No," replies Ryco. "That's all we needed to know, Ben. Thank you. You are dismissed to lunch now." He waves him away.

"But—" Ben pauses again, to swallow hard.

"You've a question?" Ryco states, "Ask it."

"If Musgrae or I didn't clean the mess, who did?"

"That is," states Zepharre smugly, "the question of the day."

"Whoever it was," adds Ryco, inspecting strewn papers on the table, "they didn't want anyone knowing of their presence on Earth."

Zepharre presses, "You didn't notice anything out of the ordinary?"

Ben just wobbles his head again.

"He tells the truth, Zepharre," states Ryco, straightening several papers, then stuffing them into a book on the table. "We'll have his full report, after lunch, and there's the end of it."

Zepharre points at Ben. "*Surely*, he remembers more than that! Why don't you—"

Ryco slams the book closed and shoves it across the table to hit Zepharre's hand. "Ben of Yharss is under *my* command!"

His glare almost matching Ryco's intensity, Zepharre shakes out his hand and rubs where the book hit.

Glad I'm not obligated to tell what I know. Liable to have my head torn off, after the interrogation.

Ryco fumes, "Do I meddle with you and your advisers, when I disagree with your methods? Name one time that I *directly* interfered."

"You know that you never have," snaps Zepharre.

"Then stay out of my way." Intensity replaced by boredom, Ryco looks to the wall timepiece and says, "Khyra works like a clock. You have ten minutes, King Talok."

"Right!" Talok snaps from his thoughts, rushing to the bay window. "We should be on our way. Want to ride a dragon there?"

Mortified, Gemma is asking, "What if I fall off and die?"

Taken aback, Talok just chuckles and then replies, "You won't, if you hang on."

16

Chatter Among the Tavern

On the back of Reign, we fly high toward the city-made-of-trees. Normally, my first time on something like a dragon would be wrought with wonder. Not today. I've questions needing answers, but I'll start out slow. At last, I ask, "Anything Gemma and I should know about cultural differences?"

His gaze lifting from my clothes to my face, Talok says, "A good question. I wouldn't recommend asking anyone to go on a Dragon Ride. Unless it's a party of three or more."

Eyes transfixed on Reign, Gemma feverishly strokes his spiked neck, asking, "Because?"

"Your intentions could be misunderstood. It's in the wording. *Dragon Ride* and *ride a dragon* don't mean the same thing."

Gemma queries, "One is going from *here to there* and the other is a ... date?"

"Essentially," replies Talok. "But *Dragon Ride* is a bit more than that. It's a discreet way of telling someone, of interest, you're willing to promise yourself to them. To bind a contract of family. When the time is right, or you're of age."

The feverish petting of Reign's neck stops, and Gemma covers her mouth in surprise.

Talok looks from her to me, asking, "Did I miss something?"

Hiding a smile, I reply, "Ben has asked Khyra to go on a Dragon Ride seven times."

Talok's eyes bulge. "He never told me. No wonder he's fidgety, when the subject of Khyra comes up."

"Ben of Yharss," rumbles Reign. "I like that one: Humble Persistence."

Staring off into nothing is Talok, saying, "I must find a way to tell him we're no longer of interest to each other."

I ask, "You were interested?"

"It's a bit of a story," says Talok, gripping the back of his neck.

Looking ahead, I shrug. "Only halfway there. We've got time."

Reluctantly, Talok begins, "With my father's death by a curse, more than three years ago. And LanSoren's over two, I became a child-king in desperate need of strong alliances."

Pulse rising, I burst out, "My dad was the King of Paragon?"

"No!" Talok shakes his head. "Though my father's advisers *did* offer the position to him. But he declined and volunteered to train me, instead; thus, becoming the first King's Advocate in the history of Paragon."

"Because he was your uncle?" I ask. Heart hammering in my chest, I muse, *Could it be true?*

Talok absently replies, "Yes." Then his eyes unsettle and close. "Cousins," he confesses, opening his eyes again. "We're cousins. I pictured that going differently, in my mind. You're not upset I forgot to tell you, when first we met?"

"That's not on you. I'm more upset that he never told me who he really was, and who my cousin is." I grin. "A king."

Gemma queries, "How's all that correlated to your interest in Khyra?"

"Correlated?" Talok flinches. "I don't know this word."

"She's means connected."

"Oh! I was getting to that. When my uncle died, familial offers started pouring into Paragon. Neighboring Sorsryn Clans were asking me to promise myself to one of theirs. Swearing to an alliance with Paragon, if I would do so."

"They didn't wait for you to grieve?" I ask.

"Three months. That's all."

"Brutal."

Gemma suggests, "Instead, you promised yourself to Khyra."

"Yes, Miss Gemma," replies Talok.

I state, "Because it took you off the bargaining table."

"Again, yes. Some within the Sovereignty told us to keep our promise a secret from the people of Paragon. When reaching my sixteenth year—the year of my adulthood—we broke it off. Agreeing that we are simply friends. Nothing greater. Nothing lesser."

"Sixteen's the new eighteen?" Gemma smiles.

"And eighteen is our twenty-one, when we gain full decision-making privileges."

I state, "I'm down with that."

"Now …" Talok says, sucking in a breath, "for some potentially bad news."

"Always a catch." Gemma clicks her tongue.

"We're vegetarian here in Paragon."

"But not us dyns," interrupts Reign.

"Well aware, Reign," hollers Talok, before explaining, "Several hundred years ago, it was ruled 'too disturbing' to hear the thoughts of our food before killing and eating it."

"You hear the thoughts of everything?" Gemma gulps.

"Mostly. Yes."

At his answer, Gemma's face goes pale.

Then Talok continues, "We try showing respect to sentient beings, by refraining from listening. But with the two of you having no shield guarding your minds, it's hard to distinguish what *is* spoken and what *is* not."

I ask, "How will we fix that?"

"Anyone in the Paragonian Sovereignty can set it in place. But Arkivy Grover is the most adept. Closely matched by Kent and his father, Arkivy Lokasi of Dysarda. We'll see Grover after lunch."

"Can't we learn how to do it ourselves?" queries Gemma.

"Once your bodies are adapted for magic."

Right then, Reign lands in the topmost tree-canopy of the city, announcing, "Welcome to the Fermata Canopy, Mr. Ravier. Where Warriors and Scouts of Paragon tread. Forever keeping a watchful eye. Be sure to get new garb befitting LanSoren's progeny."

"An excellent idea, Reign. Your clothes make you stand out. In a bad way. Both of you."

"Can I get a dress?" queries Gemma excitedly.

"Certainly." Talok matches her excitement, while helping her down.

I slide off Reign's back, landing with a soft thud onto the worn Blackwood roadway.

Talok leads us to a structure carved into the nearby tree trunk. Smoke billows out smells of vivid spice from its round window-cutouts, as Talok announces brightly, "Zima's Kitchen. My uncle's favorite tavern."

Inside, our footsteps drum on a solid-black floor. Around the tavern are several dispersed rock fountains trickling with sparkling water. Above us, floating white orbs of fire dance below a curved cardinal-branch ceiling. Inviting all who enter, they dance and scatter luminescent light within Zima's Kitchen.

Past Khyra-styled tables, chairs, and circular booths, Talok zigzags stealthily through the seated crowd of Paragonians chattering, while munching their food. Behind a high wall of intricately woven Blackwood strips, the source of vivid spice billows yet more smoke. Still in stealth mode, Talok slides into a corner booth lining the light, tangled-vine walls. Loudly, he announces, "Here we are."

All Paragonians, once oblivious of Talok's presence, now fall silent, and bow their heads in respect to him. They then resume their meal-chatter.

Across from Talok, Gemma slides in. Then me next to her. Contouring to our bodies is the shifting wooden booth. Startled by it, Gemma yanks her hand up and then cocks her head at the slight impression left behind.

Talok grins. "Glad you approve of Khyra's handiwork, Miss Gemma."

"Sorry to ask," queries Gemma suddenly, "but where's the bathroom?"

Confused, Talok's eyebrows draw together. "You need to bathe. Right now?"

Squirming, Gemma frantically twirls the strand. "I need to relieve—"

"Right!" interrupts Talok. "To negate the need for plumbing, we use magic for that. It's the first thing we learn, as children. I'll enchant some temporary rings. After you're both fitted with new clothes, we'll get permanent ones from Grover."

As Talok pushes aside his coat's center-front, I state, "Speaking of clothes, when did you get the new coat?"

"Three months ago," replies Talok, unbuckling a small pouch from his belt and setting it on the table. "I outgrew my old one. This one's a mix of young tree-bark, flower petals, and an Albino BlacKaidyn's molted skin."

"Ben's is a new design too?" I ask.

Stopping his riffling for a moment, Talok looks up to say, "I assume, Musgrae whined to you about wanting the new one?"

"And to me," says Gemma, "on the way to my house."

"Did he talk as much as you?" I tease.

"Almost," she replies.

From the pouch, Talok pulls out four small bottles and two gold rings. The first bottle holds a murky-white liquid, while the second has a butter-yellow powder; the last two are empty. Next, Talok drops the gold rings into the empty bottles. As they clink against glass, Talok glances over to Gemma. Smiling at her eyes transfixed on his hands, Talok asks her, "Would you like to help, Miss Gemma?"

"I was hoping you'd ask." She claps her palms together excitedly.

Talok slides the ring-bottles to us, then the yellow powder, saying, "Pour this in, until the rings are submerged."

Task finished, Gemma gives me the powder, asking Talok, "What's next?"

"Fill to the bottle's neck with this." He hands her the murky liquid. As she finishes, he gives us each one cork. "Now, *shake* it some."

Calmly, I rattle mine around. Meanwhile, Gemma shakes her bottle as if its contents are vermin worthy of death. Blazing are her eyes at the bottle containing her freedom from a bathroom visit.

Talok discreetly twiddles a few of his fingers in front of his mouth, motioning for me to stop, before giving a signal of silence with a finger to his lips. His voice steady, Talok states, "The enchantment hasn't taken hold yet. A little more vigor, Miss Gemma."

Harder she shakes it, blazing-eyes still on the vermin-bottle. Thinking she's done, Gemma stops with a victorious pant.

But Talok says, "A couple more should do it."

"I can't!" she whines. "My arm hurts. And now I really have to go." When glancing at him, her blaze turns to an inferno.

Talok's chin quivers, as he barely holds back laughter.

"Haven't been here a day," states Gemma, resentfully tossing the bottle at Talok, "but already, I'm the subject of everyone's teasing."

"It's your reaction that entices." Talok catches the bottle, examining the brownish liquid contents. "I'd say … it's well-done," he declares.

"What about Tyler's?"

"Same recipe. Same enchanted ingredients. Therefore, both are well-done."

"A cook," I ask, "is only as successful as the recipe?"

"Exactly," replies Talok, while flinging both bottles on the table. Shattering, they secrete a brownish-gray smoke. Waving the smoke away, Talok cups the rings. Seeping from his cupped palms are black and yellow flames. Flames fading, he gives us the rings and says, "Pick a finger you want it on; they'll resize to fit. After a minute, they'll stay that size."

I slide mine onto my right ring finger, while Gemma puts hers on her left.

"Better?" queries Talok.

"Yes!" Gemma bursts out. "What a relief!"

Just then, a voice announcing, "King Talok!" startles us. Beaming at him is a woman wearing a silky blue dress. "Good to see you. What'll it be?"

Talok smiles. "Give us a moment, Zima."

"Sure thing," replies Zima, snapping her fingers. In her grasp, a cloth appears. "But I'll clean this mess, before I go."

Talok's hand jolts out to cover the glass shards and congealed-liquid mess.

"Forgive me." Zima flushes to pink. "I forget that you're not like your father. Always wanting to be waited on." She gives the cloth to Talok.

"Thank you, Zima," he says.

Twiddling fingers toward glass shards, Talok makes them float up several inches to clean the mess below. Then he lets the shards fall, with a snap of his fingers. Rolling up the cloth holding the shards, he carefully gives it to Zima. "I'll let you know when we're ready."

"Of course, Prince Talok." Horror flashes on Zima's petite face. "I mean, King Talok."

Talok grips Zima's arm, saying, "Relax. I'm not my advisers. Nor my harsh grandfather—may he slumber in peace. To be honest, I miss being called that. I'm sure everyone can agree, it was a simpler time when I was Prince Talok. Put it out of your mind."

"Of course, King Talok," replies Zima. Snapping her fingers, she disappears.

"On to food." Talok takes a deep breath, leaning on the table. "Uncle LanSoren brought many things back from Earth, for the Paragonian Sovereignty and other Murainians to try. Name your favorite foods, and I'll do my best to order the equivalent."

I just say, "Whatever my dad's favorite was here," while Gemma lists off a myriad of foods. Finally, she picks the trio of steak, rice pilaf, and green beans fried with bacon.

Talok raises his hand, and Zima zaps next to our booth again. He rattles off words unknown. Flowing yet clipped are their sounds, as Zima takes the order and then disappears again.

Our drinks zip toward the table, seemingly by themselves. Apprehensive, my heart expects some Eel-Shock, canon-boom to go off. When the drinks just sit there quietly, I'm freed from the threat. For now.

Talok motions to the glittering-red drink, saying, "Uncle LanSoren called this Farivoo Eldyn. Fruit of the Dragons."

Taking a sip of the orange juice-like texture, I taste its tartness of lemonade. But, to the tart bite, a hint of cherry adds sweetness.

Meanwhile, Gemma frowns. "I was hoping for soda."

"Uncle LanSoren did warn of you being a little demanding," says Talok, gripping Gemma's glass.

Slowly, small bubbles appear in it, as Gemma queries, "How did Mr. Ravier know I'd be coming?"

"Not entirely sure. Over the years, he's been in contact with a few Metimoras. They're gifted in Time Magic. I suppose, it's possible one of Paragon's Arkiveis is gifted enough to see future memories of Paragonians. Although, it's unlikely. And with Tyler being half-Paragonian, it's even more unlikely. But we can ask Grover about it later."

"There aren't any Metimoras in Paragon?" queries Gemma, taking a contented sip of her drink.

Talok wags his head, saying, "Finding King Zymarc of Vitiosus would be easier than discovering where the Metimoras live."

"Are you going to war with them?" queries Gemma. "The Vitiosyns?"

"I'm not permitted to answer that yet; it will be at the end of the festival. We want to make this celebration count. Especially if it's to be our last."

Desperate to change the subject, I search for words—any to wipe the shadow from my cousin's face. "Why'd my dad call this Farivoo Eldyn?"

Talok breaks from his trance, replying, "Because the fruit trees only used to grow along the river shores near the Ruby Dragons' home. The fruit was a favorite of their former Matriarch Fayel. I'll spare you the lesson behind the words. Its direct translation means: Fayel's River Food for the Dragons. Hence, Farivoo Eldyn."

I state, "Has a nice ring to it."

When the meal-chatter fades within Zima's Kitchen, I glance around. Waltzing into the tavern's center is Quall with his triad, followed closely by Ryco with his. Trailing behind all seven is Ben, fidgeting with a new load of pouches and weapons.

Leading the others, Ryco points to our booth. Then he saunters over in our general direction. Stopping several feet away, he watches Quall sweep one hand toward some empty tables. Shifting together are six small ones, as the seven sit down in unison. A few seconds behind the others is the rookie, still adjusting his coat, pouches, and weapons. At last, he nervously sits before waving at us. All, except Ryco gulping down his drink, turn to look.

"Mud Fiend!" exclaim six of them.

A tempting smile on his face, Musgrae demands, "Come eat with us!"

Gemma hides her own smile. "Can that be intimidating and enticing, all at once?"

"Coming from Musgrae? Yes," states Talok.

Right then—greeting each Paragonian as she passes—Khyra wanders toward our table, now wearing a wispy dress. Behind her, its back edge trails on the floor; stopping a third of the way up the dress is a black-and-gray flame-pattern starting at the hem; and having the same flame-pattern are the long, fitted sleeves ending at her first row of knuckles.

Before Khyra reaches us, Gemma whispers, "She wasn't wearing that earlier."

"Dazzling Khyra!" Musgrae calls out. "You can dine with us too."

"I would love to, after discussing business with King Talok," replies Khyra, before taking the seat next to Talok. "I've finished those furnishings you requested this morning."

"Excellent!" states Talok. "You're getting faster."

"I had a few good teachers." Khyra steals a glance at Ryco. When he returns her glance, she looks away.

Mischief in his gaze, Talok says, "I have another request. Stop calling me King Talok. There's no need. We've known each other, since before we could practice magic."

"Oh! But there is," states Khyra. "Your advisers were right behind me." She motions to where Zepharre and the others sit across Zima's Kitchen giving their orders. She continues, "They've a bad habit of eavesdropping."

Talok's mischief fades. "Their insistence at all the formalities is certainly aggravating."

"At least Warren of Veldar is good at blocking them from hearing your every word. My friends say he's a bit exotic with his dark skin. A rare Kyanite specimen here in Paragon."

Warren chokes on his food, as Eli snickers next to him.

Talok scolds her. "Khyra, you can't say things like that! Not when he's listening."

Ignoring the scolding, Khyra queries, "Did you tell him?"

"What?" Talok looks to me. "Yes!"

"Tyler, want to know the best way to drive your cousin mad?"

As Talok squirms in his seat, Khyra teases, "Call him 'King Talok' for a day."

With Khyra's giggles for background noise, Talok scoffs. "Tyler wouldn't do that."

I state, "Don't be too sure."

Shock on his face, Talok complains, "Already, Khyra, you have my own cousin siding against me."

Finishing her drink, Gemma proclaims, "I'll take your side, Talok."

"She's saying that to be contrary," I state. "Don't believe her."

Gemma ignores me, while Khyra patronizes more. "You're a good sport, Talok."

"I try." He sighs. "Where is the food? Zima rarely takes this long."

"I told her to delay, until I got back."

"Back? You were already here?"

"Of course." Khyra nods. "But there was a little girl whose doll was broken. I had to go fix it. On my way back, another had a torn dress. A boy with a worn-out shoe. Then the fiancé with wilted flowers—"

"I get it," Talok cuts her off. "Next time, guide them to the Triflers. They've been bored, of late. Now I know why. You're doing their job."

On cue, our food appears. But it's suspended mid-air, right in front of our faces. Floating down to rest on the table are the plates and silverware, seeming to know who ordered what.

"Hope you like it," says Talok.

Gemma devours several bites of food, trying one of everything on her plate.

About to take the first bite of my noodle dish, I spot Gemma creeping her fork toward my bowl. Staring at her a moment, I offer her my own silverware.

She startles, asking, "You're not afraid of Gemma germs?"

"It'll be worth it, when I tell Jed Craven I got Gemma Galloway to eat off my fork."

After wiping her mouth with a napkin, Gemma states, "Assuming you leave out the part about leaving them, while taking me, to visit another world with magic and dragons; plagued by red-eyed zombies?"

"I'll tell them, at some point. You want it or not?"

She takes the bite, saying, "Tasty. You'll like it." Without another word, she goes back to devouring her own food.

I take my first bite of his favorite dish: an entree of buttery green-noodles complimented by an array of colorful vegetables. The pinks are smoky. Blackish veggies, zesty. Whitish ones, sweet. But the orange pieces are spongy. The flavors and textures are familiar, somehow, like a comforting dish always served on special occasions. Though I know I've never eaten it before.

Meanwhile, Khyra proclaims, "I require help constructing more homes. Could you spare some of your guards, King Talok? A few of them are well versed in Gendras. Are they not?"

"Ryco. Kent. Ben," replies Talok. "They're best."

"All three would be nice. Partnering off, we can build two homes at once."

Talok motions for one of his guards, and Ryco stands. After haughtily sauntering over, he answers, "My king?"

"Mind helping Khyra build new homes later?"

"Not at all. What do you plan, Khyra?"

"In addition to new homes," replies Khyra, "the tree bark's fire resistance needs improvement."

"Come discuss it," states Ryco, grabbing an empty chair, then setting it in between Kent and Ben. Khyra takes the offered seat, letting Ryco slide her chair in.

Ryco then seats himself between Kent and Musgrae, as I muse, *Ryco, a gentleman? Doubt it!* Flinching at the remembrance, I ask, "You heard that, didn't you?"

Talok nods. "But you're not alone in your dislike of Ryco. Many thought he wasn't a Paragonian at all. Due to his dark nature and yellow eyes."

"The eyes *are* a bit creepy," whispers Gemma.

"Last year," continues Talok, "he was forced to publicly admit to being one-quarter Sylvadyn—a Forest Dragon. It's one reason why he's so good with Green Magic."

"What happened?" I ask.

"When Uncle LanSoren died, suspicions were raised. Many thought Ryco was involved, since he and my uncle never got along. He's had a somewhat difficult time fitting in with many Paragonians over the years too. However, with no proof—only accusations—the theory was thrown out. Actually, right before we visited you."

"I still don't like him."

"Fair enough. He doesn't like you much, either. Maybe it's genetic."

Gemma queries, "Then why don't you mind him?"

"My father adored him. As for my mother—Uncle LanSoren's little sister—she died when I was five. Long story-short, Ryco helped me through it. Once you have his loyalty, you'll have it forever. Just don't ask him to show it."

Aunt Miriam is dead? Then who sent me—

Interrupting my thoughts is Gemma, asking, "Why's he so intense?"

"All dragons," states Talok, "even mixed bloods, have some intensity."

Gemma changes the subject. "Ever since we saw the Vitiosyns, I've been wondering ... Talok, what's a Parasogyn?"

Her question seems to ripple through the tavern.

First, a hush falls over the Paragonians.

Next, fear grips Talok's blue eyes.

Then, Reign's Roar rumbles in the distance.

At the sound, Zima's Kitchen is sent trembling.

Looking to the King's Guard, I meet the gaze of citrine-yellow eyes.

Lastly is a chill pricking my skin like thousands of needles stabbing in at once.

17

A Presence of Contradiction

I go to bolt from the booth, but Talok stops me. No one else reacts to the trembles in Zima's Kitchen; just me, with Talok's slender fingers wrapped around my wrist. Sweat beads on my forehead, as they send me their quizzical looks: tilted heads, raised eyebrows, curious eyes, or odd smiles. Some flit their gazes over my clothing, then to my face. Dozens of others steal glimpses, startling when I glance back.

Talok tugs gently, beckoning me to sit back down.

I ask, "What's happening?"

"It's Reign," he whispers. "I asked him to announce the return of our dragons sent to first help, then assess matters in Yharss and Dysarda."

Heat crawls up my neck, as I nod and sit back down. Beside me, Gemma squirms.

Across from her, Talok briefly bites his lower lip before finding the words of, "Please, Miss Gemma, never say that word again. I'll explain later. Where *ever* did you hear it?"

"On our way here." She sputters, "When we encountered Belzara. Possessed by Zymarc."

Countenance darkening, Ryco now stands by our table. "Paragonians, go back to your conversations," he commands, before looking to Gemma. "What did King Zymarc say, when referencing that word?"

As Gemma struggles to find words, I reply, "We were about to be discovered."

"Ben got nervous," she adds. "With good reason. Said something to Zymarc about never seeing a living Vitiosyn that close before."

I state, "Zymarc surmised that Ben had seen dead ones. Accused you of showing him the dead ones. Called you the Sylvadyn—"

"Parasogyn," finishes Ryco, looking down at Talok. "Then he knows."

"Knows what?" queries Talok.

"That I hunt them in the dark. Thank you, Gemma Galloway." He looks to her, saying, "You may have saved my life from ending this night. Although, done completely by accident."

Confused, she just hunches her shoulders. "You're welcome?" she mutters.

"I need to know what my uncle left behind for us." Talok's frantic eyes search the table, then he shouts over the frantic meal-chatter, "Ben! Journals! Now!"

Flying out of his chair is Ben, suffering his own heart-banging Eel-Shock. With him, all King's Guard leap to their feet and search for threats. Holding flames in their hands are Kent and Musgrae, while Quall's Triad brandish long-blades and daggers; only Quall and Khyra calmly stay seated.

"Quiet yourselves!" shouts Ryco, while sauntering back to his seat. "Ben of Yharss isn't used to King Talok yet."

Ben blushes, saying, "I put the boxes in Tyler's bag."

"Please retrieve it," states Talok.

Ben exits Zima's Kitchen, and we finish our food. Even after we're done eating, still, he's not back.

That's when Talok says, "Ryco, we're going to the tailor's. Then the Arkivara. When Ben shows up with Tyler's bag, tell him to meet us at Grover's."

In reply, Ryco sadistically grins. "You mean *the bag* that Musgrae and I tied to Awngeleik's back, after the Arkiveis and a Greyvon or two performed the cloaking spell on her—that bag?"

In exasperation, Talok wags his head. "I don't understand this extra work all of you are creating for poor Ben."

"Rookie Initiation," states Musgrae. "Got to keep him sharp."

"We won't let him search long," reassures Quall.

"I'll stay out of this one," says Talok, before leading Gemma and me onto a circular cover set aside from the rest of the tavern. Clenching his hand into a fist, Talok then splays out his fingers. Wisping over his palm are green flames that he releases down, commanding, "Deshea!"

Shifting is the cover, starting its glide down a hollow shaft of tangled black-branches.

"Talok?" I clear my throat. "Quall said I should ask you why my grandfather couldn't possibly be a pure Withrasyn."

Talok's gaze searches the black-branches, as if they'll release the words he needs. Finally, he begins with, "The White Sorsryn Clan is extinct. Any pure Withrasyns still alive are women."

"What are Sorsryns?" queries Gemma. "Are they like magicians? Vampires? Or something else?"

"Vampires is a fitting description of Deathasyns. Certainly."

"Vampire-magicians," hisses Gemma dramatically. "I like it! Until I see it." Horror flashes in her eyes, thus commencing the Strand-Twirl.

With a smile, Talok continues, "Uncle LanSoren compared Sorsryns to Sorcerer and Elf mythologies too. Magic is their lifeblood. If it weren't for them, our city wouldn't be what it is."

I state, "Thanks to Emerald Sorsryns, in particular."

"Don't let Khyra hear you say that name. They're really called Emerassas-syns." Talok pauses and rubs his neck. "I'm sure you *hear* why they started calling themselves the Emeralds."

I smile. "Sounds like assassins."

Looking up, Talok moans. "We have tried telling Khyra that. Still. She insists they be called by their ancient name."

Turning serious, I ask, "When we first met, you said something about having White Sorsryn ancestors. Are they ancestors of all Paragonians or only some?"

"All," replies Talok. "One-thousand fifty-three years ago, Queen Awleesia came to King Kailon of the Vaegons—the Dragon Tamers and Memory

Keepers—asking that they permit her Withrasyn women a new home, since their men were dying by their mid-twenties."

Gemma queries, "From what?"

Talok blows out a breath, saying, "A curse? A virus? They were never sure."

"Why did the men's age matter?" Gemma queries.

"Since Sorsryns have a decelerated-maturation, compared to other races …" Talok pauses, awkwardly searching the hollow for words again. He blurts it out, "They aren't able to procreate until their fifties."

"*Definitely* a survival problem," I state.

At near the same time, Gemma is asking, "Do they look like children for longer too?"

"In physical development. They're similar to humans, until their twenties or thirties. Then their appearance defies time. I've met many Sorsryns—centuries old—they all look forty, at most."

"This Queen Awleesia," I ask, "did she and King Kailon make a deal?"

"The Vaegon-White Pact." Talok grins. "Tonight's festival celebrates their unity. Two races—two nations—becoming one: Le Pawv'Ragaenens."

"The Paragonians," states Gemma.

"What about the Withrasyn Siveyras?" I ask. "Did those men die too?"

"It took longer, but yes. They didn't live to see the first generation of Paragonians."

That's when I muse, *Soren of the Monel is probably dead, then. How to be sure?*

Interrupting my musing, Gemma holds up the Jed-finger. "Random question: how old was Lance Ravier?"

"That's an answer I don't know. He grew up with Quall. Which would put him in his … mid-forties?" Talok nervously fiddles with his coat-collar, saying, "After the Pristine Sixteen, Privileged Eighteen, A Sorsryn's Fifty, and The Siveyra Journey, we don't talk much about age."

Gemma smiles. "That explains Ben's confusion about the birthday candles and cake."

Talok chuckles. "Yharss is the most traditional in culture and language.

Very little studying of any cultures outside of Paragon. Ben's had to learn a lot, these past two years, but he always rises to the challenge."

I state, "From what I've seen of your King's Guard, he'd have to."

"Or get stomped into the ground," adds Gemma.

Humor fades off Talok's face, and a shadow strips my cousin's eyes of happiness. "I'm glad he's strong. He'll need that strength, when the survivors arrive."

The wooden cover stops right then, and we step off onto the long wooden-roadway. Along its winding turns, we plod beneath colorful birds chirping and fluttering overhead. Down they playfully dive to the roadway, before swirling around each other on their way over the vine railing.

"How many survived?" queries Gemma.

"Not enough. My advisers tell me a quarter of our population's gone. Yharss and Dysarda in burning shambles. Only their Arkivaras were left intact."

Approaching a bustling roadway, rows of shops, which line both sides of the street, come into our view. Then Gemma lowers her head, saying, "We came at a bad time."

The bombings and aftermath trigger in my mind, but I push the horror away and refuse to think of that night. Still, I can't help wondering, *How did he really die?*

"Don't worry, Miss Gemma," states Talok, "we'll get both of you home."

"After the festival?" I ask.

"Right before the end. At its conclusion, I'm expected to announce my decision. Here we are," announces Talok. "Madeleine's Tailor Shop." He opens a dark-blue shop door, motioning for us to enter ahead of him.

Inside, wooden mannequins display an array of clothes: cloaks and dresses; corsets and skirts; coats, vests, and pants. Some match the forest. Others are vibrant and sewn with gold or silver thread. Then I spot what makes all else fade to shadows in their light; the royal-blue silks—reminiscent of vast ponchos—enveloping underlying robes of ivory edged with trim of gold and black. Both layers pool on the floor, and painting across the blue silks—like a starry night—are threads of white, ivory, and black.

Smile replacing the shadowed expression, Talok states, "The Arkiveis Robes of Paragon. You approve?"

I reply, "Robes fit for a wizard. I wouldn't ever wear them, but—"

"They're stunning!" interrupts Gemma. "Can I touch?"

"Of course." Talok beams. "Handle whatever you like. So long as no one's wearing it."

Amused, then in awe, Gemma pets the Arkiveis robes as she would a baby rabbit.

"I might use that line on Kaida." I look to Talok. "Gemma's sister has a bad habit of invading personal space."

"No joke," says Gemma, before eyeing the racks of dresses lining one of the walls.

A petite woman approaches—no taller than Gemma—in a lavish, yet tasteful lavender dress. Draping past her shoulders are locks of sandy-blonde. But it's her eyes that hold my interest. Guaranteed, hiding behind their irises of black, blue, and white are a thousand mysteries.

"Madeleine!" Talok smiles. "Meet my cousin Tyler and—"

"Gigi!" Madeleine bursts out, before hugging Gemma.

A shy-smile on her face, Gemma returns the hug, then steps back.

"You've already spoken with Khyra, then?" queries Talok.

"Yes," replies Madeleine, before grasping my hand. "LanSoren's Tyler Ravier. I'm honored to meet you. And to clothe you in Paragon's finest. A few months before he passed, I helped your father pick out a style or two. It won't be pure-black, as that's reserved for the Paragonian Sovereignty. But if you trust our taste, I'll only take your measurements here. Then deliver the final product to the castle, well before the start of the festival. How's that sound?"

I shrug. "Spares me from having to try on everything. I wouldn't know what to choose."

Madeleine holds a finger to her rouge lips, saying, "You sound like Warren and Kent. They hate fittings—pair that with their chronic indecision? I have my work cut out for me." She snaps her fingers.

Appearing out of nowhere is a black ribbon that has tiny white marks on it. Flying through the air, it stops with a smack to my chest. Next, is its whisking over my body, before I can blink—let alone react—it tightens like lacing. Flashing like a camera: Whisk-Click-Flash-Repeat, it leaves me squinting like the time Jed Craven blinded me with a strobe light in the dark. Shuddering away the black ribbon's violation, I glance at Gemma. Like most girls in a new store, she's focused on the racks. Totally oblivious to everything, including the black ribbon's pillaging of me.

I look to Madeleine and say, "I think I know why they don't like fittings."

Wrapping the ribbon around her hand, Madeleine slips it into her pocket, saying, "That? You'd prefer it, over my hands taking the measurements. Every time. Any of Withrasyn descent, so it seems, don't like their personal space encroached upon. You included."

"You're not Paragonian?" I ask.

"Vaegon." She grins. "There are a few of us left in The Eye. Although, my former home of Dysarda was bursting with us."

"Can I try this one on?" Gemma holds up a wispy purple and charcoal-colored dress with thin navy-trim along its hems and seams.

"An excellent choice," states Madeleine. "You'll look reminiscent of an Amethyst Sorsryn, especially with those beautiful slanted eyes of yours."

With the question, "Some Sorsryns look like me?" Gemma confirms both our astonishment.

"Didn't anyone mention it, when they saw you?" queries Madeleine.

"No," replies Gemma.

"Then we'll have lots to talk about, while this is fitted to you," states Madeleine, taking the dress in her arms as if it's a fragile figurine. "King Talok, to save you both the yawns of boredom, you should take Tyler to his father's favorite antique shop."

"A good idea," replies Talok. "We might even find ancient Geldryn devices."

"Geldryn?" I ask.

"Another Sorsryn Clan," he replies. "Nearly extinct, like Withrasyns."

We leave the tailor's and head farther down the path of shops.

"How many clans are there?" I ask.

"Eight." Talok counts on his fingers. "Onyx and Withrasyn. Emerald and Deathasyn. Geldryn, Kyanite, Silverian, and *then* Amethysyns—another clan who'd rather be called by their English name."

"Because they don't want to sound like a drug? Does Paragon have drugs?"

"Don't get me started on Quall and his herbs—consumed during off-duty time. He claims he's merely testing their effects for powders and tonics. But it's more than that."

"Hard to imagine him being a druggie."

Talok hides a grin. "How else is he to survive being First of the Guard?"

I shrug. "Do what you have to, I suppose."

"Hence, why I let him have his herbs." Talok shrugs back.

Stopping in front of a blood-red door, Talok opens it to a small shop crammed with trinkets. Lining glass counters are gold figurines and lamps—silver jewelry and mirrors too—among a myriad of odd bronze pieces. Along tall shelves are bottles of every color. Tall and thin, short and round—some are squares; others resemble spiked-mace balls in glass form. Overall? It could take a solid week to see everything held within this shop.

When we enter, a whisper sounds in my ear and sends my heart pounding.

It's his voice, speaking, "Fire of the Soul. Wake of the Water. How to break their laws?"

My gaze frantically searching around, it settles on a young teenage girl in a faded peasant dress of royal-blue. Partially hiding her face are her long blonde waves, and fiddling are her small hands with several odd bronze gear-pieces set with assorted jewels.

Talok follows my gaze, asking, "Did you hear something, Tyler?"

"Over by her? Are those Geldryn devices?"

"Actually … yes! Shall we go look?" Before I can respond, Talok weaves through the shop. He says, "Don't mind us," when he stands in close proximity to the girl.

Startling, she wipes away tears, then her bloodshot eyes glance at us.

Talok starts a kind introduction, but she quietly interrupts. "King Talok, I'm old enough to know who you are." She holds out her hand. "In my city,

I am called by Callie of Dysarda."

Seeming to uncover my soul are her heterochromian eyes of blue and green, now looking at me. Just then, the diving armor's interior digs in like itchy mosquito bites. Ignoring the feeling, I gently ask, "Dysarda?"

Her voice cracking, she replies, "I arrived yesterday, ahead of my parents. They wanted me to enjoy the Eye of Paragon, before it's bursting with others here for the festival."

Talok, taking a handkerchief from his inside coat pocket, gives it to Callie, saying, "You're alone? You don't look very old."

"Thirteen is old enough to travel on one's own. Is it not?"

Callie dabs away the sniffling, as my skin crawls. Reacting, I nervously clasp my hands in front of myself.

"It was," replies Talok. "But not now. Survivors from Yharss and Dysarda should be here soon; hopefully, your parents among them. Is there anything you need, before then?"

With more skin-crawling, comes more hand-tightening, before I suggest, "Why not stay with us, until they get here?"

"I could never." Callie gawks at me, then Talok. "You're the King of Paragon. You've better things to do, than tend a girl from Dysarda of no consequence."

Firmly, Talok states, "*All* Paragonians are of consequence to me. You wouldn't be bothering us one bit."

"If anything," I add, "we're bothering you."

For the first time, Callie grins. "Not at all. I was simply passing the time."

"With this Geldryn device?" Talok motions to the curved black-and-gold gear-piece in her delicate hands.

"These are Geldryn devices?" Gasping, Callie offers the one to Talok. "I didn't know. It was because of their beauty that I took notice."

"It's been told," says Talok, "that the Geldryn loved things of beauty, both living and absent of life. This appears to be a bracer or cuff. Void of enchantment, it's purely decorative."

"What about that one?" I point to a gear mechanism.

"Most likely, it opened a door. Maybe a large box."

Callie queries, "Then where's the door?"

"Who knows? Cracked in two, a thousand years ago, and still among the Geldryn ruins."

Callie adds, "During the Massacre of GroldeVa."

Talok nods, handing me the bracer. Then my skin-crawling calms, and *his* voice whispers again, "Prison of the Air. Blood of the Land. Who can truly wield the keys?"

Eyes pooling with more tears, Callie queries, "Will we suffer the fate of the mighty Geldryn, King Talok?"

"Not while I still live," Talok replies, while my breaths catch.

Abruptly, I thrust the bracer to Talok. "Here! Take it."

"You all right, Tyler?" He grips my shoulder.

"It makes me … feel weird. When can we see Grover?"

"We can go now," says Talok. His eyes concerned, he turns to Callie. "Would you like to come with us?"

"I only just arrived here; however, I know my way to the Arkivara. I'll be along, when I'm done. Hope you feel revived soon …" She pauses to study me.

"Forgive my manners!" Talok scolds himself. "This is my cousin."

"The Son of LanSoren?" Her face brightens. "I've heard much of you this day. May I attend the festival with you?"

Mesmerized by her eyes, my chest fills with comfort. Before I can stop the words, out comes, "As long as we don't go on a Dragon Ride … afterward."

I cringe inside, while she hides a smile behind her hands. "No. I've only met you." Then she turns serious to say, "Maybe in a few years?"

My only comeback for her words is clawing heat on my neck and face.

"We'd better leave." Talok snickers. "Before my cousin crumples to the floor, at your feet and mercy. If you miss us at the Arkivara, come find us in the castle."

Both of us exit the shop and stroll farther along the roadway.

While I rub my face, attempting to rid my frustration, Talok's shoulders quake with silent laughter.

"I take it: you haven't flirted much?" he asks.

"What was your first clue?"

"Do I need to assign Musgrae and Warren to teach you the art of flirtation?"

"No!" I shudder. "An alien's flirtation skills? Doubtful it'll translate back home."

"Probably not." Talok points two fingers at me, adding, "If you ever witness Musgrae flirting in a hurry, though, you must tell. Kent swears it's the funniest thing to witness." Talok takes in his whale-breath. Blowing it out like one too. "There! I've got a hold of myself. I should warn you, now. Grover talks a thousand words a minute, and I'm only exaggerating slightly. Prepare yourself, Cousin."

"Not a problem. I'm used to the Barrage of Gemma. Doubt Grover can be worse."

"I wouldn't be too confident of that," whispers Talok.

Right then, footsteps race up behind us.

"All done!" announces Gemma, hooking her arm with mine. "Wish I didn't have to wear this armor, but Madeleine managed to work it in with the design. She gave it a Sweetheart neckline. Half the time was spent explaining that it's like a curvy-heart with the top cut off. She got it, in the end." Gemma breathes in deeply, refilling her lungs' ammunition.

I glance at her chest—now free of the suffocating armor-neckline—before saying, "Looks like 'Sweetheart' uncovered your chicken pox."

"Rude! Tyler-Malik-Ravier." Gemma unhooks her arm from mine to pinch my wrist, then calmly continues, "Madeleine said they should go away before the festival."

Innocently, Talok says, "At least, you've got teasing down good."

"What?" Gemma looks at him in alarm.

"Nothing you need to know." I smirk.

"Fine!" Gemma huffs. "Keep your secrets."

18

Chills of Truth

After some time, we approach the solitary tree with turquoise leaves dancing their own rhythm. Glistening in the sunlight is its white skin, while its black crevices reflect nothing to the world. As there's no bridge, I wonder how we'll even get to the Arkivara.

In silent answer, Talok splays out his hand. Summoning—from thin air—in his grasp is a short-staff of black-and-white. Along the wooden pathway, he scrapes one end of it. At the point of contact, electric yellow and green crackles. Next, he jogs to the path's end and raises the staff to aim at the solitary tree. From the staff-tip, sparks hurl and hit the tree. Then the path starts to grow into a bridge, filling the gap. Large branches creak, as they chase after the tail of sparks.

When the spell's finished, we follow Talok across his bridge.

"Welcome to the Arkivara, forever in a state of disorder." Talok grins, before opening the dark-turquoise door.

Hanging above the door is a sign with a metal symbol reminiscent of a music treble-clef. Something about its flowing contours soothes my nerves, and when I step through the doorway, my heart fills with that strange familiarity—like I've been here before, even though I never have. I shake the feeling, as Talok ambles to a black counter strewn with old books, yellowed scrolls, and crinkled papers.

Talok, ignoring the mess, calls out, "Grover! Are you in?"

While we wait within this large Arkivara room, Gemma explores books on rounded shelves filling every bit of wall space. Then Talok clicks his tongue, before diving his hands bravely into the clutter, searching for something. Finally finding a tiny silver bell, he rings it.

"Grover!" Talok yells, then calmly clarifies, "He's a little deaf. He can hear pure-thought remarkably well, though. One time, Quall assigned what everyone was to say to Grover. *Then* we all stood there. Just thinking. Not saying a word." Talok pinches the skin between his eyes as if a headache is coming on.

"How'd that go?" I ask.

"He heard every word," squeaks Talok. "Easiest conversation we've ever had with him."

Gemma queries, "He doesn't blurt out what you're thinking, does he?"

"No promises."

Behind the counter, a short man rushes down the spiral stairs. As he pushes disheveled gray hair out of his face, his blue-and-white Arkiveis robes flutter about. Adjusting his spectacles, his Vaegon-eyes light up at the sight of us. "Master Talok! Come in! You've brought guests! What city are they from?"

Talok starts to say, "Grover, this is my cousin—"

But Grover interrupts, "Your cousin? Son of LanSoren? My word!" Grover tosses up his hands. "It's been ages. Twenty-three years. I've waited."

When Grover spots Gemma, he roughly adjusts his spectacles a second time. "You must be Musgrae's Mud Friend. What a ridiculous name! You don't have a speck of dirt on you. Pray, what is your name?"

"Gemma Galloway." She smiles.

Then Talok clears his throat to say, "He calls her Mud *Fiend*."

Grover just scowls at him. "That's what I said. Mud Friend."

Abandoning the hopeless task, Talok bites back any more arguments.

Skeptical, I ask Grover, "You've waited twenty-three years?"

"That's the same age as Warren," adds Talok.

Grover tears the spectacles off his face to clean them with a tiny cloth taken from the counter's clutter, saying, "Yes! They were born the same year. Though, I'm sure I'll like you more than most, Tyler. With everyone else, it's always: 'Grover, fetch this memory. Grover, that memory. Have you seen this-book or that-scroll?' Why do you think my counter's in such a state of disarray? My hair too. I nearly died, when I glimpsed myself in the mirror this morning. Look at it! It's like I've suffered a shock. A shock of endless requests. And *that* Warren. Always bossing me around. I'm surprised I haven't keeled over dead. Where. I. Stand."

Talok, again, pinches between his eyes, helplessly saying, "That's excessive, Grover."

Meanwhile, I muse, *Grover's acting like I'm famous.*

Jarring my musing is Grover proclaiming, "You are famous. Famous as your father. Greatest and kindest warrior, in all of Paragon. I dare say, in all of Muraine!"

Talok pleads, "Grover, he wasn't *that* famous."

"Perhaps!" admits Grover. "But those Vitiosyns left us alone, until he died. That says a lot." Cementing his point, Grover holds up the Jed-finger.

"Maybe—" Talok starts.

Yet again, Grover cuts him off. "LanSoren was even bold enough to speak with King Zymarc of Vitiosus, over three years ago. Eight months later, Awngeleik was given to him as the Vitiosyns' Sign of Neutrality with Paragon. Then LanSoren died, and Zymarc began asking for Awngeleik's return."

Talok sucks in the whale-breath. "What are you saying, Grover? That my uncle was killed by Vitiosus? We know what it does. He didn't die of that."

Grover puts his spectacles back on, before bowing his head. "So his death remains a great mystery *and* tragedy."

"What do you know of his death?" I ask.

Thinking a moment, Grover twists a gold ring—that has a single black-stone setting—around his middle finger. Then, finally, he states, "I and the other Arkiveis have searched the memory archives and found nothing to correlate with what killed your father."

Gemma startles, before exclaiming, "See! Other people use that word too."

"Grover, you may want to clarify what the Arkiveis do," suggests Talok.

"Why, we're the keepers of memories. Whenever a Vaegon or Paragonian dies, we collect their memories, then add them to the archives' heart. The Heart of the Arkivara."

"It's how you remember loved ones?" queries Gemma.

"And pass collected knowledge to the next generation," says Grover. "Only pure Vaegons have the ability to maintain and add to the Arkivara."

"How come?" I ask Grover.

"'Twas part of the Vaegon-White Pact. Several Vaegons were given the duty of producing the next generation's Arkiveis. Agreed to keep a pure bloodline. It's not to say we're better than the Paragonian's bloodline. They simply don't have a physiology for tending Arkivaras."

Someone behind us rushes into the room.

Panting for breath, Ben says, "Sorry, King Talok. Had to finish my full report. Took longer to find Tyler's bag than expected too."

"No worries," states Talok.

I take my duffle from Ben to unzip it, while he explains, "I emptied the chest contents into it. Left the locked box and large one at the castle, though. That picture frame too."

"We shouldn't need them yet," I reply, while adding duffle-items to the counter clutter.

Paging through the jade-leather journal, Grover states, "This one's in English, Tyler. Have you read it?"

"Not all of it," I admit. "From what I read, it's a recount of his life with my mom."

As if he's setting my father to rest, Grover gently places it back in my duffle. Next, he searches through the navy one, with two male figures on it, saying, "Unrecognizable" before setting it down.

"Jasper could look at it," says Talok. "He's seen a fair share of Muraine. Knows several languages too."

"That he could," agrees Grover, opening the dragon-wolf journal before exclaiming, "At last! A language I know."

Rocking back and forth on my feet, I wait and hope for something—any-thing—to be revealed from these journals. Excitement rises, and anticipa-tion closes my ribs together, making it hard to breathe.

After skimming halfway through the journal, Grover ends my misery by saying, "So far, it recaps Muraine's history: the races, forests, weather patterns, and such. Nothing noteworthy in it, except for the Greyvons' language." Grover looks up at Gemma. "They're Great Wolves, dear." He goes back to reading.

Face flushing, Gemma curls her shoulders.

Nearing the end of the journal, Grover pops open his previously calm Vaegon-eyes, then says, "Don't see this often! The ancient Sorsryn dialect. Can't decipher it. Current dialects are too dissimilar from the ancient one of the Sorshrynaks."

"Sorsryns of Old?" queries Talok. "I never took advanced history, Grover. How were the Sorshrynaks different from Sorsryns of today?"

Grover starts to answer, but pain creases his weathered face. "I forgot! I'm magically bound not to say," he states. "Everyone is."

"By whom?" demands Talok.

"No one knows, really," replies Grover. "But that reminds me, I once hypothesized that Siveyra Dezarin is a Sorsryn of Old. Never was able to extract the day of his birth from anyone or anything. The Arkivara was of no help, either. Guess I'll never know, seeing as how Dezarin went on holiday when we needed him most."

"Why do you need Dezarin?" queries Gemma.

"Why! To keep the Vitiosyns at bay," exclaims Grover. "Another mystery I'll never know is the true identity of LanSoren's father."

"No one knows who he was?" I ask.

"My mother," says Talok, "was LanSoren's half-sister. Different fathers."

Grover continues, "Until we had LanSoren's blood tested two years ago, I *really* thought Dezarin was his father. But, alas, LanSoren was Paragonian through and through," huffs Grover, paging through the dragon-wolf journal again.

I ask, "Siveyra Gyron's coming for the festival. Isn't he? Maybe he can translate some."

Grover agrees, "It's worth asking."

"What about the Greyvons?" queries Gemma.

"Alpha Jasper's coming for the Vaegon-White Festival," replies Grover. "His time of hibernation has finished. If he can't make it, he'll send Rorka in his stead. She has her own pack now and everything."

"Good for her." Ben grins. "I like Rorka."

Grover holds up the dragon-wolf journal, asking me, "May I borrow this for the night?"

"Sure," I reply, while putting everything else back in the duffle. Gripping the gloves and daggers, I hesitate. "Grover? You know anything about these?"

"Those were your father's, when he was a boy. Haven't seen them in years. Hold onto them. They're one of a kind, enchanted daggers."

"Enchanted?" I ask. "With which magic?"

"All the magics!" exclaims Grover. "Geldryn and Gendras. Red, Death, and Black. Blue and White. Perhaps, even the Crae-Shand Magic of the Greyvons. That's why the metal has those colors." He blinks at me, as if I should know this bit of information.

"But aren't the Geldryn extinct?"

That's when Grover starts zooming his face to the pages of the journal, to and fro, like a swinging pendulum. Unsure that he heard me, I'm about to ask again when he bursts out, "Yes, yes, Ben! The Silverians know limited amounts of Geldryn Magic. The rumor was, as a boy, LanSoren took the daggers to the Silverians for their enchantment."

I mouth a 'thank you' to Ben, before asking, "And other clans, for the other magics?"

"Yes! And Ruby Dragons," replies Grover, before obsessing over his spectacles again. This time, he scrubs them with one wide robe-sleeve, then on he continues, "He had to find our one and only Withrasyn Siveyra too. Avilon. Hard to find. That one. Haven't seen her in years."

"One more thing, Grover," Talok reluctantly says. "Do you have any rings these two can keep?"

Confused at first, understanding lights Grover's eyes. "You mean the bathroom enchantment, as LanSoren liked to call it? Over by the door, the rings are in that chest."

Talok opens the chest. Inside are thousands of gold, silver, bronze, and copper rings. He takes out two replacement gold rings and hands them to us, before asking "Are all of these enchanted, Grover?"

Peeling his gaze from the journal page to glare at Talok, Grover grumbles, "Got tired of the little children complaining about how their magic isn't working properly. Those are for their emergencies. Twice a year, I cook up a large batch in a cauldron."

Putting the new one in its place, Gemma slips off her old ring. After replacing mine, I give the old to Talok, then catch sight of the witch-eyes on Gemma. Stealing a glance at the three Paragonians occupied with their conversation, the witch-eyes feign innocence, and into the chest Gemma drops her old ring.

Suddenly, Grover points to us. "Make sure you don't lose those! You've no idea of the vile smells I endured while enchanting them. The wood, food, plants, and magical powders, by themselves, aren't bad. But together? They are enough to—"

Cutting him off, Talok holds up the Jed-finger. "Thank you, Grover. We'll talk later."

"Don't forget, King Talok," Grover says, "about the meal you are to cook for the Arkiveis tomorrow night, at the festival's conclusion."

"With everything that's happened," sputters Talok, rubbing his neck, "I thought we were going to skip tomorrow's tradition."

"Of course not. We will only survive this trying time, with the traditions that bring us together as family and friends."

While they're busy, I hiss, "Gemma! You'd play a prank on little alien kids?"

She rolls her eyes, saying, "No fun at all," then reaches down for her old ring.

Ben returns everything to my duffle and zips it up, before slinging it over his shoulder.

"Hurry up, Gemma," I whisper.

Talok's nervous gaze skims the counter. "What should I avoid cooking for the Arkiveis?"

Seeming to patronize his king, Grover proclaims, "The Arkiveis love creativity. Can't go wrong with that."

When someone bursts into the room, Gemma startles, grabs a ring, then stuffs it in her pocket.

"It's the right one?" I ask.

Hesitating, she nods.

With wild cobalt-blue eyes, Warren is standing in the doorway and spewing out, "Master Grover! Come with me. Immediately! Arkivy Nyrim is here. Overwhelmed with memories. They're exploding out of him. Blood everywhere. He's dying."

* * *

Hiking up robes, Grover rushes out of the Arkivara. In his scuffle across Talok's bridge, his boot cuffs slip down his skinny legs.

"Master Grover!" booms Warren. "There's no time to get to the lift."

Grover, with glowing-blue eyes, deepens the scowl on his weathered face, voicing, "Then how do you suggest I get down there to Nyrim?"

Warren's gaze creeps to the railing, then up curves his mouth. "Musgrae will catch you."

"Musgrae will do *no* such thing!" Grover crosses his arms defiantly. "I am an Arkivy! Oldest in the land."

While Grover argues, Warren cups his face. "You'll forgive me later." With a flick of his hand, he sends Grover over the bridge railing.

Fading as he falls is Grover's shrill scream. Leaning over the edge, like Warren—looking down as a spectator before a touchdown—I spot Musgrae and Ryco waiting. Musgrae readies to catch the Arkivy, and Ryco lifts his hand—the one free of a blade. Grover slows in the air, but not his flailing hands. Smacking at Musgrae, Grover's like some victim trying to rid themselves of captors and, thoroughly smacked to convincing, Musgrae obliges him by letting go.

His spectacles askew, Grover straightens them to give Warren a death-glance. With one last huff, he scuffles to the scene of shamrock-green—stained with blood—and to an Arkivy in robes of blue-and-black.

Ben starts to say, "King Talok, shall we go down the—"

But Talok interrupts, "No, please no! I hate going down that thing. Isn't there a new lift, somewhere around here, that's recently been installed?"

Warren nods. "It'll take twice as long as the Belly of the Snake, but yes. Follow me." Warren calls down, "Ryke, Mooz, we'll be down in ten, unless you need us now. The *king* doesn't want the snake."

Ryco just waves off the comment in response, and turns around to watch the scene on the shamrock-green.

Quickly, Warren leads us—Talok, Ben, Gemma, and me—along the winding roadway headed for a nearby tree trunk. We step onto a cover much like the one leaving Zima's Kitchen, except that this one's recessed in a hollowed out part of the trunk.

When we're all situated within the hollow shaft of tangled black-branches, Ben looks to Talok and says, "Forgive me, King Talok, but we'll be going down faster than usual. Warren? Keep their legs under them?" With that, Ben flicks his fingers and electrifies the cover in green sparks, commanding, "Velositas-sae-Desheados."

Warren, startling, drops to his knees and plasters his hands on the cover. Blue light emits from his palms, and we start hovering an inch up from where we stand.

That light then races to the tangled branches of the shaft, during our plummet downward.

Thrown off balance, Gemma screams.

Talok holds onto her, while clenching his jaw.

And, like a dizzying descent on a plane, my head feels as though it's floating off my body. I hold my breath and tense my neck, hoping that my legs aren't broken after the landing.

Then there's Ben just standing there, focused on the cover and sparking-green. For a split second, he balls his hands into fists.

The cover stops abruptly. And we all have to regain our footing. Except Ben, rushing out to find his way to Ryco's side. We make it there several seconds after him.

In dreaded horror, we watch the scene ahead.

At the sight inside the wall, chills prick my skin. Grover holds out a black staff, with an embedded glowing blue-stone at its tip. On his knees is the much younger Nyrim, reaching for it. On his hands are many lesions. Staining his robes to saturation is much blood. Face cut and bloodied, too, red tears pour from his eyes. Meanwhile, in variant robes, are three other Arkiveis forming a half-circle behind Nyrim.

"Where is Kent?" mutters Musgrae, while Gemma crowds closer to him.

"Had a few things to gather," replies Ryco.

Warren's about to step past where Ryco stands, but Ryco holds up a restraining hand, warning him, "Go past here, and you risk breaking the protection wall the Arkiveis put up. Only Vaegons can pass, without disrupting it."

Ben queries, "Can they hear us?"

"No," states Ryco.

Talok draws nearer to Ryco, asking, "What are we to do?"

"There's nothing we can do, other than erect another wall if this one breaks. If there was more to be done, I would've insisted that you get over your fear of *the snake*, and come down immediately."

Right then, Nyrim shouts, "Grover, stand back! More are coming."

Haunting are Nyrim's screams ricocheting within the wall. From Nyrim, dozens of ghosts of luminescent-blue burst out. Blood sprays like hundreds of bullets. It splatters on him and the other Arkiveis. Then the scarlet-eyed shadow-figures appear, extracting more blood with their escape. Away from the laughing shadows, the blue-ghosts run screaming. As all ghosts reach the farthest point from Nyrim, they fade to nothing. Only their screams and laughs remain. Left trembling are Nyrim's hands, as his robes drip with blood.

"Warren? Help him." Ben's chest heaves. "Please! Do something."

Warren solemnly bows his head, saying, "Blue Magic can't help with this."

Separating us from them is the iridescent film of protection. But it might as well be a brick wall, as only the Arkiveis, circling farther around Nyrim, can help him.

Then Kent comes up behind Ben, asking, "How strong is your Nyrim?"

"Strength doesn't matter," mutters Ben.

Ryco states, "It's his lack of experience, working against him."

"Let's hope that all those years of training with my father paid off," says Kent. With a silver staff in one hand, he places his other on the wall. In front of him, the space turns blue. Stepping through, he collects blue-ghosts into the staff's black-stone. Careful to avoid collecting the shadow-figures in it, he draws a Katana and cuts down the running shadows.

Grover presses his hand to Nyrim's forehead, and the noise quiets.

Meanwhile, I wonder, *Will the wall let me in?* Approaching its iridescence, I lift my left hand to it. Though dimmer, the wall glows blue in front of me, and Ben's eyes brighten. "It will let you in?"

"Guess so," I reply. "But there's nothing I can do. I don't know magic. Wish I did."

I grip Ben's arm, but then the ground shakes and more ghosts burst from Nyrim. Grover's thrown back, Kent stumbles, the Arkiveis fall to the ground, and wings flutter overhead. Landing behind me is Awngeleik, screeching and looking to the bloodied scene of shamrock-green.

Snake-eyes softening, she seems to understand what's at stake: Arkivy Nyrim of Yharss holding on for his last bit of life.

Petting Awngeleik's face, I stare into her eyes. "If a king would rage a war for you," I state, "you must be special. So, Awngeleik, what can you do? What did my father teach you?"

In reply, she pulls her head back to sigh. Sighing with her, I turn to face what will come.

Slower are Kent's movements, sluggish even, while collecting more ghosts into his staff-stone. Everyone, except Nyrim still on his knees, finds their footing. Tortured by it all, my mind races, thinking one thing, *I wish there was something,* anything, *I could do.*

In one swift motion—whether for good or bad—Awngeleik's nose hits my back and launches me through the wall.

Rolling in the bloodied shamrock, I stop in front of Nyrim's shaking hands and enter the tormented sound of death: explosions splitting wood and stone; Paragonians being cut down and burned; fire creeping over fabric and flesh. I cannot see any of it. But I hear all of it.

Their screams send electric pangs through my body, and I feel a shadow of their pain, their fear, their end: death by the blade and Vitiosus. At last, my gaze latches onto what's in front of me: Nyrim, Vaegon-eyes tearful.

With lacerated hands, Nyrim feels around the shamrock-grass, weeping, "LanSoren, I sense you. If you can hear me. Wherever you are. Help me. I can't hold them much longer."

Crawling my way closer to Nyrim, I grip one of his hands and whimper, "I don't know how to help you, Nyrim. But Ben tells me I have magic. If you can, take what you need. I can't watch you die."

Fighting for breath, Nyrim pants, "Your voice betrays that you're a mere boy. If I share my burden, this magic will kill you."

"Will it make any difference, knowing I'm Tyler Ravier?"

He hesitates, as chills claw at my skin once more.

"Please, Nyrim," I beg, "I feel them coming. Like a winter storm. You're already sharing some of the burden with me. Will it do you any good to resist sharing the rest?"

Nyrim gathers his footing. With one hand covering the watch-face, he latches onto my wrists, and the chills turn to flames. Burning my core first, they spread out to everywhere else.

Sounds are given faces—so many faces—screaming, dead, and burned beyond recognition. Drinking in their triumph are scarlet Vitiosyn-eyes—not just women, but men too—their twisted smiles turn to thousands of echoing laughs, mockery, and shouts of victory.

Unable to, I want to scream and make it stop.

Nyrim's hands calm, yet mine tremble. Then the Prismatic of Magic stains my left hand, turning it ice-cold. Something explodes from me. With it? A bright light and rushing-wind that launches Nyrim back through the protection wall and away from the ghosts of light.

Their hands outstretched, Kent and the Arkiveis fight the wind. Unable to hold back its force, they join Nyrim, Talok, and the thousands of others peering in at me with the ghosts and memories: the battle raged in Yharss.

Like a soft breeze, the ghosts and memories vanish.

As prismatic colors complete my hand-stain, I'm left all alone within the wall. Pressing on it from the other side is Talok, whispering, "Tyler, we're not sure what's happening. Come slowly. Gently."

I take a step. Then two and three. My stomach lurches, and I state, "I can't move."

Calling out is Callie's sad voice, "Try, Tyler Ravier." Beside Gemma, who's fighting for composure, Callie of Dysarda stands, crying for her people or me. Who can be sure of which one?

I try again, but collapse to the red-stained shamrock. Nyrim's blood smears more over my clothes, face, and hands. The scent sickens me, and I dig my fingernails past the shamrock-grass and into the grit of the ground.

When I stand, my own memories seep out from my palms. Yet, they are not blue-ghosts; they are projections. Dozens of lifelike memories—relived again—memories I never had.

While I speed through the forest on Goliath's back, near home, my dad shouts for me to go faster—to shoot this-target, to jump over that-branch—and sometimes to swing a long blade, while shielding against magic shot from his hands.

Time and again, I fall on every jump off Goliath's back, landing with ribs cracking against tree bark; with every swing, I miss; on each attack, the shield breaks.

At each projection's end, my father heals me of all wounds. Then I hear it—the explanation—my father gripping my face, saying, "One day, Tyler, you'll remember all this, when you get to Muraine with Gemma Galloway. I hope you can forgive me, for making you forget."

At once, all are gone, to be replaced by a single quiet memory in his study. He is asking, "Are you angry that I never told you of magic? That I lied for twelve years?"

My ghost replies, "You told me, yourself. That's what counts."

"What if I were to tell you of magic unknown to Earth?"

"There's more besides Earth?"

"Muraine," he says. "Where I was born and raised. You'll make it there. Eventually. But first, I need you to do something for me."

"Anything," replies my ghost of the past, as my hands pass through him in the here-and-now.

After setting the dragon-wolf journal in front of my ghost, my father opens the cover, speaking, "Read this. If you can."

The harder I fight to hold onto the memory before me, the more my vision blurs.

From the sea of gazes, Ryco's is all I distinguish.

Yet, surprisingly, he does not look to me.

Instead, with cold malice, he looks to my father.

The magic now erased from my hand, I collapse.

All fades to the pure-black canvas of unconsciousness.

19

The Art of Mensa-Div

Voices—although muffled—are concerned. Others are angry. All fade into recognition, but the one I understand first is Zepharre, seething, "When's he going to wake up? In three days? How could you let him go in there?"

Ryco states, "We didn't *let* him go in."

"It was that menace, Awngeleik," adds Musgrae. "Playing one of her pranks."

"He could've died of that prank," states EmiKal. "And why didn't she have her cloak on?"

"Irrelevant," interrupts Zepharre. "She only needs it on, when she leaves the city. Or before the looming of an attack. Quall! You and the guard are to find an effective means of confining her for the festival. I don't want more trouble. Understood?"

"Yes. I'll see to it right—" Quall starts to say.

But then I begin sitting up from a mattress of sorts, surrounded—more like smothered—by a mountain of pillows and sheets on a carved bed. I halfway expect to still be covered in Nyrim's blood. I've been washed clean of it, however.

"Tyler!" Quall rushes to me. "Someone get Talok."

Warren paces for the door, but Ryco stops him with, "No need. He's already headed back with Gemma."

Quall places his hand on my core, then my head and wrists, saying, "You've taken quite a beating. But where does it hurt?"

"Everywhere," says Gemma, as she waltzes into the room holding a cup and water pitcher colored of hematite—charcoal, sangria, teal, green, and gold—all metallic. Only tinkling of ice-cubes give away their structure of glass.

Struggling for words, I utter to Quall, "Head. Hands. Just a dull ache everywhere else."

"Just?" Gemma shakes her head. "Your wounds were as bad as Arkivy Nyrim's."

"Then where are the wounds?" I ask.

Hands clasped, Ben steps forward. "Quall and I healed you. Repaired your Mazhrein a little too."

"Although," adds Quall, "we couldn't heal you, to this level of recovery. Your magic system did some on its own."

"How long have I been out?"

"Three hours," states Talok, from the doorway. Relief etched on his face, he strides to me. "Though, we expected it to be three days."

"Three hours wasted in bed? How much longer, before I can get ready for the festival?"

At the foot of my bed, Talok sits with disbelief in his eyes; meanwhile, Gemma sets down the pitcher on a bedside table, after pouring sparkling water into the glass. Then Quall replies, "That's entirely up to your body and Mazhrein."

Siege smiles. "If you're up for it, try on the new clothes."

Warren rolls his eyes, saying, "Madeleine insisted on delivering them."

"Even though it was unlikely you'd make it to the festival tonight," pipes in Eli.

Quall hisses, "Will the three of you stop stealing what I'm going to say?"

Amusement gleaming in his eyes, Talok dips his head toward the table and chairs. Nestled on the table are crisp charcoal and fossil-gray colored clothes. On one of the chairs rest black boots, bracers, and leather lace. Beyond them, a bay window overlooks the Eye of Paragon from the castle's third floor.

Gemma holds out the glass, proclaiming, "Water for Nyrim's Hero?"

Groaning, I accept the water and say, "I'm already someone's hero? Great."

"Glad you are well, Tyler," Zepharre absently says. "You'll forgive us for leaving. We've other matters to attend. Quall, don't forget to—"

"I won't," replies Quall firmly.

I lift a hand in goodbye, while taking a sip of water to soothe my parched mouth. As he and EmiKal are about to leave, the door smashes into Zepharre, and back he goes into the unmovable wall of Ryco and Musgrae. Then, in hastens a fair-skinned woman with hair like a sunset. To Talok, her juniper-green gaze fastens. But Zepharre just smooths his coat and leads EmiKal out without so much as a nod to her.

Talok stares at the floor—oblivious to the commotion behind—while winding his hands over each other like someone lathering soap.

Oddly comforting is the woman's musical voice calling out, "King Talok! Arkivy Grover said I could find you in your bedroom. However, he didn't warn of your entourage."

"Rorka!" exclaims Talok, snapping from his trance. He strides to hug her tight—as a son would his long-lost mother—saying, "You made it."

Rorka, standing eye-to-eye with him, pulls back. "Jasper sent me out this morning. Said to hurry. Is all well in Paragon? Sadness cloaks this city more than the days after the Great LanSoren perished."

Head shaking away the shadows, Talok says, "Tell you about it later. Meet my cousin, Tyler Ravier. Only been here half a day and, already, he's saved our Nyrim of Yharss."

A wide smile is on Rorka's petite face, as she comes to shake my hand. When I take the hand of introduction, something tugs at me like the birthday card from Aunt Miriam. *Vanquished happiness? A love lost? Arising sadness? What is this feeling?*

Panic flits across Rorka's features. Still, feelings persist. And thoughts continue like a rushing-river down a mountain, echoing, *I know you, but I have never spoken to you. Familiar as my own face staring back at me. How can that be?*

Surprised by something as well, Rorka withdraws her hand, saying, "Already? King Talok found the time to teach you the Art of Mensa-div? Mind-Converse. I am astonished."

Intent on her, I state, "No one taught me anything. The words? They hint that you knew my father. That you were familiar?"

She swerves around the bed, to plod to the bay window. "I never had the pleasure of meeting LanSoren of Trauvo," she declares.

"You weren't missing much," says Ryco, under his breath.

Ignoring him, Rorka faces me. "If seeing him in the distance—as I was leaving Pariah on assignment, or as he was riding for home—is knowing him? Then I knew him exceedingly well."

"He avoided meeting you?"

"Alpha Jasper laughed at the notion. Said I was imagining LanSoren's meticulous avoidance. Claimed it was pure chance we kept missing each other. Still." She wets her lips.

Offering her my water, I ask, "What happened?"

Back she plods to accept it. Wiping where my lips touched the glass, she takes a gulp, before admitting, "Thirteen times, I devised a way to ensure our meeting each other."

Focusing on Rorka, then the colored glass, I clear my mind to project a thought to her. An emotion: *You're angry.*

Brows contorting, she continues. "Thirteen times. Something always came up. For the Paragonians. The Greyvons. Him. Me."

Crush the glass in your hand, my thoughts command.

In her tight grip, the glass shatters, and its sharp shards cut her hand. In sucks a breath, as I blink away the sudden fatigue.

Rorka, gasping, then bending down to pick up the shards, says, "Forgive my frustration."

"I'll clean it up, once I rid myself of all this resting in bed."

"If you're a Greyvon?" interrupts Gemma. "Why don't you look like a wolf?"

"Meta-Morfeis: Transformation Magic," replies Rorka, dropping the shards in distraction.

Ben, strolling to Rorka, pulls a vial from one of his pouches, then grips her hand to sprinkle the glittering-liquid onto her cuts.

Meanwhile, she continues, "We're taught as Vonsai, or rather, teenagers. Don't master it until adulthood. Perfected mine three years ago."

Testing who can hear my thoughts, I let one slip out. *Makes blending in with Paragonians and Sorsryns a bit easier.*

When all remain as they were—no flinching or remarks—I know my thoughts are safe for now, and I continue them, *Could she be the Phantom of Muraine? How to get everyone out of here, before they take away the shards?*

"How long," I ask, "before the start of the festival?"

"Two hours," replies Musgrae, "until the pre-festival events; three until dusk. When the real show begins."

Looking to Talok, I announce, "I'm ready to try on those clothes."

"Right!" Talok claps once. "Everyone out. If you need help, Tyler, I'll be at the door."

* * *

A while later, I sigh at the mirror's reflection, wishing that all-black looked back at me. Instead, it's a scaly vest of fossil-gray cloth sporting a standing-collar and five offset, angled buckles. Except for the arms, it hides the upper half of my diving armor. Next are the charcoal-gray pants with diagonal black-stitches adding depth over the plain fabric. Below each knee, the top of the black boots stop. And securing their laces are six metal, charcoal-colored buttons. Molded onto these is the same symbol as Talok's coat buttons.

From between the folds of the coat still on the table, I grab one of the pouches and drop a bloodied glass shard into it, then amble to the unreflecting black chest.

Along its sides are fluid symbols and graceful animals carved in a horizontal-wave. On the center of its top, four golden triangles rise upward to create a shallow pyramid. In each section is a different map view of Earth: north-south, east-west.

I open the creaking lid to reveal my duffle, the notes, picture frame, and other remaining items tucked inside. Except for the dragon-wolf journal and diving armor, everything's there. Even still, I count them: *three items for the locked box, three journals, and two armors; The Dark Prince, number map, and Muraine's map; daggers, gloves, and a key.*

"Fourteen," I whisper, while rubbing my forehead. "One too many. What isn't supposed to be counted? If the maps don't count, then I'm still missing an item."

Riffling through the contents, I take out the small pouch restraining Ryco's enchanted letter and the five phantom notes, then close the lid. Over the shallow pyramid, I sweep my hand, thinking, *This has to be thirteen. Why else be this ornate, if it's just meant to hold everything?*

As I'm tucking the papers into another pouch on the table, Talok's head pokes in. "Tyler? How's it coming?"

"Just need the coat." I smile and lift the mishap of separated pieces. "But Madeleine forgot something."

His mouth briefly gaping, Talok laughs. "She didn't finish lacing it? Poor Madeleine. When she heard the news, she was beside herself with worry."

Together, we lace black-cording through both tops of the shoulder and down the sleeve seams, but stop at the cuffs ending in a wide 'V.' Next, we attach the two bottom pieces with the coat's core, and form the front and back belt-line in the process.

All finished, Talok softens his gaze—admiring Madeleine's artistry—saying, "She gave you the Sleeping Dragon. Look." He points to the contours formed by the multi-shades of charcoal, fossil, and white, then continues, "The white strips are the closed eyelids. And the light-gray, along the lacing contours, forms the face."

I grin. "Definitely makes up for it not being all black."

Talok teasingly nudges my shoulder. "I'll tell her you loved it."

"I'll tell her myself," I state, while standing to slip the coat on with Talok's help.

Except for the side and front belt line, Talok tightens the cording all the way. Slipping a belt through one wide loop at the back, and adding the two pouches in the process, he proceeds to weave it in with the slack cording, before saying, "She left room for you to grow into it. But the fit's good. What do you think?"

I fiddle, first, with the hood, then inspect the rest of the coat. Curving into six points is the coat's bottom hemline. At the open front, two are adjacent—one on each side. Farther apart than the front points are two separated by the back's split center.

"Not too big," I state. "Not too small. Overall? It's perfect."

"Wonderful!" Talok beams. "Want to go—"

I interrupt, saying, "With everyone gone, there are some things I need to know."

The happiness darkens to shadows on Talok's face. "I was wondering how long it would take you."

"Guess I'll start by asking you the most nagging one." After pulling the picture from my duffle, I sit down and set it on the table. "Can you tell me who the people are, in this?"

Tears reddening his eyes, Talok bites back the quiver of his chin, then finally replies, "That was taken the same year she died." His fingers trace over the frame, then he picks it up lovingly—even longingly—like my mother's gaze on the bed's empty space that night of my deception.

"Then that's your mother?" I ask.

"And me, at five years," adds Talok, grinning weakly. "My father too, and Grover, irate with Uncle LanSoren for making him wear that wizard hat; took twelve shots, for Uncle LanSoren to be satisfied with it."

For a moment, we laugh together and share our favorite memories. Then we go silent, before I ask the hard question, "You're sure she's dead?"

Mournfully, he nods. "I watched her being carried out—by the Emerald Sorsryns—on an engraved silver-and-gold sheet of metal. The night before she died, she gave Ryco a lock of her hair; asked him to help me make flowers out of it, for placing in her hands after her passing. But before people could pay respect, during the Promenade of Death."

"You don't have to … continue, if you don't want to."

Sitting across from me, Talok sets the picture down, replying, "Actually, it feels good to talk about it. But I've a question, Tyler, why does this picture nag at you?"

"Because I get birthday cards from Aunt Miriam, every year."

Stunned at the news, Talok leans back into his chair, saying, "That *is* odd."

"If she isn't Miriam, who do you think she might be?"

Talok puffs out the whale-breath, before deducing, "*She* could actually be a *he*. Unless you've met or conversed with her."

"I haven't, but my mom's talked to her on the phone. Miriam was at their wedding too. Although, it probably *was* your mom, in those pictures."

"Most likely," Talok agrees. "Do you have one of the cards with you?"

"In my duffle." I go to retrieve it, but Talok is already snapping his fingers. In his hand, it appears. Instead of opening it, however, he just tilts his head and studies the front.

"Her writing's on the inside," I tease.

"Funny, Cousin! I was thinking that the colors—black and green, silver and white—they're clan colors of the Emerald Sorsryns."

"That could narrow down who the Miriam impersonator is," I state.

"You read my mind. Not literally, though. My Mensenglos is too good for you."

"Mensenglos?" I ask.

"Mind Block," says Talok, while pulling the card out of the envelope. "I should put up that protection spell on you and Gemma. But … Musgrae asked me to hold off."

"Why's that?"

"Because." Talok laughs. "It's hysterical hearing Gemma's thoughts, especially around Ben." Talok mischievously glances up, then continues, "She's in love with his accent. The result? Ben talks. More than we've *ever* heard him talk. He's getting snarky with Musgrae too. And we *love* it!"

"She's crushing on Ben?"

"Naw!" Talok shrugs. "It's infatuation. She's been wondering, though, what a kiss would feel like. From one of us. Eli was about to do it too. That's when I had to ask Gemma to go to the kitchen with me—before Quall strangled Eli in *this* very room."

"So that's what happened, while I was sleeping?"

"Among other things. Now! Back to this card. The writing's nothing like my mother's."

"You would recognize the penmanship after what, eleven years?"

"Not eleven," replies Talok. "When she knew she was dying, my mother wrote letters to me. Forty letters. Every year, I was given one by LanSoren. On my birthday. Whatever day that is. I don't keep track, but everyone else does."

"What about now? Who gives you the letters?"

"Quall." Talok sighs. "I'll be getting letters from her, until I'm forty-five years old. So long as I don't die before then."

"Are you in *that* much danger?"

"With Vitiosyns thriving, everyone's in danger. But after the attack on Yharss and Dysarda, they *are* required by Onyx law to give us a lull."

"A breath before the storm," I state.

In reply, Talok nods. "With any luck, though, we'll be the storm, rather than the ones fighting it. As for the cards, perhaps the one sending them was asked, by Uncle LanSoren, to look after you and your mother."

I add, "As a safeguard."

"Sure! I wouldn't worry too much over it."

"Even if it's likely she has a Vardiya-Stone that was my dad's?"

"That's different." Talok briefly squeezes his eyes shut. "I'm not sure what to do with that bit of information, except tell Quall and Zepharre. If you want, I can ask them to draw up a list of candidates too."

"Candidates for?"

"To go back home with you and Gemma; find out what's going on over there."

"After everything I've seen, I'd like that. Whoever comes with us, maybe they can figure out who keeps leaving random notes for me everywhere too."

"Notes?" Talok groans. "You mean, there's more than the Miriam cards?" He momentarily palms his forehead, saying, "I don't know if I can take more right now. Can't we talk about it tonight. After the festival?" Talok pleads.

"Sure." I shrug. "I've only waited fourteen years, but we can wait until tonight."

"Way to make me feel bad, Cousin Tyler. But if you had to suffer through a Sovereignty meeting absent of Quall. With Zepharre, EmiKal, and Ryco at each other's throats through most it … you would understand the struggle."

"Good point. Think you can get Ben on the list?"

"Ben of Yharss?" queries Talok. "Although a good choice, he's not experienced enough for an extended stay on Earth. But give him a few years. And, I dare say, his skill set will exceed half the guard."

"I bet you're right."

Talok rubs at his jaw a moment, before asking, "Shall we go down to Kent and the others? He had to wait for the critical survivors to be treated first. Quall tells me they're still getting splinters out of him from a box shattered by your blast of wind."

Gulping down a bit of uneasiness, I motion. "Lead the way."

Down winding corridors and stairs, Talok leads me. But when Kent's cries of agony ricochet down the wide hallway, he slows his pace.

Quall shouts, "Kent! Stop fighting me. You're only making it take longer."

"Look at it, Kent," Musgrae teases. "You birthed a little baby splinter. Isn't it cute?"

Skin smacking skin signals the slap Musgrae received, as Talok and I enter the castle infirmary to Kent's seething, "I'll tell you what you can do with that splinter, Musgrae."

As Quall extracts another pocketknife-sized splinter from Kent's bare chest, Kent yells at Musgrae, "I hope a dragon shoves his tail—"

Musgrae interrupts with, "Ryco! Imagine what you could do, if you had a tail."

By the infirmary entrance, Ryco leans against the wall with his arms crossed, saying, "I'll thank you to leave me out of it." Then he notices me, and a flicker of a smirk struggles to the surface.

I toil in sending a thought to him, as I did with Rorka. This time, however, it's for conversation. *Still think magic is hard on me?*

Arms uncrossing, Ryco eases off the wall, echoing, *Arrogance. You got lucky.*

What secrets did my father keep? Tell me!

Ryco, drawing a finger across his mouth, looks on at Kent, still squirming on the curved examination table. Splinter by particle, Quall removes them from Kent's chest and arms. Meanwhile, Musgrae attempts to distract Kent with horrendous one-liners. Then Ryco echoes, *Guess his belongings didn't help. Did they? Or you would know the answer to your own question. How'd the headache go?*

Heat creeping to my face, I echo one word: *Sadist!*

I've been called worse.

Like Parasogyn? You going to send me to join him in the grave, for that arrogance?

Faintly, Ryco huffs, echoing, *You don't even know where his real grave is. No one does, except Arkivy Eishal of Trauvo. When I track down that grave, I'll consider putting you in it.*

Sitting up, Kent grabs Quall's arm. "I know you want to spare me the immense pain, Quall—unlike Matron Avilon—but there's not enough left, to make me pass out from blood loss, if … you rip them out all at once, is there?"

At that moment, Gemma waltzes in with mud already speckling her black boots. Through diagonal cutouts of her walnut-colored leggings, the diving armor shows. And giving shape to her thin figure are the sides of purple and walnut-brown scales on her new coat of navy velvet. She twirls once, asking Talok, "What do you think?"

"Superb," he whispers in admiration, but whether for her or Madeleine's artistry is unclear.

Quall crosses his arms, replying to Kent, "You'll be dizzy for an hour."

"I can handle that." Kent bobs his head. "What I can't handle are Musgrae's insufferable utterings. I want to shout insults that should make me blush. I don't like this angry version of myself."

"That's the pain talking." Warren simpers. "Hurts like a Dragon's Spike."

"Not helping," seethes Quall, scowling at Warren.

To Gemma, I state, "That's not a dress."

"I know. Changed my mind. Wanted something more practical."

Meanwhile, Ryco steps forward, and aims one of his hands at Kent. Upon fingers of the Sadist snapping, all remaining splinters rip themselves free of Kent's flesh to splatter the victim and the healer with more blood.

"Ryco!" Kent shouts, flopping back to the table. "Couldn't find it in your heart to warn me?"

Sadist grin making an appearance, Ryco says, "A 'thank you, Ryco' will do just fine."

Kent just burns his gaze into Ryco. Quall relinquishes his place to Ben, to clean off the blood, letting the rookie heal Kent with glowing magic and murky creams. After a few minutes, a contented sigh escapes Kent, and he wipes sweat off his brow.

With the sigh, comes Musgrae's quaking shoulders, and patronizing words of, "All this labor, Kent. Where's the little Vaegon baby to carry on the legacy?"

Kent's face reddens to rage, his torso jolts up, and his head almost collides with Ben's. Pointing at Musgrae, Kent fumes, "That was six years ago! I had to petition my own father. Of all Vaegons. Begging that I be spared from the draft of fathering some child I'll never know."

"Wait," says Musgrae. "Some Vaegon girl could have your child and you'd never know it?"

Kent clarifies, "If I didn't have an eligible Vaegon partner—at the time draft children are needed—the young would go to an available family in Paragon."

"Were you a draft baby?" queries Musgrae.

"Mooz-grae," Ryco interrupts, "we can discuss the complexities of the Vaegons another time. For now, go assist Siege and Eli with Awngeleik."

"But Awngeleik despises me."

"That's because somebody"—Warren tilts his head to Musgrae—"stepped on her, while she was sleeping like a peaceful, baby EquiNein."

"The baby horses are so cute," slurs Kent, while his head sways. He falls to the table, saying, "This is the worst day I've had, since joining the guard."

Musgrae, pinching at his own neck, says, "At least I didn't shoot her wing with an arrow."

Calmly, Ryco states, "She got in the way of a good shot. It was too late to retrieve it."

"Who knew one creature could be so reckless," says Talok, his eyes widening to drink in much light.

"Least she hasn't topped Khyra's recklessness," states Warren, picking at his nails.

"Did you talk to her, King Talok?" queries Ryco, as if bored.

Talok startles. "You were serious about me having that talk with Khyra?"

Ryco lifts a brow. "Am I ever *not* serious?"

"Why me? Her parents made you her guardian, while they're away."

"I've tried, but she's your friend. She'll listen to you."

"Not true," corrects Talok. "Khyra listens to no one except her parents, when they're here. You, sometimes. But always for Uncle LanSoren."

"Khyra doesn't seem reckless," states Gemma.

"Not reckless?" Eli struts into the infirmary. "She's a walking disaster. Interrupted our training sessions, with her daredevil moments. Got my arm broken, once, because of her."

Following him in is Siege, raising a hand. "Broken nose for me."

Warren huffs, "Don't forget that time-distortion I was stuck in for three days. Took Siveyra Gyron and his warriors to get me out. Had nightmares for days, afterwards."

His head still in a daze, Kent slurs, "Ben's was the worst."

"Worse. How?" I ask.

Ben shudders, but allows Warren to tell the story, "During his second to last competition to be the next: Eighth of the Guard. He got his neck half-severed, because of Khyra's incessant need to show off her Gendras to Ryco."

Shocked, Gemma's mouth drops open. "Is that the real reason you stopped asking her on, you know?" She looks at Ben.

Musgrae bursts out, "You asked her seven times, Ben? On a Dragon Ride. Why's this the first I'm hearing of it? From Mud Fiend, no less."

Confusion furrowing her brow, Gemma mumbles, "I didn't say that out loud, did I?"

To Musgrae, Ryco replies, "Because you're too busy chasing a dozen women, on your days off."

"At least they're not little girls who fancy themselves in love with me."

"Infatuation," hisses Ryco, "and love are two different things."

"But their outcomes can be the same," states Musgrae victoriously.

"Here we go again," groans Quall, with his pale face turning to that special shade of angry-red.

Dazed, but sitting up, Kent blinks at me. "What was it like, Tyler? Watching Talok tame Ryco?"

All attention turns to Kent.

"Tame?" I ask. "What do you mean?"

"Ryco's part dragon," slurs Kent. "Vaegons are Dragon Tamers. Was it like watching a whipped Greyvon dog sink to the ground?"

Talok shouts, "Kent! You can't say things like that!"

"I told you," booms Warren, "it's the pain talking."

Kent queries, "What's Talok told you?"

"Not much." I smile. "Only half makes sense."

Though he says nothing, Talok playfully wrinkles his nose at me.

Side to side, Kent's head bobbles like a drunken fool. Then out slurs, "I swearrr … part o Alec's mind ceases, when anxious."

Gemma bites her lip, trying her best not to laugh.

Whale-breath turning to a hurricane, Talok states, "He's not himself. We should give him space—time to rest."

Before any can agree or object, Callie of Dysarda ambles into the fray holding a bouquet of eleven elegant blue, black, and white flowers. As worry creases her face, she queries, "Is Master Kent all right?"

Daze lifting some, Kent nods.

"Callie of Dysarda." Talok motions to Kent. "Meet your Kent: Third of the Guard. He'll be fine in a little while."

Shyness creeps into Callie's mysterious eyes, when she looks at Kent, still healing from his splinter wounds. "Your father," she says, "the honorable

Arkivy Lokasi, said I would find you here. Told me your mother's favorite flowers too. Thought they might bring you comfort."

Kent takes the offered bouquet to smell them. Then, with his slur gone, he says, "Midnight Anemones. Quite pretty. She would love them."

Holding her wrist awkwardly, Callie queries, "Your mother … was she in Dysarda, when they attacked?"

"Not a chance," replies Kent. "After my little sister passed, she and my father separated. Last I heard, she was with some Sorsryn bent on exploring Muraine. Wherever they are, I'm sure it's far from the reach of Vitiosyns."

"I'm glad to have finally met you, Kent of Dysarda. It's a name almost as famous in our city as LanSoren of Trauvo and Arkivy Lokasi."

"King Talok tells me that your parents sent you ahead, and you fear for their safety. More survivors should be arriving. Better go to the city gate. Your face should be the first they see."

Hugging Kent around the neck, Callie whispers, "Thank you, Master Kent. You've given me hope that I'll see them again."

As she pulls away from him, I state, "Waiting alone sucks. Want me to go with you?"

"I'd like that." She gives a small smile, saying, "See you all tonight." With that, she curtsies once to the guards and then to Talok.

Meanwhile, Gemma whispers to me, "I'll stay here. Fill you in on what you miss. Nyrim might be out of the Arkivara by now. Keep an eye out for him?"

"Will do."

Callie heads for the doorway; I turn to go with her. But Musgrae stops me—with his grip on my shoulder—saying, "Madeleine gave *you* the Sleeping Dragon? I wanted that design. She wouldn't tell me who got it. Thought it might be Ryco or Zepharre." Eyes calming, Musgrae releases me. "Guess I can live with you having it. Be gone with you." He waves me away. "Before I steal it, then have Ben resize it for me."

"I would do no such thing," mutters Ben.

As the banters starts, I pull Callie away to make our escape.

"Are they always like that?" queries Callie.

"Don't know." I shrug. "Just got here today."

"Really? You don't live here?"

"It's a long story. Tell me about yourself. Your parents. The festival. Anything you like."

Exiting the Castle of Sosha, we stroll down the thirteen steps and then amble on the winding path leading to the city gate.

"This is my first festival," Callie admits. "As for my parents … While I'm not very close to my mum, my father has taught me to love the beauty of everything around me. Even when I don't quite understand it all. His patience with me is unending. His love like an eternal flame."

"You're very poetic." I smile. "Can't wait to meet him. Your mom too."

When she hooks her arm with mine, her cold Geldryn bracelet presses against my skin. And I can't stop the coming echo, speaking, *Fire. Water. Air. Land. How to break their laws?*

"You bought the Geldryn bracelet?" I ask, but she shakes her head.

"The shopkeeper heard us talking—that I'm from Dysarda. Insisted I take something free of charge and trade. Does it look good on me?"

Gripping her wrist, I inspect the bracelet closer. In the sunlight, the jewels of blue, green, and turquoise sparkle, and more echoes speak, *Soul. Wake. Prison. Blood. Who can truly wield the keys?* I release her wrist, saying, "It matches your eyes. I'm almost jealous of them."

"Says he with the greenest eyes I've ever seen. Bet you're gifted in Gendras."

Strange thoughts gone for now, I ask, "Eye color determines giftedness?"

"Not always. But it can hint at it."

"Good to know. What do yours mean?"

"Fiddler of entirety. Master of naught." Callie sighs. "My father tells me, one day, I'll master the greatest magic of all."

"What magic is that?"

"Geldryn."

"Talok or Grover mentioned it," I state. "Didn't say it's the strongest magic, though."

"You should call them King Talok and Arkivy Grover; they deserve that honor. As for greatness, one can control skies with Geldryn: Wind racing over land. Clouds streaming through sky. The Rainfall, Snowfall, and Thunder bolts too. Individual Gendras spells exist for all of these, but Geldryn ones last longer. Once cast, its master can move their focus to other spells."

"Bet that takes years to learn."

"Decades," Callie corrects. "Unless you have genetics on your side. You or I can't hold enough magic in our Mazhreins, to cast even one Geldryn spell."

"Are you ever accused of being ambitious?"

"All the time." She smiles.

"Then you're in good company."

She nods, before matching my stride. "Now you know more about me. Your turn. Where are you from? The place where you got those odd clothes you no longer wear."

"Odd clothes?" I laugh, then say, "On another world—Earth—very different from here."

"I heard rumors in Dysarda that LanSoren of Trauvo had a far-off family. Didn't know you would be my age, though."

"Grover said I should be twenty-three. But time passes differently, where I'm from."

"How very strange," says Callie, while gazing to the city gate. In the distance, waves of survivors are pouring in: limping, battered, cut, or maimed.

Glancing around for Nyrim, I ask, "Do you want me to stay with you, while you look?"

Tears threatening to spill over, Callie nods weakly.

So … I've no choice, really, but to continue following at her side, as she leads the way through the fray of survivors.

20

Magically Bound

Dusk looming at the tree-line of Paragon, Callie and I wander on the path lit by hundreds of campfires. Adding to the light of celebration are Paragonians chanting, singing, or humming. Adults cook an array of vivid foods in iron pots. Adolescents manipulate the campfire flames into shapes or creatures, attempting to entertain. And the children clap and dance to the rhythm of it all.

After nudging Callie's shoulder, I glance at her. "Sorry we didn't find them. Maybe they'll show tomorrow."

"I will hold to that hope," she whispers, as Musgrae and Kent's banter drifts to us.

"Found them," I state.

We approach the camp-circle of Talok, Gemma, and six King's Guard—absent of Quall and Warren. Within their circle are two small fires, as Gemma looks to Talok, asking, "Have you ever cooked anything?"

"Uncle LanSoren once said my cooking's only fit for the palate of a dyn. Since my father never pressed the matter—saying I could learn when I was older—I had no reason to continue the endeavor."

"You can't be too awful," I state. "What do dragons like, besides Farivoo Eldyn?"

Ben replies, "Rocks, dirt, burnt trees. Creatures cooked beyond recognition. Not very appetizing. Or creative." He wrinkles his nose.

Talok rolls his eyes, saying, "Thank you, Ben. I'm *so* confident in my cooking now."

I state, "He needs lessons with Molly Smith."

"Agreed," says Gemma. "That stew needs a bit of her love. You find Nyrim?"

Looking around for a spot, I simply reply, "No."

"Take mine, Tyler," offers Siege, easing out of his seat next to Ryco.

I reluctantly take it, as Siege sits between Kent and Musgrae.

"Any luck, Little Callie?" queries Kent, with a pleasant grin.

Callie wobbles her head, and sinks to the ground at Talok's feet. Sniffling some, she leans back against his small wooden seat.

Musgrae, suddenly interested in whatever Ryco's doing, bolts up. He then goes to plop down next to Ryco's other side. "Why are you carving? Isn't that what Gendras is for?"

Knife in one hand, wood piece in the other, Ryco shaves away bits of wood. "In order to create or shape something with Gendras," he says, "first, one must know how to make it without magic."

Musgrae snickers. "I love the image of you staring at trees, sitting there, doing nothing but watching them grow."

Down goes the carving from Ryco's grasp, as he cracks his knuckles. Proceeding to run his knife-edge across a raised and parallel cylinder on his bracer, he grates metal on metal. At the sound, Musgrae cringes. Ryco digs it in harder. Resonating is the metallic-shrill sending fleeting pain over me, and left is a wake of goose bumps on my skin. Not fairing much better, Musgrae's rendered speechless.

Then an ax head slams down into the plank beside Musgrae.

Warren booms, "Too unobservant." Removing ax from the plank, he adds, "Could've had you right on the neck."

Before Warren finishes his lecturing of Musgrae, in strides Quall, carrying a satchel, to the camp-circle like a child receiving gifts.

"Hey, hey," croons Eli, running to Quall's side. "Anyone want Quall's herbs?"

Quall smacks at Eli's grabby hands. "Want some? Go pick your own! You greedy little Kirjan."

"Not everyone in Kirja's greedy," corrects Eli, a pout painting across his face. "Only the merchants."

"Are they like drugs?" queries Gemma.

Most certainly offended, Eli gawks at her.

"I mean the herbs, not merchants." Gemma cringes, rubbing her forehead. "Tyler? Want some drugs?"

"Drugs?"—Quall furrows his brow—"I don't know this word." ·

"They're not like drugs on Earth," says Ryco, carving on the wood piece again.

"How would you know?" queries Musgrae.

"First-World Medical Studies," states Ryco smoothly. "The course you failed four times."

"What can I say? I'm built for beatings," Musgrae brags. "These hands weren't meant for delicate work with a needle or syringe." Neck-pinching briefly, Musgrae adds, "You had to take that course, didn't you? Because your White Magic sucks."

When the Sadist-citrine gaze flicks to Musgrae, the charging bull retreats back to Kent and Siege.

That's when Gemma asks, "Quall, why do you take these herbs?"

Cutting off Quall, Siege replies, "To test their effects for powders and tonics. What else?"

"I was about to say," states Quall firmly, "to alter my mood, depending on the need."

"What do they do?" queries Gemma. "Wait! I want to guess."

"You mean cheat?" I tease.

"What are you going to do?" Gemma glares. "Regulate how much luck I use in games?"

Grinning wickedly, I reply, "Would if I could."

One by one, Quall hands Gemma pouches from the satchel.

"Smells like … sleepiness," she says as her first guess.

"Close. Relaxation," states Quall, replacing it with another.

"Sadness."

"Contemplation," he corrects.

"Rage," hisses Gemma for her third.

"Resolution."

Exhaling a breathy sigh, Gemma tries, "Dreamy," for her fourth.

And Quall chuckles, saying, "Dreamy works. Brings out the beauty in things."

Gemma guesses her fifth with, "Hallucinations?"

"Past memories."

"But no hallucinations?" she presses.

"Well … once, when Warren added Blue Magic—"

Defensively, Warren interrupts, "It was my rookie year. How was I to know Musgrae was joking?"

Unfazed, Quall continues, "I saw memories played out, as if they were happening again. Started calling it *The Arkivara Blend*."

When Gemma's eyes brighten, Quall takes the pouches away. "No, Miss Gemma. You're not allowed to have that one. Not until your Mazhrein has matured."

"Like Tyler's?" queries Gemma enviously.

"His Mazhrein has *not* matured," states Ryco. Now inspecting his carving of a wolf, he slips his knife into its bracer sheath, adding, "It's only just begun."

He tosses Gemma the carving, and she catches it, asking him, "Why a wolf?"

"Your aura. It's closer to that of a Greyvon than a Rubidyn."

"Aura?"—Gemma's face contorts in confusion—"What do you mean?"

Staring into the fire, Ryco thinks a moment.

But Kent clears his throat to say, "What our dear Ryco means, and I'll say for him—so he doesn't make a complete dragon's tail of himself—is that dragons, whether they've just breathed their first breath or taken their last, are powerful creatures. Anyone giving off their aura is powerful. Always will be. Without question."

I ask, "What does that have to do with the wolf?"

"The dragon's wolf counter-balance," Kent explains, "is weaker, almost frail, at birth. In time, they strengthen. But their power is in their cunning ways: meticulous and manipulative, logical and restrained, until the perfect moment when they can crush their enemies."

Ryco admits, "I'm not sure I meant all that, Kent, but you get the idea."

"Gemma." I laugh. "They hardly know you, but already, they've got you pegged right."

"Shut up, Tyler," says Gemma, fighting a smile.

Talok points to the wolf-carving, adding, "All auras lead to Greyvon or Rubidyn. Whether they're snake, horse, stag, or whatever. If you look hard enough, they can be traced back to one of the two; although, I've never understood why."

I ask, "Has anyone ever had both?"

Footsteps approach from behind, and Siveyra Gyron answers, "Prince Setharyn of the Onyx did, but he died over a thousand years ago. By means of Vitiosus, no less."

"Siveyra Gyron." Talok brightens. "Sit with us a while. Have some food. I'm working on a stew, to serve at the Arkiveis Supper tomorrow."

Suddenly anxious, Quall pauses from sipping his brewed herbs.

Gyron sits in the grass beside Talok. Motioning to the Onyx Warriors behind, he replies, "Since there's none to be had in Paragon, we had our fill of meat before coming."

Quall quietly sighs in relief, before resuming his herb-sipping. Silently, he occupies himself with watching the banter of Ryco's Black Coats. Leaning against Musgrae's shoulder, Kent sits napping. A few shoulders down, Ben scowls at Musgrae painting some black-ink on Kent's face.

"Musgrae," Ben hisses, "Kent's going to explode, when he sees his face."

"Yes! Won't it be epic?" replies Musgrae, continuing the face painting.

Meanwhile, I ask Gyron, "What's the origin of Vitiosus? Why's it so dark?"

"Go linger." Gyron waves his warriors away, before saying, "Vitiosus is an evil magic. Corrupts the heart far quicker than the dark ones of Black and Death."

"There's no counteract for it?" I ask.

"That we know of? No," replies Gyron.

The image of Soren's projection in my father's study flashes, and uneasiness sinks into the pit of my stomach. "Can a split or fractured personality be a symptom?" I ask.

Gyron queries, "Are you worried for someone, Tyler Ravier?"

Ben shifts in his seat, saying, "We saw a projection of LanSoren on Earth. With Vitiosyn-eyes. At least, they looked the same."

All attention turns to us, as Gyron states, "While he was on his deathbed, LanSoren's blood was tested by the Greyvons and Onyx. There weren't any signs of Vitiosus. Not sure what else could have caused that symptom."

Fiddling with my sleeve lacing, I add, "There was someone else with him too. Soren of the Monel."

"Soren?" Gyron gawks at me, asking, "Of the Monel? What do you know of him?"

Heart pounding, I ask, "What do *you* know?"

He starts to answer, but flinches in pain. "I am magically bound not to say," he declares. "You'll have to ask King ReNovak. Now." He looks to Gemma, then me, demanding, "Tell what you know. Both of you."

I hold his gaze, speaking, "I'm not inclined to tell. Neither is she. Who's to say the Onyx won't be an enemy of Paragon tomorrow?"

"Fair enough," Gyron concedes.

"But this 'magically bound' issue," I state. "Grover claimed to be bound, when asked about the differences between Sorshrynaks and Sorsryns. Can you say why?"

"You will find, Mr. Ravier, that magically-binding spells are tricky to outsmart. Especially for the Onyx. We are held by and uphold ancient laws of magic and warfare: The Rules of Engagement. If you want to know more, as I said, ask King ReNovak."

"This King ReNovak, is he coming tonight?"

"Briefly. Yes."

In reply, I nod. "Since it's unlikely you're allowed to translate a journal—written in ancient Sorsrynian—are other Siveyras bound by the same Onyx laws as you?"

"You *are* as bold as LanSoren," says Gyron. Quietly huffing, he continues, "With all the Geldryn dead, only the royal families of the Onyx have access to the ancient archives. My advice to you? Don't ask King ReNovak to translate that journal. He'll refuse, due to conflict of interest."

Talok queries, "What would you suggest we do?"

Hesitating, Gyron replies, "My nephew might be the answer to your dilemma. Though, I know not where he is. Have Grover search the Arkivara for Lemawr of Deivahl. He's the half-brother to King ReNovak's late wife. Devoted himself to learning the arts and history, but obsessed over language. As he has spent much of his life being a saigryn, a scholar, he's your best bet."

"I thank you, Gyron," Talok says. "We'll look into it."

When Gyron stands to leave, nodding once in goodbye, Rorka starts passing our camp-circle. Her gaze fixed on the path, her feet take long strides to some unknown mission. She's completely oblivious of our presence, until Gyron slowly looks in her direction.

Jerking to a stop, mid-stride, Rorka exclaims, "Gyron! Didn't expect to see you here. Did any of those Geldryn devices, which Alpha Jasper relinquished months ago, pique your King ReNovak's interest?"

"They were deemed decorative or useless, by Greyvons and us. We offered them to Paragon, yesterday. Should still be in their primary antique shop."

Disappointed, Rorka states, "Alpha Jasper was hoping you'd find something we missed."

"Again and again," states Gyron, "hopes are dashed, whenever searching for *anything* to stop Vitiosyns. Although we may have found something to aid us, I won't bother you with the details. I must be going, as I don't wish for the Onyx Warriors to be late this year. We're a part of the festival."

Talok stands, asking, "When was the last time they performed here?"

"Well over nine-hundred years ago." Gyron softly scoffs, saying, "When Zymarc was still a young and unproven Onyx Warrior. When he still had a face, before erasing remembrance of it from everywhere and everyone."

Rorka dips her head down. "Not even Alpha Jasper remembers his face."

Gyron nods, resting a hand on his blade hilt. "How's that for power? More terrifying than that Rubidyn, King Rentwar. No matter. We'll find a way to snuff out Zymarc of Vitiosus forever. It was done to Deezalo. It will be done to him. I only have one question for you, Rorka of Pariah."

"Which is?"

Gyron replies, "That Crae-Shand Magic of the Greyvons, how quickly does it help you adapt to your environment or someone's combat style?"

Raising her brow, she states, "If you're good? A few seconds."

"That's all I needed to know." With that, Gyron strides off into the dark.

Confused, Rorka faces the group. "What an odd question," she mutters.

"Think about it later," states Ryco. "Festival's about to start. King Talok?"

"Right! Can't be late." Talok runs off, to be swallowed by darkness.

"Kent!" Musgrae shakes him awake. "We're going to be late."

Black paint lines still on his face, Kent falls out of his seat, groaning, "Why do we always wait until the last second?"

Ben holds out a cloth and says, "Kent?"

"Not now, Ben. We've got to hurry." Kent scrambles out of sight.

As Gemma and I help Callie up, Talok calls back, "Tyler! Gemma? You coming?"

We follow streams of people, treading the same path.

We go into darkness, then into the light of magic.

Toward the festival, to start the heart of memory.

21

To the Festival

The festival's about to start. Grover and the five Arkiveis, still absent of the recovering Nyrim, sit together on a lengthy log covered by black shamrock-grass and plush white flowers. Toward the left end of it, Gemma and Callie sit beside each other, happily prattling away. On Gemma's left, the King's Guard and I stand facing the stadium fashioned of three white trees, three black, and two owning charcoal bark. Together, they form an oval-half, with ruby-vine railings separating the dozens of seat rows that angle up to a hundred feet in the back.

Far to the stadium's right is a solid ruby-stone stage. And, at its back and sides, there are shielding walls of swaying fire. Surrounded on three sides by fire, Talok's twelve advisers sit in black chairs with their mouths yawning, eyes darting, or feet tapping impatiently. Then there's Zepharre and EmiKal just sitting with transfixed gazes resting on the King's Guard and me, while they lethargically cup their faces. In front of them, closer to the stage-front, are three silver thrones glistening as scuffed mirrors. Though two are empty, Talok inhabits the center one.

When Zepharre's boredom turns to berating, Ben whispers, "Kent, your face."

"What about my face?" queries Kent, looking forward at the stadium.

Ben holds out a cloth. "You should clean it."

256

"Not now," huffs Kent, waving the cloth away.

That's when Eli leans forward—thus breaking the straight stance of the guard—to hold up a small, square mirror. Kent tilts his head out to take a peek, then yelps at his reflection and yanks the cloth from Ben's grasp. The whole time, Musgrae's shoulders quake.

Kent whips around, to scrub his face, griping, "Ryco! Why didn't you say anything?"

"It amused me," states Ryco. "Besides, I thought it best for you to pay more attention to Ben, and when he's trying to warn you."

"Musgrae!" Kent seethes. "If you survive the Vitiosyns, I'm going to kill you after the war."

"That sounds like a Ryco threat," states Musgrae. "Wait. Scratch that. Ryco wouldn't wait for a war to end to exact his revenge."

Farther down the line, Quall hisses, "Hurry, Kent, before Zepharre leaps from the stage, to wring your neck for breaking the line."

Face red and irritated like acne, Kent states, "I won't forget this, Mooz."

With that, the guard line straightens.

Talok stands to approach the edge of the stage. As he does so, the deafening stadium chatter ceases. His voice resonates, "People of Pawv'Ragaen! I and your Sovereignty welcome you to this year's Withrasyn-Vaegon Festival."

Clapping resounds, then quiets for Talok to announce, "We have special guests this year. The first? All the way from the Nyxane: King ReNovak and his Onyx Warriors!"

Applause erupts, louder than before.

Talok trails back to his throne, and looks over the scene as a lion would his pride. At that moment are fourteen figures, all dressed in hooded black cloaks, strolling from the path. They then move onto the Blackwood field, and cross over a Vardiya symbol painted in white at the center. First, five align. In front of them, four more. Then three, and one. Meanwhile, the fourteenth stands between the formation and front of the stage. Out wave his arms once, like a powerful dancer, and his cloak tears away. The thirteen follow suit. Then, into eight black doves, each cloak transforms:

one-hundred twelve doves in all.

Overhead, the graceful doves fly close together. Without warning, they ignite and morph into a dragon of pure flame. High above the stadium, the dragon explodes to falling ashen embers that cover the field of Blackwood.

The stadium applauds.

Yet Gemma's hands are unsure, as she's asking, "Those weren't real doves? Were they?"

"Spirit doves," replies Callie. "Conjured from the cloaks. We don't allow animal sacrifices in Paragon."

"What a relief," states Gemma, now clapping harder.

"I'm dying," moans Musgrae enviously, "to have one of those Onyx Warrior coats. Look at them. Enchanted scales and weapons on every centimeter."

Kent states, "I swear, Musgrae, if you weren't in the guard, you'd have every coat style and color imaginable."

"All dark Onyx scales, buckles, and belts," Musgrae corrects. "No Vaegon frills, satin, and glittering thread."

Ignoring them, Quall beams. "Our King Talok doesn't look as small next to ReNovak this year. Does he?"

On the stage, Talok rises from his bow to the tall fourteenth warrior—apparently King ReNovak—and offers him a vacant silver throne. ReNovak, looking like a younger and lesser Gyron, chooses the one on Talok's left. Then *down* sit the two kings. As ReNovak waves his hand out, his deep voice resonates, "Siveyra Gyronawv, I leave you to entertain Paragon."

Gyron, standing at the formation's front, bows to the stage, then whirls to face his twelve warriors grasping their hilts. Double straight-blades unsheathing, the warriors cross them in an 'X' in front of their chests. Stabbing blade tips into the ground, at their sides, they kneel before Gyron. With a snap of the Siveyra's fingers, black blindfolds cover the eyes of all thirteen warriors.

Burning away are their coats of black, revealing the garb of Onyx: unreflecting black boots, pants, and vests similar to mine. With arms and hands now exposed, Gyron draws out two blades. Then advancing toward him are the twelve, but Gyron jumps onto the stage and back-flips over them—avoiding their swings and sparking magic. He lands to safety and rises to stand tall.

In harmony, the blindfolded twelve rush Gyron. Before reaching him, however, Gyron's blade tip scrapes the Blackwood, and a fire wall blazes across the breadth of the field to protect him. In sets of two, the twelve work to douse the flames like dance partners; six release ice spikes, then trade places with six spewing water from their hands. Over and again. They trade out with each other.

Gyron then sheathes his blades and, while still blindfolded, faces the ruby-stone stage. Using his fingers, he proceeds to draw four luminescent circles in the air. First on north. Second to clockwise on east. Third for south. He ends on west. As the fire wall dies down, the top billows black smoke. Unconcerned, as if time is meaningless, Gyron presses on with his task of painting symbols in each directional circle.

When the fire wall sputters, Gyron finishes the symbols. He draws out his blades again. Across west and east, he slices first. Turning ninety-degrees, he then cuts north and south.

Through the dying wall burst the twelve, as all directional symbols fade to nothing. Gyron swings the Northwest blade at them. Dripping with water is its edge, before wind gales to send the Onyx Warriors back toward the stage.

With swift precision, they collect their footing and surround Gyron. In retaliation, he stabs the Southeast blade into the Blackwood field. From its edge, surges fire and stone to rapidly roll across the field. Although the warriors manage to dodge the elementals, they miss the avoidance of Gyron's lightning-fast swings. In the span of one full breath, he has drawn blood from the arms of six warriors. On clash the remaining six against Gyron—two almost bettering him—as the defeated six amble to the center field and wait like statues.

From where I stand with the guards, I glance to Rorka across the field. To my surprise, she's staring back, and it makes me uneasy, though I've no idea why. Just as fast as the fighting began, the remaining six stop to fall in line with the waiting statues.

The confusing wait of what's happening isn't long, as Gyron—still blindfolded—smiles charmingly in front of Rorka, before holding out his hand, requesting, "A dance? My lady."

Startling from her stare at me, Rorka gapes at Gyron. She hasn't time to stop him from grabbing her wrist, and pulling her onto the field. Closer to his twelve warriors, he flings her to stumbling and fumbling out-of-sync with them, while they clash their blades together and into the field—drawing symbols, both with blades and feet.

The ground hums.

Paragonians begin a soft chant.

In six heartbeats, Rorka snaps out of her awkwardness. Her movements now matching his warriors', Gyron falls in step with her. He hands off the Northwest blade, imbued with Air and Water. Together, the fourteen begin their own chant. Starting as deep-chilling intonations sinking into the soul, they shift to songs rising higher to warm the air.

Even after their voices cut out, all blades continue clashing a melodic harmony. Sounds of metal digging up rocky land. Blades skating on ice. Above the field, the swinging blades sound as water and crackling embers. All end with angled blade-edges, united in 'X's' to their adjacent partners.

A thick fog blankets the field, yet a soft wind chases some away.

Around the field's perimeter, stones form. Fire hovers over them.

Of the four elements, the last utterance is water, filling the Blackwood field ankle-deep.

Taking the enchanted weapon given to Rorka, Gyron stabs both blades into the field's center: the heart of the white Vardiya. When he stands back, a pillar of fire shoots up from the blade hilts. Dropping the other weapons are Rorka and the twelve aiming at Gyron. They shoot magic. With open arms, he accepts the blows. And his olive skin starts to glow. Across his exposed skin, black-ink paints into etchings akin to tribal tattoos.

The thirteen stop.

The Siveyra's hands clench into fists, and his knuckles press together. Relaxing fists, he releases the absorbed magic from his body. That's when the marks and glow leave his skin. Now made of only light and tattoos is his mirrored-figure beside him.

Gyron removes the blindfold; his warriors follow suit. Standing among the twelve is Rorka, while Gyron looks to King ReNovak.

Almost smugly, the Onyx King rises from the throne. He waves out his hands, proclaiming, "People of Paragon! Which Sorsryn shall I summon from our ancestors of old?"

Eyes locking onto ReNovak, I hope with all hope that he'll hear me and grant my request. To him, I echo, *Soren of the Monel, if you dare.*

Unflinching on the stage, while looking over the Blackwood field, ReNovak echoes back, *Don't you know with whom you Mensa-div, boy? The Onyx King does not* dare. *He does and does it well.* Pointing to Gyron, ReNovak resonates rather loudly, "I summon one Sorsryn of Old: Soren of the Monel."

On his light-figure, Gyron lays his hands, speaking to it, "Invitios! Soren-el-Monel."

The last syllable spoken, the pillar of fire goes out.

Bolting to her feet, Gemma whispers to me, "I think Gyron planned that. To give you what you asked."

I reply, "Could be."

When the light-figure takes shape, he's clothed like an Onyx Warrior in all white. Eerily, it's the same Soren as the one projected in my father's study, now standing on the Blackwood field, and turning away from Gyron. Toward the path leaving the field saunters this Soren. He starts his count. The Count of Despairion. "One. Two. Three. It goes … to King Kailon." He whirls around.

A conversation resonates out from him, and into the field. Then everywhere. Pleading with another is Soren's voice, "As my Withrasyn king is dead, I answer to Queen Awleesia and you. Grant me my request: to cut Vitiosus down, once *and* for all."

"We are young and weak, Soren," replies a man. "We've barely established Paragon, a united race. Would you ask me to risk everything? What if you fail?"

"My King Kailon, I won't fail."

Kailon scoffs, "Heard that before."

"I am the oldest Siveyra this world has seen. Yet you doubt me?"

"Give me one night, in the Arkivara," offers Kailon. "You'll have my answer tomorrow."

"There's no time!" shouts Soren.

"That's my final offer. Don't like it? Leave Paragon and never come back. I swear, Soren, you will be her death. If not now, then later. When she's strong."

Soren cries, "You break my heart."

Coldly, Kailon says, "You've already broken mine."

The conversation switches.

From the unmoving projection's light-figure, out steps Soren's lifelike ghost to walk the field. He continues counting, "Four. Five. Then Six. Adair—Tomatsu—Galloway. Gather your courage. This night. We defy a king, to kill another. One, Zymarc of Vitiosus."

Beside me is Gemma, with terror in her eyes, while she cups her hands over her mouth. Adair wanders over to her, dressed as an Onyx, except for the hints of purple on his sleeves and coattails. When the irises of his eyes seem to bleed, to what Ben calls Vitiosyn-eyes, Gemma stifles a scream.

"Seven. Eight," continues Soren. "What's that, Adair? You see your great-granddaughter?" To Adair standing in front of Gemma, Soren approaches. "Gemma Galloway?" He says, "What a pretty name. For a pretty girl." With murder in his eyes, Soren pushes Adair aside.

That's when Gyron starts panicking. Hands outstretched, and unsteady, he shouts, "I can't sever the link! No one move. Soren must choose to end it."

Fighting back her own panic, Gemma huddles closer to me. As she trembles, Soren leans down to her eye level, cooing, "Do you remember? The first time we met?"

Trembling almost turning to sobs, Gemma refuses to look at him. Then Soren taps on his temple, mocking, "You don't, do you? The conversation you heard, on your eighth birthday. The one I made your father forget.

The one LanSoren fought so hard to keep intact in you. Nine! Gone. Like ash." Soren's hand reaches, to touch Gemma on the face.

Something thrusts me into a reaction, and I clamp a hand on Gemma's arm.

Startling, Soren searches around as if *nothing* is before him. "Crafty LanSoren. Always getting in my way. No matter." Soren turns, to continue the count. "Ten. Eleven. I have a confession." Now standing in front of Gyron, Soren smiles his twisted grin. "I know the real face of Vitiosus," he proclaims.

Gyron keeps his hands motionless at his sides—even though sweat drips from his brow—while Soren voices, "Twelve and thirteen. Beginning. End. Everything in between." He motions to the elements within the field. Boredom briefly replaces the vicious intent in his gaze. "Now, Siveyra Gyron of the future, *you* may sever the link. Do it now, or I will kill you where you stand."

Extending his hand, Gyron grips some invisible rope. He then cuts through the air in front of him. Appearing, as Soren twiddles his fingers at me, is the linking rope of light between him and Gyron. Just as it's severed, Soren and his murderous eyes fade to nothing.

Gemma crushes my hand, whispering, "Tyler, you wave like that to Jed and Jaxson. Every day. After school."

Knowing she's right, my heart stops, and I rasp out, "I know."

"Quick," whispers Kent, reaching for me, then Gemma. "King Talok doesn't want your backs exposed. You too, Little Callie. Go in front of Ben."

Repositioned to stand in front of Ryco, I look to Gemma—safe beside Kent and Musgrae—then to Callic, holding her wrist.

Down from the stage leaps ReNovak, calling out, "Cease your alarm, People of Paragon."

Meanwhile, Gyron kneels at his king's feet, waiting for something.

The Onyx King continues, "I must use a bit of Death Magic, to get an answer I've longed for." Ending with that, ReNovak stabs a dagger into Gyron's chest.

The Siveyra falls dead to the field.

Screams resound from the stadium.

But Talok bolts off his throne, and holds up a hand to quiet his people. Though obeying him, they refuse to sit back down.

Ticking by are twelve seconds.

On thirteen, ReNovak bend down to remove the dagger. His chest now free of it, Gyron wheezes in a breath of renewed life, and the Paragonians give cries of relief.

Gyron stands, his eyes glowing-green, and speaks in a reverberating voice akin to the Vardiya, "With you, we will stand waiting for your Victor's Call. When we hear it, in all of the Nyxane, we shall ride to your aid. Hold fast! One more trial to be won. People of Paragon. Until the Vitiosyns are no more!"

The stadium cheers, the glowing-green fades, and Gyron's eyes return to normal.

Satisfied, ReNovak saunters back to the stage. He takes his temporary throne, commanding, "Siveyra Gyronawv. Give me two victors, to finish the tradition. Then you are released of your duties, for the night's remainder."

The fourteen reposition on the field, once again. They battle each other with blade and magic, until only two remain: Rorka and Gyron. Each take one enchanted blade.

The defeated warriors exit up to the stage, and stand behind the Advisers.

Then ReNovak is telling Siveyra Gyron to remove his marred heart-armor. Twice, Gyron snaps his fingers, and the cut vest disappears. Re-vealed is Gyron's battle-scarred, muscular skin, before his king commands, "Begin."

Powerful are Gyron's blows matched by Rorka's cunning swings. His blade nicks against her legs, forearms, or sides. But, mid-dodge, she leverages her swings to cut deep into Gyron's skin: his arms, thighs, but not his face and core. On one of his swings, she trips him to falling on his knees. With her blade tip at his throat, Gyron holds up hands of surrender.

"You gave me that victory," states Rorka. "Come at me again, Siveyra

Gyron."

She backs away, and Gyron tosses aside his blade. Gathering his footing, he releases fire from his hands. In one of her palms, Rorka catches it and pushes back the flames.

Attack after element, Rorka outsmarts Gyron. Wearing down his stamina, until he hesitates, she takes the opening and knocks him to the ground. One foot pinned on his chest, her other digs into the field. Rorka holds her blade-edge to the Siveyra's throat a second time.

Quieter is the Paragonians' cheering, even strained, as if a darkness of the mind has fallen over them. The darkest shadow, however, is cast over my cousin's face.

How to make them smile again? I muse. *How to make my cousin laugh?*

Straightening to attention, Rorka announces, "At last, a victory earned."

Standing up, Gyron ambles to the foot of the stage. As he looks up at his king, ReNovak resonates, "What shall our victor's reward be?"

When I catch sight of Rorka yearningly staring at Gyron's bare back, I feel it in my veins: her warmth, then her love and anticipation for him. An idea dawns, and I echo to ReNovak, *The kiss of a Siveyra? If you dare.*

To me, ReNovak flicks his heterochromian gaze—a mirror image of Callie's own—before stating, "I know what she needs. A Siveyra Kiss."

The stadium hollers cries of agreement.

Huffing, Gyron turns around and ambles back to Rorka without verbal complaint. Peering away, she shyly brushes a hand to her cheek. When Gyron draws close to her, he tenderly grabs under her chin, mouthing the words, 'thank you,' before planting a soft kiss on her cheek.

The people clap, and back Gyron ambles to his place in front of the stage. Far behind him, Rorka stands stiff as a board.

"If I didn't know better," says Musgrae, "I'd think Paragon craves a good romance."

"No need to give them one of your *many* expeditions," states Ryco. "They'd want to gouge the memories away."

Kent smacks Musgrae on the chest, with the back of his hand. "Both of you. Shut up. You'll ruin it."

I echo to ReNovak, *That wasn't a real kiss. Didn't you say an Onyx does it well?*

Wagging one finger, ReNovak states, "A *true* Siveyra Kiss, dear Gyron."

Shoulders slumping, Gyron turns a second time to plod back to Rorka.

Paragonians begin to holler their encouragement, from the stadium.

"Kiss the Greyvon!"

"We love you, Gyron."

"Rorka! You lucky dog!"

"Own that Siveyra."

All around, laughter resounds. Lighting the stage, and my heart with it, is my cousin's smile. His laugh too, as Gyron and Rorka break out their compliant grins.

Turning serious, Gyron cups her face and looks into her anxious eyes with nothing but admiration in his own. After parting his lips to take a breath, he kisses her long and slow.

Her shoulders relaxing, Rorka runs her hands from Gyron's bare core to his backside. Kissing him back, she pulls him close.

That's when the stadium whistles and some patronizingly howl.

Her face matching her sunset-red hair, Rorka's left breathless when Gyron pulls away.

His face tinged pink, Gyron whirls around and strides confidently back to the stage. But ReNovak flicks his hand at him, saying, "I don't think our victor was done, Siveyra. Again! Until she's had her fill."

Jaw clenched, Gyron mutters, "But I am done. My king."

Rorka, catching her breath, faces the stadium. "People of Paragon!" she calls out. "A round of applause for King ReNovak and his magnificent Onyx Warriors."

The crowd chants, cheers, and claps, but Rorka just heads for the path exiting the field. That's when ReNovak drops down from the stage, calling to her, "Rorka of Pariah. In Alpha Jasper's stead, your position's on the throne next to King Talok."

After escorting the reluctant Rorka to her place, ReNovak takes his, with Gyron standing to his left. The Onyx King pleasantly grins at Talok, waiting for him to initiate something.

When Quall shakes his head slightly, Talok lathers the invisible soap twice. He then rises off his throne.

The stadium quiets.

"My fellow Paragonians," Talok begins, "as our Nyrim of Yharss is not well enough to assist with our long-awaited surprise, we will close early this night. But, first, there is *one* I must introduce to you."

"Get ready, Tyler," Gemma whispers.

Motioning to me, Talok calls out, "Tyler Ravier, Son of LanSoren. Our Hero of Nyrim."

"And there it is," I state. "What I was dreading: the hero title."

Gemma teases, "Now you can sympathize with *King* Talok. And I thought they went nuts for the Siveyra Kiss," she adds, while releasing my hand.

In my roam to the stage, the applause is deafening. Even the very air vibrates with it. When Talok raises his hand—as if catching a falling, brittle leaf—the thunder ceases. The only noise filling the air now are my footsteps, creaking like ice on a lake, as I ascend the ruby-stone stairs.

Facing me, Talok beams. "Say hello to Paragon, Tyler."

When I lift a hand in greeting, the undertones turn to chattering hums.

"Already, they love you," whispers Talok, reaching to give me a small metal-sphere. "Since you can't yet control magic, use this to close the night with a bang."

Taking to his throne, Talok relinquishes the stage to me.

Unsure for a moment, I repeatedly turn the sphere over in my right palm. Deciding that I'll get more answers this night, I speak, "To new beginnings. To the people and world I never knew existed. To a love for magic. To the death of Vitiosus."

I toss the sphere back to Talok, surprising him, yet he catches it. Then, clenching my left fist, I whisper, "In memory of my father."

This time, the Prismatic of Magic is summoned to my hand effortlessly. Eyes unblinking, I hold my breath. On the exhale, I throw an expanding white ball of light toward the field. Even though I long to, still, I do not blink. Burning are my eyes, but not with tears. With something else. Smoke?

Dust? Magic? How can I know?

At last, they close.

Something explodes.

Gasping, the people then sigh in delight.

When my eyes open, ice-flakes fall from high above. No ball in sight, the flakes melt on water still trapped within the Blackwood field.

That's when I echo to him or, maybe, even to the Vardiya, *If you can hear me, wherever you are, tell me why you lied. How you died?*

Something unseen races down the path. It splashes onto the field. Then, like discarded trash, a cloak drops into the water. Awngeleik flaps her wings, screeching. She prances around like a dog proud of a fetch, and flails her head. She mocks us.

Quall exclaims, "That menace! How'd she get out? Someone catch her, before she flies off into the night."

Loathing in his sadistic yellow eyes, Ryco breaks the guard-line. The first action he takes is to aim a drawn arrow right at Awngeleik's head.

22

A Hint of Citrine

The ruby-stone stage shudders. I leap off, shouting at Ryco. Ceasing are the falling snowflakes, as I land hard on the Blackwood field. Footsteps splashing through slushy water, I'm too late. The arrow has been shot. Erupting with its release is shrill chaos. That's when the magic fades from my hand, and a chest-pang sends me to my knees. I'm drenched by the freezing water.

As the arrow's about to hit her, Awngeleik sways her body toward me. The arrow grazes through her mane. It continues toward the stadium, but Khyra—standing at the perimeter opposite of Ryco—leaps up to catch it.

Warren and Musgrae scramble into action, trying to corral Awngeleik in her game of chase. Storming my way, Ryco hauls me off my knees. His strong grip tight on my arm, he proceeds to drag me to the stage. He pushes me against it, then commands, "Stay put. You'll only get in our way."

Passing by us—on their way to Talok, Rorka, and ReNovak—are Kent and Siege, leading Gemma and Callie up to the safety of the stage.

Ryco starts to walk away. But I grab his arm, and dig my nails in, fuming, "That arrow was going to hit her!"

"Don't be ridiculous," seethes Ryco. "The shot was meant to startle her—"

Quall interrupts, "Ryco! Stop defending yourself and get out here."

Eyes flashing in anger, Ryco states, "Now we have to do this the hard way. Want to help? Get the abomination to come to you."

He turns on his heel, to saunter into the mayhem of Musgrae and Eli dodging Awngeleik's kicking tantrums, all while Warren and Quall pull her down mid-flight. Looking on from the sidelines is Ben, waiting for someone's signal.

From the stage, ReNovak gives the command, "Onyx Warriors, retrieve the Paragonians' prized possession. No need to let her escape. Thus ending this war, before it's begun."

Off the stage, and onto the field, Gyron leads the twelve. When I go to join them, he cuts in front of me. His warriors continue forward to encircle the Walking Terror's havoc.

Gyron grabs my arm, saying, "You're a prized one of Paragon, too, Tyler Ravier. I've witnessed Awngeleik use magic, when she's playing. Your Mazhrein is weakened. One hit from her and you'll be sent into a coma for a few days. Best to sit this one out. Or I'll restrain you, myself."

I try pulling away. But he holds tight, and I state, "I'm not yours to command."

"But you're mine to protect!" shouts Gyron. "LanSoren was a great friend to the Nyxane. To me. I would give my life to save you. To serve you."

Serve? I muse. *Forever at your service. Could it be him? The one who knows more truth of what happened than anyone. But he is magically bound not to say?*

"Clear out!" commands Quall. "Reign's coming."

Quall's all the distraction I need to break free of Gyron, and sprint for Awngeleik. Save for Ryco—standing a safe distance from her—everyone scampers away. When Reign lands hard on the path leading out of the field, Awngeleik stumbles. Looking to her, I know the familiar sight of thirteen steps to a goal. My goal? To catch a Walking Terror.

First thirteen and twelve, I take eleven.

Getting closer, something warms me. Is it the heat of magic coursing through Awngeleik, as she takes on her demon form? Its crawl starts from her hooves, then to her legs, the black finishing its stain on her scaly sides.

"Reign!" I shout. "Distract her. Make her afraid!"

Ten then nine to closer, as Reign lifts his head to the night sky. He quakes out his roar.

Eight then seven to halfway, while the water on the field vibrates. With Reign's inhales, the water rises into air and then crashes down on the exhale.

Six and five see that the magic returns to me, unnoticed by all watching the disorder.

Four and three to musing, *It was her and the Vardiya—the ones who did this to me—gave me magic I know through emotion, rather than words. By instinct, instead of spell-books. But how could they have done that?*

On two, I stop. My legs tremble from the quaking ground.

The last might as well be a lifetime away.

But then, the demon form fades to a cowering dragon-horse covering much of herself under her wings. As Reign's Roar ceases, rustling branches that resemble slithering snakes grow toward Awngeleik. The branches soften to vines. With a flick of Ryco's hands, glowing a gentle-green, they strap Awngeleik's wings and body to the field. Thrashing, she screeches a tormented cry. Taking his signal, Ben rushes to her side and tries to soothe her. "Calm, Awngeleik. Be calm. Everything's going to be all right."

One to crawling, I rest a hand on her. She struggles against the straps, and snaps a few.

"Both of you!" shouts Ryco. "Get back. She's casting an electrical spell."

Ben leaps up to rush away. Yet I stay, even as her scales begin sparking colors of white-and-blue.

"Tyler? Come away," Ben pleads.

Right as I pull away, the bindings ignite and burn to ash. Awngeleik's irises swirl with blue-fire, and strip away any thoughts of safety, as she stares into me. She slowly stands. Though a chill settles in, I hold her gaze. I've no choice, really.

All sound fades.

The sight shifts to nothing but my father standing in front of me. Tears flow down. No words. Just tears. I'm in shock, wondering if he's here or if it's only an illusion.

He starts the dialogue. "In case you think I'm trapped inside Awngeleik. The answer is, no. Like in my study, I'm merely a projection."

Chest aching, I hold back bitter anger.

On he continues, "I've hidden messages. Memories for you, Tyler, in many places. It was the only way to keep them safe from his reach."

"Please," I beg, "tell me something, to help find truth in all this."

His sad face is unchanged by my voice. That's when I know he can't hear me.

I step closer, but still, his tall posture is unmoved by the sight of me. Can't see me, either.

"For now," he states, "all I can say is: follow where the journals point. That Rubidyn-Greyvon one, in particular."

How does he expect me to do that, when no one can read its entirety? Let alone the others.

Though Mother has her Chess-Bluff, my dad was armed with the Chess-Grin. He has that same grin now, before saying, "The journey will be hard. But you'll have help. Take care of her and she'll take care of you. Now, Tyler. It's time to wake up."

Reaching out, I scream for him. It doesn't stop him, however, from fading away.

Just like that, my screams cut out. The sight of Paragon seeps back into view. In the exact same place as before, I stand. Hands trembling, I wipe tears off Awngeleik's face. "You saw him too. Didn't you?"

Blue-fire now gone, Awngeleik's sad, large eyes break my heart. Pulling her face to rest against my chest, I speak, "Sleep, Awngeleik." At the words' utterance, her legs buckle. And she slips from my grasp. Now at my feet, she lies in a heap of scales. Disheveled are her mane and feathers, as her eyes close. Sleep takes hold.

Fighting composure, I stumble back. A gentle hand steadies me.

It's Talok, at my side, his face ridden with a storm of concern. "You all right, Tyler?"

Struck speechless, I just wobble my head, trying to clear it for an answer.

"What did you see?" he presses.

Recovering slightly, I respond, "We should get her to safety."

"Yes! Of course. Guards! Take her to the castle infirmary." Climbing onto Reign's back, Talok reaches for me. "Come, Tyler. We'll get there ahead of them."

* * *

In a corner of the castle infirmary, Awngeleik sleeps on a wooden platform, while Gemma is asking, "Will she be all right?"

Quall affectionately looks at Awngeleik. "Nothing can keep this beautiful menace down for long," he says.

"What's going to happen," I ask, "with the Onyx King knowing she's here?"

"Nothing," replies Talok. "Because they're still neutral."

Quall states, "Vitiosyns would have to gain physical proof, to present to King ReNovak—"

Siege interrupts, "That Awngeleik's in Paragon."

"Without proof," continues Warren, "Vitiosyns can't attack without Onyx reprimand."

"They," finishes Eli smugly, "must wait until the conclusion of our festival. After King Talok has announced his decision."

"I swear," Quall seethes, "if the three of you don't stop interrupting me, I'm going to have Ryco cut your tongues out."

Ryco, leaning up against the wall, has a grin tugging at his mouth.

"Do you know," I ask Talok, "what you're going to say, at the end?"

"I do not." Talok sighs. "To war, negotiate, or flee? All decisions. All outcomes—in one way or another—are stacked against me."

Easing away from the wall, Ryco states, "King Talok, you should prepare for tomorrow."

"Yes, but first. Miss Gemma? I'd like to cast protection spells on you."

"What for?" queries Gemma, in alarm.

Talok wrings his hands. "What I saw of this Soren of the Monel," he pauses, "greatly disturbs me. I feel it's my duty to protect you. However I can."

"What about Tyler?" queries Gemma, curling her shoulders.

"He doesn't need them. I'm sure my uncle had something to do with that. You, however, aren't safe. Come. I'll help you settle your fears." Talok extends his hand to her.

Hesitating, she mumbles, "Glad you're okay, Tyler."

"Don't worry," I reply. "We'll find out why Soren's so interested in you."

Forcing a grin, she grips Talok's hand.

He leads her out.

"The rest of you," says Quall, "may go to the makeshift quarters. I'll stay with Awngeleik a while."

Smiling at Quall briefly is Kent, grabbing an elegant vase—holding Callie's Midnight Anemones—and proceeding to lead the others from the infirmary. One by one, the King's Guard spill into the fire-illuminated hallway. Farther behind the others is Ryco, lingering at the back, almost taunting me to confront him. Instead of following the others to the stairwell, he disappears through a doorway on the left.

Careful in my pursuit of him, I stay out of sight. Each footfall of his wide gait, I match so the sounds are in unison. First, up a narrow, spiraling set of stairs, we go. Then down a twisting corridor. I follow, until his footsteps suddenly stop. To the right or left, I look but he's nowhere in sight.

Shrugging in defeat, I slink into the circular room straight ahead. Though small, it's packed with cases of books. Bound and old are the books aligned on shelves like a library. Their old parchment fills the air with musk, while mixing in with it is a hint of pinesap drifting in through the open window. Creeping to stand in front of it, I glance down from the second floor and search for where Ryco may have gone.

"Let's agree on something," states Ryco.

Startled by his nearness, I whirl around to face him.

Less than an arm's length away, he declares, "You don't like me. Nor I, you. Still. Think you can fake tolerance of me?"

"Why should I?"

"For Talok's sake. If you're anything like LanSoren, you shouldn't have a problem with faking."

"Leave my dad out of it," I seethe.

"I will." Ryco nods. "When it suits me."

"Talok knows how I feel about you. Why would I need to hide it?"

"Because he values me. But he adores you. He already has enough contentions. There's no need for us to add to his grief. Is there?"

"In his presence, you mean? What about when he's not around?"

"You're free to say whatever you like. But prepare yourself for the consequences of your words."

"Hypothetically speaking," I ask, "what will happen, if he dies in this impending war?"

"No need for us to be civil anymore." Ryco smirks. "Nor see each other. Ever again. Once taken back to Earth—where you belong—you and your friend will remain there. No more Muraine to worry over. Nor family to fear for."

"That's not your decision to make. From what I can tell, my father was higher in the Paragonian Sovereignty than you. As his son, I won't be cast aside so easily."

"The little boy is flexing his muscle," Ryco mocks. "How cute! You know what I see? When I look at you?"

Through grinding teeth, I ask, "What?"

Ryco leans closer. His breath hot on my face, he whispers, "That stupid boy ripping himself free of Gyron's protection. Potentially sprinting toward his death, by Awngeleik's magic, without any regard for what his death might mean for Paragon and Talok."

"I couldn't let her get away."

"If you hadn't distracted her, I would've had her the very second after the arrow startled her into a new position. Already. You *are* getting in the way, because you're inexperienced and weak!"

"I'm not as weak as you think, Ryco of Paragon."

"Yes, yes. So you shared a mere fraction of Nyrim's burden and recovered remarkably well. You learned the Art of Mensa-div, all on your own. And you command that menace to sleep. Bravo. You're so strong."

Fists clenching, I counter with, "I shielded Gemma, from Soren's view."

"For a few seconds," Ryco agrees. "That was a little impressive. Outsmarting a Sorsryn of Old. But that wasn't your magic. That was LanSoren's. Undoubtedly imbued to you by way of an enchanted item you touched first."

"Like your letter?" I scowl.

"Mine was meant to be an annoyance." Ryco grins. "Like you. But yes, the concept is the same."

"Stop!" I shout. "I've had enough of this." I storm out of the room.

Striding not far behind, Ryco grabs my arm. He shoves me against the wall. "Glad that's over. Now we can join the others crammed into one room. Because. What was the reason?" He thinks a moment. "Right! Two of our cities were burned to ash this morning, leaving hundreds of survivors in need of new homes."

23

Stroke of the Razor

In the makeshift quarters for the King's Guard, I lie on one of nine beds. Brooding, with my arms crossed, I'm still fully dressed in the Sleeping Dragon coat, vest, pants, and all.

To the left, Musgrae and Warren occupy an empty corner of the room. Blade-dueling akin to some type of dance, their need to outdo each other is evident from the inferno in their eyes. To the right, the Midnight Anemone vase has found its home on the potions' half-circle table in front of Ben. Sitting reverse of him, Kent and Siege help decide on herb and liquid variations to mix. Opposite of the battling human-tanks, water splashes behind the barrier of an L-shaped, high wall, as Eli's singsong hums drift out with the mist.

Mid-swing at Musgrae, Warren grumbles, "Don't start your singing, Eli."

"By all means, do," says Musgrae, clanking his weapon against Warren's. "'Tis the best way to distract Warren in a duel."

Forlornly sighing, Eli states, "Not feeling a song tonight."

"Hopefully, no rhymes either," mutters Ryco, a good distance across from where I brood on the bed. At a Khyra-styled desk, he sits poring over pages of a blue, leather-bound book. Every few minutes, he cross-references scrolls and other books fanned out on the surface.

Water dripping down his bare torso, out struts Eli from the bathing quarter of the room. Proudly, he wears damp, gray pants. He passes four of the beds, leaving a trail of water behind him.

From across the room, Kent asks, "Don't you ever dry off?"

"Effort," replies Eli, running a comb through his soaked hair.

"Let me know about effort," states Warren, "when someone uses a freezing spell on you, immediately out of the bath."

Eli starts to retort, but Ryco interrupts with two snaps of his fingers. At the sound, Eli's attention cracks to him like whiplash.

Ryco taps on a page of the blue-leather book, then says, "Come tell me what's wrong with this Blue Magic combination of yours."

Eli moonwalks over to Ryco, thus provoking a deep citrine glare. "It's not as awesome as Warren's spells?" he answers.

Unamused, Ryco taps the end of his quill on the desk. "Why have you put the miniaturization of an item, before the weight reduction spell?"

"Because," replies Eli, glancing to the ceiling, "it doesn't matter that much."

Setting his quill down, Ryco slides his chair back to ease out. He grabs a metal ingot off the bookcase behind the desk. To Eli, he gives the ingot, stating, "While it won't matter with small, lightweight items, why might it matter with something of this weight or greater? If you were to reduce its size to, say, a grain of sand? Right now. In your hand."

Shoulders slumping, Eli replies, "It would cut through my hand."

"Then continue through the floor," adds Warren. "And whoever's below you, if you throw it hard enough. Not stopping, until it loses momentum."

"Or hits something impenetrable on impact," says Kent.

When Musgrae heads for the bathing quarter, right then, Siege glances from him to Warren, asking, "Done already?"

Warren huffs, "Too worked up."

From the bathing quarter, Musgrae adds, "Might be hours, before I prevail once again."

Warren, his huff altering to fuming, watches Musgrae's clothes being tossed over the high wall. They land in a heap on the floor.

"Musgrae!" Ryco seethes.

Warren leans his hip against Ryco's desk, stating, "We're not one of your expeditions, Mooz."

"Your point?"

"Ryco doesn't want to see your dirty laundry."

"His problem. Not mine." Musgrae goes silent, and water splashes on the tile floor of the bathing quarter.

Gripping the ingot harder, Eli brightens. "Could I use this like a weapon?"

"It's called"—Warren laughs—"smashing it over someone's head. Like Musgrae's, for instance."

"I already suffered a Ryco headache," hollers Musgrae. "Thank. You. Very. Much."

"You're welcome," states Ryco, now somewhat amused.

Eli complains, "You didn't let me finish, Warren! After throwing it at a line of enemies, could I use *Resilios* to cut through several in one shot?"

"Yeah!" Warren booms. "I've done that countless times. With weapons, though. Love resizing, while it's embedded inside them."

Cracking his knuckles, Ryco adds, "If your timing isn't adept enough for that—or weapons are far out of reach—you could shape something simple, like that ingot, into a weapon: a spike, blade, or mace. Then, reduce it mid-air."

"That way," Ben says, "the wounds would be harder to heal."

"Shall we test it?" suggests Ryco, removing his coat. He reveals the black scales of his heart-armor. His combat-weathered arms too. "Warren," he says, "keep it from going through the floor."

As instructed, Warren prepares a blue-tinted sphere around him. Ryco sits down, holding the unaltered ingot. He touches it to his right forearm. Curling his arms apart, as if he's preparing a shot for an arrow, his left hand starts to throw it. At a third of the distance to his opposite arm, he lets go. Mid-air, the ingot seems to disappear. Then it exits out of Ryco's forearm. With it? A pinprick of blood spurting out and a few drops forming at the tiny wound.

At the sound of Ryco's fingers snapping thrice, the bloodied ingot grows to full size on the floor within the sphere. Picking it up, Ryco fashions it into a jagged oval-mace. As it has no handle, he's careful how he manipulates it. Then, hesitating for seconds, he proceeds to throw it into his left arm, only flinching when a dime-sized chuck of skin explodes out the other side.

Sphere now gone, Ryco states, "Now to heal these, Ben."

Approaching, Ben starts on the first wound. In seconds, he closes up Ryco's pinprick wound with the white-glow emitting from his palms.

Ryco then offers his bleeding left arm, instructing, "Now the other."

To a pale-yellow, Ben's glowing palms shift.

Grimacing, Ryco says, "You missed healing the chipped bone. Do that first. Then replace the missing tissue."

Turning to a brighter-yellow is the glow of Ben's palms, as he works for a few minutes.

Nodding his reassurance, Ryco instructs, "Close the wound up, from the inside, out."

Another minute passes, before Ben announces, "Finished."

Tightening and relaxing his fists, Ryco taps the first injury point. "This doesn't hurt a bit. The other's still sore and bruised, however. I'll have to wait for it to heal on its own."

Right then, Musgrae wanders out from the bathing quarter wearing only fitted athletic-shorts. His muscles bulge as if his skin belongs to someone a size smaller, such as Siege.

"Musgrae," Ryco harshly commands, "put your clothes on."

"We're all men, here, aren't we?" Musgrae defends.

Pink tingeing his face, Siege steals a glance at Eli, and whispers, "Debatable."

"I suppose," Ryco states, "if you don't mind Miss Galloway seeing you naked, Musgrae … run naked in the room, for all I care."

Like a crack of thunder, Eli's gray eyes pop open.

Musgrae takes a staggering step, asking, "Mud Fiend's sleeping in here? With all of us? I thought she'd sleep with Khyra or something."

Creeping his fingers on the desk, Eli grabs the blue-leather book and says, "Going to work on some hypothetical combinations to test first thing in the morning. Want to help, Ben?"

"Need to practice more White Magic," mutters Ben.

To Musgrae, Ryco replies, "For the night, I suggested both visitors slumber with the Onyx Warriors. It seems, however, that it would bring *great comfort* to King Talok, if both slumbered near some of Paragon's best. His words. Not mine."

Chest huffing once, Musgrae trudges to the wardrobe that's adjacent to the bookcase. Yanking the doors open, he digs through the mess of clothes spilling out, hollering, "What chaos? Look at this! Creases everywhere. And can't find anything."

"I'll free up Quall for you, Ben," states Ryco, sharing a triumphant look with him. "Back in a bit."

He saunters out, then clicks the door shut.

Taking a large book off the case, Warren ambles to the nearest bed and lounges on it like an athlete soaking in a hot bath. On the corner bed—three away from Warren—Eli busies himself with penning spell combinations in his book.

When I spot Ben intensely studying me, I sit up on the bed. "Something wrong?" I ask.

"Your face …" Ben pauses, seeming unsure of what words come next.

From the potions' table, Kent is asking, "What's this face obsession you have, Ben?"

Warren's own is hidden by the book in his hands, as he states, "Ben was wondering if Tyler had those few man-whiskers on his face this morning." Slowly, the book lowers, and the amused cobalt-blue eyes peer over the top of it.

Kent, like a crazed fan to their idol, rushes toward me. Curiosity overcoming him too, Siege roams over. But Eli—from the farthest corner of the room—launches his spell-book across the floor, during his mad dash. He beats both, and gets to me first.

Inspecting my face, Eli announces, "Yo, brothers! He does."

"Sorry, Tyler," says Ben sheepishly. "Didn't mean for my thoughts to blurt it out."

"Blurt what out?" queries Musgrae, now donning black pants and a shirt.

"Man-whiskers, apparently," is my good-humored reply.

Musgrae barrels to me. He grips my shoulders. "So you do have a few."

He smiles, stepping back to ask, "Kent? Where does Quall keep LanSoren's shaving stuff?"

"In the trunk, at the bed's end."

By the lonesome bed near the bay window, Musgrae marches to the one wooden trunk in the room, then kneels down to open the lid, shrieking, "This is worse than the wardrobe." After smoothing his hair back, he takes the plunge. Moments pass, before he's announcing, "Here it is: little black box."

Musgrae starts to stand. But he's shoved to the floor, by Eli yanking the box away. Opening it, he then dumps its contents upon Ryco's desk.

"You little Kirja punk!" Musgrae fumes. He whacks Eli's ankles, and the Kirjan plummets to the floor.

In horror, Kent cups his face. "Ryco's going to murder you, Eli. You know the desk is off-limits."

Popping up like a jittery squirrel is Eli, racing out of Musgrae's grasp and waving off Kent's warning. "He went to relieve Quall of duty. We'll have it cleaned up, before he's back. Honestly, Kent, stop being our mother," says Eli, while lifting out a straight razor from the clutter.

"If you get your back whipped tonight, don't say I didn't warn you." Kent starts smelling the Midnight Anemones.

Musgrae plops into Ryco's chair, then digs through the pile. Like a curious cat, I wander over to stand at Musgrae's side and stare at them: the pre-shave oil, aftershave, and alum block.

Though unwanted in this moment, memories fade in. Like the time I caught my dad in the middle of his routine. A year before he died.

His tall figure hunched over the sink vanity, a black towel wrapped round his waist. He gazed into the mirror. That was when I glimpsed the tribal-wolf tattoo on his back, for the first and last time. "You have a tattoo? Does that mean I can get one in a few years?" I asked him.

He jumped to the side, startled by my voice, and hit his head on the wall. The towel started slipping off his naked body, but he grabbed it in time to regain composure. "Can't you make more noise, when you walk," he complained, "instead of sneaking up on me all the time?"

"If you closed the door, during the Beethoven-Blare, maybe I couldn't sneak up on you."

"It's Mozart," he corrected, while readjusting the towel. "Your mother wouldn't approve. Of a tattoo, that is. Music's fine. So she's told me."

"So … tattoos? You would approve?"

Staring up at the bathroom ceiling, he raised the Jed-finger. Come to think of it, Jed may have learned it from him. At last, he said, "I have the right to remain silent, on that subject." Turning back to the mirror, he rubbed lotion on his face. "As for closing the door. I had a bad experience. Once. With a closed door."

"Care to share?" I asked.

"Another time, perhaps."

Kent's exclamation breaks the memory. "Wait, Eli! You need the—"

Straight razor already pressed to his neck, Eli snaps his attention to Kent, then out spurts Kirjan blood. Dropping the razor, Eli compresses the deep cut. His body thrashes, yet he stays standing.

Jaw clenched, in anger, Ben gathers cloth and powders from one of his pouches. With steady hands, he proceeds to heal Eli. Meanwhile, Musgrae picks up the razor. He wipes it clean of Eli's blood.

"You're supposed to angle it," states Musgrae, pressing the razor edge against his oiled neck. He slides the sharp edge up. With the slide, a flap of skin is flayed almost completely off.

Siege goes death-pale. But Kent just rolls his eyes, as only a mother of reckless daredevils could. A second time, the razor falls. Musgrae holds his wound. Eyes clamped shut, he sways back and forth.

Ben's steady, glowing palms pause from healing Eli. He scowls. "You couldn't wait until I was done?"

Eyes now bloodshot, Musgrae squeaks, "It's okay. I'll wait my turn."

"I've got it from here," says Kent. "Go heal the big lug, before he whines and cries."

Right then, Warren's bed jiggles. He peeks out from behind the side of the book, to look at me. A bright grin contrasts with his dark skin. Then he goes back to reading, and hiding his amusement.

Ben, meandering to the razor's second victim, flicks Musgrae's hand. "Get your hand away. I need to see what I'm doing. And no talking."

Musgrae pries his blood-smothered hand off his neck, yelping when the skin-flap gets pulled. The sight is too much for me to contain some laughs cackling out. In reply, Musgrae tenses his neck and points at me, saying, "Stop it, Ravier."

From the tense neck, blood spurts onto Ben's face. He flinches. Then his eyes blaze at Musgrae. "I said, *no* talking. Don't you ever listen?"

Jackhammering his head, Musgrae shuts his mouth.

"Somebody," states Ben, "get a chair for this monstrosity."

Color coming back to his cheeks, Siege drags one from the potion table. Musgrae sits on it. Ben heals him, in silence. When he finishes, Musgrae stands up and then thanks him.

"The only thanks I need," replies Ben, while dampening a white cloth, "is for your blood to never violate my face again." With that, Ben scrubs his face and hands clean of the offender's blood.

"That's what he said," states Warren, letting a deep laugh escape.

"Shut up, Warren." Musgrae throws some bloodied rags at him. "I can't help that my blood has a trace of the Greyvon stench."

"You're part Greyvon?" I ask.

"Way down the line. Thousands of years, from what my aunt told me. Before passing me off to another Paragonian family."

"Pass off?" I ask. "Didn't she want you?"

Almost pinching his throat, where the wound was, Musgrae stops himself. Picking up the razor, instead, he offers, "Want a go, Warren?"

"Do I look like a fool?" replies Warren, his nose still to the pages.

"Siege?" Musgrae queries.

But he replies, "I like my skin where it's at."

Then Ben, before Musgrae can ask, says, "Don't trust any of you, to heal me free of scars. Except Quall."

Kent reaches for the straight razor, and Musgrae surrenders it.

Looking to me, Musgrae clears his throat. He starts with, "Her family couldn't figure out why my mother was carrying me so badly. Eventually, they had Jasper's research pack test her blood and my father's. Found out that my dad had a trace of Greyvon. Dog stench. As my mother called it, when last I saw her." He forces a smile. "My aunt and uncle tried to love me. But never did, really."

I ask, "Do Paragonians not like Greyvons, or something?"

Musgrae claws at the back of his neck. "Queen Awleesia and her Withrasyns never liked the Greyvons, after Alpha Jasper and his council refused them a new home. Back when the Withrasyn men were dying in droves."

"That was over a thousand years ago," I state.

"But the grudges," replies Musgrae, "are as fresh as ever. Particularly, if you're raised by the right Paragonian family."

"You mean the wrong family?" says Kent, wincing when the razor leaves skid marks on his neck. Folding it, he sets it down. "I think it best, to put the razor to rest. Use magic for Tyler's face, instead."

I ask, "Is that why you're all so terrifyingly bad with a razor? You only use magic?"

"Except," replies Siege, "for the typical Trauvo-Truists."

Face still behind his book, Warren adds, "They prefer using magic out of necessity."

"Every day," says Eli, staring into nothing. "Quall makes it look so easy."

Warren lowers his book.

The bedroom door swings open.

Striding in, Ryco states, "Ben. Quall will be in—" Trailing off, Ryco stops at the sight of his desk, then pivots his attention to the blood-splattered scene, asking, "Care to explain why it reeks of Musgrae's blood in here?"

"Forgive my sweat and blood"—Musgrae scoffs—"for not smelling like a Sylvadyn's pinesap."

I interrupt, "They were trying to shave, so they could teach me."

Kent beams. "Little Tyler's got his first man-whiskers."

Inspecting the desk-clutter, Ryco states, "*Obviously*, the lesson was unsuccessful. Where's the soap and brush?"

Except for Ben collecting blood-soaked rags, and Warren lifting his book to shield the smile playing across his lips, all guards just shrug at Ryco.

"Very well." Ryco grinds his teeth, before asking, "Who dared to put, not one, but *four* things on my desk?"

Eli reddens to the shade as Siege's red hair.

But I take the blame, replying, "That was me," before echoing to Ryco, *What are you going to do about it?*

Striding to Quall's trunk, Ryco fishes out the soap, porcelain dish, and small shaving brush bursting with fine bristles. Tossing me the pre-shave oil, he states, "For you," then dumps all supplies in the black box and closes the distance between us. Catching the oil, I rub some in, then add it to the box.

Ryco forces the box into Musgrae's grasp, then takes out the brush. He soaks it, with water seeping from his palm. Next, he swirls the brush over the soap and in the dish, preparing a thickened foam. Offering the frothy brush, he states, "Put a generous layer everywhere you're going to shave away the fuzz. Eli, a mirror for Tyler Ravier. Please."

When Eli speaks, "Argentus!" a rectangular mirror appears in his hands, and Ryco snaps his fingers once. I fall into the chair, suddenly hitting the back of my knees. Then a sickness creeps down into my stomach, as the mirror shows that some fuzz, indeed, has turned dark-brown. After slathering foam on my face and neck, I give Ryco the brush. He hands me the clean razor.

Now holding the frothy brush and porcelain dish, Ryco states, "Well, Mr. Ravier. Begin. We're all waiting on you. Make sure you angle it right."

Starting near the base of my neck, I run the edge up as I've seen my dad do countless times. When it pricks my skin, I stop. And Ryco, tapping his foot twice, states the obvious: "You're not angling it right."

That's when branches grow up from the floor—seeming to have no master—and fashion into a rough table in front of me. Ignoring the table, I adjust the razor-edge angle and try again. Then, similar to Kent's attempt, it starts the skid.

"Stop," states Ryco firmly. Frowning, he runs one of his palms on the rough table surface. In front of his fingertips, a layer of wood peels up.

Then he sets down the brush and dish on the smooth surface.

Still struck silent is Eli, holding the mirror in his now-wobbling grasp.

Next thing I know, Ryco takes the razor from my grasp. He grips the lower part of my face. That first stroke he runs across my neck is the worst—the stroke of a sadist. Eli's sliced-open neck, and Musgrae's flayed one are all I see. Breaths catch in my throat, like bits of powdered-sugar on a gasping inhale. Though needing to cough the powder away, I know I cannot. Not with a razor literally to my throat. At the stroke's end, my breaths calm. My heartbeat evens, to that comforting rhythm of imminent sleep.

Relaxing, I echo to Ryco, *Ironic. Instead of my dad here for this step—from boyhood to manhood—it's you, Sadist.*

Arrogance, again, he echoes, in return, taking the second stroke. *Sure that wise, while the Sadist has this to your neck?*

Is it arrogance, to speak the truth?

Eli's mirror trembles more.

Ryco takes the third stroke. Sighing, and his gaze softening, Ryco states, "There's no need to force the razor to do what it doesn't want to. What's needed *is* for you to have the razor do all the work. Harmlessly, and without effort." Taking the fourth stroke, then the fifth, he continues, "All you do is keep moving it. Finding the right angle, then turning the edge, to match the contours of your face." With that, he starts along my jawline, echoing, *I won't deny what I am: a sadist, as you call me.*

Is there anything else to call you?

I suppose not, as I enjoy inflicting pain on those deserving of it. Why do you think Zymarc of Vitiosus would even take notice of me? Of my methods? If I was not as ruthless as he can be.

It takes a monster to know one, I echo.

Hence, little boy, why *I become one when I need to.*

Ryco glances at Eli's clammy face, saying, "You may put the mirror down, Eli."

After he obeys, more branches grow up from the table surface to encase the mirror in a frame.

Releasing his hold on my face, Ryco sets the razor down. He takes the white cloth from Ben, to wipe residual foam off my face. Into the beckoning mirror, I look. Aside from the marks left by me, there's not a scratch.

"Is it not better," queries Ryco, "to let experienced hands guide you? Rather than the inexperienced?"

You're still a sadist, I echo.

Would a sadist leave you unscathed?

I echo, *Until an opportune moment.*

Cutting our Mensa-div short, with their entrance through the open doorway, is someone creeping shyly into the room.

Ryco, tapping his foot once, makes the table disappear. He catches the mirror, before it shatters on the floor. "Gemma Galloway," he says. "How may we be of service?"

"I didn't come for anything. Just to …" she trails off, unshed tears in her eyes.

Ryco hands Eli the mirror, then nods once at the others. Save for Warren and himself, the guards skulk to the bathing quarter without a word.

The steam rises. The water splashes. Then the guards begin their whispering banter.

Musgrae mutters, "Ben, aren't you going to show us?"

Sounding surprised, Eli butts in with, "Musgrae, you know?"

"Don't touch my clothes," Ben hisses. "I already washed, and no! You don't get to see it."

"Quall hasn't finished it, yet," adds Kent.

Ignoring them, Ryco glances from Gemma's sad face to the stubborn box in her hands, asking her, "That the last of LanSoren's items?"

"Talok said you might be able to open it," replies Gemma, taking a few more steps into the room. "He also told me … what *that* word means."

"Parasogyn?" Ryco states for her.

"Please." She cringes. "Don't speak it. Don't think it. No one should *ever* be called that."

Glancing my way, Ryco states, "I've been called things worse than that."

"No one deserves the degradation of that name. I'm sorry—"

Chair clattering back against the bed, I bolt up, scoffing, "You're apologizing to *him?*"

"I know you don't like him, Tyler, but—"

A jeer is all I have for what's happening: Gemma Galloway—the Rich Witch—apologizing to the Sadist. To the one almost undeserving of all kindness. He who would taunt and threaten me from the beginning.

She slams the box down on Ryco's desk, asking, "Who do want me to be? The Gemma who hurt you? Or the one I'm trying so hard to be?" Taking the key from her pocket, she lets it thud to the desk.

"Then, go on!" I yell. "Apologize to the one who shot at Awngeleik. The one who threatened me. Before even trying to get to know me."

"You're not being fair, Tyler!" Gemma shouts back. "I can't help what makes me feel bad. What makes me sorry." She looks to Ryco. "I'm sorry for even speaking that word."

My head pounds. "I can't be hearing this right."

"You don't know, Tyler. It's an insult to his father. His mother taking a brunt of the shame for it. And Ryco—along with any and all of his descendants—is accused of being cursed, simply for being born. It's not right."

"You know," interrupts Ryco, inspecting the box, "the last time someone apologized to me with words, I was a year younger than you are now."

He looks to Gemma, and she queries, "Thirteen?"

Book now in his lap, Warren sits up. "Maybe I should leave?"

"No need," states Ryco, taking the key in his hand to open the box. When unsuccessful, he queries, "Were there any other keys?"

Coldly, I reply, "That's the only one we found."

"Yet, it doesn't fit the lock."

"It has to."

"Are you sure?"

"Yes," I seethe.

When Ryco lays the key sideways on the box-lock, I ask, "What are you doing?"

"Opening the box. What else?" He frowns. "You said the key is for this box. So it must be, as you seem to know everything. Hero of Nyrim."

Thrice, he snaps his fingers. Then, like the thrown ingot, the key disappears. One palm glowing green, Ryco waves his hand over the stubborn box. Brightening the impenetrable box is the glow now cracking and splintering the wood. Shattering out are metal shards, as the key grows from within the box. At the exploding sound, Warren leaps off the bed. His chest heaving, he holds his book by the flap and watches Ryco reduce the key to its normal size once again.

I'm at the desk, in a flash, digging through the shards and box contents. My hands shake, until brushing over the cover of another journal. Now resting among the desk-clutter are the other contents of a folded paper, Enigma Star, and long, scarred key. Though all items are unscathed, I still shout at Ryco, "You couldn't have known what's inside. Ben couldn't see past the lining. What if you had broken something?"

"I'm a bit more versed in Gendras than Ben of Yharss. No need for me to make things harder for you, by destroying what your father left behind. He made learning the truth hard enough as it is."

Just as the mist fades, and water splashes cease, Gemma pleads, "Will the two of you stop it?"

The guards trail out of the bathing quarter, all wearing black pants and tank tops—except for Ben, who's still in full-uniform.

That's when I take the new Enigma Star, and stomp toward the door.

"Where are you going?" queries Gemma.

"Out," I reply. "Can't think with all this noise. First, a razor to my neck. Then, apologies to he who threatens me. *Now*, you're trying to create a truce?"

When I continue for the doorway, Gemma whispers, "I can't win. Can I? You'll always hate me for something."

Stopping mid-stride, I quiet my voice to say, "You're the only one I know here, Gemma. The only one I trust never to lie to me. Or hide the truth. So, no, I don't hate you. How could I?"

"Then why leave?"

"Because I need to think. Alone."

"Ben. Sorry I took so long," says Quall, sauntering in and almost stumbling into me. "Tyler? Were you headed out?"

"Yes! Or am I not allowed to leave anyone's sight for a little *alone* time?"

"I think it's best you rest for the night," he says. "You've had a long day. If you must go, you'll need your cousin's permission."

"Am I a prisoner?"

"Of course not, Tyler!" exclaims Talok, wandering in with a shadow looming in his gaze. "Go take a walk. Clear your mind. Uncle LanSoren did it all the time."

"He did that back home too," I agree.

Talok grins. "Especially when he needed answers to evasive questions. Or to walk off a storm of frustrations." Gripping my shoulders, he adds, "I would love to go with you. But … I think you need to take this walk alone. Keep an eye out for Callie of Dysarda too? I lost track of her, after Awngeleik's commotion."

"Sure. And feel free to look over the last items, from that box Ryco was kind enough to open."

Talok beams at Ryco. "You opened it? Wonderful!"

From across the room, Kent calls, "Check for Callie at the Midnight Anemones. I believe there's a field, near the Arkivara's base. Should be glowing in the moonlight, by now."

Lifting my hand in goodbye, I state, "I'll look there first. Won't be long."

24

Midnight Anemones

Bathing in full moonlight is the empty scene of bloodstained shamrock-grass. It's where memories exploded from Nyrim, then me. Memories I still can't remember, no matter how I try. What currently disregards my grievance now, though, is this mocking object resting on the rock. The second Enigma Star, beside me. Still unsolved. Aloud, I state, "Even with everything I've been able to do, I can't figure you out." Silently, I continue, *Not my dad's secrecy, nor his death. This Enigma, or the Vardiya's message. Awngeleik, or the journals, either. But Soren's interest in Gemma disturbs me. How does everything fit, in what my dad was running from?*

The field of Midnight Anemones beckons me to look, and I do. And when I do, something deep within my soul is brought to the surface. An inner summon, which calls from across the stained grass.

It is a cool breeze and warm sunlight.

It is fear and courage.

A contradiction of sensation, all felt at once.

Sighing, I seize the Enigma Star. Whether I'm ready, or not, I prepare myself for the presence of contradiction: the Geldryn device displayed on her wrist. Though Callie of Dysarda's out of sight, I sense the device nearing with every step.

The cool breeze turns to ice.

The warm sunlight to a scorching desert.

Fear to horror.

Courage to carelessness.

Sweat beads on my brow, and I claw at my neck, until a gentle wind carries the calming sugar-musk scent of Midnight Anemones. At the field's border I stand, taken aback by their glow. Blue toward the center of unreflecting black, each flower boasts of six glowing petals edged with white.

Sensing that I've been here before, once again, familiarity fills me. Through the intoxicating knee-high flowers I wade, calling for Callie. The one uniform reply is from the Arkivara's leaves rustling their own rhythm. It's like thousands of little replies, really. Unable to resist, I flop down in the elegant flowers the same way I would in my favorite patch of grass back home. With a long, single inhale, my lungs soak in my new favorite smell of Midnight Anemones.

Time passes, though I know not how much, when I sit up to think, *If she's not here, where would she go?*

A grove of fruit trees, nearby, looks promising. Reluctantly getting up, I wander deep into its dark shadows, echoing to her, *Callie. You in here?*

Behind me, hurrying footsteps rustle through the Midnight Anemones. Someone's in the grove with me. Fear takes hold, when heat returns to my veins. That same heat felt near Mirror Lake. I dash farther into the grove. But I collide with something. Someone. We plummet to the ground, together.

The Enigma Star is knocked from my grasp.

Rolling on top of me, the figure clamps small, strangling hands round my throat. Like a ghost sensation of that first razor-stroke gliding on my neck, I'm choked more. That powder seems to fill up my lungs. Not one breath am I able to take. My heartbeat goes wild. Too erratic for me to count its beats. My heart should be exploding in my chest; yet, it does not.

Struggling, I manage to grasp hold of my offender's wrists. The ice-cold metal of the Geldryn device touches the skin of my left arm. That's when the stroke sensations cease. Though hoarse and coughing, I'm able to speak the words, "Stop, Callie. It's me."

When it registers *whom* she is choking, Callie lets go. She springs to her feet, to help me up, then hands the recovered Enigma Star to me. Masked by darkness, the deep blush is still unmistakable on her fair skin. "Many pardons, Tyler Ravier," she whispers. "I heard a hushed voice and it frightened me. I thought it might be someone else."

With the remembrance of ReNovak's eyes, I am unnerved. He's a Sorsryn, and she? A Paragonian. Yet their unusual eyes are mirrored. Pushing nerves aside, I simply ask, "Who?"

Before Callie answers, rushing footsteps loom nearby. She tugs me to the shelter behind a tree, as two figures pass. Their footsteps crunch on the grove's fallen twigs and leaves.

One of them giggles. Not a girl. But a woman. Rorka. She whispers, "Sh! Gyron. Someone will hear us."

In the moonlight, Gyron stops a short distance away, from where we're hidden in the darkest shadows of the grove. He presses Rorka's back against a tree. His hold on her shoulders, he leans down and kisses her on the mouth more passionately than he did, earlier. He then finds interest in kissing her tenderly on the cheek. Then along her jaw. The whole time, Rorka's breaths are heavy, but her hands are steady while grasping Gyron's forearms. Only seconds pass, before she releases the Siveyra's arms to roughly grab fistfuls of fabric at his hips. When she yanks him closer against her, Gyron lets out a soft groan. Desperately, almost wild, he starts kissing her harder on the neck, working his way down to the nape.

And then he bites her.

At least, that's what I assume, because Rorka is grumbling, "Ow! That hurt!"

"Sorry." He pulls away, saying, "Got too eager."

"Sorsryns still drink blood?" Rorka seems surprised. "I didn't know."

Healing her neck, he replies, "It's mostly Deathasyns, who still enjoy blood as a main part of their—"

Cutting him off, Rorka says, "It doesn't matter." Gripping Gyron's coat-collar, she tugs him down to kiss her again.

Smiling inside, I take hold of Callie's hand and whisper, "Now that we know we're not going to die, we shouldn't keep eavesdropping."

We start to leave, but stop when Rorka breaks away to ask, "How did your King ReNovak know of my interest in you?"

"He didn't," replies Gyron breathlessly. "It was that little Tyler Ravier. Goading him with Mensa-div. Daring him to request a Siveyra Kiss. For you. Our victor."

Hearing my name, I stop in my tracks. Callie bumps against my back.

Teasingly, she whispers, "But eavesdropping is entertaining, when you're the subject of discussion?"

"Maybe?" is my simple reply, while narrowing my gaze at her.

"LanSoren's Tyler?" queries Rorka. "The oddest thing happened, when I met him today. He thought he read my mind. Which he did. But he didn't realize we had the exact same thought, when we shook hands."

Stepping back, Gyron grips Rorka's hand, then pulls her toward the field of flowers. "You're sure you weren't imagining it?"

"Now, you sound like Alpha Jasper. In all seriousness, Gyron—as you're a Siveyra—have you ever heard of something like that happening?"

Partway through the wade of flowers, Gyron pauses the progression forward. "When you met LanSoren the first time, did anything similar happen?"

Rorka declares, "Never met him."

Gyron faces her. "You're one of the Greyvon alpha candidates. And you never met King Sosha's Waking Dragon?"

"Actually, I'm a Matriarch Candidate. One of few born, since the War of Ichors Von."

"Interesting," states Gyron, while fiddling with a lock of Rorka's sunset-red hair. "How is it that candidates are chosen? Matriarchs, in particular."

Ignoring the Siveyra's toying with her hair, Rorka replies, "The first requirement is the Alpha Howl—solely obtained through genetics. I got my all-consuming one, when I was a thirteen-year-old Vonsai."

All-consuming howl? I muse. *Has to be Jack Wayeland's Bear-Wolf. Then a Greyvon* has *been to Earth. Why?*

"I've heard it." Gyron chuckles, brushing his fingertips along her tinged cheek. "Not yours, but that Mekka's. Sounded like a pack of angry Vonsai."

Could Rorka be the Phantom of Muraine? Or was that Mekka? Still possible for it to be Gyron. And what about the Miriam-imposter? Too many! I groan inside.

"Mine's the same, although higher," says Rorka, resting her hand on Gyron's blade hilt. "Ever since my thirteenth year, Alpha Jasper has personally trained me for the position: to be the first Greyvon Matriarch, since the death of Shena."

Gyron suddenly pulls his hand away. "That makes the lack of introduction between you and LanSoren even more bizarre. Especially considering the great friendship those two shared."

Earlier, Rorka sounded obsessed with meeting my dad. Would she resort to spying on him? Killing him? What reason would she have?

Gyron resumes the walk, stating, "No matter. You Greyvons can keep your secrets. Although, I'd like to know a few more of yours this night. Before the wake of dawn and my resumed duty."

"Would you now?" queries Rorka, a calm in her voice belying the color brightening her cheeks.

Somewhat shrinking back, Gyron says, "Though, perhaps, not the howl."

"No promises, Siveyra. Lead the way."

Toying with his hands shyly, Gyron states, "I was hoping you would. I'm not familiar with the Canopies of Paragon."

"Astonishing!" she exclaims. "The Warrior of the Nyxane wants to be led?"

Gyron grins. "Only by the future Matriarch of the Greyvons."

Their voices fade away, but not the heat in my veins. Attempting to ignore it, I state, "We should head back to the castle."

"Yes, but ..." Callie hesitates. She fiddles with the crisscrossed cording of my sleeve, then asks, "Can you do me a favor? When we get there?"

"Like what?"

"Introduce me to Awngeleik? She's the most beautiful creature I've ever seen."

"You wouldn't be saying that, if she nearly killed you three times. Still want to meet her?"

Plodding for the stained grass, then to the path, Callie follows at my side, saying, "She doesn't mean any harm. She's merely bored. Most neins don't like playing with the dyns. And only some dyns enjoy the antics of neins."

I nod. "They don't want to play with her."

"Exactly," replies Callie, hooking her arm with mine.

Clearing my throat, I ask, "What did you think of the festival?"

"It was terrifyingly-beautiful."

"Or was it beautifully-terrifying?" I counter.

She thinks a moment. "Depends on perspective, and what is felt more strongly: beauty or terror?"

"Terror," I state.

Callie smiles, saying, "Beauty for me."

"I can see it, Miss Poetry."

Smile diminishing, Callie presses closer. She matches her strides with mine, asking, "Why are you so cold? Your skin's like ice."

I shrug. "Don't feel cold. I'm actually too warm."

She reaches for my left hand. When her Geldryn bracelet grazes my skin, the haunting thoughts echo, *How to break their laws? Freedom from the grave. Who can truly wield the keys?*

That's when Soren's odd words come to mind, as well: *Twelve. Thirteen. Beginning. End. Everything in between. He motioned to the four elements. That Geldryn device could be pointing to the same thing. But what could it really mean?*

"Callie?" I ask. "Will you take the Geldryn device off?"

Her eyes glass over with tears, and she whimpers, "I thought you liked it?"

Gently, I state, "I like how it looks. Not how it makes me feel."

Blinking away the glassy eyes, she states, "You shouldn't worry. Both Greyvons and Onyx test Geldryn objects for imbued magic, before they are free to give them to us. To Paragon."

"Even still. They missed something with this. I think it's absorbing magic from anyone wearing it."

Wrenching it off, Callie declares, "Then I shall never put it on again."

"I'm probably being paranoid. I just want someone to take a look at it. Make sure it's safe for you to wear."

"After seeing what you can do," she says, "I trust your judgment over mine, *wholeheartedly*. As I said, I shan't put it on again."

We stroll in silence, the rest of the way: on the winding path; through the castle entry; then down a few corridors, until we arrive at the infirmary entrance.

Within the dim room is that glowing yellow gaze watching the entrance. Before I can back away from it, he sees me. "Thought you wouldn't be long?"

I reply, "Had to erase the razor-strokes, so I could, you know, fake tolerance in front of Talok."

"Fair enough," states Ryco. "But what brings you down here, instead of up there? Do you prefer a cold cobblestone floor, to a warm bed?"

Fuming at his reference to dumping me on the barn floor that first night, I just twist the watch round my wrist furiously.

"Master Ryco?" queries Callie, her gaze searching the room. "I wanted to see the Equidyn."

"Over there." He motions. "In the corner, still asleep."

To Awngeleik, Callie strolls; when I go to follow her, Ryco grips my arm, asking, "What happened?"

"Don't know what you mean."

"I could feel your cold skin, before you even entered the castle. And, for the first time since you arrived, *real* fear is in your gaze."

I smirk. "It's nothing I would tell you."

"Then Talok, perhaps?" Ryco stands.

"Where do you get off?" I seethe. "You threaten to send me to the grave. Then you imply my death would crush Paragon. So which is it? Do you want me dead or alive?"

Clawing at one of his arm bracers, Ryco states, "I will show you the same courtesy that you give to me. You laid the first judgment. I replied in kind. It is the nature of Sylvadyns, to balance the scales. As you cannot control your nature, I cannot deny mine."

Shaking my arm tiredly, Callie yawns out the words, "Suddenly, I am overcome with fatigue. Where am I to go for the night, Master Ryco?"

I grit my teeth. Hearing her call him that, lights a different kind of fire. A thought of, *Master Pain-of-My-Life. That would be a better title.*

Regaining composure, Ryco says, "This way."

Out toward the stairs, he leads us on the route the others took before. Upon entering the illuminated quarters, all guards have my dad's remaining items strewn across Ryco's desk. Not even the potions' table is safe from the clutter.

"All this," says Eli, "just from LanSoren's Last Poem?"

"Seems excessive," Siege adds, "to have the poem *and* the numerical guide."

"Safeguarding." Warren yawns, from Ryco's desk chair. "Always have another plan."

Louder than necessary, Ryco announces, "Look who finally decided to come back."

Asleep on my bed is Talok, his body half-hanging over the edge. On the one next to it is Gemma, in the dead-doll pose. Contorted to broken, she still wears her new coat of navy, purple, and brown. Together, the two are the very picture of *slept wrong last night.*

Shaking my head at the sight, I go inspect the last and thickest of the four journals. Its glistening cover of leather is bronze-colored, with black-edged pages. On the front are two dragons, intertwined. The larger one of black displays a rack of spiral horns, while its feathered-wings fan out. Halfway down the tail, three velvety-tails split off. Adding the most magnificence, however, is its long neck similar to a giraffe's. In contrast, the much smaller dragon is copper. The four wings of it are reminiscent of a bat. But its head is fox-like, and its tail is as bushy as a fox's too.

Flipping to the inside cover, his writing reads:

To my son. Tyler Malik Ravier.

You will know the truth. One day.

By my words or another's.

When I turn the page, foreign symbols taunt me to remember. Frustrated,

I close it. My attention moves to the Rubidyn-Greyvon journal. I ask anyone who's listening, "Grover's done with this, already?"

"No," replies Kent. "We brought it here for Rorka to look at. Still waiting for her to come back for the night."

"You'll have to go looking for her, in the Paragonian Canopies," I state, while sharing a look with Callie.

She sets the Geldryn device on the potions' table.

"We don't know what this opens," states Ben, handing me a long key. "But agreed that you should keep it on your person."

Taking the scarred key in my grasp, I study the top of it, where four tiny triangles are enclosed within each of the four circles.

Right then, Ryco calls out, "My king."

Stuck in the dream world, my cousin remains placid. Only his chest rises and falls.

Determined to wake him, Ryco shouts, "Talok!"

Scrambling from the bed with stumbling footsteps is Talok, suffering the bang of the Eel-Shock. "What's happening? Are we late again?" he hollers, eyes now wide-awake.

Calmly, Ryco states, "Tyler found Callie of Dysarda."

"Excellent!" Talok blinks away the fog, then looks at Callie by the potions' table. As she fiddles with the closed buds of Midnight Anemones, he says, "You'll be staying in here. Safe with the King's Guard. Hope you don't mind sharing a bed with Gemma Gal—" At that moment, Talok looks to Gemma on the bed. "Dragon's Spike!" he exclaims. "Did she die?"

Not waiting for an answer, Talok leaps onto my bed and then to the floor at Gemma's bedside. He lifts one of her limp arms up by the wrist.

"She's fine." I shrug. "That's how she sleeps."

Surprised at my implication, Talok releases Gemma's wrist. Back to the bed her arm flops, as his attention pivots to gawking at me. While I cringe at him, Talok is asking, "You know how Gemma sleeps?"

Pinching the bridge of my nose, I reply, "It's a long story."

Smirking, Ryco echoes, *If I'm a sadist, what are you? A night creeper.*

"So," Ben interrupts, "that is the dead pose you and Gemma were fighting about? You're right. It is disturbing. Though, I still don't know what a doll is."

Talok grins. "I think both of you have some stories to tell, over breakfast, tomorrow. But, for now, I'm going to bed. Before I fall over." Talok's feet drag, on his way to the potions' table. "Anyone have luck, making sense of my uncle's belongings?"

Quall lounges on his lonesome bed, and answers for all by stating, "Not a bit."

"Callie. Isn't this yours?" queries Talok, right as he picks up the Geldryn device.

Fear rises up my throat so fast, I'm strangled to speechless.

A moment too late, Callie calls out, "King Talok, don't!"

Flashing briefly with light are the device jewels, like some vindictive beast. Shifting and twisting as a living creature, the bangle clamps onto Talok's right wrist. He shrieks, then thuds to his knees.

25

Device of Uncertainty

On his knees, Talok's unresponsive when Callie grips his wrist ensnared by the device. During the turmoil of bodies clambering to reach him, the bronze-bangle begins the same scarlet glow of Vitiosyn-eyes. Talok slams his eyes shut, and starts to hyperventilate.

"It's burning hot!" Callie exclaims. "Someone do something."

Ryco's at Callie's side, yanking her away. Everyone watches him kneel in front of Talok, and fumble with the device. Jolting up, he announces, "It's not activated by Gendras. Warren! Check it for Kyanist."

Musgrae hauls Talok's writhing body up from the floor. He sets him on my bed. At the same time, Warren presses his dark hands on the device. In horror, Callie watches.

"Master Quall," she cries, "it's my fault. I shouldn't have taken it off."

Warren's hands tremor, right then, and Callie wails. When Warren lets go, Talok stops breathing. The room plunges into silence, after Callie ceases her wails. Everyone holds their breath, as if doing so for the King of Paragon will release him of his plight.

Gasping to consciousness, Talok opens his eyes. We take breath with him.

Across the king's forehead, neck, then chest, Quall sweeps his hand, asking Warren, "What did you do?"

He stammers, saying, "Nothing. It stopped absorbing magic, is all."

Paralysis gone, I rush to my cousin. Gripping his arm, I refuse to let go. "Are you hurt? How do you feel?"

Talok, sitting up to rub his head, pushes Quall's hand away. "I'm fine, Cousin Tyler," he says. "Have the worst headache, though." His mischievous eyes betray his calm.

"This is no time for jokes, Talok," Siege scolds. "We were truly worried."

Ryco confirms, "If it's given you a headache, then it absorbed some of your magic."

"Is that dangerous?" I ask.

"Depends on how much it absorbed," replies Warren. "None of us are familiar enough with Geldryn devices, to know for sure."

I suggest, "Then we need Rorka and Gyron. Someone should go find them in the canopies."

Quickening for the doorway, Ben volunteers to go.

"That will take too long," states Ryco, as a longbow and two arrows appear in his grasp. He opens the bay window.

When cold air zips in, and reaches Gemma, she springs up, exclaiming, "Cold! Close the window!"

Mischievous eyes dancing more, Talok says, "You sleep through chaos, Miss Gemma. Yet waken to the cold?"

"What chaos?" queries Gemma, shaking away the fog of sleep.

As they update Gemma, Ryco whispers something into the two arrow-tails and then aims toward the night sky.

"You only need one," I interrupt.

Glaring back at me, Ryco lowers the bow a moment.

I continue, "They were with each other, around the time I found Callie."

"That was a while ago," says Ryco. "You're sure they're still near each other?"

Shrugging, I echo, *Yes, but go ahead. Release both. See if I'm wrong.*

Aiming again, he releases both, then shuts the window firmly.

In the distance, a howl rings out. And Musgrae cocks his head, stating, "That was fast."

Clearing his throat, Ryco states, "They can't reach their mark that quickly."

Quall starts to talk, but Warren cuts him off with, "Unless you've been expanding your Blue Magic repertoire, Ryke."

Quall tries again, but fails when Siege says, "We would know it, if he has."

His eyes lighting up, Eli adds, "Ryco can't help but use all magical knowledge, to razzle and dazzle. Razzling Ryco!"

Turning deep-red is Quall, doing everything he can to keep his rage at bay, while Ryco states, "That doesn't rhyme, Eli. Try harder."

"Wasn't trying to rhyme. Just thought it catchy."

Kent says, "Whichever life-partner gets stuck with you, Eli, we're telling her she's in charge of naming your children."

Smirking, Ryco echoes, *While our Eli may be annoying, at least he isn't a night creeper. Like you. Watching Gemma Galloway sleep.*

Turning back to the window, Ryco watches and waits for the answer all want to know this night. What havoc might the Geldryn device be doing to my cousin, the King of Paragon?

* * *

At the window is Ryco, while my gaze burns into his back. The King's Guard continue their banter. For now, time ticks safely away. Void of the shadow, my cousin rests on my bed, while Gemma giggles. "Hettie and Lettie! For twin girl names?"

Musgrae laughs. "Eli, those are terrible."

Kent adds, "What are their nicknames going to be? Let-Het?"

The room roars, save for Ryco, Callie, and me.

Eli mutters, "Didn't think about the nicknames."

Ryco rotates around, to face the door. When two raps sound out, Quall opens it. Striding in first is Gyron, announcing, "Came as quickly as we could."

Rorka enters, then closes the door. "Something happen?"

Words burst from Callie. "It's that Geldryn device the shopkeeper let me have. Tyler asked me to take it off. Thought it might be absorbing my magic."

"King Talok will be fine," reassures Kent. "Settle your fear, Little Callie."

On opposite sides of the bed, Gyron and Rorka lean down to examine the device.

Hands jerking back in alarm, Gyron states, "That's one of the devices I brought this morning. It was dormant. Perhaps even void."

Rorka sweeps her gaze over the room, asking, "Did someone use magic on this?"

"After it latched onto him," Ryco says, "and wouldn't come off."

"Which ones?" She straightens to standing.

"Gendras and Kyanist."

"That shouldn't matter," says Gyron, brushing a thumb across his brow. "Unless it's a—"

Interrupting him, Rorka asks, "Device of Old?"

"What were those meant for?" queries Gemma.

Gyron starts to form words, but stops, and I ask, "You're magically bound not to say?"

"You're learning," replies Gyron, before looking to Talok. "I must get back to the Nyxane. To King ReNovak. He should have access to more knowledge on this than I."

Rorka states, "Are you saying, he isn't here?"

"He had other matters to attend to."

Ryco interrupts, "Wouldn't he have already seen it?"

"Not from this last cargo," says Gyron. "As my king was absent for a few days, I cleared several devices for delivery myself. I figured—since Jasper personally inspects all of them—it was safe to release them to Paragon, without King ReNovak's blessing."

Rorka's eyes widen, in fear. "Jasper's been hibernating for eight months. Had to, after he gave some of his soul-essence to LanSoren, trying to save him."

Talok sits up. "What are you saying, Rorka?"

"Jasper hasn't inspected the last five deliveries to the Nyxane. It's been some of the council members and me."

Striding for the doorway, Gyron grumbles, "Why were we not told of

Jasper's absence?"

"It's Greyvon business. If word got around that our alpha was hibernating, it could embolden our enemies to attack us, or … our allies." Rorka glances at Talok, with even more fear sinking into her eyes.

Gyron sharply inhales. "Let us hope our errors won't prove fatal to Talok or Paragon."

"I will send for Jasper, immediately," says Rorka, looking down in shame.

Ben observes some unspoken cue, and pulls out a small paper-square from one of his pockets. He gives it to Rorka. But Warren's the one to relinquish a quill to her.

Talok states, "He's back, then?"

"A few days ago?" replies Rorka, second-guessing herself. "Two weeks? I'm not sure. I was out on assignment. He was there, when I got back." With that, Rorka starts to push aside the dragon-wolf journal, but her hand briefly lingers on it. Next, she puts quill to paper and scrawls a few symbols; one symbol matches Talok's etched coat buttons.

Because the penned symbols aren't words, it's unclear whether she wrote the phantom notes or not. Ripping away my chances to study her pen strokes more, Rorka folds the note into an origami bird. Opening the window, she tosses it out. The paper lights into a bird of fire that descends to glowing embers. She speaks, "To Jasper of Pariah." Then the bird vanishes out of sight like a bullet. Fading with it is the sound of its flapping.

Across from me, Gemma shivers on the edge of her bed. "Why's it so cold?"

Musgrae dumps his massive coat on Gemma's shoulders, and she's swallowed up by it. Now sandwiched between him and Callie, Gemma hugs the coat tight. She soon stops shivering.

"The Midnight Anemones are closed," declares Callie to Gemma.

"What's that mean?" I ask.

"Rolling in rainstorm," replies Kent, plopping down beside Callie.

Quall adds, "With the quick temperature drop, it should be quite the storm."

Ryco, standing beside Rorka at the window, asks Gyron, "Will the storm delay your return to the Nyxane?"

"Not if I take a Mystadyn."

Some of Callie's gloom disappears, as she states, "Though lightning may crash around them, they're as steady as a breath before the plunge. So says my father."

"Wise words." Kent smiles.

Quall commands, "Siege, go with Gyron. Summon that Mystadyn friend of yours. Claudys, wasn't it? Afterwards, attend to Awngeleik until dawn."

The two hurry out, during Kent's instruction of, "Rorka, go wake Grover. Relay what's happened."

"Where is he?"

Ben replies, "Still attending to Nyrim, in the Arkivara."

Before she leaves, Talok says, "Earlier, Rorka, we heard you howl. Was something wrong?"

Juniper eyes unsettling, she replies, "I was demonstrating one of my howls, for an Onyx Warrior. Made a bet that I couldn't break through his sound-proofing barrier."

"A bet," states Ryco, "that he should openly regret."

Doubtful that he regretted anything, I echo, to anyone listening.

Except for Gemma and Callie, concerned with their hushed conversation, several in the room glance my way. From where Musgrae sits by Gemma, he smiles like a devil at Rorka. "Was it a howl of prowess? Or pleasure?"

"Kinky," mutters Warren, as the hushed conversation ceases.

"If there isn't anything else…?" Rorka starts to say, but pauses nervously, when Musgrae approaches her.

"What's that on your neck?" Musgrae taps his own, cooing, "Rorka of Pariah."

Rushing to Rorka is Eli, sticking his face not even an arm's length away from her neck, announcing in a squeaky voice, "You have a Sorsryn hickey."

"I'll go find Grover, now." Blushing deep-red, Rorka scuttles out.

"Guess she really liked the Siveyra Kiss," states Gemma, doing her nervous Strand-Twirl.

Looking down at her restless hands, Callie hides a smile.

Eli whirls around, exclaiming, "Her and Siveyra Gyron? No!"

Kent rolls his eyes. "Whom else would it be?"

Quall shudders. "Ryco, I leave the hopeless-incurables in your capable hands." With one last look at Talok fast asleep on my bed, he starts to leave.

But Musgrae queries, "Where are you going?"

"To check on Awngeleik," he replies. "Then to keep Siege company, when he gets back."

With that, Quall makes his escape.

Glancing around, Ryco states, "Best we rest, before dawn."

"Hey!" exclaims Eli. "You made a—" When the citrine gaze turn sadistic, Eli stops short. Sheepishly, he finishes with, "Rhyme." Like a scolded child, he trails to his corner bed.

Everyone follows suit, one by one, taking to their own beds. Gemma and Callie share one. And, since Talok has claimed mine, I settle for Quall's lonesome bed.

After Ryco fiddles with the door, the lights go out. Only streams of moonlight seep in now.

Ben, coming over to look out the window, whispers, "Don't worry, Tyler. I'm sure that device is nothing to worry about."

"Hope so," I reply.

In the silence of the room, my heart aches for answers, my body for rest, and mind for reassurance that everything will be all right. Still, the sensation of contradiction pricks at my skin. In the end, I can't fight it. Sleep consumes me.

III

The Victor

*"Think of this moment we share,
as both of us reaching out
across the pages of time."*

26

Until Tomorrow

A deep chill sinks into the room, and I wake to Eli hissing, "Ryco, somebody opened the window."

At the window, stands Callie of Dysarda. Dragging myself out of bed, I join her in gazing out to the night sky. Quietly, I ask, "Waiting for something?"

"The rain," she whispers, hooking her arm with mine.

In that moment, my father's whispering echo speaks, *You will know the truth. One day. By my words or another's.*

"You a tattle now, Eli?" Warren grumbles.

Glancing over my shoulder, I see Talok illuminated by the moonlight. Still clamped on his wrist is the mysterious device, while he sleeps amid the noise.

If the device is over there, why are these thoughts still invading?

Kent teases, "If somebody dried off all the way."

"I'm dry, Kent!" Eli hollers.

"What?" says Musgrae, faking heartbreak. "There isn't going to be any little Hettie and Lettie? Devastating."

Laughingly, Warren mumbles, "You could help him out, Mooz."

Still groggy, Ryco groans, "You *are* no help, whatsoever, Warren."

From somewhere in the room, a bed creaks. Shuffling footsteps sound out, next. Then water splashes from across the room. Eli shrieks.

A groan, coming from Warren's direction, deepens to a growl. "Quiet!" Ryco demands.

Ignoring the demand, the heckling banter of the hopeless-incurables ensues.

Then Gemma, still drowning in Musgrae's coat, grips my hand. "I couldn't sleep, anyway," she whispers.

Heavy footsteps march for the door. When it opens, full light races across the vine-ceiling. Standing there, his grip on the knob, is Ryco. Eyes looking to inflict harm, he slams the door.

Squinting, Talok sits up to ask, "Morning already?"

Voice steady, Ryco states, "*Callie* of Dysarda, do you have a valid reason for opening the window? Thus, awakening the little vermin called Musgrae and Eli?"

Soaked head to toe, and glaring at Musgrae, Eli peels his black tank-top off to wring it out. Ignoring the Kirjan's glare is Musgrae, peering round the room innocently, until he sees Kent's scowl. That's when a devious grin breaks through the facade of innocence.

"The smell before rain," says Callie, glancing to Ryco. "It's a favorite of my father's."

"Very well," states Ryco. "Eli, put more clothes on. Or incubate under a sea of blankets. Your choice."

Eli's stormy-gray eyes turn to blazing. Though he murmurs no complaint, his steps bang his every displeasure. Vanquishing his usual strut, to some sort of angry-shiver, Eli stomps to the wardrobe. Ignoring the Kirjan-Stomp, Ryco traipses back to bed and then whips the covers over himself to go back to sleep.

Easing up to stand, Talok queries, "Did you and Gemma see the rain this morning?"

"No," I reply, wondering why, of all things, Callie and my cousin care so much about rain. Like my name, there's nothing special about it.

"Master Ryco?" calls out Callie.

Rolling over, Ryco props his groggy face on his fist.

"Is it too much trouble," queries Callie, with a breathy sigh, "for you to put the light out? The rainstorms, at night, are breathtaking without—"

Unamused, Ryco cuts her off with a snap of his fingers. The ceiling light goes out, but not the lights flashing outside. Except for Ryco, all gather to watch the lightning fracture and boom across the sky. Talok, dragging a chair to the window, sits down to breathe in the crisp air of Midnight Anemones.

Electrifying the clouds are more thundering bolts shaking the castle, as they catch a handful of outlines. Weaving in the brewing storm are luminescent dragons, attracting the lightning and splitting the clouds with their long tails. Can they be anything other than the Mystadyns Callie spoke of? With roars more like calls of giant eagles, they seem to fear nothing.

Looking toward the ground outside, Talok taps the windowsill. "Didn't Gyron say King ReNovak already left? What's he doing here, leaving the castle this late into the night?"

"With the Onyx," Warren replies, "who knows?"

Kent suggests, "Maybe his matter to attend, was a stroll in the rain."

"On Muraine!" exclaims Eli. "I made a rhyme."

"Bravo," Ryco grumbles. "Want a medal for it?"

"Nah! They're worthless for trade."

"Spoken like a true Kirjan," states Ryco. "How you must make them proud."

Drowning out conversations, the rain begins its hail down like fire. First are the sapphire-blue droplets. Next glisten the white then black likened to flashing cameras. Finishing is the showering of crimson and canary.

Gemma looks to me, asking, "You know what it reminds me of?"

"A painting you wish your mom had?"

Grinning, she reaches behind my back to unsheathe one of my dad's daggers. She holds it at arm's length away, letting the black-peacock handle balance on her palm. "It's like your dad's sleeping-dagger."

Agreeing, I take the dagger and ask, "Talok? Didn't Grover say these were enchanted with all types of magic?"

Captivated by the rain, Talok dimly answers with one nod. No words.

Just that. A nod.

I ask, "Is that magic, collecting in the falling rain?"

Callie teases, "Isn't it terrifyingly-beautiful?"

I shrug. "As long as it doesn't burn. No."

"It's a good kind of burn," says Kent. "Like warming your hands at the fire, after being out in the freezing cold of winter."

"Can we go out into it?" queries Gemma.

From under his bedcovers, Ryco coughs twice, signaling what someone's answer should be. Catching the signal, Talok shakes his head. "You and Tyler are still adapting to Muraine."

"The magic in the droplets," Kent states, "is concentrated."

"Might make you both sick," adds Ben.

Musgrae proclaims, "We don't want a sick, puking Mud Fiend. If that happens, I might have to come up with a new name for you."

In reply, Gemma punches Musgrae square on the ribs.

Snickering, then fighting off Gemma's pinching hands, Musgrae hollers, "Mercy, Mud Fiend! Already had the wind knocked out of me, by one of your Judo kicks."

"Gemma?" I ask, in surprise. "You kicked Musgrae?"

"It was deserved! While you were passed out, he decided to be a food hoarder. Wouldn't let me have any. Unless I could read his mind."

"Big mistake," I state. "Don't get between Gemma and her food."

Musgrae replies, "I won't. Ever again."

Ryco sighs yearningly, before saying, "*Words* I wish to hear from you every day."

"You would. If you'd put in a good word for me, to that Rozeth of the Aeown. I could bask in her beauty all day."

Ryco grumbles, "Musgrae, for the last time. Believe me when I say, to bask in the beauty of Rozeth of the Emerassassyns, *one* must tolerate the constant ten conversations swirling about in her head, while two spew from her mouth. Trading off with each other like night and day, every few minutes. Her presence is exhausting."

"Hence, Ryco's reason for never basking," says Kent.

"A small price to pay," states Musgrae, "to be with beauty made flesh."

"Stop it," Warren whines, "you're making me sick."

Jerking the covers back, Ryco sits up to ask, "Are you telling me, Musgrae, if we survive this war … you'd make Rozeth one of your expeditions?"

Musgrae starts to answer, but Ryco continues, "If you do, forget about chasing anyone else in the same span of time. You may not even have time for guard duty. For one day spent in the company of Rozeth, will take the same energy as all your other expeditions. Combined."

Kent interrupts, "Wasn't she supposed to be at the festival?"

"She was," Ryco confirms. "But I convinced a former friend in the Aeown, to detain her for a day. She will be here, tomorrow. Made it expressly clear that she's *elated* to meet LanSoren's Tyler Ravier. Best to get some sleep, Mr. Ravier. And you, Musgrae. You'll both need it, to face her in the morning."

Musgrae smacks my back, saying, "We'll just block her spilling thoughts with Mensenglos. No big deal."

One laugh bursting out, Ryco quiets himself to say, "Like me, Rozeth was one of Siveyra Dezarin's apprentices."

"At the same time?" queries Ben.

"The same three years. Yes. You cannot alter her mind, Musgrae. Her thoughts will invade. When she wants them to, or when she's overly excited. Which is most of the time."

"I'd still love to be formally introduced."

Ryco smirks. "Then you're a hopeless fool. Tomorrow, I will introduce you as my *personal* favorite one in the Paragonian Sovereignty."

"If you resent her as you do," says Musgrae, "I'm bound to adore her."

"We shall see, tomorrow. Shan't we?"

"On that note," interrupts Talok, "I vote we go back to bed."

"Agreed!" Warren booms.

"Callie of Dysarda," states Ryco, "if you are finished with smelling the rain, close the window … if it's not too much trouble?"

She obeys, then joins Gemma in their shared bed. I recline on the lonesome one. Within our darkened room, we're safe from the torrential sheets of magic-stained rain sweeping over the Eye of Paragon. Staring at the fire-turned-to-liquid, I'm captivated by the raw magic raining down. It provokes a myriad of emotions, as water streams down the glass.

Hopes trickle up to my heart.

The hope of tomorrow's end never finishing.

The wish that an orphan is not made in Callie of Dysarda.

Then there's the third and greatest desire of knowing the truth. For Gemma and me to stay long enough to find it, before going back to the lives we've always known.

* * *

When something booms above the castle, the room shakes.

Warren groans, "Was that a fire-bomb?"

"It's barely light out," Musgrae complains.

"It's too early, for the practice of tonight's events," Ryco mumbles, before his bed creaks.

"Smells like smoke." Eli's voice quivers. "Something's on fire."

Footsteps pad across the floor, toward me. Callie shakes me into full awareness, shouting, "Tyler Ravier. Wake up!"

Ryco rushes to the bay window. He gulps in a horrified breath, before rasping out, "Vitiosyns! They're attacking the city."

Pacing to Ryco's side, in shock, Kent adds, "Already started on the Fermata Canopy."

"Everyone!" shouts Ryco. "Get up. Paragon's under attack."

While Talok and Gemma are still the picture of contorted-tranquility, the King's Guard rush to action: out of their beds and dressed in full-uniform within minutes. When the door slinks open, the vines' light illuminates the room of anxious faces.

In trudge Quall and Siege.

Talok moans. "Can't I sleep a little longer?"

"Why's everyone up this early?" queries Siege.

"Ryco!" Quall says, through a smile. "You couldn't have known we were coming, for a menace-watching replacement." When he registers Ryco's wild eyes, the smile creeps away. With it? The little color Quall's pale skin has.

Peeling off Musgrae's coat, Gemma yawns out, "Were those fireworks?"

Heart pounding, I answer, "Vitiosyns."

Clenching her throat, Gemma's yawn is cut short.

Quall exclaims, "Vitiosyns?" He leaps over me, to get to the window, saying in disbelief, "It can't be."

"Your coat, Miss Gemma," says Kent, helping her up. "It needs quick enchantments."

Ben adds, "Wish we had time for absolute ones."

"Some are better than none," states Musgrae, slipping his coat on.

"What about Callie and me?" I ask.

Siege answers, "LanSoren enchanted the fabric of your coat."

"Keep that hood on," Warren adds, "and you'll be fine."

"What are we going to do?" queries Gemma, hugging herself and shivering.

Ben mutters to me, "Your father's things. Miniaturized." He hands me a small pouch. I add it to one of mine, somehow managing to flash a pathetic grin at him.

Oblivious to it all, Talok grips his head, muttering, "It's like I haven't eaten all week."

"Musgrae," Ryco commands, "go let the Onyx know what's happening. They're down the hall. See if they can stop this assault, before it escalates."

Musgrae rushes out.

Kent hands Gemma her coat. "Now for Little Callie," he says. "One of Ben's old coats should fit fine."

Retrieving a tattered, black one from the wardrobe, Ben tosses it to Callie.

"They've disappeared!" Musgrae hollers, before emerging in the doorway, breathless. "Beds look untouched. All their things. Just. Gone."

"Eli. Siege." Quall commands, "go get Awngeleik."

They rush out.

Ryco turns to my cousin, declaring, "King Talok, you have two options: to flee Paragon *or* huddle in one of the protected bunkers below the city."

"And hope," adds Warren, "that the Arkiveis and LanSoren's barrier spells hold."

Head still in a daze, Talok states, "We had one more day." He looks to Ryco. "Why have they violated the laws of the Onyx? It doesn't make any sense."

Quall rushes for the door. "We can't think of that, King Talok. You need to make a decision."

"Now," Ryco demands.

Just sitting there on the bed, Talok stares at the floor. He holds his breath, and fights rising emotions.

I step toward him, saying, "I vote that we flee. Relying on magic, alone, to save us? Sounds like a bad idea."

Device still on his wrist, Talok clenches his fists. Seeming to break from his battle, he nods in agreement. "It does. Doesn't it? Being trapped? Waiting it out? We're not prepared for it. Because of the festival. Because we assumed we had one more day. What fools we've been! Thinking the Vitiosyns couldn't outsmart the Onyx laws."

"Talok," Ryco pleads helplessly. "Your decision?"

Standing to straighten his coat, Talok states, "To flee."

With that, he rushes out the door. Hurrying after him, I'm next. Quall and Ryco are hot, in pursuit. The others follow behind us. Together, we make our way to the castle entrance room. There, we meet Siege and Eli.

"She's gone!" announces Eli, in horror.

I state, "We can't leave her."

Ryco replies, "Any attempt to chase her down, will result in her thinking it a game."

"We'll try spotting her, once in the air," says Quall.

In one fluid motion, Ryco forms a bow to shoot an arrow up at the ceiling. Behind him, Talok softly grips the arrow's tail of light-rope. He lets it slide within his grasp, until the arrow thwacks into the ceiling. With the thwack, Talok tightens his grip. He yanks down, as if slicing at an opponent behind him. When the rope grows into a pillar of light, he and Ryco step back.

With the pillar at its center, Siege and Eli etch a circular platform, on the castle floor, big enough to hold all of us. Then, like a mime drill-sergeant, Quall herds us onto it. Though silent, he has one chief call: the call of duty to save us.

Huddling close to me are Gemma and Callie, while Talok's hands release fire into the pillar. With embers it now sparks, as Talok speaks into it, "Awb-Sheados."

The platform cracks away from the first floor. Creeping past the second, it gains momentum in its rise toward the third floor. However, the ceiling of it still bars our freedom.

Eyes closed, Talok hovers his palms inches away from the ember-pillar. In the air, his fingers strum as if playing an instrument. With each strum, the ceiling is peeled away. Our path is made clear.

The platform stops on the third floor.

Ryco steps off first, stating, "Talok, open the roof. Reign's already here."

Confirming Ryco's words, a giant shadow spreads out on the floor. Talok forms his short-staff, to cast fire up to the roof. In reaction, it slithers back an opening. Reign's enormous face emerges above that space.

Talok calls to him, "Reign! We're fleeing the city. You are to escort us."

Dipping his head in understanding, Reign turns to let his tail hang from the roof opening.

"Climb!" Ryco commands.

"But it's a dragon's tail." Eli cringes.

Clawing at his own face, Ryco shouts, "Do you want to die today? If so, I'll end you this very moment!"

Startling into action, Eli climbs as if death is snapping at his heels. With the look Ryco has, he might as well be death. Citrine-Death. Next, Musgrae and Ben climb. Then Siege and Warren. With their ascent, the Citrine-Death calms. Ryco looks to us, asking, "You sufficient at climbing, Gemma?"

"Horrible at it," she admits. "Ask Tyler. Can't even catch a box thrown down to me."

Handing Gemma an arrow, Ryco states, "I thought as much."

When she takes it, Ryco twirls his index-finger in the air, instructing, "Spin once."

After she obeys, he takes the arrow from her and then forms a bow in his hand. That's when she starts asking, "What are you going to do?"

"Something I'll need your forgiveness for," replies Ryco, aiming the arrow between the waiting Musgrae and Warren.

"We're ready," calls Musgrae. "For Mud Fiend."

"What?" Gemma shrieks. "You're going to launch me up there? But I'm afraid of heights. Wait! Can't I—"

Mid-sentence, Ryco releases the arrow. Gemma screams. Cinching round her waist is the tail of light-rope, as she's flung up to Reign's back and into Musgrae's waiting grasp. Next to them, Warren cuts away the rope. When released of his grip, it disappears into nothing.

Offering an arrow to Callie, Ryco states, "You're next."

"But I'm a good climber," she argues. Not waiting for a response, Callie begins the climb with a rhythmic pace of quick-quick-slow.

"Climbs like a true Dysardan," states Kent proudly. "Meet you at the top." Repeating the same rhythm, Kent goes next; then Talok and me; Quall and Ryco last.

All of us upon his back, Reign bursts from the castle roof.

Rising in unison with Reign is a smaller BlacKaidyn, carrying a female rider. A woman dressed in garb colored of jade-green.

Either irritated or relieved, Ryco utters one word: "Rozeth."

Shielding part of her unblemished fair face is her sable-black hair being tossed in the wind. Meeting his gaze, Rozeth calls, "Ryco of Paragon! You do live, after all."

"For now," he states ominously.

Following his omen—like black clouds on all sides, blocking out the sunrise—is the chaos of sooty-black Vitasadyns and their female Vitiosyn riders. Their scarlet eyes dance with laughter, as their mouths utter the chorus of screeching, bellowing, and chanting.

The Vitasadyns are as formidable as Reign, with their breaths of black and red flames. Like molten magma, the space glows between their thick scales. When the molten-glow extinguishes, ash collects in its place. Adding more soot to their scales, some ash falls to the green pastures of Paragon.

When a target meets with the Vitasadyn-flame, they explode into white-fire. Unable to withstand the flames, the smaller BlacKaidyns screech and cry. In the air, they writhe like noble dogs incapable of defending their assaulted masters. Riders—both Paragonian and Emeralds—attempt to douse them in water spells. Yet, the flames wisp out like insatiable beasts.

Imprisoned in unquenchable fire are several falling BlacKaidyns. By the time their bodies hit the ground, they are nothing but ash. Unable to control myself, I tremble. Too shocked to cry out; yet, too heartbroken to be angry. I am nothing but … speechless.

Behind me, Gemma digs her hands into the fabric of my coat. Against my back, she buries her face. Though her cries should be near, their echo is a world away.

Tears stream down Callie's blank face. She takes my hand, saying, "Settle your fears, Tyler Ravier. The King of Paragon is far too valuable, to meet an end such as that. We will not be struck down in the air."

Searching for words, I reply, "Wish I had your confidence." That's when thoughts pervade. Unwanted ones. Disturbing ones. They chill me to my core, yet I cannot stop them. *If the roles were reversed—the Vitasadyns on the good side—all this would be terrifyingly-beautiful. But how can I think that? I'm not a monster like them. Like Zymarc of Vitiosus. Or Soren of the Monel. Am I?* For now, I push the thoughts away and refuse entry of more.

Fading back into my hearing is Ryco and Rozeth's conversation.

"Which one," Rozeth says, while scowling, "do you want me to seek: your ward or Awngeleik?"

"Talok?" Ryco turns to him. "It's your call."

"Khyra would want us to *first* find Awngeleik."

Bowing her head, Rozeth declares, "Then I shall do my best to find her. Before they do."

"One more question," states Ryco. "Did you and the others pass the Onyx Warriors, on your journey here?"

"No," she replies. "Even though I was very much hoping to. All the warriors, together? They're magnificent."

Talok states, "They must have left hours ago."

"Unless," counters Rozeth, "they were avoiding the usual paths."

"King Talok?"

"What is it, Reign?"

"I cannot go higher," he rumbles. "They've made the air too thick. Too heavy. If I were a younger dyn, I would have the bursting strength to do it."

"Ryco," Rozeth chatters, "can one of you raise an undetectable cloaking-shield, while airborne? I would. But dragon physiology? It's a bit of a mystery to me. It shouldn't be, with all the scrolls I've read about them. But, alas. It still is."

"Only Jasper's spell works," states Ryco. "Takes a dozen of us to cast it too."

"In the best of circumstances," adds Quall.

During the chatter, Talok comes to my side. Resting a hand on my shoulder, he echoes, *I am glad to have met you, Cousin Tyler.*

My attention snaps to him. The shadow's absent. The fear? Gone. Only sheer determination is etched on my cousin's face.

Talok? Don't do anything crazy.

No promises.

"King Talok," rumbles Reign. "What are my orders?"

Before anyone can stop him, Talok sprints across Reign's back to leap onto the smaller dragon with Rozeth. Missing by a step is Quall, stumbling forward to grab him.

Ryco shouts, "Talok! What are you doing?"

Calmly straightening his coat cuffs, Talok commands, "King's orders: you are released of duty, for the remainder of today."

"Don't do this," Quall pleads. "We'll find another way—"

Talok interrupts with sadness in his voice. "There is no other way. I'm as valuable as Awngeleik. Therefore, my surrender into their hands can create a ceasefire. Thus, giving all of you long enough to get to safety. To the bunkers, below."

"But Talok," Quall pleads again.

In reply, Talok shouts, "Those are your orders! First, to safety. Then, protection of my cousin and his friend. You are to guard them, as if they are me."

Stripped of all emotion, Ryco replies with one word, "Understood."

Though we hate it, that one word finalizes what's going to happen. Talok of Paragon will give himself up to the Vitiosyns. This. Very. Day.

Talok commands, "Reign, take them back to the castle. Rozeth of Aeown, if you will, please drop me at the city entrance. From there, find Awngeleik. Then Khyra."

"If you are sure, King Talok."

"I am sure."

With one last chance to wipe away my cousin's sorrow, I call out, "Talok?" But then I glance to the Geldryn device on him. My spoken words cut out. My mind races with the unspoken. *What if this is it? My chance to say goodbye to someone I hardly know, but long for a chance to get to know? Death and goodbyes ... are they always this unfair?*

After Talok dips his head down once, his gaze meets mine. For a second, we share that look of knowing. Knowing what the other is feeling. Talok breaks the silence to say, "Yes, Cousin Tyler. But I'll see you again. Tomorrow. All of you."

"Your cousin?" Rozeth perks up. "LanSoren's Tyler Ravier? Always my luck. Meeting famed-ones, under the worst of circumstances."

"Gives you more reason to stay alive," states Ryco.

"Tyler Ravier?" Rozeth pleads. "Do us a favor? Don't die. I've anticipated our meeting for many Rentwa-Novas."

I reply, "So I've been told."

On autopilot, Quall sighs out, "She means days and nights."

Smiling, I state, "Until tomorrow."

Transfixed on my face is my cousin's gaze, as he replies, "I'll be here."

Nodding once, Rozeth grins back. "He means, *we*."

Together, on the dragon, Talok and Rozeth fade out of sight.

That's when more thoughts pervade to torment.

What if tomorrow comes?

But no Talok?

Just people.

Broken at the loss of their young sovereign.
My cousin.
The King of Paragon.

27

LanSoren's Last

Below the castle, within the damp bunker illuminated by torchlight, we wait. Fury carves deep into the contours of Zepharre's face. He demands to know, "Where's King Talok?"

Ryco, emotions unreadable, states, "He released us of duty, before surrendering services to Tyler Ravier and his friend."

"How could you let this happen?"

Ryco's calm cracks away. "He is of age, Zepharre. As king, it was his right."

Quall leans against the stone-wall, admitting, "There was nothing we could do, but obey."

Lowering his voice, Zepharre says, "LanSoren never would have let him surrender to those gray-skinned wretches."

In torment, Quall sinks to the bunker's damp dirt-floor. "Please, Zepharre. Arguing won't change what's happened."

"Besides," interrupts Kent, from his spot between Gemma and Callie, "King Talok is surrendering himself. Not all of Paragon. We do have that to hold onto."

"*That* is not much, Kent of Dysarda," states Zepharre. "And wherever did Musgrae and Siege run off to?"

"Collecting weapons for sharpening," replies Ryco. "Looking for Yigoshi, too, while they're at it."

After a huff, Zepharre turns on his heel. He marches deeper into the dim bunker. That's when Paragonians start staggering down into the main tunnel. On down, they continue deep into the safety of torchlight. Although some are unscathed—others cut and burned—many are carried down. They scream in pain, or are limp with death. Ragged are their breaths, in the struggle for life.

At the tail end of the line is Rozeth. Her eyes teary-red, she wipes at the blood and soot-smears on her cheeks.

Ryco ambles toward her. "I see that you're uninjured, but did you have any luck?"

"No sign of them. Though I searched high and low."

"What of King Talok?" queries Ben.

"Still at the city gate," replies Rozeth. "When last I saw him, he was running around. Ordering his warriors to get everyone to safety."

Warren braves the question, "How bad is it out there?"

Rozeth sucks in a held breath, bursting out, "I've spoken with the Warrior of the Nyxane."

Quall sits up straighter. "Gyron? What did he say?"

Eli stand, asking, "Will he help us?"

Tears break free. They run down Rozeth's tormented face. She searches for words, but none form. Gripping her arm, Ryco presses, "Rozeth. What's the verdict? Tell us."

"Stop!" She wrenches free of Ryco. "Your Mensa-div will not work on me. I've a message from Siveyra Gyronawv, to all of you. I will, but speak it once. Gather your Sovereignty. Only then, out of me, will you get another word on the matter."

"They're headed this way now," Warren mutters. "Might take a bit, though."

That's when I ask, "What was it, Rozeth, that you wanted to tell me?"

Her face calms at the sight of me. She replies, "It's a dream I've been having, since the death of your father. Every Novas, it is the same."

"What would that be?" queries Ryco, sounding far from intrigued.

"LanSoren's Last," Rozeth declares. "The complete version. I would have spoken it before now. However, against my will, LanSoren bound me to silence. Commanding I only tell it, after his son arrived on Muraine."

Standing, to brush off dirt, I approach Rozeth. "It must be important, then. You'd better write it down."

"Already thought of that." She hands me a sealed envelope. "I'll quote it for you now, though. If you like."

"Please do." I motion.

She begins, "You will find her, at dusk: my Despairing Marion. The miller of the woods. The tamer of the dyns. The first and last of her kind. Who is she? A foreigner or a warrior? A stranger or a friend?"

"Marion?" interrupts Quall, confusion on his pale face. "That's the mother of LanSoren and Miriam. She's been dead for years."

"I'm merely telling you the words of the dream," says Rozeth, gripping her jade-colored collar like a nervous model before their first walk. Tighter round her hourglass-figure, she pulls the coat.

"Go on, Rozeth," states Ryco, crossing his arms.

The nervous model is erased from Rozeth. She continues, "Into the future, you must reverse the clock. Acknowledge the ever-present danger. The fading light of death's gaze. You cannot escape them. Death and time. They wait. Then turn. And shift. Only at the solar eclipse, will they flee."

Ryco smirks. "I think you meant more cryptic. Not complete."

Ignoring him, she goes on, "Dance with Gendras. Race to the place of Mirrors. Only then can reflection tell all, but no more. There's the end," huffs Rozeth. "I've delivered his message. Completed my duty to LanSoren. I can only hope, Tyler Ravier, that you know its true meaning."

In frustration, I shrug, saying, "I don't. But Miriam? She's Talok's—"

"Mother," finishes Ryco.

I shake my head. "Talok said she passed away. How can I receive birthday cards from someone who's dead?"

"Talok mentioned the card and notes," states Quall. "Sure you want to talk about all that, now, Tyler?"

"What else are we going to talk about, down here? How lovely the dirt-floors are?"

"Not that he's complaining," Gemma adds.

"Very well," says Quall, rising up from the dirt-floor. "Ben, resize the contents."

As Ben resizes the box and contents, I start visualizing the card in my hand, the one boasting of the clan colors of Emerald Sorsryns. Snapping my fingers, fire briefly ignites between them. The card appears in my hand.

All eyes turn from Ben, completing his magic, to me. That's when I offer Rozeth the card and make my request of, "Tell me whose writing this is."

Dead quiet is the room, as Rozeth opens the card from the Miriam-imposter. She pinches at one of her temples, finally announcing, "I'm not sure whose writing it is, but I recognize it."

"What about—" I start to say, but stop to think, *Should I ask if she has my dad's Vardiya-Stone, the one Jack Wayeland had? Being an apprentice to an Emerald Siveyra must mean she's talented. But how talented is she, in a room of King's Guard and Dezarin's other apprentice?* Courage rising, I ask, "How was Jack Wayeland last year? Or was it two years ago? I don't remember."

Rozeth's forehead creases. "I'm not sure what you are suggesting, Tyler. But you'd best be out with it. I can't read your mind. No one can. Unless you want us to. Which is, really, quite astounding, considering—"

Ryco shouts, "Rozeth! Shut up. Let the boy talk."

Mouth still open, Rozeth then draws it into a tense frowning line.

Twisting the watch round my wrist nervously, I state, "I was hoping Jack gave her my dad's Vardiya-Stone. That's all. But it seems you didn't write that card. Which means, you can't be the one posing as my aunt on Earth. So! Back to square one."

"Possibly not," states Ryco, taking the card from Rozeth's crushing grip. "This was penned with an enchanted quill—"

Before he can finish, Rozeth gasps out, "That's where I've seen it! The writing. It's one of LanSoren's enchanted quills."

"Tyler?" Quall queries smoothly. "Permission to peruse everything in that box and bag?"

"Why not? Just don't dump—" Before all words leave my mouth, Eli has emptied my duffle contents *all* over the dirt-floor.

"Eli of Kirja!" shouts Quall, turning red. "Must you make a mess of everything?"

"What? It's faster this way. Besides, the rookie's good at cleaning off every speck of dirt."

Through clenched teeth, Ben asks, "Is that why you and Musgrae need your coats magically cleaned every day? To create more work for me? Well, I'm not having it anymore. Clean it yourself. If you're no good, I'll teach you how."

"Way to go, Rookie!" Kent grins.

Warren booms, "Yo, Quall! Ben's found his voice, just in time for us to die. How 'bout that!"

"No comment," says Ryco, checking the front pages of each journal.

Eli queries, "Ty?" as he holds up *The Dark Prince* book. "Why'd you bring a children's book? And what's it doing in your bag, instead of the box?"

"That's item number nine. It kind of goes hand in hand with Gemma. Long story."

"Here's something LanSoren wrote at the end," announces Eli, proceeding to read aloud. "To Gemma. May she one day find her perfect Dark Prince." Gasping, he whispers the closing, "Your friend, Soren."

As if stunned into paralysis, Eli drops the book. Warren picks it up. There beside him is Rozeth, comparing the imposter's card to the book's endnote. Warren, also examining the endnote, says, "This version of LanSoren's Last was, indeed, written with an enchanted quill."

Rozeth adds, "The strokes have similarities enough to this card. Therefore, both quills had the same enchanter. Not entirely sure if it was LanSoren's, though, as I never witnessed him enchant a quill then use it immediately, thereafter."

Offering Kent the phantom notes from my pouch, I look to Warren and Rozeth. "And the part Eli read?"

"No enchantment. No quill signature," states Warren. "It was penned by its author."

Kent fans out the phantom's notes, for Quall and Ryco to see. Until that moment, I didn't know what fear looked like on Ryco's face. Yet, with his eyes wide and fading to a pale straw-color, there's no mistaking it. Even Ryco of Paragon is afraid.

He looks to me, asking, "Where did these come from? Was this *phantom* on Earth, before Talok and I arrived that night?"

"Don't know. But that bloodstained one is—" I start.

Interrupting, Kent says, "From the night he died."

"Which reminds me." I take out the shard with Rorka's blood on it. Handing it to Quall, I ask, "Is there any way to match *this* to that stained note?"

"You think the phantom is Rorka?" queries Ben.

"She's worth ruling out, isn't she?"

When Ryco gulps in a breath, Quall snaps his focus onto him, asking, "What is it, Ryco?"

"Ben," Ryco begins, with panic edging his voice, "Yharss had the only medical center in Paragon capable of performing genetic testing, correct?"

"The Genome Center. Yes. That's where I studied medicine and potion-making. Never got into genetics, though. Too complicated."

Ryco continues, "They ever get a sample of LanSoren's?"

Ben replies, "The medical team begged him to give one. He never did, until …"

When Ben trails off, Ryco states, "The night he died. That's why Yharss was destroyed. The Genome Center and two years of study on LanSoren's genetics. Gone, most likely."

Warren scoffs, "Guess the eighty-eight medical and potion centers were bonuses to them. The wretches!"

"No sense lingering on it," says Quall. "There's nothing we can do about it now. Except survive."

Pointing at me, Warren states, "You keep that shard, Tyler."

"Those Greyvons," Quall adds, "are the best, at everything to do with research. Rorka is one of theirs, however. Jasper will protect her, at all costs."

"Assuming we survive all this," states Warren, "don't give away the importance of that shard or note, when asking Jasper to test them. Best to wait, until after he gives you the results."

"Back to the impersonator," states Ryco, glancing at me. "You ever meet or talk to her?"

"No and no."

"Yet, you receive cards from *her* every year?"

I reply, "So it seems."

"It appears," Ryco says, "that he's been planning something, for quite some time."

"But what?" queries Rozeth.

"You're the one delivering messages," states Ryco. "You tell us."

Zepharre strides into view, right then, complaining more than asking, "We were summoned?"

Absent of Grover and Nyrim, the Advisers and Arkiveis follow him in.

Ryco motions to her, stating, "Rozeth has a message."

"From Siveyra Gyronawv of the Onyx," she declares. "He told me …"

She pauses, when Musgrae and Siege come up behind the Sovereignty. They lay several collected weapons down, then organize them by type.

"Well?" snaps Zepharre.

Startling, Rozeth continues her message, "The Vitiosyns. They have proof, that Awngeleik was here of recent."

"Utterly ridiculous!" shouts Zepharre. "They would have to send a spy. But we would surely sense them, if they had."

Rising to her feet, Callie whimpers. To Zepharre's coat sleeve, she clings, while wailing, "Is King Talok going to die this day?"

In contempt, Zepharre looks to Quall, asking, "Who's this?"

Kent replies, "Callie of Dysarda."

"Presumably an orphan, now," coos Zepharre. "How unfortunate."

Callie's soft wails break into sobs, and Ryco seethes, "You are out of line, Zepharre."

"I see no wrong, in speaking the truth," he defends, while patting Callie's fist clenching the black fabric of his coat. "Take comfort, Callie. For you will have Arkivy Lokasi and his son, Kent, to care for you. While Ryco and I are the worst, I dare say, the Dysardans are the best of us."

"What's left of us," states Kent, now peeling Callie away from Zepharre to hold her close. As she sobs, Kent's scowl pierces the very air Zepharre breathes.

Overhead, something rumbles. And seeming thankful for the distraction is Quall, stating, "Reign's Roar."

"Best we be quiet, for a bit," states Ryco. "I'll make the first trip, to the infirmary for supplies." He races up the stairs leading to the castle.

Warren adds, "I'll go with him."

Meanwhile, Kent helps Callie ease down to sit with Gemma, who's just staring at her hands fiddling with her coat hem. Callie hooks her arm with Gemma's, and both girls fall into some kind of trance.

Back to the darkness slink the Advisers, summoning Rozeth to follow them, as Eli, Ben, and I gather my things.

Advisers and Rozeth now out of sight, Kent paces to the bunker entrance, stating, "You do know that Ryco hasn't gone for supplies, but to seek out Khyra or Awngeleik. Right, Quall?"

He nods. "I let him think he has the mask pulled over my face. When, in fact, he does not. I need Ryco to *informally* disobey me, without *formally* disobeying me. If that makes sense."

Quall grins, as I state, "In a world of Paragonian Advisers—with Zepharre at their head—it makes perfect sense."

With that, we just wait.

28

Fading Light

Overhead, rattling and booming quiets for short intervals. Then come more assaults.

Undaunted are Musgrae and Siege, busily sharpening the collected blades and axes, as Eli and Gemma fill them in on everything.

A short time ago, Gemma saw a Katana being sharpened by Siege. Her unusual silence ended, soon as she did. She started prattling away about her dad's collection. But I didn't catch most of it, because, it seems, the only one able to drown out the Barrage of Gemma is Eli of Kirja, jabbering away a slew of foreign words, and telling her what the Paragonian names are for each and every weapon. Gemma asked about some spells too; I only caught the ones familiar to me. Desheados for descend, and Awb-Sheados for ascend.

To Callie, beside me on the bench, I whisper, "Looks like Gemma found her long-lost twin in Eli."

Unresponsive, Callie just sits there. For a second, her mouth twitches with a hint of a grin. Then back she goes to having a blank face.

Warren returns with medical supplies. Absent of Ryco, he gives Quall and Ben supply bags for dispersal.

"Eli," Quall calls out, handing him two bags. "You are to divvy out food and water. While you're at it, Kirja, do what you do best."

"Gemma, want to help?" queries Eli, taking the bags.

Before she answers, Quall states, "She needs food, first. Her desire for it, I'm afraid, has exceeded Talok's protections on her mind. I speak for all in saying, her thoughts—of how starving she is—will drive us to madness."

From one of Eli's bags, Kent takes out a small bread-loaf. He gives it to Gemma, saying, "Gigi, I command you to satisfy your hunger. If even, a little."

Blushing, but accepting it, Gemma states, "Didn't realize everyone could hear me thinking of Molly's cooking."

"Yes!" Kent smiles. "Whoever this Molly Smith is, we're all envious of her cooking."

"You should be," I state. "It's divinity."

A short blade clatters to the floor. Musgrae, from where he sits—either amused, irritated, or both—points at me. "Stop it, Ravier!" He says, "We're already starving, after Mud Fiend's listed off an entire menu in her head."

"I don't know what lobster is," adds Ben, coming back from his round. "But the bisque sounds nice."

Desperate for a distraction, an idea pops up, and I state, "Gemma? Here's a, Would-You-Rather. A mountain of Molly's cooking right now"—I pause long enough to glance at Eli—"or a kiss from Eli?"

Gemma drops the bread. Kent catches it, but a cackle escapes from him. Then there's Warren, deeply crooning out one word: "Kinky."

"Who tattled?" shrieks Gemma, cupping hands over her mouth.

Mid-step, Eli gawks at me: mouth open, eyes bulging, and everything.

Quall reddens; Ben begins his typical Handclasp-Fidget; and Siege frowns at the snickering Musgrae.

Eli squeaks out, "I'm going to go divvy." With that, he slinks away to cheerily chatter at the Paragonians stuck waiting for their freedom or their end.

To Gemma, I reply, "Talok, after we finished sewing the Sleeping Dragon."

She spews, "He'd better come back now, and face the consequences. Argh! When I see him!"

I grin wickedly. "There's the bully."

"Bully my face, Tyler!" growls Gemma, pounding a fist to her palm.

"If I have to go to therapy when we get back, you're coming with me."

"I don't need therapy," Gemma argues. "Just some Judo kicks to Musgrae's chest, if he doesn't stop laughing!" She glares at him.

Cutting his laughing short, Musgrae complains, "That really hurt, you know." He rubs his chest, seeming to relive a ghost-pain of Gemma's kick.

Through it all is Callie, still unmoving like a statue. I glance from her to Kent, swallowing hard. I hope he notices how pale she suddenly is.

Handing the loaf back to Gemma, Kent calls out, "Little Callie, you all right? Perhaps you need food, as well."

Briefly shivering, Callie answers, "Yes, Master Kent. Food? Sounds lovely."

Calmer now, Gemma sits by Callie's other side. She shares bread with her. Kent picks that moment, to glance down the tunnel at Eli grudgingly divvying to Zepharre and the Advisers.

Meeting Zepharre's glower, Kent nods once, then says, "Musgrae. Zepharre's orders: we are to start collecting the wounded nearest the castle."

"'Bout time!" says Musgrae, as he hoists up from the floor.

Before they leave, footsteps stumble down the stairs. Someone shouts, "Quall! Take her."

At the bottom of the stairs is Ryco, clutching Khyra's limp body in his arms. Blood flows out from several of her wounds. The worst of them are on her arms. Kent is the first to reach the two. He takes Khyra from Ryco. Ben, with a wave of his hand, fashions a delicate-looking examination table. Made of a web of contoured metal strings, in appearance, it's unlike anything I've seen in Paragon.

As Quall, Ben, and Kent work to heal deep cuts on Khyra's neck and arms, Ryco sits in a heap at the foot of the stairs. Covered in blood, he crawls his way to the nearby bench with Gemma, Callie, and me.

Gemma is the first to ask, "Are you hurt too?"

"I'll heal," replies Ryco, leaning back against the bench.

Callie eyes the half-loaf in her hands, then offers it to Ryco. But he waves it away, saying, "You need it more than I."

"We must all make sacrifices this day, Master Ryco," Callie says. "Kent infused it with a bit of magic. Should help revive a little."

"If you insist," says Ryco, as he tears the half, and gives her the quarter back.

About to take a bite, Gemma stops to offer hers as well.

Ryco bites into his quarter-loaf, replying, "Save some for Khyra. Besides, Siege tells me you've been commanded to eat, so they don't have to hear all about Molly Smith and her cooking. Whoever that is."

I clarify, "She's the family cook."

"She's more than our cook. She's my best friend and ally, in that monstrosity of an art museum. Wish she was my mom. Can't stand mine." To me, Gemma hands her quarter-loaf. "Take this, so I'm not tempted to eat it."

"Sure thing."

I take it, right as Gemma changes the subject. "I've been wondering, Ryco. You're not that old. Certainly not old enough to be Khyra's dad. How did you end up being her guardian?"

Ryco finishes his bread. Then thinks a moment. Wiping at the blood smears on his face, he starts with, "Khyra's parents ... such odd people. When Khyra's mother, Eva, was carrying, she caught me practicing a bit of Gendras and Taming Magic by myself."

"Is that a bad thing?" interrupts Gemma.

Tiredly, Ryco replies, "At eleven years old, it's unusual to practice advanced magic. By yourself, no less. I was preparing to go to the Aeown. To compete for an apprenticeship with Dezarin. Thought taming an imperial Sylvadyn would give me an edge. So, that's what I did that day."

"Imperial, meaning pureblood," says Quall, on his correcting autopilot.

"Such a showoff," says Siege. "Taming the untamable and illustrious Sylvadyn."

"It helps being part Sylvadyn. Can't do it otherwise, unless you're Talok. Long story short: Eva was adamant about learning Gendras from me. Later, she insisted I forever be a part of their family. So, she and Dhavin named me as Khyra's guardian. At sixteen years old, I never thought it would amount to anything more than the occasional child-watching of a pesky little girl."

Warren's gentle, in whispering, "She's a bit more than pesky to you. Aye, Ryke?"

Ryco swallows hard. "I'm not sure what she is to me. But *soon* she'll be sixteen, and it won't matter. I'll be free of her *and* she ... free of me."

"Who's less prepared for that?" queries Siege. "You or her?"

"Her, most likely. She's the type who'd lose her head, if it weren't attached. Every year she forgets her own birthday, while remembering—to my dismay—every single one of mine." Sighing deeply, Ryco braves to ask, "How is she, Quall?"

"Stable," Quall replies, wiping his hands on a white cloth. "Who wants to learn stitching?" From me to Gemma then Callie, Quall looks. Daring us to volunteer are his amber-colored eyes, as I raise my hand and accept. "Then come," he says.

Kent motions for Musgrae to follow him. The two leave the bunker.

Now next to Quall and Ben, with Khyra unconscious in front, I stand waiting for instructions.

"Needle and enchanted thread." Ben offers them to me.

"No need to knot the ends," adds Quall. "Twist them together. They'll know what you want. Start the first stitch, before the cut; end the last, past the wound."

Ben states, "Because it's enchanted thread, simply use a wide-stitch."

"He means whip-stitch," corrects Quall. "All that's needed is to loosely bind the wound. The enchantment does the rest for you."

Curved needle in hand, my fingers struggle to thread it. Then they twist the ends. My needle's ready, but I'm not sure that I am.

Quall points to the long gash seeping on Khyra's forearm. "Start on this one."

I swallow back nerves, before pricking the needle-tip into her skin. Though my heartbeat hammers in my eardrums, my hands are steady. In sinks the sharp tip, then it pokes out of the skin two millimeters away. Oozing out with it is more blood, as Gemma comes to peer over my shoulder. Whether it's her presence, or the sound of thread sliding through Khyra's skin, my nerves calm to an even rhythm.

"With enchanted thread," states Quall, "use wider stitches. After the first, don't bother pulling the thread slack tight."

Ben instructs, "Until getting to the end."

Several minutes tick by. Upon doing the last stitch, I tighten the slack. Quall snips the thread with tiny scissors, but lets me twist the ends. In seconds, the thread cinches the wound closed. All that's left behind is a faint scar.

"Show me, Ben?" queries Gemma, moving to Khyra's other side.

Carefully following Quall and Ben's instructions, Gemma and I bind Khyra's wounds in silence.

* * *

Except for the gloves and daggers, all items are now miniaturized and back in my pouch. As we wait for the healed Khyra to wake, I fiddle with my dad's daggers. Repeatedly, I turn them over in my hands. Then come the gnawing thoughts: *Dance with Gendras. The place of Mirrors. The elements? How to break their laws?*

Across the tunnel—in proximity to each other—Ben and Gemma are passed out, exhausted after his quick lesson in potion-making. I tried listening, but nothing sank in. I could only worry. Obsess, really, over what might be happening to my cousin. Now, I just think one horrifying thought, *What if he's dead?*

My horror breaks when Ryco eases out of his coat, and says, "You have to know magic, to use those to their full potential. When I was a boy of twelve, I observed LanSoren's use of a similar set. They came with gloves. Did they not?"

After he adjusts the strap across his black vest of heart-armor, which holds glass vials and small weapons, I toss the gloves to him. He slips them on, then grips the daggers. They unsheathe, on their own.

"I remember those," states Quall. "They belonged to LanSoren's father.

338

In our youth, however, they didn't have near that level of enchantment."

Feeling the edge one dagger, Ryco states, "Yet he never shared his enchantment tricks with you."

Quall answers, with only a shake of his head.

"And you knew him how long?"

"Since we were ten."

Ryco clenches his jaw, then slashes one arm open with the sleeping-dagger. While blood gushes from the self-inflicted wound, he states, "The Great LanSoren of Trauvo. If I had a weapon for every secret he kept, I could fill Yigoshi's armory."

Giving back the sleeping-dagger, Ryco echoes, *How can you put faith, in someone with so much to hide?*

What do you want me to say? That you're right? You know you are.

There it is, he echoes.

There's what?

A breath of humility. Now, I can simply tolerate *you. Instead of faking.* Gripping the waking-dagger, Ryco places its edge in his wound.

But I echo, *If you don't mind, I'll keep faking.*

Though he doesn't look at me, a grin tugs at Ryco's mouth. Slowly, the splattered blood on the floor floats back into his wound, and he removes the blade-edge. The wound seals itself up, leaving no visible scar. "This one," states Ryco, "has enough enchantment to bring life back in the midst of a battle. But only if the wielder knows the highest level of White Magic."

Quall states, "Matron Avilon must've helped enchant that."

"Replenishes its enchantment too," adds Ryco. "Even now, it's drawing my magic."

It's mostly quiet, until a scream shatters it.

Ryco drops the waking-dagger.

Off darts Khyra from the examination table, plowing into me. We tumble to the ground. Rushing to us is Ryco, prying her writhing body off me. But she escapes his grasp.

Scrambling up, I just watch like a frightened creature. Unsure of what to do, I sit on the bench between Callie and Eli. Back in her trance is

Callie, staring into nothing. Then there's Eli, transfixed on studying his spell-book. He completely ignores Khyra's commotion. Perhaps, he even holds a grudge against the daredevil.

Ben and Gemma are still sleeping alongside each other, until Khyra crawls onto Ben's lap and startles him into awareness. Hitting the back of his head against the wall, Ben holds his hands away from Khyra as she squirms on his lap He acts as if touching her will shock him into unconsciousness. Ryco's about to get her off Ben. But the crazed Khyra cups Ben's face, and pulls him into a frantic, sloppy kiss.

Ryco stops. He moves away, licking his lips. He then smirks at Quall, whose eyes are wide. He notices Eli's mischievous gleam too. But then he sees Gemma. And that's where his smirk ends. Turning to a wince, he observes the sight of Gemma resting in the contorted doll pose. Half on the floor and half on the wall, she's oblivious to the pair making-out beside her.

Meanwhile, Ben doesn't know what to do. Half-pulling away and half-holding still is Ben, struggling not to kiss Khyra back. As her fingers claw at his coat-collar, her lips skim from his to kiss his chin, then slowly on down to his neck—there, she lingers for several seconds. With a long exhale, Ben seems to give in. Licking his lips once, he closes his eyes for a moment of ecstasy. When Khyra stops, his russet-brown eyes dare to open and watch her curl up further on his lap. Khyra then rests her head on his chest and falls asleep.

"What's wrong with her?" queries Ben, quietly taking ragged breaths.

Ryco sits down, smirking again. "She was thanking you for saving her life."

"Don't be absurd," states Ben, wiping Khyra's spit off his mouth and neck. "She didn't know what she was doing."

Ryco explains, "Her mind doesn't know how to cope, with what she's witnessed this day. Her parents have forbidden the teaching of *anything* more than intermediate defense and attack magic."

"What they failed to realize," adds Warren, "is that learning higher magic levels, allows for better coping and stress management. That reaction happened, because her mind doesn't know what else to do."

"Most likely," says Ryco, "she won't remember any of this. As her guardian, I give you full permission to kiss her again … if you like."

To Khyra resting in his arms, Ben looks down and says, "That wouldn't be right. To take advantage."

"But potentially worth it?" Ryco suggests. "Especially if it's a swift, direct way of sharing someone's burden, whether it be emotional *or* physical turmoil?"

Looking to Ryco, Ben replies, "It is her burden to carry. How else does anyone become stronger?"

"A wise conclusion," states Quall.

Tiredly, Ben is asking, "Did I pass the test?"

"Beautifully," states Ryco.

Ben shakes his head, asking, "How did you plant the test? When you couldn't know what her reaction would be, beforehand?"

"That's the thing with my tests. I use present issues, in a controlled environment. I'm certain that *I* can help her, no matter what her reaction is. But I wanted to see how *you* could handle it."

Suspiciously narrowing his eyes, Ben states, "Somehow, Ryco of Paragon, I think you are … stealing my sword?"

Hiding a smile, Ryco simply replies, "Maybe."

That's when Khyra decides to wake up again. This time she sobs, and provokes an eye-roll out of Eli, as he's still attempting to study his spellbook. "Here we go," he mutters, flipping another page.

Wrapping arms round Ben's neck, Khyra wails, "Ryco, my parents. Don't let them leave me. Please! They always leave me! Why am I always left alone?"

Ben tries soothing Khyra, by brushing at the frazzled hair plastered to her sweaty face.

"Give her to me." Ryco sighs.

Ben starts to push her away. But Khyra thrashes, thus awakening the contorted doll from the wall. Gemma's hands jerk to the side, and smack Ben in the face. She asks, "Khyra? Is she okay?"

In reply, Ben wobbles his head. Pressing his smacked nose, he blinks away tears of pain.

Then Ryco—while his palms glow a soft-blue—cups Khyra's face, speaking, "Khyra, you're safe. Be calm. It was merely a nightmare. A bad dream you can wake from."

The glow fades, and Khyra's terror eases enough for her to ask, "Ryco, where are we?"

"The castle bunker. It's a drill, in the event of an attack. We've moved some of the survivors here, to act as our wounded. Go tend to them."

"But have some food, first," states Gemma, offering the bread I put next to her while she slept.

Brightening, Khyra takes it. Then she glances around. "Where's King Talok? I'll share some with him, before we begin the task of healing."

"Somewhere around here. Most likely, playing keep-away with Awngeleik."

"Then I shall go find them." Khyra prances away, with the bread in hand, not a care in the world.

"Can you make me forget too?" queries Gemma.

"I could," Ryco replies. "However, you don't need to forget, Gemma. You are strong enough to remember."

She sniffles. "I don't feel like it."

I state, "But he's right, Gemma. You are."

"You're agreeing with Ryco?" She gawks at me.

"Just this once. For you."

Ripping the moment of peace away is more turmoil on the stairs. Kent rushes from them, to start clearing the examination table of everything.

"What's happened?" I ask, in alarm.

"It's Madeleine. Vitiosyns slit both her wrists right in front of us. Then Talok was taken. My quick spells were undone, just before the ceasefire, when an arrow—"

Kent stops, out of breath, while Musgrae barrels down the steps carrying Madeleine in both arms. Skewering their necks together is a single arrow.

"Ben," Ryco commands, "when I break the arrow free, tend to Musgrae."

"Understood," replies Ben, before preparing potions, needles, and cloth between himself and Gemma.

Ryco breaks the arrow-tail off, and Musgrae winces. As the shaft is pulled out from the back of Musgrae's neck, Madeleine chokes up blood. She tries touching her face with trembling hands, but Quall stops her, commanding, "I'll bind wrists. Kent, her neck. Then get those shards out from her eyes and face, before they embed deeper."

Obeying, Kent cups one palm over Madeleine's neck and the other over her bleeding eyes. Quall—running hands over her wrists—closes his eyes. He begins a quiet chant.

Calming, Madeleine whispers, "Kent, if I am to die soon. There's something I must say."

Musgrae, his neck now mostly healed, bolts up to plead, "Don't say that, Madeleine."

"You're not going to die today," soothes Kent, while his glowing palms work out a few fragments from her eyes.

Rasping and coughing, Madeleine says, "It's about LanSoren's little sister, Miriam."

"Sh! Madeleine," Kent quiets her. "Save your energy."

Ignoring him, she continues, "Miriam could tend the Arkivara, as if she were an Arkivy. She and LanSoren: they were different from other Paragonians."

Drawing closer to her, I ask, "Different how?"

When Kent removes another shard from her eyes, Madeleine screams, "The light hurts! Please! Make it go out."

"She needs darkness. This way," commands Quall. "The rest of you? Stay here."

Musgrae lifts up Madeleine, then follows Quall, Kent, and Ben deeper into the bunker. Left in suspenseful agony are the rest of us, wondering what will happen to the one with a thousand mysteries behind her Vaegon-eyes.

29

Of My Eyes

Into the tunnel entrance, Quall and the three trail back with shadowed faces claiming a hidden truth; something they are reluctant to relay.

Musgrae's the first to utter anything, asking Quall, "Will she remember us?"

"Once she finishes healing—" Quall ends his answer abruptly, too distraught to finish; instead, he goes silent. Clamping his lips together, he stops their trembling.

Kent continues for him. "She will have to relearn how to walk. How to speak. Everything." He takes a ragged breath. Then glances down at his blood-covered hands, asking, "Ben, do you have a—"

Already, Ben offers him a damp cloth. Taking it, Kent nods his thanks.

I start asking, "May I—"

Ryco interrupts, to say, "She needs rest."

Slowly, even forlornly, Quall instructs, "Ben, please attend to her. Ease her pain, but don't numb it completely."

Ben adds, "Because the pain is keeping her fighting?"

"Exactly," Quall replies.

To Ben, I echo, *Ask that I go with you?*

During a Handclasp-Fidget, Ben asks, "May Tyler keep conversation, while I work?"

Quall nods his approval.

I follow Ben down the tunnel. Into a room lit with blue light, we enter. At the sight of her, tears sting my eyes.

A white-stone table is what Madeleine rests upon. Her blood stains the rock. On the floor, her blonde hair lies in a heap. The worst sight is her face. Her head too. It's been shaved of all hair. Stitched seams show along her scalp. And, though cloth covers her eyes, lesions are on her face. Once beautiful were her Vaegon-eyes, swirling with blue, black, and white. I shudder, aching inside, imagining how they must appear now.

Ben sits on the bench, by a simple table, to arrange bottles from his pouches. Joining him—too shocked to say anything, initially—I just watch, as he smears ointment on her cheeks and forehead.

He sniffles some, then ends the silence. "I never thanked you, Tyler, for saving Nyrim. He's the closest I have to family, along with our guardian, Symovi: The Warrior of Yharss-Rawshuen."

"Honestly?" I shrug. "I had no idea what I was doing."

"Even still. Thank you."

I softly say, "Thank me, by healing her. It's what we both want."

Tears glisten, in his eyes. "It should've been me they took. Then Talok would be here. We were to protect him. I have failed the highest purpose of the King's Guard."

"No, you haven't. Talok bought us more time. There would've been no ceasefire with the Vitiosyns, without him or Awngeleik being handed over. In his mind, he picked the better option. We have to respect that. Whether we want to or not."

"You're right," Ben agrees. Tears diminishing, he slides a jar of cream to me. "Use this on her arms and face. But not her skull. I must go prepare another cream, to ensure her hair grows back even."

I state, "We'd still love Madeleine, even if she was bald."

"But she will want her hair back." Ben grins. "Especially where the stitches are." With that, he leaves, and I start rubbing cream on Madeleine's blood-speckled hand.

At my touch, she grips my left hand with one of hers. She removes the cloth from her eyes, with the other. "I don't have long," she says, "before everything is gone forever."

"You'll be fine, Madeleine. I wanted to tell you, though, I love the Sleeping Dragon. It's the best gift I've ever received."

"It's only fitting, you have that one," she rasps. "Your father had the Waking Dragon. King Sosha? The Dragon in Flight. One day, I'll make a special one for King Talok."

Now curious, I ask, "Is there a Vision of the Dragon?"

"I'm unsure. That phrase, however, has to do with Rubidyns. They see visions of the past, present, and future. Dragons can be quite prophetic, at their choosing, in times of great need."

I sigh. "Seems like we're in great need, now."

"Yes," she agrees. "But there is something else you must know, Tyler. When the time is right, you will see Rentwar."

I ask, "What do you mean? Muraine's star?"

Madeleine tightens her grip on my arm, stating, "Not the star."

"You mean the Rubidyn, King Rentwar?"

Madeleine manages a slight nod. "He is an old dragon. Over six-thousand years, though you would never know it. He's so magnificent."

"Then you've met him. Did my father know him?"

"Quite well. That Soren of the Monel knew him well too."

"What do you know of Soren?" I ask. "Why didn't you say anything, after the festival?"

"I thought we had more time." Madeleine coughs. "But it seems, my time is up."

"Don't say that," I beg.

Fighting for words, Madeleine speaks, "Soren and Adair, they …"

"Gemma's great-grandfather"—I nod my encouragement for her to continue—"How is her family connected to Soren and my dad?"

Wheezing are Madeleine's breaths, as if they will be her last. While her eyes flicker to stay open, mine sting with defeat.

Like never-ending rain, the tears pour down my cheeks. My eyes burn, with the sensation of smoke. My heart is cut to torment. All the while, chills sink into my skin, and I shiver.

"Madeleine," I command, while clutching her hand, "don't you dare die."

In desperation, she puffs out the tormenting words, "Twenty-two to slumber. Thirteen to conquer. Eight to rise."

I want to scream for Quall to save her—for Kent to heal her—for Ben to stop this from happening: The death of Madeleine.

But no words escape.

Only breaths.

Only heartbeats.

I whisper, "I don't know what that means."

"Thirteen. We're done." Speaking her last, Madeleine's eyes flicker shut.

Holding my breath, I wait for her Vaegon-eyes to open. When they don't, my screams beg for release. Yet my aching chest restrains them.

Though longing for this moment to be different, it seems, I can't stop the inevitable.

My last hope for Madeleine dies, with that last rasping wheeze. Her chest is as undisturbed as a sunset on Mirror Lake, while she appears to have caught her breath.

Unable to move, my thoughts race, *If I have the power to call her back from the edge of death, how do I use that power?*

In reply, the Prismatic of Magic returns to my hand. While its colors race over my palm, color drains from her face. My trembling hand touches her forehead. I sweep back, then to the base of her neck. I lean over, speaking words in her ear. Words of: "*Forget*, Madeleine. You must forget the pain. *Remember* happy times. Simpler days. When there was *no pain* in your life."

Quiet—even peaceful—she's unmoved by my words.

"Open your eyes, Madeleine," I speak. "You're not done."

The prismatics fade, and I gaze at the minutes ticking away on my watch one by one.

Holding onto her limp, cold hand, I list off my many hopes.

The sound of her breath.

The rhythm of her heartbeat.

Color returning to her.

Warmth of life awakened in her veins.

Still, nothing happens. Giving up, even though it strangles me to do so, I take both of her hands and rest them on her chest. Turning to leave, my heart is *utterly* broken.

Behind me, a voice speaks.

So quiet, I cannot discern the words.

Then it is louder.

Younger and indignant, Madeleine's voice is asking, "What happened to me?"

Rushing back to her side, I cannot believe it. Staring at me, confused yet happy, are her gorgeous Vaegon-eyes. No thousand mysteries hiding in them. Only the bright bliss of Madeleine. Her lesions and scars now gone, as well, she's healed of all wounds.

I state, "You seem more than all right, but what do you remember?"

"Baking pastries with my mother, in celebration for my eighteenth birthday."

I smile. "Happy birthday."

"You're cute, Green Eyes." Madeleine's face brightens to a sunrise. "Have we met before?"

"No." I sigh. "But you can call me Tyler Ravier."

Wrinkling her eyebrows together, Madeleine prattles out, "Ravier? Never heard of it. Is it an interesting city?"

"I'd like to think so."

Her lips pouting like a child deprived of dessert, she seems disappointed in saying, "Then you're not Paragonian or Vaegon?"

"I don't know what I am."

"With those eyes?" Madeleine thinks a moment. "You must be of the Aeown. Or, perhaps, a special Onyx?"

"Don't know." I shrug.

"Such a tease, you are, Tyler of Ravier." Madeleine giggles. "No matter. I'll figure it out, somehow."

"Let me know, when you do." Squeezing her arm, I start to leave again.

But her complaint stops me. "Why's my head in such pain? It was that Dragon Ride with Kent, wasn't it? He let me fall off. I warned him of my horrible balance."

"A Dragon Ride with Kent?" I slowly bob my head, stating, "That was it."

Struggling to sit up, Madeleine prattles on, "Tell that Kent of Dysarda, he owes me an apology. I'm certain, this is his fault."

"I'll tell him."

Striding out of the room, I turn a corner and bump into Ben.

"Sorry, Tyler," he says. "I was just headed back. She is resting, then?"

"Sort of," I reply. "I'll explain."

We make our way back to the others.

Ryco looks up, asking, "Ben, back so soon?"

I start with, "It's Madeleine. Her mind—"

Standing up, Kent interrupts, "She can't be gone this soon."

Quall agrees, "It should've taken days for her memories to fade."

I state, "She thinks she's eighteen. That her injuries are from an accident involving a Dragon Ride—"

"With me," interrupts Kent again. "That was eight years ago."

Musgrae fumes at Kent. "You were once engaged to Madeleine? And you let me flirt with her all those times? In front of you. Without saying anything?"

"It didn't matter, Musgrae!" shouts Kent. "I broke it off six years ago."

"It's going to matter, after the war," mutters Musgrae. "Now that she thinks it was like yesterday."

"I'm not going to stand here and argue with you." Kent starts hurrying past me.

But Ryco question of, "What did you do, Tyler?" stops Kent mid-stride.

I blow out a breath, replying, "I told her to remember happier days. To forget the pain."

"Did you touch her skin?" queries Ryco.

I hesitate, then say, "Her forehead."

"How 'bout that?" Warren states, "Power of suggestion, paired with time-distortion."

"Why didn't you call for help?" Ryco presses.

I stare down at the floor, as my quivering voice replies, "Tried, but couldn't. I only wanted to save her. I'm sorry—"

"Sorry? Tyler!" Kent grips my shoulders. "You saved her memories. She was going to lose *all* of it."

"But I don't know how I did it. I don't even know what I am. Do you? Do any of you?"

"You're Paragonian," Quall replies.

"I don't think so," I disagree, shaking my head. "I'm not just human, either."

"We'll find answers for you, Tyler," says Kent. "For now, we should go to Madeleine. See what she remembers. *Whom* she remembers."

All follow Kent to the room, except for me. Gemma stops beside me, and grasps hold of my arm. "I wish I had been able to say goodbye. Now, she won't even know who I am."

"At least she's here."

Before I know what Gemma's doing, she stands on tiptoe to kiss my cheek. Her lips linger there long enough to warm my heart and ignite my wicked grin.

Grabbing round her waist, I pull her against me. "What is it you want, Gigi?"

Undaunted by the teasing in my voice, Gemma cranes up farther to whisper in my ear, "To thank you, on Madeleine's behalf."

When her breath tickles my ear, the skipping heartbeats betray my feelings toward Gemma Galloway. Now my friend and ally, the Rich Witch is gone. With any luck? Forever.

Easing down, Gemma pushes away to ask, "Do you forgive me?"

"For what?"

"Taking Ryco's side."

"You didn't take sides. You took the Onyx way of neutrality. I can't blame you for it."

Twirling a sweaty strand of hair in that way I have come to love and hate, Gemma states, "I'm going to see her now. And if you're thinking of sneaking out—while everyone's away—in the voice of your mother: Don't you dare, Tyler Malik Ravier."

I lean down, whispering, "No promises."

"Then give me a few minutes?"

"How about … I stroll out of here. If you run, you'll catch up with me."

"Deal!" Gemma smiles, handing me the waking-dagger. "See you out there."

* * *

Through the debris within the castle. Out through the cracked front doors. Down the stairs. But now frozen on the last step of the castle, I stand looking out to the surrounding chaos.

Rancid enough to turn any stomach is the air, reeking of burning wood and flesh. I start gagging, but snapping me from the paralysis of sickness is the castle, echoing, *Take heart, Son of LanSoren. We are wounded, though not defeated. The Vitiosyns think they have won. But the war has only begun.*

Not if they get Awngeleik. Help me find her.

The castle starts answering, *The Midnight Anemones has—* Before it can finish, its voice abruptly cuts out.

Shivering off fear pricking my skin, I take the last step.

In the protecting tree-wall of the city are several breaches, and within the expanse are many great trees resting in flaming piles of splinters too. Half the city-made-of-trees is gone. What remains has a remnant of BlacKaidyns on top of the canopies. With their wings, they cover the embers to starve the fire of its oxygen.

In the distance, among the wreckage, one tree stands pristine. The Arkivara. Undaunted by the horror all around, its rhythm is never-ending.

Taking to the path, I pass countless Paragonians weeping for their fallen men, women, and children. Many sob, too, while hunched over the bodies of dead, bleeding neins, dyns, and small creatures.

On the ground, the able-bodied BlacKaidyns burn away lifeless Vitasa-dyns and their fallen Vitiosyn riders. In the air, several wispy-white dragons blanket the sky in mist with each flap of their wings. They clear away some of the smoke.

The whole way to the Midnight Anemone field, I scan for Reign and any sign of Awngeleik. When I'm halfway there, footsteps drum behind me. Slowing to match my stride is Gemma, catching her breath. "We won't have long, before Quall or Ryco realize we're gone. Better hurry."

We take off, sprinting toward the Arkivara. When Reign's massive black scales catch a glint of light, we slow to a jog. There at the Arkivara's base is Reign, impaled by dozens of spears and metal spikes. At the sight of him lying contorted in a heap, we stop in our tracks.

Sickened, I'm barely able to whisper, "We're too late."

"Wait!" Gemma exclaims. "He's still breathing!"

"But what can we do? We don't know magic."

We move closer to Reign. He sputters up blood and rock, weakly rumbling, "Tyler. Gemma. Leave. You shouldn't be here, to watch me die."

Gemma says, "I'll hurry back. Get help. Back soon."

She runs off.

Left to tend Reign, alone, I touch his tear-streaked face. I tell him, "No one should die alone."

"They took my king." He coughs. "Those possessed wretches. I tried to accompany them. To ensure Talok's safety. But they attacked, before the ceasefire was called."

A voice rings out behind me, calling my name. Whoever it might be, is livid and set on the path to murder. Turning around, I spot Ryco charging my way.

Citrine gaze set to the kill-switch, he shouts, "Do you have a death wish, Ravier? If so, I will grant you that wish, if you don't come back with me *right* now."

He's an arm's length away, when I stubbornly state, "Not until Reign's healed."

Teeth gritting, Ryco's lashes out to grab hold of me.

At the same time, Awngeleik screeches from somewhere nearby.

Ryco almost has hold of me. But some unseen attacker clamps down on his arm, cutting through his coat sleeve. Sylvadyn blood is drawn.

Ryco shouts out a deep, resounding cry, and wind rushes forth from him.

Losing my footing, unable to withstand the airstream, I'm launched back toward Reign and into one of the protruding spikes.

30

More Time

At first, I feel nothing. Not the metal spike embedded into Reign; now protruding from my pierced shoulder. Nor the bloodied end of it sticking out, which I clutch onto. As my feet are kicking and struggling to find a foothold, I'm left helpless … only able to watch Ryco trying to wrestle his arm free of his unseen attacker.

When his opposite hand snags the cloak off his attacker, standing there is Awngeleik. Between us, she guards me as would a growling dog bent on protecting its master. She would, with her very life. However, in this moment, it seems Awngeleik's more of a threat than Ryco of Paragon ever was.

I scream at her to let him go, but she refuses to relax her tight-clamped jaws. That's when pain finds my nerve endings and surges from the wound. I cannot cry out, as her snake-eyes are fixed upon Ryco. She growls and hisses a deep-demonic sound, like the reptile brood she is.

There's no reasoning with her.

To his advantage, Ryco isn't one to gently reason with a menace. Digging his fingers into Awngeleik's mane, he slams his body against her shoulder. Awngeleik, knocked off balance, releases his arm in her fall to the shamrock-grass. Collecting himself, Ryco drags one boot-tip along the ground. From his made mark are vines and branches, racing to Awngeleik to wrap themselves around her limbs. Before she can run away, they pin her tight

354

to the ground.

Meanwhile, with no foothold, my weight pulls me down. The skin splits more. Adrenaline wears thin, and throbbing pain swells throughout my body. It spreads like the bite of infection in a prolonged wound. In pain so great that I can't breathe, I somehow manage to rasp two words out: "Ryco. Help."

Still facing Awngeleik, Ryco spews, "You psychotic beast."

Further, my wound rips. Hot tears stream down. Unsteady breaths catch in my throat. Though I try, no words come out.

Turning, Ryco faces Reign and me. All color drains from his features. He rushes to my side. His gloved hands tremble. Assessing the wound, he then says in relief, "It missed your heart. But not by much."

One hand of Ryco's grabs my uninjured side. He lifts, to support me. A fraction of pain subsides. Using his teeth, he removes the glove off his other hand. He wraps his bare fingers round the protruding spike. At the point of contact, some metal melts away and drips to the ground. Breaking the weakened spike off, Ryco tosses it aside. He now supports me, on both sides, saying, "I'm going to pull you off. Ready?"

Grimacing, one nod is all the answer I have in me.

Swiftly, Ryco frees me of the broken spike. With it? A scream from my lungs, as he lays me on the ground. He presses a glowing-yellow palm to my wound. More pain is eased away, while he says, "I can't heal you all the way. But I can stop the bleeding."

"Then you can't heal Reign?"

"His wounds are too extensive. He would bleed out, before I could heal him enough."

"Ryco of Paragon," rumbles Reign, "do not worry for me. I've lived long enough. Attend to young Tyler."

Seizing hold of Ryco's healing-hand, I ask, "What about his surface wounds? Can you heal those?"

Glancing back at Reign, Ryco starts to say, "Yes, but—"

I shove his hand away, demanding, "Then do it. While we wait for the others. I'll be fine."

Cocking his head, Ryco starts to say something else, but decides against it. Eyes amused, he pulls a cloth out from one of his pockets, replying, "As you wish, Mr. Ravier. Ben will be here soon. In the meantime, keep pressure on it." With that, he gets up, and tosses the cloth on my face.

His footsteps fade, as he goes to attend Reign.

The cloth I swipe off my face, and wad it up. Obediently, I press it to the wound, groaning when I do. Somewhere out of sight, the welding sound starts its crackle.

Thrashing near my feet, Awngeleik glares at her thin captors. Even with her struggle against them, Ryco's vines hold strong. Giving up—at last—she just screeches and screams, as would a bird ensnared in a trap. It's not a typical trap, however. It's a Ryco trap. With any luck, it's the best kind of trap there is: one fit for a dragon-horse.

Staring up at the sky, I'm exhausted. My free arm I let flop, to the shamrock-grass, before I muse, *More and more, this Ryco of Paragon is a contradiction to himself. Feigning hate, but caring for many in reality ... unless you're Awngeleik.* I rasp out, "Let's hope, Walking Terror, that this day doesn't get any worse or *more* confusing."

* * *

"Shoulder: good as new," Ben announces. "Shouldn't hurt anymore."

Standing up, I state, "It doesn't. Thanks."

"You won't fly for a year," states Quall, patting Reign's side.

"Least I will fly again," rumbles Reign, standing on wobbling legs.

He digs his wings into the ground for support, while Gemma stands, horrified at the sight of five-foot spikes piled next to Reign. "So, those are Dragon's Spikes," she states.

Ryco nods. "Don't ever be near one, when it first hits. A clean batch is electrocuting, within a certain radius. Unless you're a dragon, forget about surviving them."

To the twelve Paragonians standing by—dressed in gray, white, and red coats—Quall commands, "Mages, you are dismissed to attend others."

With a wave of Quall's hand, they disperse. Turning back to Reign, Quall continues, "Do you need another dragon or two, for assistance back to the castle?"

He rumbles, "I must aid with the burial of death. That is my servitude to Pawv'Ragaen, now."

"But you need rest," Ryco argues.

"Do Vitiosyns rest, in the wake of dawn?"

Ryco sighs out his displeasure.

"Then neither shall I," proclaims Reign, staggering away to the dug-up pastures of Paragon and toward the other dragons hauling the dead there.

Down into hollows, dotting the pastures like a vicious disease, they will be buried. Forever to rest. The tamers of dyns—now Paragonians—with all their beautiful, yet destroyed creatures, will be buried by the very ones they claim to tame.

I wonder, *Noble dragons burying the dead: is it beautiful or is it terrifying? I do not know. Perhaps, it is both tragic and poetic. Altogether? Ironic.*

Right then—pulling me from the horror of death, to the horror of orders—is Zepharre, storming our way with the remaining King's Guard in tow. He stops in front of Ryco to say, "You are to accompany Tyler and Gemma to the portal. Get going!"

Before Gemma or I can object, Ryco laughs. "You can't be serious. It's far too dangerous to take them there now. We'd be leading the Vitiosyns straight to Earth. We've been lucky, in hiding the portal this long."

Smugly, Zepharre states, "That's the verdict of the Advisers. You would defy us, therefore putting yourself at risk to being found guilty of insubordination?"

"You voted on it?" hisses Quall.

Ryco motions behind Zepharre. "Here's six of the Arkiveis now. Shall we put it to a proper vote?" Not waiting for Zepharre's reply, Ryco strides toward them, calling out, "Grover? King Talok passed his safety clearance to Tyler and Gemma. I ask all of you: would we take King Talok to Earth. In Paragon's current condition?"

"Of course not!" shouts an astonished voice, from amidst the six Arkiveis.

Emerging out is Arkivy Nyrim, asking, "Whose idea was that?" When Ryco covers a cough, Nyrim nods. "Zepharre of Paragon. Of course, it would be you."

"Nyrim of Yharss," croons Zepharre, in surprise. "You're alive and well?"

Blazing are Nyrim's Vaegon-eyes, as he steps closer, stating, "No thanks to you."

"I vote," Ryco states, "that Tyler Ravier and his friend stay. Amid the protection of our warriors and dragons."

Quall adds, "Those agreeing with Ryco, step forward."

Toward Ryco, all King's Guard and Arkiveis take one step, then Nyrim turns to Zepharre. "Request? Overruled. Zepharre, go feed the sick."

"You do not command me!" Zepharre shouts.

During Zepharre's tantrum, Nyrim's tattered black and blue robes burn away—revealing warrior-garb identical to Ben's—then he shouts, "Nor do you command us, without a proper vote!"

Rushing from Nyrim is wind, sending Zepharre back several steps. Somehow managing to stay on his feet, Zepharre straightens to stand tall.

Meanwhile, next to me, Ben whispers, "Nyrim found his voice again."

"And it's wonderful," hisses Gemma, in delight.

"Fine, Nyrim! Have it your way." Zepharre turns on his heel and stomps to the path.

Through a victorious smile, Nyrim exclaims, "Ben! It does my heart good to see you."

"Likewise." He grins back. "But where's Symovi?"

"Still in Yharss. Protecting it, and the Arkivara, like a faithful city-warrior should."

Sheepishly glancing at Nyrim, Ben is signaling someone with his Handclasp-Fidget.

The Arkivy of Yharss turns. Looking my way is Nyrim, saying, "It seems I am in your debt, Tyler Ravier. How can I ever repay you?"

"By living," interrupts Gemma.

"Gigi, is it?" Nyrim holds out a hand of introduction, and she takes it.

"Something like that," she replies.

Nyrim states, "I will do my best, to follow your suggestion."

I clear my throat to say, "Glad I could help share the burden, earlier. Although, I still don't know how it happened."

Nyrim studies me in wonder, asking, "Then you don't know?"

Kent interrupts, "Don't know what?"

"He didn't share my burden"—Nyrim looks to me—"Tyler, you took it. Then threw me to safety. Or something did."

Twisting the watch nervously on my wrist, I undo the clasp and hold it out to him. "Could it have been this?"

Nyrim takes it, for further inspection, stating, "It has no magic that I can sense."

"What's that?" queries Quall, pointing at it.

"My dad's watch. Didn't he ever wear it, here?"

Casting his gaze down, Quall shakes his head.

Taking the watch from Nyrim, Warren states, "If it had magic, it's gone now."

As I clasp it back on my wrist, Nyrim startles. Off to the sky—past the city gate—he gazes, and Ben takes in a sharp lungful of air, asking, "What is it, Nyrim?"

"Vitiosyns approach."

Ryco adds, "Still a few kilometers out."

"We should get Awngeleik out of sight," I state, while hunting around for her cloak. That's when I realize someone's missing from our group. "Where's Callie?" I ask.

"With Khyra," Eli declares. "Passing out bread and cheering Paragon with her sweet Dysardan song."

Ryco commands, "Warren. Musgrae. Get Awngeleik."

"Like that?" Musgrae points at her. "Aren't you going to put her to sleep, first?"

Disdainfully looking at the Walking Terror, Quall mutters, "Warren, you ever finish that muzzle for the menace?"

"Nope!" is his reply, as Awngeleik—in the midst of gnawing on her vine-branch captors—spits out gobs of wood chunks and leaves every few minutes.

Crossing his arms, Ryco states, "That will only make her more unruly, when she wakes."

"Wonderful!" Musgrae complains, "Now Ben will get to heal my neck half-chewed off by an Equidyn."

"There are worse things in life," states Ryco, glancing at me.

I echo, *Like being impaled on a Dragon's Spike?*

Would you believe ... it was an accident?

Not a chance.

Glad you'll live.

Are you, Sylvadyn?

With a faint smile, Ryco ends the Mensa-div with, *Guess you'll never know for sure.*

* * *

No sooner do we reach the Castle of Sosha, then ringing out in the near distance is a deep horn. Rushing down the thirteen steps is Rorka, asking, "Was that the Onyx Horn?"

"Rorka," says Quall, in surprise, "where've you been this whole time?"

"Trying to contact Alpha Jasper."

"Any luck?" queries Siege.

"No response, yet."

All displeased smirks on smug faces, Zepharre with the other advisers occupy the castle's doorway. "How nice of you to bring the wretch back," states Zepharre. "Who's to watch her?"

Bound and squirming atop Musgrae and Warren's shoulders is Awngeleik, as the two human-tanks push past the others.

"Since you asked first, Zepharre," Quall states, "you and the Arkiveis get to watch her."

Though they grumble and complain, Zepharre and the Advisers slink back into the castle like skittish mice in the wake of the Equidyn's angry screeches. For a moment, I almost pity them. Then I remember Zepharre, in all his arrogant glory. Under my breath, I mutter, "Serves him right. Hopes she bites him."

"Me too," Gemma agrees.

When thunder crackles overhead, I ask, "Do Gemma and I need to get out of the rain?"

"You'll be fine," replies Quall. "We and our opposition have temporarily depleted the air of magic."

No sooner does he finish then drops of rain, absent of color, start spotting the ground. Before long, it pours down its damp cold. It adds to the misery of the day.

Rozeth and her dragon land beside our group. "Get on," she commands. "Gyron and the Onyx Warriors are approaching the gate with the Vitiosyns."

"Is Zymarc with them?" queries Quall, getting on first.

"No. In his stead," replies Rozeth, "he has sent his Prince-General, Azabahk."

I ask, "Any sign of Talok?"

"I didn't see him."

The rest of us clamber on, with Rozeth and Quall.

"What about Musgrae and Warren?" Gemma asks.

"They'll catch up," states Kent, as Rozeth's dragon bursts from the ground.

In minutes, the city gate's in sight and we're landing just before the field of Midnight Anemones. We clamber off. Forming a straight line next to each other are Rozeth and the King's Guard, refusing to step past some imaginary barrier in line with the Arkivara.

All eyes watch the shamrock-grass.

Before long, Vitasadyns come scaling over the city wall like crawling shadows of dusk.

Riding on the backs of wingless, charcoal-colored neins are the Vitiosyn men and women pouring in through the cracked gate, as the largest Vitasadyn—twice the size of Reign—soars in like a king of dragons. Down, toward the ground, he lands across the empty, bloodstained shamrock. Flecked with blood is his spiked-snout, while he shakes out his neck as would a black horse ruffling its mane. Exuding from his scarlet gaze is desire. Lust for more blood. Paragonian blood. Perhaps, even, my blood.

Stroking this king Vitasadyn's neck is Belzara, sitting atop his long back. Behind her, with features shielded by a large hood, sits an unmoving black-cloaked figure.

Several Paragonians and BlacKaidyns come protectively behind the King's Guard. They arrive in time to hear Belzara call out, "People of Paragon. I give you, Talok. Your child-king." She motions to her side.

Beside the Vitasadyn stands a massive black nein fanning out his wings. Revealed between its wings, is a figure with hands bound by rope. Though his cheeks are bruised, and he holds back tears, he's alive.

My cousin sits, muzzled by a bronze piece with inset jewels matching the Geldryn bangle still on his wrist. Two female Vitiosyns proceed to drag him off the EquiNein, as Belzara dismounts her Vitasadyn. Shoving the two away, Belzara takes hold of Talok's arm. No one moves. Not the Paragonians, or BlacKaidyns. Nor the Vitiosyns, or their Vitasadyns.

All is quiet.

All is still.

Then Belzara, with malice in her scarlet eyes, hurls Talok forward to the shamrock-green. Still bound and muzzled, he trips. Into a mire of blood mixed with mud, he falls forward.

From the Vitiosyns come resounding roars of haunting laughter, as the rain suddenly stops.

The cloaked figure slides off the massive Vitasadyn, and saunters toward Talok.

On the path leading into the city, hoofbeats then thunder. One by one, thirteen riders enter the scene. They spread out to the sides of shamrock-green like referees. Whom else could they be, but Onyx Warriors?

Peering from between Kent and Ryco, I ask, "Why are they here? Now and not before?"

Quall, at Ryco's side, replies, "To negotiate? To announce a victor? We're not sure."

Standing apart from the thirteen is one rider cloaked in thunder-blue, rather than the unreflecting black of Onyx. When that figure dismounts, the one approaching Talok removes his hood. Covering her mouth, Rorka sharply inhales at the sight of him.

The black-cloaked figure is none other than Siveyra Gyronawv, staring at us. His eyes turn apprehensive, when he focuses on Talok.

My cousin tries to crawl his way out, from the mire.

"Oh no." Quall winces.

I dare to ask, "Why is Gyron standing with Belzara?"

"They're not here to negotiate," Ryco whispers tensely.

I ask, "Then why?"

"To trade Talok for Awngeleik," states Rozeth. "What else would they want?"

"Guard your thoughts, Paragon," Kent whispers. "They're searching for her."

Just then, Musgrae and Warren approach. A few steps short of them is Callie, trailing in among the Paragonian line.

Musgrae queries, "What's happening?"

"Nothing good," replies Quall.

Together, we watch the blue-cloaked figure whipping his arms out as if he's clawing at something in his grasp. His thunder-blue cloak shreds away to shift into six screeching owls of blue in search of a resting place. Their search isn't long, however, as they find refuge atop the massive nein.

"Azabahk!" Rorka hisses, "Can I kill him now, Master Quall?"

"Not yet." Quall lifts his hand, trying to quiet her rage.

A bronze mask-muzzle covers much of Azabahk's face. He approaches the Vitiosyn line, while scanning the scene with his bright-scarlet eyes. On his arms and chest—torso and legs too—are cords, chains, and belts covering him. The only piece of clothing providing an ounce of modesty are his tight brown pants, torn as if by some wild beast. Yet Azabahk does not bleed.

Hand motioning to Gyron, Azabahk's distorted voice commands, "Siveyra Gyronawv. If you will … announce the verdict to Paragon."

Briefly bowing his head, then standing tall, Gyron finishes sauntering to

Talok, now covered in muck. Helping my cousin to his feet, Gyron escorts him eight steps past the Vitiosyn line.

Hoping Gyron will hear me, I echo, *Do something, Siveyra.*

I have, Tyler Ravier. You've been procured with more time. Don't waste it.

31

Flames of Betrayal

Ending his Mensa-div with me is Gyron, calling out, "People of Paragon! Before the break of dawn, proof by King Zymarc's hand—to my King ReNovak—has been given of Awngeleik's recent whereabouts."

Restless are the Paragonians, with solemn faces. Some whimper, others cry, but most stare out to their King Talok and the Onyx Warriors. In utter shock, they fix on Gyron.

"This dawn," states Gyron, taking more steps. He pulls Talok along with him, voicing the verdict, "A victor has been announced, by the Onyx King ReNovak."

Ryco scoffs, "It can't be us. Start thinking of a plan, Quall."

"We're in no position to fight," mutters Quall, wiping the sweat off his brow.

"This won't end well," adds Siege, fearfully.

I state, "Gyron said he bought more time, and not to waste it. What could he mean?"

Gyron continues, "Though it has nothing to do with proof, it has everything to do with wit and cunning. The Vitiosyns have outsmarted you twice-over—therefore proving their worthiness to the Onyx, this day and thereafter. We must bear arms with Vitiosyns. Against Paragon and all her allies."

365

Paragonian by-standers struggle to hold back cries of horror and anger. Through clenched teeth, Rorka says, "Yet he calls himself a Siveyra."

"Are they going to kill King Talok?" Callie whimpers. "Master Ryco, you are a great warrior. Do something."

Gemma grips Callie's hand, stating, "As King Talok would say: settle your fear. We'll get out of this, somehow."

"I shall hold to that hope," states Callie. "And I will never forget the great courage you showed, Gemma, when I could not." Together, they look back to the scene.

Beside Belzara and the massive nein, Azabahk stands, demanding, "Give our King Zymarc the Equidyn. Then you shall have your child-king back. In one piece."

"The alternative?" calls out Quall.

"Refusal," states Azabahk, "will result in King Talok's death. However, it will be staved off for a time, as requested by King ReNovak." When Azabahk nods twice at Gyron, the Siveyra strides back to the Vitiosyn line.

Thirteen steps from their line—and thirteen steps from us—is Talok, left all alone in the center of shamrock-green. Close enough for me to feel his fear, yet too far away for me to help share his burden, my cousin seems an ocean away.

"Paragon!" Gyron calls out. "You have twenty-two days, to make your final decision: to trade Awngeleik for Talok's life, or to refuse—thus leading to war, destruction, and the death of a king."

"Your King Talok will die," interrupts Azabahk, "in the wake of your refusal. This very day, however, we shall but leave him in your great care." Azabahk motions to Talok. "What say you, Pawv'Ragaen? Shall you come collect the king for preservation, of twenty-two days more?"

Tears from my cousin's eyes collect on the muzzle-rim of the bronze mask. As they buildup, some spill over. To me, he looks with the gaze of a forgotten dog half-starved to death. That's when I find my voice to ask, "If they're offering for us to take him, why are we just standing here?"

"They wait," states Ryco, "for the First Approach. The first to cross the unseen line we stand behind. In the Rules of—"

I cut him off with, "Then I'm not waiting any longer."

One-two. I step forward.

Three-four. Ryco then Quall reach for me, but miss.

Ryco shouts, "Tyler! The first to approach is the first die!"

Five-six. I go on, even though Gemma begs, "Tyler, come back."

Seven-eight. I won't stop now.

Callie wails, "Someone save him."

Ryco commands, "Musgrae, stay where you stand! Their thoughts permit only the boy's approach."

Nine-ten. I reach out to Talok, but he stays planted to the center of shamrock-green. Eyes frantic, he slightly shakes his head as if trying to warn me of something.

Eleven-twelve. The mask muffles Talok's screams.

Thirteen. With fear wrenching my stomach, I stop an arm's length away. Then, neither giving in to fear—nor letting it shake me—I boldly demand, "Give the King of Paragon to me."

Unreadable are Azabahk's eyes, watching me from across the sea of green. At last, he gives the command, "Release the child-king, dear Belzara, into the boy's hands."

Belzara approaches. She grips Talok's arm, then thrusts him against me.

As soon as his fingers briefly grip a piece of my coat, Talok warns with an echo, *They're testing the Rules of Engagement. Take my right arm. Then don't move. Whatever you do, don't move. They'll kill us all.*

I heed his warning, doing as he says. His bound hands clutch the front of my coat, while Belzara starts removing his muzzle. Her hands then linger on the side of Talok's neck. Igniting with hatred are her eyes, as her clawed-gloves split the neck's skin. He screams. Holding tight to me, he doesn't take even one step from where we stand, together.

Belzara hisses in Talok's ear, the words, "How unlucky that Vaegon broods squeal like baby dyns."

"Belzara, stand down!" shouts Azabahk.

She spins around, defending, "With the boy, he was practicing Mensa-div."

"That matters not. King Zymarc was explicitly clear. We were not to leave another scratch on the child-king, when *once* we delivered him home."

Belzara starts asking, "What of the Rules—"

But Azabahk cuts her off. "I did not give the command for his reprimand. But you disobey. Again and again. Vitiosyns, mark her for disobedience."

Two female Vitiosyns rush to restrain her.

Resisting their clutches, while still holding Talok's removed muzzle, Belzara shouts, "You would punish me, before all of Paragon?"

"Your disobedience was witnessed by them. Therefore, they shall see your punishment."

After the two females drag her back to the Vitiosyn line, Azabahk commands, "Kneel, Belzara, and accept your punishment."

She throws Talok's mask at Azabahk's feet, before the two restrain her arms with cords, and force her to kneeling.

A mere step away from Gyron, who's standing expressionless, is a male Vitiosyn brandishing a heated metal-piece, and approaching Belzara. He presses it hard into the skin of her forehead.

No other sounds escorting it, her tormented screams ring out.

The dyns are silent; the neins are still.

No Vitiosyn jeers.

No Paragonian cheers.

Without end are her screams, until the metal-piece is lifted off.

The two release their hold. They leave Belzara there, on her knees, panting and gasping.

Azabahk starts sauntering toward Talok and me, while the straps, cords, and chains fall off him like limp snakes. Hitting the ground, they seem to take on life. Writhing in erratic waves, they cling to each other. Then, up they rise to form legs and arms—a torso then chest—they finish with the neck and head. Standing there, now, is a lifeless body.

Sensing my emotions, Talok echoes, *They smell your fear. Fear, to them, is for the weak, and the weak are worthy of death. Whatever you do, don't cry. Tyler. They'll kill you.*

I fight the inner battle, while Talok gazes over my shoulder. He starts to take in the sight of his magnificent city, now in shambles.

"Don't, Talok," I whisper. "Look away."

"I can't. You see what they've done?"

After Azabahk casts crackling black-and-gray lightning onto the lifeless body, emerging from its fog is a cloaked figure dressed in black and thunder-blue, spreading its arms out wide. The cloak rips away to roll into bats, ravens, moths, and other small creatures. Together, they whirl in place. Something starts taking shape.

Silver light flashes. A figure similar to Azabahk appears. His eyes, however, are not of scarlet. They are of crimson-red. His skin, instead of gray, is pale as if untouched by sunlight. Upon his shoulders, rest two black snakes like the ones on Belzara. Covering the lower part of his face is a midnight-blue metal muzzle. It continues on, to wrap around the back of his shaved head. What skin of his scalp is exposed, boasts of symbols and tattoos.

No other Vitiosyn stands like him.

Beautifully-terrifying doesn't quite describe him, either.

Azabahk, kneeling on one knee, bows to the figure. "My lord, King Zymarc. I present: Eyo'el de Pawv'Ragaen."

This Zymarc approaches Talok and me, but stops eight steps away. "Twenty-two days, I give you." He soothes, "To let you rebuild your city. To change your minds. To give me what is rightfully mine: the dragon-horse, Awngeleik. Even now ... if I see the Equidyn, I will not go back on my word to King ReNovak."

Twenty-two days to slumber? I wonder. *Is that what it meant?*

Zymarc glances around. "Where is he, for this momentous occasion? To witness that a Vitiosyn *can* be reasoned with? That a Vitiosyn *can* show pity, for such a frail race as seen in Paragon?"

"He sent me, instead," is Gyron's cold reply.

"A pity," states Zymarc, turning to face the Paragonians. "I had hoped for it to be different, Little Paragon. For you to produce a worthy adversary. But, with the Great LanSoren's death, there is now none in all of your land. Such an embarrassing death, he had too. One none can explain, though

I've asked many."

No longer able to resist, I hiss out one word: "Stop."

With his gaze piercing into me—trying to glimpse into my intentions, my thoughts—Zymarc states, "Azabahk said you had the audacity to break the Rules of Engagement. I had to come see this brave boy. Sadly, I see now. You are nothing but brazen."

"Then, go on. Leave Paragon. Don't come back, until your twenty-two days are up."

"*My* twenty-two days? You mean his." Zymarc points to Talok.

"I said what I meant."

Taken aback is Zymarc, asking, "Who is this, King Talok, that he would comfort you? Yet dare speak out of turn to me?"

Talok replies, "He's no one but a boy. A brazen one, as you said."

"Yes. With much love for his king." Zymarc nods. "I will forgive your insolence, this once, but you really should go back to the early training. Learn how *not* to address Sorsryns."

"I will, but it wouldn't make any difference in how I speak to a vacant, Vitiosyn shell."

Talok echoes, *Tyler! You're going to get us killed.*

Zymarc stands taller, saying, "Vacant. Vitiosyn. Shell? That's a new one, isn't it, Parasogyn? No matter. I shall take my leave now, as I'm not welcomed here." He turns to go, and the two snakeheads lift off his shoulders to stare back at me.

"A question, before you go?" I ask.

"Now he dares to question me, Parasogyn. Do the marvels never cease?"

To Zymarc, I speak those feared-four-words, "Soren of the Monel," like they're salt on my tongue. With Zymarc's flinch, it seems, those feared-four-words mean something to even the worst of them. Upon hearing the name, Zymarc's eyes flicker in recognition.

With any luck, he and Soren are one *and* the same.

Beckoning someone forward is Zymarc, holding out his hand, before commanding, "Come get your king, Parasogyn. But leave the boy. He amuses me."

As Ryco comes to fetch Talok, and take him back to the Paragonian line, he brushes against my arm, echoing, *Be careful what you reveal. You don't know who you're dealing with.*

My echo replies, *He knows something I need. I have to know what.*

Talok and Ryco are back in line, when Zymarc raises a translucent-yellow wall around the expanse of shamrock-green with a twirl of his hand. Sauntering the rest of the way to me, he stands slightly shorter than my dad did.

Second-guessing myself, I muse, *Could Zymarc really be him? Soren looked taller.*

"They can't hear the words," states Zymarc. "Can't see them spoken. To them, we are simply moving, looking, or standing. Don't try speaking to them. They will only see you staring blankly into their eyes: soon to be nothing."

Nodding, I state, "Answer my question."

Zymarc begins, "Soren? It's a name I've not heard spoken in centuries. Am I he? What's it to you?"

"You can't be him." I shake my head. "Soren's too arrogant to dodge the accusation. He would claim the name, without hesitation."

"You seem to know this Soren quite well. Yet you are young, and he's been dead for decades. There's no possibility of you being his son, even though you look remarkably like him. Save for your skin. So, who are you? You don't talk like a Paragonian. You don't act like one. And you don't look quite like them, either."

I answer with the plain name: "Tyler Ravier."

Sulking, Zymarc states, "A name that means nothing to me. Perhaps a rephrase? *What* are you? Dare avoid answering and I'll cut your throat, take the Equidyn—bound to be in the city somewhere—then end the Paragonians forever."

"You can't cut me, here or now, because you're not really *here*. You can have one of your Vitiosyns do the deed, in your place. Yet, somehow, I don't think that's good enough for you. Letting someone *beneath* you have the pleasure of killing me, capturing the dragon-horse, and then ending the Paragonians? No. *You* want that recognition. You crave it."

While I'm talking, Zymarc circles around me. He stops, when I'm done, but then holds down the index and middle finger of his hand with his thumb. Using his ring finger, he skims along my left cheek. Eerily, he whispers to me, "A wise deduction."

Hot is his touch on my cheek—almost intoxicating—as I liken it to the warmth of the beast near Mirror Lake. Though my face burns, my body's cold, and I'm overcome with the presence of contradiction.

Could it be his mask, or is it something else? Licking my lips, I state, "Your touch is an illusion. But even if you're here, you still can't kill me this day."

Startled, Zymarc pulls his hand away. "You cannot be certain of that."

Glancing around, I spot Gyron holding his head high. Prideful, he watches me. By his held-back smile—telling me that I'm right about something—I'm lit with confidence, in stating, "Siveyra Gyron's face says otherwise."

Absently, Zymarc states, "I shall reprimand him later."

"You mean, King ReNovak will? This day, perhaps not tomorrow, I'm protected by Onyx law. Therefore, you cannot kill me here-and-now."

Circling me again, Zymarc thinks a moment. "Tyler Ravier, you said? Surely, I've heard that name before."

Looking behind Zymarc, I notice that the Vitiosyns grow restless. They flinch, at the slightest movement among the Paragonian line; and, searchingly, they gaze to the sky above.

On, I continue like the Barrage of Gemma. "You may be able to breathe your essence into the spirit before me. But you take a great risk. It requires effort: Magic. Your Vitiosyns grow uneasy, with each step you take. Why not end Paragon now? Why wait?"

"I have my reasons," he replies, snapping his fingers. By some invisible hand is Belzara dragged to Zymarc kicking, choking, and screaming. Around her neck, he tightens his grip, before remarking, "You want more bloodshed this day, Tyler Ravier. How about killing a Vitiosyn?"

I stare into her eyes. Then into his. Yet all I see is Soren threatening my father, mocking Gemma, and taunting me.

"Belzara meant much, to the former King Deezalo of Vitiosus. She was one of the first he turned. The first to serve him faithfully. But she means nothing to me. Now a mere thorn in my side, she's almost as bad as that Soren was … all those years ago."

The presence of contradiction returns.

A breeze cools my skin's surface.

Sunlight warms my veins.

Yet fear numbs my mind.

Courage ignites my soul.

"Cut her throat," Zymarc speaks soothingly. "You'd be doing me a favor."

I clench my fists, and close my eyes. I refuse to let him control me.

The sound of a blade scraping across Belzara's skin sickens me, though, far worse than the razor-strokes on my neck ever could. She yelps. Then I smell it: her blood. It's intoxicating.

The breeze turns to ice.

Sunlight to a scorching desert.

Fear to horror.

Courage to carelessness.

Zymarc's smooth voice speaks again, "Drink her blood. Bathe in it. You know that's what you want."

My eyes flash open to the sight of Belzara kneeling at my feet, with a symbol burned into her forehead. Her eyes beg me to end her misery, but I shout, "No!"

Rushing from me is wind, throwing Belzara back to the Vitiosyn line. Then, for a moment, it flashes a rippling gale-storm against the Vitiosyn's offense. Through it all Zymarc stands unmoved, unnerving me, while I muse, *I swear he's smiling behind that mask. But why would he be?*

Waving the tinted-barrier away, he states, "Paragon, you may heal your king."

Desperately, Callie replies, "Please! Let me free him too?"

"Very well," replies Zymarc calmly. "Remove his bindings."

I get to Talok's side, as Callie undoes the bindings. Halfway through healing him, she says, "Almost done."

Turning on his heel, Zymarc strides back to his Vitiosyn line, stating, "Come-come, stop petting the King of Paragon. You'll see him soon enough, Caleiso. The time has arrived to admit you into the next level, for I need an opening to admit a *new* apprentice."

Right in front of me, Callie brushes a hand across the Geldryn bangle still latched on Talok. That's when her skin turns pale, looking similar to Zymarc's. Her heterochromian eyes shift to match his own of crimson-red.

"You," I jeer. "You were the spy? *You're* the reason all this happened!"

Smiling wryly, her deeper voice states, "Outsmarted Paragon. Twice-over."

Burning me to an uncontrollable anger is the betrayal of this girl no older than I was when he died.

My hands ache to hit her.

To strangle her.

To wrench the blonde strands from her scalp.

I hate her, because I cared about her; even started to trust her.

Summoned to my left hand is the Prismatic of Magic. Before I can think twice, I wrap my fingers round her small neck and squeeze hard.

She thrashes in my grasp, choking and gagging and struggling for breath.

Then I ask her, "What's terrifyingly-beautiful now?"

32

Across the Pages of Time

Chaos erupts. A distance behind Callie, in my strangling hold, Vitiosyns stand ready to shoot on Zymarc's word. At me, they aim longbows. Red flames wisp in their palms.

"I did not command reprimand," states Zymarc, lifting a hand. "Stand down, Vitiosyns."

He takes a long step toward them, and they obey as his figure explodes into the bats, ravens, and moths. They fly away, leaving Zymarc nowhere in sight.

Gemma cries out, "Tyler, let her go! This isn't you. You're not one of them."

Ignoring the call to honor, I practically spit in Callie's face, "You liar. You never had any parents. You let me go on and on about my life. All while you sought out a way to destroy Paragon."

My hand tightens more on her neck. Her lungs are deprived of air. She cannot cry out. Instead, she gags and coughs. Replacing her recent paleness is a pale-pink, while her hands wring on my left wrist. She tries to free herself. But I grip tightly. Then I take hold with both hands. Ragged is her breath on my face, as I spew out, "It was you, making those odd thoughts rush into my head. Not the device. You. Callie of Vitiosus. I hate you for what you've done."

Standing atop the shamrock-grass, two steps past the Vitiosyn line, is

375

Azabahk with a blank glint in his gaze. For an instant, his bronze mask darkens. Then its color returns.

Loosening my grip slightly, I ask, "Do you have any remorse at all?"

Callie, clutching to my wrists, wheezes out the proclamation, "This is not your war, Tyler Ravier. I suggest you leave. I can convince King Zymarc to let you and Gemma go back to your real home."

Releasing her neck, I shake her by the shoulders. "We're not leaving. Nor will we be stupid enough to reveal the way to my home." I shove her back.

But she regains her footing, to stand as tall as a small girl of thirteen can. Though she utters nothing, disappointment creeps into her sad eyes.

In the distance, an approaching Sorsryn strolls down the path leading into the city. Onyx, by the looks of him, in the black coat uniform. With his slow gait and hands in his pockets, from his view, this day must be lovely and bright. Though rain has started drizzling down again, and Vitiosyns embrace the line of offense, all while Paragon holds its breath—perhaps its last—on goes this Onyx, strolling closer.

Yet there's one piece out of place. A bronze mask on his face. It covers all: save for his poised ears, exposed scalp, and the crimson-red eyes of Vitiosus. On the mask are intricate symbols and lines, adding contours to his face. Starting right before his ears, the mask dips down to wrap behind. At the base of his skull, they join together and then split up into five metal veins. Looking like a clawed-hand encasing the back of his head, the five fingers form a 'V' above his brow-line: two angle on his temples, two curve above his brows, while one is centered on his forehead.

Though this bronze mask deepens his voice more, it's unmistakably Zymarc calling out, "Thrice. Tyler Ravier. You have broken the Rules of Engagement. *You* made the First Approach, and escaped death for your insolence."

Continuing his happy stroll toward Callie and me, Zymarc goes on, "Again, for your *lack* of respect in addressing me. Commanding me to stop, twice, when I have every right to destroy Paragon and kill her king, for the lies they've told and the Equidyn they have withheld."

One hand still in his pocket, Zymarc's other beckons for Callie's approach.

"And last, you *attack* my apprentice. An act worthy of death-where-you-stand. But she tells me you are a foreigner. That you don't know any better."

I watch as Callie, ignoring my hateful glare, ambles to Zymarc's right side. Pivoting on her heel, she faces the Paragonian line.

Then Zymarc, like a player on their winning move, is clasping his hands in front of himself. "I will ask this, one more time. Who are you, Tyler Ravier?"

"Why don't you ask your apprentice? She knows who I am."

"I did not ask her. I asked you. A third time? Answer me."

I state, "What if I were to tell you that LanSoren of Trauvo isn't dead?"

His eyes lighting with interest, Zymarc replies, "I'd say, you're lying."

"What if I wasn't?"

"Then I would leave Paragon this moment. Never to return, without his permission."

I ask, "You feared him that much?"

Zymarc thinks a moment. "It was more of a fascination for him, rather than fear."

"What was so special about him?"

Even beneath the mask, this time, I know Zymarc is smiling. The amusement in his eyes says it all, as he states, "In my centuries of living, I've learned who can survive the Call of Vitiosus and who will die by it. Until LanSoren, there was only one who resisted me. Resisted the call *and* the death."

I state, "Soren of the Monel. Is that why he was a thorn in your side? Because you couldn't possess him with Vitiosus? So you killed him. Killed LanSoren too?"

Laughingly, Zymarc rants, "LanSoren and I? It was complicated. But I would never kill him. I don't think I could, even if I tried. Respected him too much. That Soren, however … Though it was not I who committed the glorious deed of ending his essence, I wish it had been. In the end, he was psychotic, illogical, unreasonable. Altogether? Dangerous. If you discover the cause of his death, be sure to let me know. It would be enough to end this war between us."

"It's that important to you?" I ask. "Knowing how a Sorsryn of Old died?"

"It's an impossible task. You'll never find the truth of Soren's death. But you can try."

To Zymarc, I echo, *You already know how he died, don't you?*

Of course! It was quite beautiful. He plotted my death. But walked into his own, instead. One of the greatest ironies I've ever witnessed.

If you know how he died, why would I need to find out the truth of it?

Zymarc echoes, *To show tenacity and sharpness of mind. Oh! But I did tell one, little lie.*

And that would be?

He wasn't walking. He was running. Quite like a desperate soul. I was the one walking. Trying to find a good spot, to watch the sun ascend after the rain.

You mean, after the wake of a slaughter?

With the pause in our Mensa-div, my veins warm with hatred. The pulse rises. The watch twists round.

Zymarc's mask distorts his escaping titter, as he considers aloud, "Slaughter or Victory? It all depends on perspective, doesn't it … LanSoren's Tyler Ravier? That's who you are. His son. Thank you for letting your hate bring your guard down. You are gifted in Mensa-div. Not so much with Mensenglos. You should work on that."

"I will, if given the time."

"Your father's Mensenglos was exquisitely good. You'll have a good teacher, in him. Wait!" Zymarc gales in a breath of surprise. "You can't learn from him. Because he's dead!"

His Vitiosyns roar their haunting laughter, but Zymarc just watches me.

When fury burns in my heart, Ryco echoes, *Tyler, do not provoke him more. You've already said far too much.*

I clench my teeth to stop the words, before they start.

Zymarc wipes away his horde's humor, with one raise of his hand. Silent they go, as all scarlet gazes are on me. Zymarc then ends the silence with, "Knowing who you are, Tyler Ravier, I'm going to wager a bet with you."

"It's not one you'll win. Not with me."

"You haven't heard it yet," remarks Zymarc. "Though you may hate me now, before your cousin's end, you'll be giving me Awngeleik. And taking your rightful place, as my new apprentice."

I seethe, "Never going to happen. Besides, you already have one."

"Contrary to belief, a Vitiosyn can have two. After this day, however, she won't be my apprentice. She will join one rank below my Prince-Generals; a Prime-Warrior, such as Belzara."

Callie's eyes light with pride, as she side-glances at Azabahk.

He crows, "Caleiso! You've done your duty in deceiving Paragon." Snapping his fingers twice, he then demands, "Now change out of that ridiculous outfit."

With red-fire, her palms ignite. Down her torso sides, Callie sweeps the fire. As she does, the dress and Ben's tattered coat burn away. Only pants, boots, and a heart-armor of black and thunder-blue are left in place. "Better?" She scowls at Azabahk.

"Hardly," says Belzara boredly, easing atop the king Vitasadyn's back.

Ignoring the exchange is Zymarc, still watching me. "I know how you can restore the Rules of Engagement," he says, "And stop me from destroying Paragon with her king this day."

"Then, go on. We're waiting."

"A duel," proclaims Zymarc. "With you."

"No!" shouts Talok, taking a step forward. "If you duel anyone, as I am Paragon's King, it will be with me."

"You misunderstand. That brazen boy is not my match. There is no one here, to match me. However, I want a duel between my current and my future apprentice. That is my term. The recompense for his insolence, in order to restore our agreement."

Talok begs, "Think of something else."

"There is nothing else!" shouts Zymarc. "I am the one who has been slighted and insulted. Therefore, I am the one to name recompense. Even if you were to uncloak that Equidyn beast for an offering, this very moment, I wouldn't accept her as payment. There shall be a duel between my apprentice and him!" He points at me.

"But neither are sixteen," says Quall. "Surely, that breaks some sort of Onyx law. A duel between minor-pristines?"

"Siveyra Gyronawv?" Zymarc looks to him. "Am I breaking any laws, in my request?"

His gaze like ice, Gyron replies, "You know that you are not."

Zymarc demands, "Then let it commence."

From Azabahk's offering hand, Callie takes the wavy Kris daggers. She advances to the shamrock's center, to wait for me.

I glance back at the Paragonian line, then to the sea of worried faces looking back. Fear bangs inside my chest, until I catch sight of a face that ignites confidence in me again. To my surprise, it isn't my cousin. Nor Gemma. But Ryco of Paragon, echoing to me, *Trust those daggers, Tyler. They were your father's, after all.*

Unsheathing them, I then face the presence of contradiction.

Zymarc commands, "Advance to the center, Mr. Ravier."

Obeying, I stop a step away from my betrayer. Coldly, I ask her, "What are the rules?"

Azabahk answers instead, "Neither of you are of age. Not yet, true Sorsivytes. Therefore, no fighting to the death. Although, you may come close."

"But accidents happen," remarks Zymarc. "And some Sor-Nefawgytes *have* died."

I ask, "You'd risk her dying? In a duel?"

"I'm confident that if one dies an accidental death, this day, it will be you. Not her."

I smirk. "I'm not Soren. If I die, it will be on purpose. Nothing accidental about it."

"Already, I see it," states Zymarc. "You, joining me. Standing at my left side, and accepting the Call of Vitiosus, before burning Paragon to the ground."

I state, "Keep thinking that. See where it gets you."

Now shifting to impatience, Zymarc yells, "Begin!"

Tight I hold to the daggers, and dig my boots into the shamrock-grass.

Anticipating yet dreading the first strike from Caleiso of Vitiosus, I wish she had not done what she did.

In her hands, the long Kris daggers resemble slithering snakes frozen in place. Jabbing at me like a snake, too, are her movements—fast and erratic, then slow and precise. She's quick, but I manage to dodge the blows and match her speed.

Metal starts striking metal and, with each contact of our blades, my fingers ache. But my wrists hold strong. Like a dance, she swings. I dodge. Down she wears her own stamina thin, and I take the opening to grab one of her outstretched wrists.

In one swift motion, I slice.

Not without consequence, though.

While the sleeping-dagger's tip exits her forearm below the elbow, she lunges with her free hand at my face. Across my cheek and nose, her dagger rips the skin open.

Hot blood runs down.

I drop the sleeping-dagger to shove her back, as blood continues over my jaw and then down my neck. It seeps into the collar of my coat. My hands tremble. I gasp for breath. Yet, somehow, I manage to push through the excruciating pain and blink away tears. I regain the dropped dagger, and my footing, forcing myself to focus on this traitor of my heart.

"Caleiso, no healing or magic!" Azabahk yells. "Not until Zymarc gives the command."

From her left arm, blood cascades down. Landing on the now very red shamrock-grass, it adds more to the stains of today. Undaunted, Caleiso grips both daggers tightly. Not a flicker of pain on her face, she scowls.

My breath calms, and my heartbeat steadies. Without fail, the con-stants—which prove I'm alive—are with me. While the sting of my own wound subsides, the deep glower of Caleiso's gaze turns into terror.

"He said no healing!" she shrieks.

"I didn't use magic." I scoff. "Don't even know how to heal myself, without potions."

"No one," Zymarc remarks, "not even the boy has used magic, Caleiso.

Continue."

The scowl returning, she huffs, "I underestimated you. I won't again."

"Good! I was wondering when I'd get to see the real Apprentice of Vitiosus. Instead of this girl taking pity on me."

Her speed twice what it was, Caleiso runs at me, screaming. Only luck saves me from the worst. Across my hands, face, and neck, she slashes dozens of times. Deeper into my arms she cuts. Though relentless, she seems careful in avoiding my eyes and mouth.

Each slash stings, mere annoyances more than anything. But the deep ones, on my arms, bleed two rivers of blood.

I stumble around, disoriented.

Caleiso's about to trap my neck between her daggers, and hold me at her mercy, to win this duel. But something stops her from doing so.

Like Midnight Anemones, I smell her fear. It warms my veins. Lifting my soul. With it? The disorientation too.

The stain of blood disappears.

Pain diminishes to nothing.

I straighten to standing.

"I don't understand!" she cries out. "How is it that you are healing? Yet you do not use magic? King Zymarc! He is cheating!"

"If he's cheating, Caleiso, then he is a master of it."

Huffing, she comes at me, slashing over and again. With each passing minute, her speed slows. My wounds heal, time and again. But fatigue's brought with it.

Desperate, I echo out to any listener, *I don't know how much more I can take.*

Sensing my exhaustion, Caleiso begins fluid movements. Circling me are her steps, likened to a vulture waiting for a meal to drop dead. Her eyes are wild, in anticipation.

On the path outside the city, heavy sprints get nearer. Everything goes quiet to listen. Even closer now, its deep, beast-like breath approaches. Running past the gate, it's a blur of gray and black.

When it bumps past Zymarc, he stumbles a few steps off the path.

Slowing to a trot, the dark blur circles around Caleiso and me.

Emerging into view is an enormous black-wolf, peppered with gray and white. He's a fraction smaller than Jack Wayeland's Bear-Wolf. Though, still terrifying. His movements are a mix of a wolf cornering prey and a lion stalking a victim. Stretching his neck out, he lowers his noble head to dip below his shoulders.

He's ready to pounce.

I'm ready to run in the other direction.

His emerald eyes lock onto me. He seems to strip away my defenses, with one gaze. I'm terrified, but in awe of him. Respect, he commands without an utterance of a single word. He's the sort of creature, which can't be described fully.

On Caleiso, he focuses. His low growl resounds. Instead of shaking the ground as Reign's Roar does, the growl sends tremors to my chest and then my throat.

Ignoring the beast, which is one leap away from her, Caleiso takes a swing at me.

In reply, the wolf wails at her. His voice is like a dozen beasts trapped inside one form:

The utter terror of a tiger's roar mid-lunge.

The shout of a gorilla about to rip his enemy limb from limb.

The screaming of a fox tormented by ghosts.

The screeching of a horse being whipped.

A warrior's cry on the battlefield.

Below it all is a deep, mesmerizing howl of a great wolf holding the voices together, and blending them. Friends of his need not fear. They are free to be captivated. It's his foes whom should worry. I'm not sure which one I am, yet.

Behind me, Paragonians take to one knee. Behind Caleiso, Vitiosyns bow at the waist. Even Zymarc ducks his head down once, in acknowledgment. All pay homage to this great beast parading on the shamrock-grass stained red.

Except, that is, for Caleiso of Vitiosus. She's crumpled to the ground.

Eyes slammed shut, she covers her ears. Yet, she still screams in terror at the wolf's voice.

I grab her injured arm, and pull her up. Oozing between my fingers is her blood and iridescent colors. All the colors: save for green, purple, and orange. They stay divided from her blood, like oil in water. There's black liquid, and white; both shimmering. Brass, ruby, and cobalt-blue too. Magic from her Mazhrein; what else could it be leaching out with her blood?

The wolf ends his wail. Caleiso opens her heterochromian eyes, now absent of crimson-red. Something then scorches into my veins.

Too weak to hold onto her, I have no choice but to let go.

Voices turn to whispers, before all sound is gone.

Everything fades away like ghosts.

Caleiso's face is the last I see, as it goes black around me.

Left all alone, I call out, "What's happening? Can anyone hear me?"

Getting no answer, in reply, one horrifying thought starts surfacing.

I whisper to the darkness, "Have I died?"

I can still breathe a breath.

My heart can still drum its beat.

But maybe I was right.

Even after life is gone, they may follow in death.

"Beginning. End. And everything in between? Is that what Soren meant?" I muse aloud, if for no other reason then to fill the void. Yet the sound does not carry. It's confined to as far as the breath can transmit, but no farther.

A light turns on, in the distance. Brightening my chances, my way to freedom emerges in the outline of a door. Perhaps it's unwise to shed the blank canvas and replace it with what lies beyond the door. But, here-and-now, I do not care. I want out, and my feet take me there. On the way, cold mist swirls around me. When my steps stop, halfway there, the doorframe's seeping light catches on the mist and illuminates my darkness to a soft-charcoal.

Determined again to abandon the void, I continue with a step ... then two, and another—all the way, until I'm standing at the black door etched with white scrolls.

I knock. Nothing happens.

Because there's no handle to grasp, I place my left hand upon the door's center. The Prismatic of Magic stains my hand. This time, however, the colors bleed out. Onto the black door and over the white scrolls, they race, then go out. The door cracks in half. It peels away like the city gate of Paragon. Beyond is a room lit with bluish light and torch-fire.

When I enter, I gasp at the sight of a figure leaning over an intricate desk.

Not noticing my company, he studies one of the journals: the Rubidyn-Greyvon one. He whispers to himself, "If only I could remember."

Taking the step, one word escapes me: "Dad?"

His attention gradually lifts off the journal, as if the weight of a lifetime holds his head down. Our eyes meet, for a moment, before his glance continues searching the dim space trapping us.

Crushed inside, and rasping out, "He still can't see or hear me," I then echo, *Why ... does this have to be so hard?*

At last, lighting my father's copper-colored eyes is recognition. He beams as if he's experiencing sunshine on a frigid day, saying, "Tyler? Is that really you?"

My pulse quickens. "You can see me?" I ask.

"And hear you now, yes. What are you, fourteen? Surely, you can't be fifteen yet."

"Fourteen," I reply, smiling. "Where are we?"

Approaching, he states, "The Arkivara of Trauvo. The heart is dark, when she sleeps. Just now, I thought you were an illusion of her dreams."

"Are you trapped? Are *we* trapped?"

He squeezes my shoulders, asking, "Trapped? No. Why would you think I'm trapped? Aren't you with a Borrower of Time? Visiting me from the future?"

"I don't know what a Time Borrower is. But you died a year ago. Almost to the day."

His strong hands pull me into an embrace. And he crushes me in his tight hold, stating rather than asking, "Then I died when you were thirteen."

The sting to my eyes threatens to break me, but I pull away to say, "Thirteen. Done. That's what it meant, right? That you'd die when I was thirteen. No matter what you did, to escape fate?"

"That is a logical assumption. But that's not what it refers to."

"Then what?"

He starts to answer, but stops when pain tightens the contours of his face. Giving up, he replies, "I am bound—"

"Not to say," I finish. "Is that your reason for secrecy? For not telling the truth? Because you couldn't?"

"Yes and no." He looks away, pacing around the dim space. "Some secrets are guarded by strong magic," he says.

Indignant, I ask, "How am I supposed to figure those out? Through a process of elimination: getting only *no's* and *maybes* in response?"

Forever patient with me, he says, "That will only work, until three options or answers are left. The other secrets, you're not ready to know. But the rest?" He pauses. "I let fear keep me from telling you, your mother, and many others. Those give me no excuse, but a need for your forgiveness."

"Then you have it," I cry. Tears spill over. I beg him, "Please! Tell me there's a way to save you. I can't bear living without you."

He grasps my left hand, declaring, "Yes, you can. Because you are *my* son. I have seen a thousand ends of a thousand paths. Of the ones, where you survive beyond a certain point—" Again, he pauses, too distraught to continue.

Taking that moment, I argue, "But I want you here with me. With Mom, and Talok too."

My father's face ignites with determination. He finds the courage to go on. "At the end, Tyler Malik Ravier, you are terrifyingly and beautifully *extraordinary*. Far greater than I ever could be. All you have to do is … survive."

"I don't want to survive. I want to be with you."

Mournful, he states, "That will never be. Didn't the Vardiya speak to you? What did he say?"

Finding my voice, I quote, "You care. Because I have the answers to what you seek. Though I have not breath or magic enough to tell. Forgive that all I have is how much he loved you. Enough to die for you. It's last words were: 'Thirteen. Done.' Then it died."

"That's all he said? There was so much more. He wasn't supposed to die, either."

"I think Soren had something to do with that. Who is he?"

"I can't," he replies, in frustration. Closing his eyes, he drums fingers-to-forehead, as if it will make the right words hum inside his head. Aloud, he muses, "What does one say? When words on a page, *simply* are not enough?"

I suggest, "Maybe you can answer what this means: I know you, but I have never spoken to you. Familiar as my own face staring back at me. How can that be?"

The drumming fingers stop. His eyes light in fondness. "Where did you hear that?"

"It was a poem I started, but never finished."

Excitedly, he presses, "Where did you start it?"

"The lake." I pause to smile. "Where the Vardiya was. That was part of its message?"

My father laughs. "He was trying to get you to go into the water. To hear the rest. Did you really not swim in the lake for a year?"

I shrug. "I couldn't bear to."

Waving his hands, he replies, "It's all right. I have an idea. It's not the message you were supposed to hear. But it'll have to do. The words are crucial to remember. Ready?"

Nodding, I close my eyes. I prepare to listen to each and every uttered sound.

He begins, "Happiness is vanquished with mortality and the days of zeal are now rime."

Focusing on the vibrato of his voice—the rhythm of the words—the sensations they provoke, I count.

One: It is fire. It is ice. The presence of contradiction, ignited to an all-consuming inferno and an arctic winter.

His voice fractures, at the words, "Love is lost in the sea of time."

Two: It's heartbreak. It's death. It's hopelessness. My battle against tears.

He spews forth the words, "Sadness arises out of failure!"

Three: Utter death, disobedience, and destruction. Ruled by pure fear and hate.

Gentle is his voice, saying, "Hatred's pain turns to nirvana, never again to remember."

Four: It rises. The hope after wars. The light after storms.

His voice quickens to utter, "Anguish stays after memory."

Five: Fight or flight to survival.

His voice deepens to say, "Fear of the obscured. Is near and last of the end."

Six: To level the scales.

Prideful is his voice, whispering, "Reflection gazes into the ages. Confirming it and seldom more."

Seven: To the answers I seek. To the one I need.

He sighs. "But reason and resolve can mend it all. There's the last of it."

Eight: To the mystery. To my story.

My eyes open, and I ask, "Beginning, end, and everything in between?"

He lifts a shoulder, saying, "Something like that."

"Did Soren kill you?"

"I'm not sure, Tyler. I haven't died yet. Remember? Whatever you do, though, don't make the mistake of underestimating him. For in that moment, *everything* you love will die."

I state, "There's so much I want to ask you. Where do I even start?"

Sucking in a whale-breath like Talok, he announces, "Our time is near its end, I'm afraid. Take care of her. And she'll take care of you."

"She? You mean, Awngeleik?"

Smiling that Chess-Grin, he playfully replies, "Maybe."

"So, she," I state, "is more than three. Good to know. Just tell me this, before I go. Who is Despairing Marion?"

"I can't tell you that."

I ask, "What about despairion? Is it anything special?"

He briefly cringes, replying, "I can't give you a straightforward answer.

Sure you want the riddled ones?"

When I nod, he sighs out, "Okay. But know that I warned you. Although there are others, this one makes the most sense. Words for riches." He flashes that special smile.

"That makes *no* sense. Pick a different one."

A few moments pass, before he's announcing another hint, "Despairion is kindling for thought. Is that any better?"

"Worse," is my frustrated reply.

"All right"—his sigh is deeper—"last one."

When he pauses, I ask, "Well?"

He slightly waves his hands, speaking, "Forget it. It won't do. Just remember the two. *No* forgetting. You'll figure it out."

"If you say so." I shake my head.

He rubs at his neck, then asks me, "Are you ready to wake up, Tyler?"

I shrug. "Wake up? What do you mean?"

"Time has stopped for you, on the other side—wherever you are—because of the powerful being I've hidden a bit of magic in."

"You mean that giant wolf?"

After exclaiming, "Jasper?" he narrows his eyes, teasingly saying, "Maybe."

"What!" I seethe. "You've hidden magic in more than three people?"

Pursing his lips in a guilty manner, he answers with one word: "Maybe."

Sounding like Jed, I complain, "You've got to be joking. That's messed up."

"It's hard, Tyler," he defends. "Outsmarting a Sorsryn of Old, among others. It requires being more crafty. Let's hope I was successful, in outsmarting him."

I sigh. "What do I have to do?"

"For now? Wake up and remember a piece of what I made you forget."

"And that would be?"

"When you wake up," he states, half-chuckling, "you will know."

Indignant, I cross my arms. "Then I'm ready."

He smirks. "You're ready? Ready to trust all that I've laid out for your journey to truth?"

"Yes. But one *last* question, before I go? Will I like the end?"

"I've made many preparations, to ensure the best for you, but no one can be sure of your end. Ultimately, it's up to you to forge your fate. Goodbye, Tyler."

I whisper, "I don't want to say goodbye."

In good humor, he replies, "Then don't. But be sure to tell that cousin of yours, he'll be a mighty King of Muraine one day. As was his father, Sosha. Especially with you at his side."

"I will." I grin. But the sight of dim light withering into the blackened canvas tears away my joy. Like a ghost, my father's fingers start slipping away.

Tears pour down his face like rain. Yet he stands tall and proud, while watching me fade away. Between us, the distance widens to a black ocean. Reaching out to me, he echoes across the expanse: *Think of this moment we share, as both of us reaching out across the pages of time.*

Cherishing every moment, I echo.

He continues, *Hoping for brighter days to come.*

Love is lost in the sea of time, I echo. Readying myself, I wave goodbye.

But reason and resolve can mend it all, he finishes.

"Wake up, Tyler," he commands, and I'm summoned to close my eyes. When they open, only the misty black greets me. Then faces start emerging.

On my right is Talok, his face etched with brokenness.

In front of me is Jasper of Pariah. No longer in wolf-form, he stands as tall as Quall. His garb is likened to the colors of his fur: mostly black, with gray and some white. Two leather belts are crossed over his chest in an 'X.' Dark fur accentuates in all the right places, giving way to the truth that he's still a beast. He stands as a simple warrior, with a single weapon upon his belt. Yet his short hair of pepper-gray is frazzled. His gaze has lost that confidence too. His eyes now dance with fear.

But what fear? I wonder. *For Paragon, me, or of me? Who can know?*

On the left is Zymarc, reappearing, as he adjusts his coat. He then leisurely stuffs his hands in his pockets. Victory is in his gaze, fixed on me. And it unsettles me.

More unsettling, however, is a fourth face emerging one step behind Jasper. Shifting from the back of Jasper's head to my face is his murderous gaze. There he stands like a demon. The feared-four-words made flesh. Soren of the Monel. He has hold of my father's daggers, as he leans over Jasper's shoulder. Maliciously, he speaks two words: "Thirteen. Done."

Afterword

Dear Reader:

I hope you've enjoyed this first installment, in The Journals of Ravier series. If you want to help me out, I would love for you to write a review of my first book. Just go to where you bought it online, and leave it there. Or you can email me your review, and I'll post it on my website. My email is: jrvaineo.news@gmail.com. There's also a contact form on my site, you can use, instead.

I know, I know! The cliffhanger ending was killer. I'm sorry! But I had to do it. There was no other choice. Believe me when I say, it was an *agonizing* decision. Maybe you hate me for it. Maybe you love me for it. Or a mix of both? Just so you know, I'm hoping for both.

In parting, I wish you luck in discovering authors and books to add to your favorites' list. I sincerely hope I've made it on that list.

All the best,
Julie

P.S.
Always remember . . . no matter how bleak life gets, smile through the tears, fully knowing that it does get better.

About the Author

J.R. Vaineo is a self-published indie author, residing in Salt Lake City, UT. In 2018, she published her first book: Kings of Muraine. When she's not writing, she and her husband, Jessie, have many adventures together. Mostly in cooking, hiking, photography, analytical talks, and fawning over their two adorable fur-babies.

While J.R. Vaineo writes mostly fantasy fiction—combining elements of epic, portal, paranormal, and dark fantasy—she enjoys reading all genres; except, perhaps, for horror stories. After finishing a creative writing program, through the Institute of Children's Literature, she continued to improve her craft of writing. In 2013, she graduated with her AA degree in psychology. During that time, she expanded on many things, especially focusing on what would prove invaluable for fleshing out characters and plot twists. What started out as a writing prompt, in 2005, has now become a nine book series she is currently working on: The Journals of Ravier. Sometimes, she is quite jealous of the characters' abilities, found within her own writing. If that is a sign of anything, it is this: Obsession.

You can connect with me on:

🌐 https://www.jrvaineo.com

🐦 https://twitter.com/JRVaineo

📘 https://www.facebook.com/j.r.vaineo

🔗 https://www.instagram.com/j.r.vaineo

🔗 https://www.goodreads.com/JRVaineo

🔗 https://www.bookbub.com/authors/j-r-vaineo

Subscribe to my newsletter:

✉ https://www.jrvaineo.com/newsletter